Also by Alafair Burke

CLOSE
CASE

CLOSE
CASE

A SAMANTHA KINCAID MYSTERY

ALAFAIR BURKE

HENRY HOLT AND COMPANY ▪ NEW YORK

Henry Holt and Company, LLC
Publishers since 1866
175 Fifth Avenue
New York, New York 10010
www.henryholt.com

Henry Holt® and ® are registered trademarks of
Henry Holt and Company, LLC.

Library of Congress Cataloging-in-Publication Data

Burke, Alafair.
     Close case : a Samantha Kincaid mystery / Alafair Burke.—1st ed.
          p.   cm.
     ISBN-13: 978-0-8050-7784-1
     ISBN-10 0-8050-7784-7
     1. Public prosecutors—Fiction.   2. Women lawyers—Fiction.
     3. Portland (Or.)—Fiction.   I. Title.
     PS3602.U755C58 2005
     813'.6—dc22   2004060903

Henry Holt books are available for special
promotions and premiums.
For details contact:
Director, Special Markets.

First Edition 2005

Designed by Paula Russell Szafranski

Printed in the United States of America

10   9   8   7   6   5   4   3   2   1

For my remarkable grandmothers,

Mrs. Margaret Pai and

Mrs. James L. Burke, Sr.

CLOSE
CASE

He called it quits earlier than usual. He'd heard about the troubles downtown, but in Northeast Portland the streets were quiet. Cruising his contacts and getting nowhere was discouraging. Less admittedly, it was disconcerting. He couldn't help but wonder whether sources were mum because they had nothing to say or because they were nervous.

The truth was, he was worried too. As he drove the familiar route back to his condo, he found himself watching the rearview mirror for headlights. He also kept an eye on the speedometer, even as cars passed on either side. He was tired of cops pulling him over for speeding while he was following the traffic flow.

It wasn't like him, but damn if this one wasn't getting to him. He had the confirmation he needed, but he'd been holding off, trying to decide whether to keep his mouth shut or go forward. But it was time to put an end to this bullshit. Laying low was for punks. Here he was, watching his back while he'd been

1

spinning his wheels. Tomorrow he'd go with what he had. He'd dealt with worse and lived to face the day.

When he could see the lights of the Burnside Bridge glowing over the still Willamette behind him, he felt some of the tension ease. He was on the west side now, almost home. He continued monitoring the mirrors for lights as he climbed the steep hill to Vista Heights, looking forward to a quiet night alone. A little ESPN, then the clean sheets he'd placed on the bed that morning, would hit the spot. In the morning, he'd start taking control. Rise up and get this motherfucker over with.

He'd given so much attention to the approach of other cars that he didn't notice the feet step from the parking lot into the darkness of his carport.

"Nice car, Snoop," he heard, as he climbed out of his Benz.

Three minutes later, he felt a pool of his own blood warming the cement beneath him. He thought about his phone, still in the car, but knew he would never get to it. *I'll be fine,* he told himself. *Someone's calling for help, and by this time tomorrow I'll be writing a story about this shit.*

1

Hotshot reporter Percy Crenshaw died on the last day of my thirty-second year.

I'm crystal clear on the timing, because I remember precisely where I was when I got word the following morning. I was slogging away in the misdemeanor intake unit, issuing criminal trespass after criminal trespass case, thinking to myself, *This is a shitty way to spend my thirty-second birthday.*

The way I saw it, I had no business working at intake. I have been a prosecutor for seven years, three federally as an Assistant U.S. Attorney in New York City, and four in my current position as a Deputy District Attorney for Multnomah County. Only someone with a local connection would know where Multnomah County is, let alone how to pronounce it. It's the county whose seat is Portland, Oregon, the rainy city in the Pacific Northwest. Not the big one with the needle in the skyline, the smaller one south of there.

Before hearing the news about Percy, my big complaint of

3

the morning—and the reason I was at intake—was the protest-ers. Outsiders might not recognize the county name, but they know about these people, even if they've never made the Ore-gon connection. My hometown's protesters are the same nuts who stirred up the masses outside the World Trade Organiza-tion talks a few years ago. In a smaller local show, they tried to make a lost point about our soldier-a-day situation in the Mideast by upchucking red, white, and blue ipecac when the President showed up for a campaign stop. Some of them are rumored to be responsible for the arsons in California targeting suburban housing developments and SUV dealers.

The political causes may vary, but one thing remains the same: These kids love to protest. And the night before my birth-day, the chosen cause was the fatal shooting two weeks earlier of Delores Tompkins, an African-American mother of two, by a patrol officer with the Portland Police Bureau. Like all police shootings, the Tompkins case would be presented to a grand jury before any official determination was made regarding jus-tification. Unlike most, however, this one's purpose would not be simply for appearances. Tompkins had no criminal history, was unarmed, and was shot through the windshield of her car during what should have been a routine stop. And, as often seems to be the case with these things, the police officer in question, Geoff Hamilton, was white.

As the newest member of our office's Major Crimes Unit, I was not working on the investigation into the Tompkins shoot-ing. But even I could sense a more than theoretical possibility that our office would be going for charges against Officer Hamilton. The public must have sensed it too. With each day since Delores Tompkins's death had come another related event—a prayer vigil, a town meeting, a conference with the police commissioner—each occasion an opportunity to apprise the city that its small community of color was fired up and paying attention. And as their message trickled its way each morning into a new edition of the *Oregonian,* the odds of an indictment reading *State of Oregon v. Geoffrey Hamilton* increased just a little more.

Until the Sunday night before my birthday, however, the pressure to indict had been quiet, subtle, and largely behind the scenes. All that changed when the state's band of semiprofessional protesters selected Delores Tompkins as their cause du jour, drawing a riled-up crowd of several thousand downtown on Sunday afternoon for a hastily planned March Against Racism. Supporters of the police bureau organized a counterprotest, not because they were marching *for* racism but because they interpreted the anger over the Tompkins shooting as a general attack on law enforcement. When a pack of militia types from eastern Oregon announced that it would piggyback onto the counterprotest, downtown Portland became the official magnet for every disgruntled wack job in the region.

At last count, the bureau had arrested 212 protesters for various counts of criminal trespass, reckless endangerment, vandalism, and disorderly conduct. Clashes among and between opposing political groups and police officers continued until 2 A.M. And, on Monday morning, extra available bodies in the District Attorney's Office—including mine—had been summoned to misdemeanor intake for the overload.

So that's why I was at intake when I found out that hotshot reporter Percy Crenshaw had been killed.

"This is a shitty way to spend my thirty-second birthday," I said, this time not to myself but to Jessica Walters. Jessica was the head of the District Attorney's Gang Unit. She had just walked in, forty minutes behind me, grande mocha latte in hand, trademark pencil tucked between her pearl-studded ear and her sporty frost-tipped haircut.

"Could be worse, Kincaid. I got ten years on you, it's not even my birthday, and I'm stuck drinking decaf because of this little fucker." She gestured with her Starbucks cup at the swollen belly hidden beneath her black maternity pantsuit. Leave it to Jessica to find a way to drop the f-bomb as a maternal term of endearment. "I guess intake is Duncan's idea of a reward for coming in early."

The boss of all the bosses, District Attorney Duncan Griffith, had left an office-wide voice mail for all of his deputies that morning. The gist: Intake needed help issuing custodies from Sunday night. The rule: The first deputy to arrive in each unit was to report to misdemeanor intake immediately to help, unless the lawyer had a trial scheduled to go out.

It takes a lot to make me yearn for a trial, but that did the trick. Doing someone else's work is bad enough, but this was mundane stupid busywork. Not to mention the fact that the intake unit was located in the Justice Center, two blocks from the courthouse, so in this case doing someone else's work had started with a walk back out into the rain.

"I guess the early birds really do get the worms," I said, handing her a misdemeanor intake file. "When I got the boss's message, I was tempted to hightail it out of the courthouse. Let someone else take the bullet."

I left Jessica with the misleading impression that my conscience had gotten the best of me. In truth, it was my paranoia, combined with my ignorance of technology. For all I knew, Griffith could be keeping track of who had logged in to voice mail and in what order. I didn't need to furnish him yet another opportunity to accuse me of not being a team player. Or, better still, to unleash my very favorite motivational phrase: "There is no 'I' in *team*."

Maybe not, I say, but there is a *me,* and that "me" had little interest in churning out another misdemeanor complaint. Jessica Walters, on the other hand, had little sympathy. "Cut your whining. If I can pull this duty, you can suck it up for one morning."

Known in some circles as Nail-'Em-to-the-Wall Walters, Jessica was a career prosecutor, a fixture in the office for nearly twenty years. Before her promotion to supervise the Gang Unit, she'd preceded me as the only female lawyer in the Major Crimes Unit, handling some of the toughest capital murder prosecutions in the state. She was right. It had been only six months since my promotion into MCU. If she wasn't too good for intake, I guess I wasn't either.

I counted another four files from the large stack we were facing, handed them to her, and then plucked out five more for myself. "Want to race to make it interesting? Winner on each set of five cases buys a drink?"

"Rub it in, Kincaid. You have no idea how much I miss my amber ales." She looked down again at the contents of her maternity suit.

"Sorry," I said sheepishly. "Starbucks?"

"You're on," she said, opening the first folder.

Jessica and I *each* issued fifteen separate cases in the next fifty-six minutes. I won two prosecutorial sprints of the three. A quick read of the police report, a few taps on the ten-key pad for the badge numbers of the arresting officers, and a few more strokes for the applicable sections of the criminal code, and— voilà!—out popped a criminal complaint.

If the pace seems callous, don't blame me; blame the system, at least when it comes to issuing custodies. These are the cases filed against suspects who were booked the previous night. If a custody case isn't ready for arraignment by the time the suspect is called on the 2 P.M. docket, the court cuts the suspect loose. Free lattes weren't our only motivation for rushing.

As eight-thirty was rolling around and the rest of the office was finally strolling in, a young woman I recognized as the intake unit's receptionist interrupted our case-issuing sprints.

"You're Kincaid, right?" she asked.

I nodded, scrawling my illegible signature at the bottom of yet another complaint.

"You've got a call from an officer. I'll transfer it back," she said.

"Who is it?" I asked.

"Who pays attention? They asked for you, though."

"Thanks a bunch," I muttered, under my breath. I couldn't figure out who would be calling me at intake, but for the moment it was an excuse to ditch my post, at least for a few minutes.

I picked up the transferred call. "Kincaid."

"Good morning, Ms. Kincaid. It's Jack Walker." Otherwise known as one of my favorite Major Crimes Team detectives. "So my sources were right. You've worked your way all the way up into the glorious misdemeanor unit."

"Rumor's out already, huh? You calling to gloat?"

"I'm busting you out of there. We got a body up in Hillside. I'm told you're our gal."

"Yeah? By whom?"

"That'd be one Senior Deputy District Attorney Russell Frist." He enunciated my supervisor's name in the deep booming staccato voice used widely in law enforcement circles to mimic Russ Frist. Apparently Russ had decided this call-out would be mine.

"You need me to come up there?" I asked.

"Definitely," he said. "This one's gonna be a doozy."

As my Jetta putted up the steep incline on Burnside toward what Walker had helpfully described as "the parking lot of those big pink condos," I considered the scenarios possibly awaiting me at the top of the hill—none of them good. Protocol requires the bureau to connect with our office immediately on every new homicide, just to be sure a DA works the case from the start. But most cases don't warrant the physical presence of a prosecutor at the crime scene. What made this one so special?

When I turned into the parking lot of sprawling Vista Heights, I silently cursed Jack Walker. There must have been eight hundred condos perched on the overlook above north-west Portland, surrounded by acres of parking lot. I cruised the main road surrounding the complex—as well as its various offshoots—at a steady five miles per hour, thanks to the frequent and enormous speed bumps spread throughout the property. I finally knew I'd reached the right place at the dead end of one of the side roads when I spotted a flurry of cop activity behind the familiar yellow crime-scene tape.

I found an open spot, grabbed my briefcase, and climbed out of the car, cinching my raincoat more tightly around me. It was the first week in November, and the autumn dampness had already begun to settle into the air and into my bones.

As I walked across the parking lot, I noticed neighbors peering from behind their blinds at the obvious bustle. A few had stepped outside their condos, some still in robes and holding coffee cups, trying to ascertain what could have brought so many uniforms and marked vehicles to this quiet enclave.

The learning curve in the Major Crimes Unit had been a steep one, and by now I knew the ropes on a call-out. I showed my badge to the officer monitoring access at the scene, watched as he logged my entry onto his clipboard, and then ducked beneath the tape that roped off about a quarter acre surrounding an open carport.

Jack Walker caught sight of me in his periphery and waved me over. He stood with his partner, Detective Raymond Johnson, in front of a black Mercedes S-430 sedan. The personalized plate read SNOOP. Even in a lot stocked with late-model yuppie-mobiles, that one stood out.

As I approached, I saw two crime-scene technicians rise from where they must have been kneeling next to the front driver's-side tire. A blur of crisp white linen flashed between them; then they carefully maneuvered a covered gurney through the tight corner in front of the vehicle. I nodded as they passed on their way to the medical examiner's van.

Johnson and Walker met me just outside the carport. Some of the other detectives referred to the pair as Ebony and Ivory. Even beyond the obvious contrast in melanin, the two couldn't have been more divergent physically. Walker wasn't much taller than my five-eight, but about twice as wide, testing the buttons of dress shirts that were almost universally short-sleeved. Johnson's frame, on the other hand, was tall, fit, and always tucked neatly into whatever suit he'd brought home that month from the Saks men's store.

Regardless, the partners were two peas in a pod. I couldn't imagine them working with anyone but each other.

"So who's our dead guy?" I asked, glancing back at the techs loading the gurney into the van. The MCU culture required a kind of nonchalance toward death—or at least the appearance of it.

The two detectives exchanged a glance. Using whatever silent language partners tend to share, they must have decided to let Johnson break the news.

"The one and only Percy Crenshaw."

"The reporter?" I asked incredulously.

"Didn't I just say he was the one and only?" Johnson retorted.

I shook my head. "This is *not* good."

"Try telling that to Crenshaw," Walker said dryly.

Percy Crenshaw started out doing "on your side" pieces for the *Oregonian*'s Metro section. If a restaurant fed you bad meat, or your used car oozed mystery melt, or your new hairdresser surprised you with a blue mohawk, Percy Crenshaw was the go-to guy. More recently, though, he had managed to make a name for himself as a celebrity muckraker in this relatively quiet little city. Of course, like all good muckrakers, he had done that by turning what usually would have been relatively quiet stories into salacious tales of sex, greed, and corruption.

Last year, just for instance, I had worked on a case involving the murder of an administrative law judge. Sure, it had all the ingredients of a good scandal: bribery, betrayal, adultery, the works. At its heart, though, it was the sad story of a woman whose own mistakes had gotten her killed. Crenshaw had nonetheless managed to sell his version of the story, including every last irrelevant detail of the victim's sex life, to *L.A. Magazine*.

"That's some damn shameful timing," Johnson said. "The man was right about to hit it big."

"Didn't he just sell the movie rights to that magazine article?" Walker asked.

"Yeah, he did," Johnson said. "Got a nice chunk of change from that one actress, the blonde in all those legal thrillers."

His partner didn't read the entertainment section as thoroughly as I did. Walker wanted to know if she was the same actress who "gained all that weight for that one role." Nope, they just looked alike.

I guess that's the way the entertainment industry works. The victim dies, her family loses a daughter and sister, and I nearly get killed. But who sells the story and drives an S-Class Benz? Percy Crenshaw.

"I actually met him once," Johnson said.

"I hope you weren't the target of a story he was after," I said. "From what I've heard, the guy left no stone unturned."

"Understatement of the century," Walker added. "More like he'd crawl over his dying mother to get to the last stone left unturned."

"Nah, nothing like that," Johnson said. "We had a real quick 'Hello, how are you?' kind of deal about a year ago at a Boys and Girls Club thing. There's not too many brothers in this white-bread town with real jobs. Once you find yourself on the list of people to call for mentoring panels and whatnot, it's probably inevitable that you end up meeting Percy."

Fewer than 7 percent of Portland's half a million residents are African-Americans. Take into account the predictable decision of the upwardly mobile to live with similarly situated others, and you don't find many black professionals who move to or stick around the Pacific Northwest.

"So what was he like?" I asked.

Johnson's eyes darted briefly to the ME van, the doors now closed. He paused, then shook his head. "Not what you'd expect," he said. "You know, none of the 'tude he puts on in his interviews. Pretty down-to-earth. He talked to the kids about being one of the few black journalism majors at U of O. They were more interested in his work digging up the dirt. I remember him looking me right in the eye when he told them he'd thought of being a cop but wanted the freedom to do what was right."

"I know the guy's dead," Walker said, "but fuck that noise."

"No, he was all right. You get stopped a hundred times for being in a nice car, and you eventually develop a chip. Imagine what he would have written today about the protests. I feel bad for Hamilton," he said, referring to the cop who shot Delores Tompkins, "but if this shit keeps up, the city's going to burn."

I could tell that Walker was poised for rebuttal, so I brought us back to the subject at hand. "Any theories yet on who might have had a chip against *him*?"

They shook their heads. "Way too soon to say," Johnson said. "I suppose there's always the chance he finally ticked off the wrong kind of nut job—"

"Well, you *know* that's what they'll be saying tonight on the six o'clock news," I interjected.

"Of course I know that," he acknowledged, "but I also know what you've been around long enough to know too: By the end of the day, we're probably going to learn that Percy Crenshaw had something kinky going on behind the public persona."

You've seen it before in high-profile murder cases. Early speculation about a motive usually gives way to a dirty little secret, lingering somewhere in the victim's life: shady business deals, a tryst with someone else's wife, a hidden life in Internet chat rooms—something to put the case squarely in the "comfort zone" of murder, where people toeing the straight-and-narrow are safely off limits.

"Unless," I wondered aloud, "it's a carjacking gone wrong?"

"A definite possibility," Johnson said. "The guy who found the body says he noticed a couple of guys in the parking lot last night. He didn't think much of it at the time, but maybe it plays into the carjacking angle."

"I don't suppose he recognized them."

Johnson smiled, familiar with my impatient tendency to hope for early lucky breaks. "Nope. Two white guys in jeans and rain gear. He thinks he might recognize them, though, so we'll sit him down at the station with some mug shots. The poor guy's kicking himself, feeling guilty as shit."

"For what?"

"He's the superintendent for the whole complex." He checked his notebook. "Peter Anderson. He found the body in the carport when he went to replace the motion-activated light that's supposed to be there. Percy put in a maintenance request for the burnt-out bulb a week ago, and Anderson was running behind. I didn't have the heart to tell him he'll be lucky to avoid a lawsuit."

A holler from across the parking lot interrupted us. "Detectives, when you got a sec, we got something you might be interested in."

After exchanging glances with Walker, Johnson volunteered—"I'll go"—and started a slow jog toward the patrol officer.

"Anyway," Walker continued, "we're keeping the carjack scenario as a possibility, but usually they take the car, plan gone wrong or not. We found the keys right there." He pointed to a numbered evidence placard marking a spot by the driver's side door. "Crenshaw probably dropped them during the attack."

I looked more closely then at the area surrounding the Benz. Low spatters of crimson marred the barren white Sheetrock of the carport. A wet stain that might otherwise be mistaken for oil spread beneath the front tire like a Rorschach test. I suspected that the matte smear down the side of the car's waxed front panel was also blood.

I turned back to Walker. "Was he shot?"

He shook his head. "Doesn't look like it. He was beaten real bad. Unclear whether the technical cause of death's going to be the internal bleeding or some real nasty damage to his head, but I'm guessing there was a weapon involved. Maybe a bat or a crowbar."

I swallowed, relieved that I hadn't arrived a few minutes earlier, before the gurney was covered. "So what are you working on?"

"We've got patrol officers canvassing the complex in case a neighbor saw something. Doubtful, though. In a place like this, someone would have called it in."

"Did you notify the family?"

"Not yet. We're working on that as a priority. We've got the place closed off, but it won't be easy keeping this quiet. I assume everyone in the complex knows whose car that is, and it's pretty obvious what's going on here."

"He's single, right?"

"Yeah. Ray put a call in to the *Oregonian* for next-of-kin information. Hopefully his family'll hear it from us before it hits the news."

"Have you gone into his place yet?"

"Working on that too. He lived alone, so we're getting a warrant. Should be easy."

"Who's working on the applications?" I asked. Judges routinely sign warrants for a homicide victim's home and office, so the paperwork was straightforward.

"Mike and Chuck are taking care of it now, back at the office. They'll page you when they're ready for you to look at it." Detectives Mike Calabrese and Chuck Forbes were partners, also in the Major Crimes Team. I'd seen the latter just three hours ago when he rolled out of my bed, pulled on his clothes, and kissed me goodbye. In addition to his position in the bureau, Detective Forbes also filled the role of my current boyfriend. And, technically, I suppose he rolled out of "our" bed, because as of a week ago we were officially shacked up.

"Any legal work you need me to do?"

"Not yet." He squinted at me, anticipating what was coming. "So why am I here?"

15

"Appearances," he said bluntly. "I called Frist as part of the usual procedure, but I told him we didn't need anyone at the crime scene."

"And he said?"

"Something along the lines of"—Walker channeled his best Frist—"'Uh, that's fine, Detective Walker, but, you know, the news'll be all over this one. Why don't I go ahead and ask you to get Kincaid out there; it'll be easier down the road if something comes up.'"

"Your impersonation's better than ever."

"I'm pleased that you're pleased. Now, as for why he dimed you up instead of someone else in the unit, I can only guess."

"And your best guess?"

"Honestly? To see how you'll cut it. You've got to admit, the one other time you got handed a hot potato, your approach wasn't exactly traditional."

He was referring, of course, to the aforementioned case of the missing judge. By the time that one played out, I had leaked information to a defense attorney and helped him subpoena some of the biggest muckety-mucks in the county. Yes, I suppose Walker was correct: My boss wanted to put me to the test.

Ray Johnson walked back to the carport with his black leather steno pad open in front of him, Montblanc pen in hand.

"They find a neighbor?" I asked.

"Looks like we've got a possible girlfriend."

That got Walker's attention. "I thought the guy at the paper told you there was no girlfriend."

"So maybe Percy didn't tell the guys at work everything. A couple nights ago, one of the neighbors came home late to find a car parked in her designated spot. She got ticked and took down the plate so she could complain the next day. Later on, she saw Percy walk the lady to her car. He gave the neighbor the mandatory apologetic wave, so she let it go, but she's still got the plate for us."

"Good," I said. "Run it and find out her story. Anything else?"

"That's it from the patrol so far, but Chuck just called. He and Mike are working last night's PPDS entries from the area." The Portland Police Data System is the clearinghouse for every piece of information collected by the bureau. Generating a list of arrests, stops, and traffic tickets in a given location during a stated time range was a snap.

"Anything worth following up on?" I asked.

Johnson glanced at his notes. "Yeah, maybe. They're still culling through the full list, but there's a couple that jumped to the top. A broken taillight on a two-time car thief down on Twenty-third Avenue. A stop-and-talk with some kid at the bottom of the hill; we still need to get the details from the patrol officer." He flipped a page of his notebook. "Another stop farther up Burnside; that one's for drugs. We'll see, right?"

He closed his notebook and switched gears.

"Also, I finally got through to the human resources chick at the *Oregonian*. Crenshaw's local emergency contact is just a friend. Closest family's his parents down in Cali."

"I'll do this one," Walker said quietly.

Johnson tucked in his lower lip and nodded. I knew how much they hated notifying the families. "Oh, before I forget," he said, pointing at me, "when I talked to Chuck, he and Mike were just finishing the warrant applications."

It was time for me to head down to MCT.

2

On my way up the Justice Center stairs to the Major Crime Team's fourth-floor offices, I passed Jessica Walters on her way down.

"I'm afraid to ask," I said, looking up at her.

"You should be. The custodies still aren't done, but at least we got things sufficiently under control for intake to finish on their own. Now I've got to deal with whatever the hell's waiting for me back in Gangs."

I looked at my watch. Nearly eleven.

"How could they not be done by now with all those extra bodies?"

She scoffed. "Yeah, right, all those extra bodies." She ticked them off on her fingers one by one. "Jennifer Loving came over from Child Support and spent the whole morning. So did some new guy from the misdemeanor trial row, but he was so slow it barely made a dent. Harding came over from General Felonies, but was suddenly paged back. Kessler was over from DVD, but, lo and behold, he was mysteriously paged away too. Anyway, you get the picture."

Rocco Kessler was my former supervisor in the Drug and Vice Division, before my promotion to the Major Crimes Unit. I had no problems picturing him, Peter Harding, and most of my other colleagues cooking up fake pages to weasel out of intake duty.

"Even worse, it turns out I'm probably going to have to take a bunch of those dog cases over to Gangs."

I gave her a puzzled look. The Gang Unit rarely handled misdemeanors, even when they involved gang activity.

"Looks like we had a pack of kids totally out of control up on Northwest Twenty-third after the protests were dying down. They did a shitload of property damage. Bashed in a mess of parked cars, even smashed in a couple of storefront windows. The neighborhood association's freaking out, so Duncan told me he wants me to handle them as felonies."

"Good luck," I offered facetiously. She'd need it. Unless it's a domestic situation where the victim knows the perpetrator, finding the culprit in a property damage case is nearly impossible. That would not be the answer the public wanted, though. Twenty-third Avenue was the crown jewel of Portland's burgeoning collection of quaint but happening hot spots. Pillaging there was equivalent to taking a can of spray paint to the Lincoln Memorial. There would definitely be pressure to find the culprits.

"What about you? I take it you had a real reason for leaving?" she asked expectantly.

I looked around to see if anyone was in earshot. For the Justice Center, the place was remarkably quiet.

"You could say that." I lowered my voice to a whisper. "The call-out was on Percy Crenshaw."

Her eyes widened. "Percy Crenshaw killed someone?"

"No," I said, shaking my head. "He's the *victim*, bludgeoned to death in his carport up on Hillside, right in those big condos on the heights."

She looked genuinely stunned and placed a hand on the underside of her extended belly. Reading her expression, I immediately regretted what must have come across as an excited tone.

"Oh, God, Jessica. I'm sorry. Did you know him?"

She sighed and seemed to snap back into character. "No, I guess I wouldn't say I knew him."

"But?"

She paused. "Sorry, I just kind of freaked for a second. God, this kid must be making me hormonal. Anyway, Percy did some work on a case of mine about a year ago. He was friends with the vic's mom, I guess, and I wound up talking to him a few times on the phone. He came in for grand jury too."

"You called a reporter into grand jury?" I asked. Jessica was known for her doggedness, but dragging information out of a journalist involuntarily was nearly impossible.

"Not as a reporter," she said. "It was a gang shooting, and he was poking around on the side. He managed to get a lot more out of the victim's gangbanger buddies than the police ever did. Apparently he was a PI before we all got to know him as a reporter. Still had his license and everything."

"Raymond Johnson from MCT had crossed paths with him too. Said he was a pretty good guy."

"Yeah," she said, nodding, "I think he was. Unless, of course, they've found out otherwise already."

"Nothing yet, but it's still early. The police haven't even looked through his place. I'm headed up to review the warrants now." I pointed up the stairs.

"Well, let me know if you need anything. This one's going to get some attention."

■   ■   ■

Chuck and his partner, Mike Calabrese, were gathered at the unofficial MCT powwow spot, a small conference table situated in the middle of a cluster of detectives' cubicles. Both were in familiar positions, Chuck teetering his chair at a 45-degree angle, his fingertips pressed against the table for balance, Mike centered solidly in the seat nearest the minifridge.

I paused in the doorway and took a good look at Chuck. After adjusting to my divorce a few years ago, I had sworn that my French bulldog Vinnie would be the closest thing I'd ever have again to a housemate. But last spring Chuck and I took the leap from gratingly platonic flirtatiousness to an in-your-heart-and-guts thing that had begun a decade and a half ago at Grant High. I resisted the change at first, but somewhere over the summer I stopped analyzing our budding relationship and resolved to enjoy the ride. By the end of August, Chuck was dropping hints that the rent on his apartment was going to waste, and by October I had invited him to move into my Alameda bungalow. We celebrated our first night as live-ins by dressing up Vinnie in his cow costume and doling out candy to the kiddies on Halloween. I suspect Vinnie found the whole thing emasculating, but Chuck and I had a blast.

"There she is!" Mike hollered out, when he saw me lurking. "Ray told us that Frist was putting you front and center on this one."

Chuck eyed me mischievously but maintained his promise not to spill the beans about my birthday. "And we all know how much Samantha Kincaid loves to be in the spotlight."

"Well, that all depends on what it's for, doesn't it? Hopefully, this time around it'll be because you find the bad guys and hand me a slam-dunk case."

"We're trying," Mike said. "Meanwhile, though, Frist's looking to shine himself by going after our boy Hamilton."

My boyfriend's protective tendencies kicked in. "C'mon. If Sam could control Russ Frist, there'd be a whole lot about her office that would change."

"What? I can't kid her like any other DA?"

This was precisely why I had insisted from the very beginning that Chuck leave the rest of the law enforcement crowd out of the loop about the change in our domestic arrangements. Our ability to maintain a professional distance was questioned enough as it stood. Chuck being Chuck, he was more cavalier about the line between our personal and professional lives, seeing the subject as one more humorous opportunity to see me sweat.

"Hey. Guys. Yoo-hoo." I threw in a little wave. "Still in the room. And for what it's worth, Calabrese, as the new kid in the MCU sandbox, I haven't exactly been consulted on the resolution of your *boy* Hamilton's situation."

Cops are never happy when their use of force is questioned, but they are especially incensed when the criticism comes from prosecutors who bill themselves as the real crime fighters without ever dealing with the rough stuff. Mike Calabrese wasn't ready to let the subject of the bureau's most recent police shooting drop. "Yeah, well, you got to admit: Every fuck in your office creams at the idea of going after one of us. It's a direct route to superstardom in this PC little hippie town."

Mike was a transplant from the NYPD and would probably never fully adjust to a population that favored community policing over Giuliani-style street-crime sweeps. He may have been right that a few cop-prosecuting DAs had jumped on the fast track to become judges and politicos, but I still resented the accusation.

"Maybe you should rethink your meaning of *us*, Mike. I would certainly hope you'd never put a bullet in an unarmed woman's head during a traffic stop."

"Unarmed, my ass. A moving car's just as lethal as a loaded gun, and if you were ever on the street—"

"Yo, time out." Chuck made a T with his hands, bringing his chair back down to all fours. "Why don't we agree to disagree, since the last time I checked we had other things to deal with. Besides, none of us know a damn thing about what happened out there with Hamilton."

"Knows," I said, after a pause.

"What?" Chuck didn't hide his irritation.

"None of us *knows* a damn thing. Singular. You said *know*."

Mike laughed. "Now *that's* fucking funny. If the two of you ever decide to tie the knot, you should have one of those reality shows, like that girl who asked her husband if Chicken of the Sea was really chicken. I could watch this shit for hours." He folded his arms in front of his chest and smirked.

"Glad we could amuse you," I said, throwing an uncomfortable look at Chuck. "You guys done with the warrant applications?"

"Hot off the presses," Chuck said, handing me a set of papers for review.

It was the standard packet of forms we used for searches after a homicide: a warrant authorizing a search of the victim's home, cars, and office and a bare-bones affidavit about the crime. I signed off on the DA line, and Mike volunteered to find the nearest judge for the signature that actually counted.

"How's the birthday so far?" Chuck asked, once Mike had left.

"Word hasn't leaked, so it's been fine under the circumstances."

"Why are you being so secretive?"

Maybe this guy didn't quite get me after all. "Because."

It seemed like a perfectly satisfactory explanation to me, but Chuck was clearly looking for more. "Why in the world do my coworkers need to know that I managed to live another year?"

"Beats the alternative, right?"

"Trust me," I said, "those guys at the courthouse are always looking for an excuse. They get one inkling that it's my birthday, and my office will be plastered with birthday cards featuring five-by-seven glossies of naked geriatrics."

"Hmmm," he said sheepishly. "I may need to run out and get you another card."

"Funny. Hey," I said, changing the subject, "you weren't kidding about your buddies having a bee in their bonnet over the Tompkins shooting." I glanced toward the door Mike had just used. "What's up with him? Are he and Hamilton tight?"

"Not that I know of." He pulled a PPDS report across the table toward him.

"So what's his deal?"

"He's a cop. Hamilton's a cop. Delores Tompkins was not a cop. That's enough for some people."

"Some *cops*, maybe."

"Are you trying to start a fight with me? I told you last night, people are getting pissed that your office is even looking into this. They expected Griffith to have issued a statement by now saying the shooting was good."

"With what's been going on in the streets? You have to know that's ridiculous."

"I see both sides. I just told Mike that, right?"

"Not really. You said we should agree to disagree."

"And I also said we have work to do. I'm still going over the PPDS entries from last night." He waved the green printout at me.

He was right. The two of us weren't going to settle the question of whether Officer Hamilton should be prosecuted for shooting Delores Tompkins. Better to focus on Crenshaw.

"Anything interesting?" I asked, sitting on the tabletop to get a better view of the printout. "Johnson said something about a few stops near the condo."

"Maybe. It's been slower going than usual, though. Take a look at how thick this thing is from just one night. Fucking protesters."

"Tell me about it. Until I got called up to Crenshaw's, I was stuck at intake dealing with the custodies."

"So you understand what a cluster fuck it is. When I restricted the search to just a few blocks around Crenshaw's up on Hillside, I only got a few hits." He pulled a different, thinner printout toward him. "Nothing obvious, but I circled a few worth looking into. Best one's probably a traffic stop on a guy with a couple UUV pops."

"Johnson mentioned that one." Given the carjacking-gone-bad scenario, the proximity of a defendant twice convicted of Unlawful Use of a Vehicle was at least interesting.

"I don't have high hopes, though," Chuck said. "The guy was stopped heading east, which would put him on his way *to* Crenshaw's place. Possible a guy would try to pull something off right after being stopped by a cop, but—"

"Not likely," I agreed.

"Right. So then I expanded the search to include a mile around the vic's place. That's when I got this massive thing," he said, holding up the thicker report again. "We wind up hitting downtown and all the crap from last night. It's taking me awhile to get through it all."

"You going out on the warrants?"

"You bet. Ray and Jack will take the car and the condo, but Mike and I are doing the office."

"Call me if you find anything?"

"But of course, madame."

"And make sure the other boys keep me in the loop too?"

"No one's out to get you, Sam."

"Just make sure they don't shut me out."

"Consider it a birthday present."

Chuck was right. Even for cops like Calabrese, the ribbing I was getting was just collateral damage from bombs directed at the man who walked into my office a couple of hours later.

Russ Frist is best pictured as a young Kirk Douglas in a Brooks Brothers suit, if Kirk had been built like a side-by-side Sub-Zero. I told him the other day that any more time on the weights and his seams were going to burst open à la Dr. David Banner, but without all the incredible green hulkiness.

Frist rapped his knuckles against my open door before plopping his dense body down in my guest chair. "You keep any aspirin in this dump?" He grabbed a mail-order running-gear catalog from the corner of my desk and started flipping through it, propping one wingtip on the unoccupied chair next to him.

"You comfy there?" I asked. "Can I get you a pillow? Maybe some chamomile tea?"

"Tea's for wusses." He looked up from the magazine to give me a self-mocking tough-guy look while he shifted his weight to rest both feet on the ground. "Got an aspirin?"

"Sorry, can't help you."

"I feel sore all over. Advil, Tylenol, Aleve, anything?" I was shaking my head as he rattled off pharmaceutical products. "Come on, Kincaid, even you must get the occasional ovary-induced cramp."

"And just when I was feeling sorry for you. Besides, you probably did this to yourself. Did you lift yesterday?"

"Yeah, that's probably it."

"Then suck it up, Mister Marine. Don't you jarheads always say that weakness is wanting pain to leave your body?"

He laughed. "I think you mean 'Pain is weakness leaving the body.' But point taken: All whining will cease. So did you make it up to Vista Heights this morning?"

"Yes, I made it up there, thank you very much. The trip was a total waste of time. I'll be requesting reimbursement for mileage, you know."

"What are you complaining about? It saved you from intake, didn't it?"

"Speaking of which, it was mighty convenient that I drew our unit's short stick on that one. Where were you this morning?"

He interrupted the browsing again and laughed, shaking his head. "*Convenient*, you say? You don't know me at all by now, do you, Kincaid? What time do I usually get in?"

Russ was the only attorney in MCU who often beat me into the office in the morning. "You are such a little shit."

"It was a near miss, though. I actually saw you walking to the courthouse just as I was sneaking out to Marsee's. Nestled into a cozy little table in the back, I almost felt guilty, knowing what was waiting for you on your voice mail, but the cheese Danish got me past it."

"Did you come in here just to torment me, or is there actually a purpose to this little pop-in?"

"I wanted to see how things went on the Crenshaw case this morning."

There was no right answer to that question yet. Early in a case, it's impossible to tell if an investigation is getting any traction. You go through the usual motions of checking out the victim, scouring the neighborhood for witnesses, and shaking down any shady people whose names crop up along the way. You're working the case, but for all you know you're climbing the down escalator. But once you hit the right piece of evidence, all the early effort pushes the case into hyperspeed, potentially hurling the investigation forward *too* quickly from its own momentum.

It was too soon to tell if we'd get to that point on this case, but we certainly weren't there yet. I told Frist as much, bringing him up to speed on where the investigation stood.

"Here's a question for you, though. When Walker called you about the case, why'd you send him my way?" A high-profile murder like this one would usually be hoarded by the head of the Major Crimes Unit.

"Give yourself some credit, Kincaid. You're a good lawyer. You're thorough with the cops, you're one of the very best around here in trial, and you're great with victims."

"Would you mind repeating all of that while I transcribe it for my next evaluation?" I said, pretending to grab for my legal pad. "Seriously, I wasn't questioning whether I'm qualified to handle the case. I know I am."

"Modesty never was your forte."

"What I mean is—unless you're saying I'm better than you at all those things—why didn't you keep the case for yourself? You're not exactly someone who backs down from publicity."

A frustrated defense attorney once told the *Oregonian* that the most dangerous place to stand in Portland was between Russell Frist and a TV camera. Apparently, his fascination with the media began early. According to the rumor mill, when Russ was still on misdemeanor row, he grew impatient waiting for the spotlight that often singles out career prosecutors. Halfway into a trial against a medical school professor accused of picking up a prostitute on Sandy Boulevard, he recognized a crime-beat reporter at Veritable Quandary, a favorite downtown drinking institution. Russ forwent his regular VQ booth, planted himself at a table behind the reporter, and gabbed away to a coworker about every last detail of his pending trial, down to the good doctor's impounded Porsche 911 with the DR LOVE personalized plate. The morning after Russ got his guilty verdict, that same reporter ran the story on the front page of the Metro section, "exposing" the blur between Portland's elite and the city's seedy side.

Ever since, Russ's trials have had a way of grabbing headlines. If he was ducking a case as big as Percy Crenshaw's murder, there had to be a reason.

"Is there a problem I should know about?" My question was blunt, but I can be blunter—and I was. "If you've set me up to eat a plateful of shit you're trying to avoid, the least you can do is tell me it's coming."

The straight tack—coupled with the requisite prosecutorial profanity—always did the trick with Frist. "It's not quite that bad, but there is something. That's why I came in, actually." He leaned back in his chair and shut the door behind him. "I talked to the boss about the assignment this morning. We're taking heat on this Tompkins shooting, big time. Duncan's just being cautious, but he figured it would look better if we had separate DAs working on the two cases."

I was still suspicious. "You've had two big cases going at once before. What gives?"

"This is not two garden-variety big cases."

I gave him a blank look.

"You know," he said.

"I really don't, Russ."

"The African-American thing," he said, whispering the hyphenated adjective the way you might say *cancer* under your breath during proper dinner conversation. At least he hadn't used air quotes.

Still, I laughed at him. He deserved it.

"I'm trying, OK?" he said.

29

"Fine, but the logic's still just plain stupid. So what? We've got two black victims. Since when is that enough to warrant calling in the big boss himself to separate the two investigations?" As District Attorney, Duncan Griffith was the public and political face of this office and supervised all hundred-and-some-odd deputy prosecutors. He rarely involved himself in individual cases, let alone the micromanagement of doling them out.

"It's not just their race. Jesus, Sam, haven't you picked up a paper in the last week? Hamilton stuck three bullets into that woman's head through a fucking windshield. People are seriously pissed. Those same people love Percy Crenshaw. Duncan's being cautious, is all. Having two bodies on the cases might keep them from getting clumped together out there in the public mind." He tilted his head toward the window, as if the glass were all that separated us from the ignorant and manipulable masses.

"Your call," I said, sounding unintentionally dismissive. "I'm happy to have the case."

The ring of the phone saved me from any further paranoid political overanalysis. According to the digital readout, the call originated from Lockworks, a hair salon owned by my very best friend, Grace Hannigan. Grace and I say we're like the sisters we never had, even though she in fact has a screwed-up half sister who turns up occasionally for money. The day I pass up a call from Grace for run-of-the-mill work talk will be the day I officially deserve a smack upside my Lockworks-coiffed head. Fortunately, Frist took this as his cue to leave, mouthing *I'll talk to you later* as he headed out the door. I picked up.

"What's up?"

She got straight to the matter at hand. "Percy Crenshaw's dead?"

"I would've told you tonight." One of the defining ingredients of the friendship I share with Grace is gossip. I hear the city hall and court juice first, while she keeps me up-to-date on the socialite scene. "It's going to be my case, actually."

"Yeah? Well, your case is on the news."

"Already?" Senior prosecutors pine for the good old days, when they could rely on a tight lid until at least the five o'clock news cycle. No such thing anymore as a safety period, given today's nonstop informational stream. Thanks to the cable news practice of designating programming time to local affiliates, even a regional story like mine could pop up any time, 24/7. "What channel?"

"Headline News," she said. "Oh, and before you hang up, happy birthday, girlie."

One of the advantages of a best friendship is the license to be rude when necessary. As she knew I would, I cut the call from Grace short and rushed down the hall to the conference room, the site of the office's only television set. A couple of the guys from Drug and Vice were watching a repeat of *Pimp My Ride*, where humble little Corollas are transformed into full-fledged pumped-up badass-mobiles. Picture a vehicular makeover by Snoop Dogg but without the class. I silently cursed Chuck Forbes and his cable addiction for poisoning my brain.

Ignoring the protests of my former DVD colleagues, I grabbed the remote and started flipping for the news. I didn't recognize the correspondent, a perky, twenty-something brunette positioned at the periphery of the parking lot. From the looks of her enormous umbrella and rain-inappropriate clothing, she was probably new. Soon enough, she'd have a hooded Gore-Tex jacket like the rest of them. Behind her, I did recognize the carport where I had stood just that morning. The carport, I reminded myself, where Percy Crenshaw had lost his life last night.

The news now had one more crime story to add to the pile of coverage about Delores Tompkins and last night's protests. She covered the basics: location, apparent cause of death, the early morning discovery of the body, the victim's semicelebrity standing, the lack of any current suspects. It was pretty much what I would've expected, given the investigation's early status. Until, that is, she began interviewing a self-described neighbor.

The neighbor was definitely new to Portland. Or, as she put it with a nervous smile, "We're new to these parts, so this whole thing's got us darn near ready to head back down to Louisiana."

One of the DVD peanut gallery couldn't resist. "Right, because I hear purt' near nothin' goes wrong in them thar parts—"

"Jesus, you sound like Jethro Bodine," I said, turning up the volume.

"Wait, you didn't let me get to the punch line. There's no crime there unless you count the pumpkin cases. Get it? Pump *kin*?"

I shushed him and turned up the volume some more. All of Russ's cautious talk had gotten to me. Leave it to the local news to transform one anomalous case into a sign that the entire city had become a war zone.

"I feel just awful today wondering if there was something I could've done," the neighbor continued. "Percy lives upstairs from us, so I'm right across from his carport. I was taking my dog Quincy out for his nighttime tinkle, and I saw Percy coming in. He waved at me, which was his usual way. As I was going through the door, I heard someone say something like 'Nice car, Snoop.' You know, that's what he had on his license plate, the word SNOOP. Well, I didn't think anything of it, but now I'm wondering whether it could have been whoever . . . well, whoever did this to him."

Great. Reporters were finding our witnesses before the police. I'd need to call MCT right away to make sure they interviewed this woman.

As it turned out, MCT got to me first. The voice-mail light was on in my office. My pager, which I had left on the desktop, had vibrated its way onto the floor. I picked it up: four missed pages, all from Chuck's cell. I assumed he was checking to make sure I knew the news had broken, but I called him right back anyway.

"Kincaid?"

The voice was familiar, but it wasn't Chuck's.

"I was calling for Chuck Forbes?"

"Yeah, it's Mike. We've been trying to call you."

"Sorry, I just ran down the hall to watch the story. A friend of mine actually beat you to the punch."

"About what?" Mike asked.

"The news. She saw the story and called me."

"The news about what?"

Talking to Chuck's partner was making my head hurt. "The Crenshaw case. The news got hold of it already. I thought that's why you were calling. Someone needs to get out there and interview Crenshaw's downstairs neighbor, by the way. Or has it been done already?"

"Shit. I dunno. We're dealing with something totally different."

A beeping on my phone told me I had another call coming in. I let it go to voice mail.

"What's up?"

"We've got a problem searching the vic's office."

"I signed off on that this morning," I said, specifically remembering that the warrant application included not only the victim's house and car but also his office at the paper. "The judges should all know it's standard."

"That's not the problem. Judge Schwartz signed it this morning, right after I took it in. We called the *Oregonian* a couple hours ago to make sure they knew what was going on and that we were coming." That probably explained how the media had found out about the case before the bureau's public information officer had released it. "Now that we're here, they're telling us not to go in."

"They know you've got a warrant?"

"Faxed over a copy this morning to the facilities manager. It didn't sound like a problem then, but it must have hit a bump somewhere up the road. They say they've got their lawyers looking at it."

"Shit." The involvement of lawyers is always bad. Unless, of course, the lawyer is me. "Did they say why?"

Another beep for another call. When it rains, it pours. I ignored it again.

"Not really. Sounds like a load of bull to me. We don't let anyone else pick and choose whether we execute signed warrants. Chuck thought we should call you before we barged on in, though."

He thought right. Even though the warrant entitled the police to use any reasonable means necessary to conduct the search, the bureau was already stressed about the front-page photographs of cops in riot gear dispersing tear gas into last night's crowds. We didn't need Chuck and Mike splashed across the paper tomorrow, strong-arming their way past a pack of Jimmy Olsens and Peter Parkers.

"Did they say who the lawyer was? Maybe David Bever from Dunn Simon?" I was pretty sure Bever's first-amendment practice included work for the *Oregonian*.

"Yeah, that sounds right," Mike confirmed.

"OK. Hold tight. I'll call him and see what's up. In the mean-time, can you call Johnson and Walker? I just saw Crenshaw's downstairs neighbor on the news. They need to talk to her."

When I hung up the phone, I realized that Alice Gerstein was standing patiently at my door. Of course, Alice always appeared patient. As the senior paralegal for the Major Crimes Unit, she had learned to maintain her cool.

"Judge Wilson's clerk was trying to get through. An attorney from Dunn Simon's down there asking for a temporary restraining order on one of your cases."

I was already out of my chair, knowing exactly which case she was talking about.

3

Late Monday morning downtown at the *Oregonian,* Heidi Hatmaker was fact-checking an article in the paper's research dungeon. She was enjoying the silence, but the day's pace was definitely slower without the ordinary activity of the newsroom. She glanced at the clock, eager for a lunch break, and saw Tom Runyon at the door. Unfortunately, Tom spotted her too. Whenever Heidi's editor laid eyes on her, it meant more work for Heidi.

"There you are," Tom said. "I've got a special project for you. It's a little sensitive. My office?"

Heidi followed her supervisor, dubious about how special this project would turn out to be. Three years ago, she had thrown everything she owned into her hand-me-down BMW 2002 to leave the East Coast and work for this paper. To date, the only break she caught from endless photocopying, line editing, and fact-checking was the occasional fluffy sidebar about yet another useless community activity.

Tom closed the office door behind him and drew the shades.

"I know it's been a hard morning for everyone. I'm still reeling from the news myself, but I need you on this. I just got a call from our legal counsel." Tom was fiddling with the blue lid of his Bic pen. "The police are here to search Percy's office."

Heidi couldn't believe that Percy would be wrapped up in anything nefarious. "What did he do?"

"Nothing," Tom snapped. He was clearly upset. "Geez, I had no idea you were so jaded."

Heidi looked at him blankly. "So why are the police here?"

"I just told you."

"I know, but why would the police search Percy's office if he didn't do anything?"

"Oh, boy. You haven't heard?"

Heidi shook her head.

"You're a reporter, all right," he muttered. "Percy was killed last night. Channel Twelve just broke the story."

"I was in the dungeon all morning," she said. Before she had a chance to let Tom's words sink in, he was telling her to go down to Percy's office. "I don't know what's going on, but I just got a call to make sure no one goes into Percy's office. Someone from building maintenance is there now, but I guess they want someone from the news department to be there too, just in case something happens. I'd do it myself, but it sounds like it might be a while before legal sorts things out with the cops."

"So what am I supposed to do?"

"Stand outside Percy's office and page me if something happens. If you can't find me, get Dan Manning."

His implication was clear: If someone's time had to be squandered, it should be Heidi's. This was precisely the kind of meaningless task that had filled her weeks and months at work, not exactly what she expected when she agreed to move to Oregon. At the time, Heidi thought she'd hit a journalist manqué's jackpot. After graduating from Yale, she had taken a job at a small-town paper in Vermont. From there, she'd gone to a not-quite-as-small small-town paper in Rhode Island.

The chain of events that brought her to Portland began with a visit from her parents, checking up on her quiet northeastern reporter life. The weekend started out well enough: brunch at the B and B, a peek at Slater Mill, and then Heidi would put them back on a plane as planned. But during a final afternoon stroll in Waterplace Park, up the street rode a buddy of sorts, Brent Last-name-unknown, straddling his Harley, his mop of curly hair wrapped in a bandana.

"Hi-diddly-ho, Heidi Ho," he called out, apparently oblivious to the likely relationship between Heidi and the older couple accompanying her. "I left my belt at your place. I'll swing by later?"

Heidi's parents stared at their daughter as she watched Brent ride away with a friendly horn blast to say farewell. "If it makes a difference, it's nothing serious," she said.

Not long after, her father called with an offer. His Skull and Bones buddy had just become the Editor—with a capital E— at the newspaper in Portland, Oregon. The two had met for rib eyes at Ruth's Chris Steakhouse when Dad was in the Pacific Northwest for a merger. A job was waiting for her if she wanted it.

Despite her father's obvious ulterior motive, that conversation had meant the world to her. Daddy was a corner-office partner at a big New York City law firm where former senators went to serve "Of Counsel." Corben Hatmaker, although not a former lawmaker himself, was nevertheless not the kind of lawyer who had to bill hours. He was one of the privileged few whose name on the letterhead justified his enormous annual draw. And Mom—well, Mom was a woman who'd married her dad. In short, they hadn't understood her drive to be a journalist.

So when her father told her he'd used his contacts to secure her not a publicity job with *Vanity Fair* or an events-planning position at *Vogue* but a real line-entry job at a plain old regular city newspaper, she knew she would have been nuts to say no.

Three years later, facing yet another one of Tom Runyon's mundane chores, she wondered why she hadn't stayed put.

On the way to Percy's office, Heidi saw Lon Hubbard from the facilities department talking to two policemen. The beefy darker one was also the more animated. He was holding a piece of paper in front of Lon's face, pointing at specific words for emphasis. The younger, fitter, and, in Heidi's opinion, hotter one appeared to be maintaining his cool. He was simultaneously attempting to calm his friend and convince Lon to read a document. Heidi assumed it was the warrant.

The cute one's cell phone rang. He flipped it open and handed it to the angry one, who answered it and stalked off down the hall. With the confrontation temporarily on hold, Heidi let Lon know that she'd been sent down from the newsroom.

Heidi doubted a cop would disclose details about Percy's death, but it was worth a shot. She put on her friendliest smile. "Do you know anything yet about what happened?"

"It's too soon to tell."

"It can't be too soon if you've got a warrant, right?"

The cop took a second look at Heidi, like maybe she reminded him of someone. "Yeah, but it's a warrant for the victim's office. Standard operating procedure, so to speak."

"But it must be based on something. You had to have told the judge what happened to Percy, at the very least." Heidi was a firm believer that any reporter who coveted a crime beat needed at least a basic knowledge of how the court system worked.

The detective smiled. To her surprise, he handed her the papers he was holding. "Here. Knock yourself out."

She eyed the document. Cops didn't hand over summaries of pending investigations. The papers would simply establish the fact that Percy Crenshaw was a homicide victim. Still, she'd take what she could get.

The description of the evidence lacked detail, but just a few words were enough to give Heidi a sense of Percy's terrible last moments. A carport. A blunt instrument. Repeated massive blows.

"You OK?" the detective asked.

"Sure. I hardly knew the guy." She returned the pages to the detective as if she'd seen it all before.

The dark-haired detective emerged from the hallway, seemingly more calm. "Your girl says to hold tight while she calls this friggin' lawyer we keep hearing about."

Two minutes later, the dark-haired cop's patience was apparently exhausted, and he told his partner he needed to get some air. Heidi took the opportunity to excuse herself as well and head to the restroom. There, she found a stall and cried quietly for a coworker she'd hardly known.

4

From the look on her face, I could tell that Judge Abigail Wilson was not a happy camper. Seeing David Bever's tall thin frame standing before the bench with a stack of papers in hand, I had a pretty good guess as to the source of her discontent.

Judge Wilson was currently assigned to handle the ex parte docket. For judicial types, this gig was about as close as you get to winning an extra vacation day. The body might need to be there in its black robe, but the brain could check out.

Why? Because the only sure way for a judge to avoid the usual bickering between litigators is to leave one of them out of the room, and ex parte is a fancy way of saying that one party is talking to the judge outside of the other party's presence. For simple things like uncontested extensions of deadlines and trial set-overs, head over to the ex parte docket, assure the judge your opponent has no complaints, get your order signed, and you're out of there. Easy work for the lawyer, even easier for the judge.

But David Bever's unusual request was anything but simple, and any hopes Judge Wilson may have carried for a day of mental coasting were quashed.

"Ah, Ms. Kincaid. You're here." Wilson's long gray hair was pulled back loosely at the nape of her neck. Although she sat at her bench, she hadn't bothered throwing the judicial robe over her cream-colored silk blouse. "David, why don't you provide Ms. Kincaid with a copy of your papers so she can get up to speed."

They were precisely what I expected after my conversation with Calabrese. The *Oregonian* was asking for a temporary restraining order to prevent the Portland Police Department or the Multnomah County District Attorney's Office from entering their building. The end goal was to permanently quash the search warrant authorizing a search of Percy Crenshaw's office.

Wilson had the authority to issue the order ex parte but, like most judges, had chosen to hear at least a preview of what both parties had to offer. From the tone of Wilson's voice, I was not off to a good start. Consciously or not, judges sometimes hold a grudge against the lawyer responsible for bringing them work. I thought of that lawyer as Bever; he, after all, was the one asking for the TRO. Unfortunately, Wilson seemed to hold me responsible for this intrusion, since the police had sought the vexing warrant in the first place.

Once my quick and casual flip through the papers made it clear that I didn't place much stock in them, Judge Wilson asked for my position.

"What it would be in any other criminal case involving a lawfully obtained search warrant. The police are authorized to execute the warrant. If the search yields incriminatory evidence against a suspect, that suspect can challenge the search in his trial. I don't understand why Mr. Bever feels entitled to commence such a highly unusual proceeding in response to what is truly a run-of-the-mill search."

"There's nothing run-of-the-mill about it," Bever said, removing his wire-rimmed glasses to maximize the appearance of scholarly pontification. "The police are entering a building owned and operated by a newspaper for the express purpose of searching through a reporter's office. They want to search—and *seize*, don't forget—quote: '*Any* documents, notes, files, papers, *or* photographs, including *but not limited to* those in computerized, digitized, or electronic formats, that *pertain* to the murder of Percy Crenshaw.' Apparently it is left to the officers' discretion to determine what does or doesn't *pertain* to their investigation."

I had to hand it to Bever; he'd earned his reputation as a fierce protector of the Constitution. Coming from him, our standard warrant language sounded downright Big Brothery.

"With all due respect to Mr. Bever's thespian talents, his dramatic reading failed to emphasize the fact that the reporter in question, Percy Crenshaw, is a homicide victim. Searching the victim's home and office is a vital part of the beginning of an investigation, and the clock is ticking."

"But here's my problem, counselor." Shoot. I was right. The judge had a problem. "This particular victim was a reporter, and that means you're searching the offices of a newspaper. I find that very troubling."

Fortunately, I had more to argue. "Your honor, *Zurcher v. Stanford Daily* is directly on point." I recited the facts and controlling law as if I'd read the case minutes earlier: The police executed a warrant to seize photographs that a campus newspaper had taken of political demonstrators who assaulted a police officer. The paper balked at the search, but the Supreme Court didn't. Evidence is evidence, even if it's in the hands of a newspaper.

I couldn't help but feel satisfied. I have never been able to memorize anything—strike that. I have involuntarily cemented thousands of failed Hollywood liaisons and sappy love-song lyrics into my brain matter, but much to my frustration I cannot memorize the names of cases. Meanwhile, scores of lawyers routinely dupe judges into thinking they're smart by rattling off the case names, regardless of what they say or whether they're relevant. Today, though, I caught a break. I knew this particular case because it had occurred on the very campus where I had first read it in law school.

Bever knew it also. "*Stanford* is distinguishable. In that case, the paper's cameraman had actually been present at the scene of the crime, taking photographs while the crime was committed. Here, the police don't even know whether the victim's death had anything to do with his position at the newspaper, so how can they possibly know whether his office contains evidence?"

I knew in my gut the police should be allowed to get in there. How could they know if there was a link between the murder and the paper until they checked it out? I gave it another shot. "I find it hard to believe that Mr. Bever's client would want to impede the investigation into the murder of one of its employees. More importantly, I find it even harder to believe that Mr. Crenshaw would agree with this maneuver if he were around to hear about it."

"She does have a point, David." Then why did I feel so lousy? Because apparently my opponent was on first-name terms with Judge Abigail Wilson, while I was the pronoun prosecutor, She. "We're off the record. Why in the world would you want to stop the police, given the circumstances?"

Bever's gaze alternated between me and the judge. "I'm not trying to be an obstructionist. I have absolutely no problem with the police looking at anything that might lead to whoever did this, but the warrant is so broad that it amounts to a fishing expedition. I'd be a heck of a lot more comfortable with this if the police had something—anything—tying this terrible crime to Percy's reporting. My concern is that they'll scour all his notes and files, many of which will undoubtedly reveal confidential sources and pending stories, and then find nothing relevant to their investigation. Maybe once the TRO is in place, Ms. Kincaid and I can hammer out a compromise."

The only reason Bever wanted a TRO while we sought a compromise was to put me over a barrel in negotiations. And if all he was after was some middle ground, why hadn't he just picked up the phone? Before I realized what I was doing, I spoke the latter objection aloud.

I knew it was a mistake the second the words left my mouth. Courthouse gossip gets around fast, even with the judges, and Wilson wasn't going to let the moment pass.

"As I recall, Ms. Kincaid, you were accused of pulling a similar stunt not so long ago." On my first case in the Major Crimes Unit, the one Percy Crenshaw had turned into a movie option, I had sprung a surprise confrontation on the City Attorney himself. He had refused to let me examine a missing judge's files, and without any notice I had hauled him over to the courthouse to defend himself. I had won the battle, but Dennis Coakley hadn't kept the incident to himself. In the longer war of professional reputations, I had suffered a hit.

Bever had an additional reason for heading straight to the courthouse. "To be frank, your honor, I'm not precisely certain what you're referring to. But, since you've asked, Ms. Kincaid, I'll tell you why I didn't call you directly. In light of my firm's past dealings with you, I had the perception that you might not be receptive to working something out between the lawyers."

Various people had warned me over the years that my antics would eventually catch up to me, and today seemed to be the big day. Bever was referring to the same case, different conflict: My shitbag of an ex-husband, Roger, worked at Dunn Simon and had represented the missing judge's husband. Let's just say we butted heads a few times, and now the three hundred or so lawyers at prestigious Dunn Simon think I'm a snake.

I could see where this road was heading, and I wanted off.

"I'd be happy to try to work something out with David," I said, trying to join the first-name club, "but it shouldn't be with a groundless restraining order in place. Your honor, Judge Schwartz issued the search warrant this morning after a thorough review of the affidavits supporting the warrant request. Perhaps she would appreciate the chance to rule on the motion?"

Wilson had been a rainmaker at one of the big firms before coming to the bench, which meant she didn't know a lick about real-life police work.

"Trust me, I'd love to dump this on her, but she just started a monthlong trial so I'm stuck with you. I see what the state is saying about the routine nature of searching a homicide victim's property, but I don't like the idea of the police having unfettered access to a journalist's office. Crenshaw could very well have been working on something critical of the city or even of the police, and there would be nothing to preserve the confidentiality of that work once the search warrant was executed." She paused, and I could tell that she truly was torn about what to do. "You don't have *anything* suggesting a link to his work?"

She was looking for a way out. I suppose I could have told her that the police viewed a link to a recent story as the most likely scenario. But it wouldn't have been true. And she and Bever would know it wasn't true once they got wind of the interview I had just seen on the news moments ago. Six months from now, this moment too could come back to bite me.

Better to repair the damage. "No, we don't. In fact, it may have been an attempted car theft that got out of control. One of the neighbors heard someone say something to the victim about his car last night, and another witness saw some kids in the parking lot. It's too early to tell, though, and it's vital that we explore all the possibilities." After forty-eight hours, the odds of solving an unsolved homicide start slipping fast.

"And they say lawyers are never honest," she said. "Here's what we're going to do. I am persuaded that there is a risk of irreparable damage to the *Oregonian* if I permit this warrant to be executed as written, so I am going to enter the TRO. But I don't want to halt a valid step in an ongoing murder investigation. So, Mr. Bever, have your client choose an employee to work with Ms. Kincaid to search the victim's office. Ms. Kincaid, you can choose one police officer to assist you, and I'm entering an order that requires confidentiality from all those involved for any information that isn't relevant to your investigation. Any problems?"

On my way back to the office, Frist stopped me in the hallway. "Alice said some Dunn Simon fuck was trying to get a TRO on something?"

"Yeah, a search on the Crenshaw case. We worked it out, though." He wanted the play-by-play, but I explained I had detectives in the field waiting for instructions.

Chuck was uncharacteristically glum when he answered the phone.

"What's wrong with you? Worried I'd blow the restraining order?"

"No, I knew you'd handle it."

"So what's the problem?"

"I don't even know how to put it," he said lowering his voice. "It's just so unbelievable. Johnson called. Matt York's wife has been cheating on him."

"Alison was cheating?" I asked in disbelief. Chuck and Matt had met the day they both sat for the bureau's civil service exam. They stuck together through the police academy and had been friends ever since. Chuck had been a groomsman at Matt's wedding to Alison, and just last week, Matt had been one of the few buddies willing to work for pizza and beer when Chuck loaded the U-Haul and moved to my place.

"Did Johnson tell you that Percy had a woman over a couple of nights ago? She parked in someone else's spot?"

"Yeah. A pissed-off neighbor wrote down the license plate."

"Right. Well, the plate came back to Matt, and the neighbor's description of the driver matched Alison. Ray called her. She'd been seeing Percy for a few weeks."

"Oh, my God." I suppose I should know from my own experience with marriage that you can never tell who might be cheating, but it seemed hard to imagine with the Yorks. As I understood it, Matt had fallen so hard when he met Alison Madison working in the precinct records room that his sergeant made him choose between a transfer or a shift change to avoid the romantic distraction. Matt chose the transfer so he and Alison would still have the same schedule. I'd had dinner with them a couple of times since Chuck and I had become an item, and I could have sworn that same intensity was still there. Last I heard, they were trying to get pregnant. In retrospect, maybe it had been a last ditch effort at happiness.

"So now," Chuck said, "just to make sure we're squared away, we've got to nail down where Matt and Alison were on Sunday night. Alison was at a baby shower with ten other women, but no one has talked to Matt yet. I told Ray I'd do it."

"I'm sorry, Chuck. I know that'll be hard."

"It'll suck, basically. But, hey, what are you gonna do, right? Where are we on the warrant?"

I knew Chuck well enough to know he desperately wanted a change of subject and mood. "Have you been fretting over there?"

"When are you going to get it, babe? Worrying gets you nowhere. It's all about the zen. We good to go?"

"Nope. Say bye-bye to that warrant."

"Yeah, right."

"No, I'm serious. Judge Wilson granted the order; the warrant's void until further notice."

He waited for the expected "just kidding." When he didn't get it, the cussing commenced. "What the—"

I had to smile. "What about the zen, babe?"

"I apparently lost it with the contents of my bladder."

I walked him through the compromise Judge Wilson had hammered out.

"So when are we supposed to do this thing?" he asked.

"Soon, I think. The attorney will call me once he knows who's going to help us on the newspaper's end."

"And you can only have one person with you?"

I needed to pick between Mike and Chuck. I cringed at the thought of publicly opting for my beau, but I trusted Chuck's discretion more than Mike's. The son of a former Oregon governor, Detective Charles Landon Forbes, Jr., might choose to eschew political niceties, but he understood them enough to tolerate them when necessary. With Mike, what you saw was what you got.

"Why don't you find something else for Mike to do? You and I will take care of the files."

"Sounds hot."

"You say that about everything."

"With you? You know it."

49

■   ■   ■

I was still smiling while I disconnected and dialed Johnson's cell number.

"Hey, it's Sam. You get my message from Mike about the neighbor?"

"We're on it."

It had been six months, but the MCT detectives were still getting used to my style. I kept a closer watch on investigations than a lot of the other DAs. "Did you talk to her?"

"Just walked out, in fact. Nice lady, but not real helpful. She didn't bother turning around to look at whoever was talking to Crenshaw, so there's no way we're getting an ID from her. She can't even remember anything about the voice, other than that he had an Or-uh-gahn accent." He emphasized the last syllable of our state's name, the way people from the rest of the country pronounced it. The wrong way.

"How's the search of the vic's apartment going?"

"Nothing obvious yet. Did Chuck tell you about Alison York?"

"Yeah."

"Can you believe that shit? I guess you never know, huh?"

No, you never did. I thought back to the shock of finding my ex-husband Roger atop his extramarital conquest on our dining room table.

"Lucky for all of us, we can avoid what could have been an even worse scene," he went on. "I just called Central. Matt put in OT on the swing shift Sunday, working the protest crowd. Chuck's going to talk to Matt about the details, but it looks like he's clear."

"So we finally find Percy's dirty little secret, and we've still got nothing."

When victims' messy entanglements are responsible for getting them killed, we usually get a whiff of it right away. Last year, we had a family mowed down in a home invasion in Sellwood. According to the family's neighbors, coworkers, and fellow parishioners, they were plain old regular folks. A quick sweep of the house revealed otherwise. Plain folk don't hide forty grand and nearly a kilo of heroin in the sofa cushions. Needless to say, the discovery helped MCT narrow the investigation considerably. In the odd case where the victim isn't hinky, developing a theory to guide the investigation is a lot tougher.

"We're still digging," Johnson said. Of course they were. The truth was, until you knew who did it, everything about the victim's life remained in question. After all, which was more likely: that the case truly was the statistically improbable random killing, or that the police just hadn't stumbled across the right dirt yet?

"Anything helpful?"

"Well, we've got the super I told you about this morning."

"The one with the generic description of two white guys in the lot."

"You got it. Peter Anderson. The guy's seriously stressed. The condo owners are paging him incessantly, wanting every light in the parking lot replaced in case it burns out. Meanwhile, we've got him downtown looking through the books."

"Needle in a haystack," I said, recognizing that it wasn't anything Johnson didn't already know.

"I'm trying to get someone in ATTF to work up a montage of some likely candidates, but I'm not holding my breath." It was a good idea. Members of the specialized Auto Theft Task Force could help. With the bureau's fancy state-of-the-art X-imaging software, officers could now search a database of mug shots electronically, pulling up photos of perps with similar crimes with a few keystrokes. The problem was that Ray had no idea which known car thieves were most likely to get violent with a victim.

"What's the problem?" I asked.

"I just don't know anyone over there anymore. You know how it goes."

If interdepartmental cooperation at the bureau was anything like it was in the DA's office, I wasn't surprised that ATTF hadn't dropped everything for a faceless member of the MCT. I offered to call Heidi Moawad, ATTF's assigned prosecutor. I was pretty sure she'd help me; she had a reputation as a good egg, and I'd shared my friendlier side with her at a couple of tipsy happy hours. Most importantly, I had saved her two weeks ago from walking out of the courthouse elevator with a bra hanging out of her gym bag. We're talking serious female bonding.

"If all else fails, what about bringing in a sketch artist?"

"Too early. We don't usually get into something like that until everything else has dried up and all we've got left is an eyewitness and no suspect. We're sort of in the reverse situation right now. Lots to look at still, and a witness who may not have seen anything helpful."

"All right, keep me up-to-date. I need to go brief Frist."

"Damn. Tell him to give you some breathing room already. It's been six months."

"Yeah. How about you tell him for me?"

Russ was still waiting for assurances that David Bever's pop-in with Judge Wilson wasn't going to derail the investigation. Jessica Walters was splayed generously in one of his office guest chairs, her Rockport loafers kicked off to expose obviously swollen feet, her suit jacket draped open around an enormous mass that was once a flat abdomen. I realized I was staring at the buttons that threatened to pop from the crisp white cotton stretched across her impressive girth.

My gawking didn't go unnoticed by Jessica. "Christ, Kincaid. Get a good enough look there?"

"Sorry," I said. I forced myself to lift my gaze from her belly to her eyes. "I guess I didn't realize you were that far along."

"The magic of a black jacket," she explained, momentarily holding her blazer closed in front of her. She was right; the move took off a good trimester. "Yep, I've only got one more month, and I'm not going to lie. I've gained fifty-two pounds."

Frist nearly spit up the water he was guzzling from a sports bottle. "Well, you better hope you're giving birth to a four-year-old, because I've never heard of a fifty-pound newborn."

"Tell me about it. Julia's been accusing me of using the pregnancy as an excuse to eat all the shit she normally keeps away from me. I keep telling her I'll take it off breast-feeding, but she's threatening to withhold sex if all this fat sticks around." She grabbed her stomach for emphasis.

"Uhh, I know you like fucking with my head, Walters," Frist said, with his patented introductory gravel, "but that's a little too much information."

I wasn't sure if Frist was referring to the mammary activities or to Walters's intimate mention of her longtime partner. Either way, his discomfort was ironic, because I had heard Frist and his buddies fantasize about both. Apparently, a big pregnancy bosom was sexy only if it wasn't going to be used as intended, and the idea of Walters with her beautiful girlfriend was hot only when discussed among her male coworkers.

"Deal with it," Jessica retorted. "If your half of the species had to go through this shit, doctors would have invented an artificial womb fifty years ago. Anyway, Sam, this is what awaits if you too decide to enjoy the miracle that is human childbirth."

I silently added the physical discomforts of pregnancy to my long list of reasons for being squeamish about motherhood. Nine months of sobriety. The mall-hopping required for a whole new wardrobe of maternity clothes. No way could I swing a club past a belly like Jessica's, so bye-bye to golf. Apparently indescribable physical pain. Stretch marks. Diapers and upchuck. Not to mention the idea of a little independent person who can't talk, understand, or reason; who at the slightest sensation of discontent, could afford to pour every last drop of oceanic baby energy into a penetrating scream that convinces you—rationally or not—that you are an incompetent parent who fails to anticipate and satisfy your child's most basic needs. No, thank you.

"Not to change the subject, ladies, but what was the deal on that Dunn Simon thing?" Russ asked.

I told him about David Bever's motion to halt the search of Crenshaw's office and Judge Wilson's order.

"You should've made Bever go through the City Attorney's Office," Russ suggested. "They're the ones who represent the police, and the motion was aimed at the bureau, not us."

True enough, but I couldn't see any advantage in involving Dennis Coakley's office. "We're lucky the judge called anyone at all, since Bever waltzed in to the ex parte docket. Besides," I added, "most of the city attorneys don't know anything about search and seizure anyway."

Jessica and Russ exchanged a knowing glance. Jessica was the one to speak the shared thought. "Not to mention the warm fuzzies between you and Dennis Coakley."

"And there's that," I said, with a sigh. I wondered how long it would take to heal the damage inflicted by one rash decision. OK, make that two. Three, maximum.

"Well, don't sweat it, Kincaid," Russ said. "I'm not exactly Dennis Coakley's favorite person right now either. Duncan and

I had a meeting with him this morning about the Tompkins shooting."

"Is he worried about the police union?" On the rare occasions that the city tried to discipline a bad apple in the police barrel, the PPA went into overdrive. Two years earlier, the city tried to fire a vice unit lieutenant for having sex on duty in the back of his bureau-issued Crown Vic with a self-described *escort*. He chalked it up to a "lapse of judgment," even though the activity had occurred thrice weekly for an eight-month period. The Portland Police Association beefed the termination, and the state Employment Relations Board eventually ordered the bureau to reinstate the backseat lothario, albeit with a demotion and a transfer out of vice. Ever since, I've wondered what a cop needs to do to lose the protection of the powerful PPA. That, and I always checked the upholstery before accepting a ride in a bureau car.

"If my MCT guys are any indication, the union will balk if the city tries to go after Hamilton on the employment front."

"Are you kidding?" Frist jeered. "The city would love to see this thing go *away*. Coakley's pressuring us to call the shooting clean, so the heat will come to Griffith instead of the mayor and the bureau. And don't forget the money. The city's already looking at major liability. A criminal indictment will add a couple of zeroes to the civil demand."

"So are you going along with it?"

"We'll send the case to the grand jury like all police shootings. But we haven't decided yet which way to steer things."

Any prosecutor who tells you that the grand jury acts independent of the prosecutor's office is relying on legalistic niceties. Sure, as a formal matter, the grand jury has its own powers to call witnesses, gather evidence, and decide whether, when, and which charges should be brought against a defendant. But there's no judge or defense attorney in the grand jury room, only the prosecutor and the jurors. It doesn't take a legal eagle to figure out the real dynamic.

The opposing theoretical and practical realities are what make the grand jury the perfect vehicle for police shootings—or any other sensitive case, for that matter. Behind the sealed confines of the grand jury proceedings, we nudge the decision, subtly or not. Then, in the public statement announcing the grand jury's decision, we proudly declare that we presented the evidence to a pool of independent citizens and entrusted them with the final call. It's the ultimate CYA.

Jessica had strong feelings about the Delores Tompkins shooting, and she wasn't hiding them. "Fuck Geoff Hamilton. Some time in the pen would do that idiot good."

Russ was obviously more torn. "Maybe you should have this case, then. My whole problem with an indictment is the mandatory minimums that would apply if he actually got convicted."

"Listen to Mr. Lefty Lou over here." Jessica hiked her thumb toward Frist. "It's not like you've got a problem with those sentences when we're doling them out against the rest of the docket."

"Oh, come on," I interjected. "You can't seriously believe Hamilton's like the rest of our docket. He's got piss-poor judgment, but it's not like he went out looking to shoot someone. He was just doing his job when a situation got out of control."

I'm funny that way. Put me in a room with Mike Calabrese, hailing Officer Hamilton as the great American hero, and I'm ready to slam the cell door myself. Faced with Walter's unsympathetic excoriation, I become Hamilton's defender. When confronted with extreme positions, my tendency is to run to the center. Some might call it waffling. Chuck calls it contrarian. I choose to see it as fair-mindedness.

Jessica was unpersuaded. "Maybe I'd give the benefit of the doubt to another officer. But Geoff Hamilton's a thumper. Something wrong with that boy upstairs."

"I don't know anything about him," I conceded.

"Well, one thing about working in Gangs, you have witnesses and victims who are usually the defendants on our cases. I take most of it with a grain of salt, but, trust me, Hamilton's name comes up so often there's got to be something there. He came into Northeast Precinct a couple years ago, and it was, like, immediately the neighborhood knew his name. One story has him complaining when the precinct's fleet manager cleaned blood off the hood of his patrol car after a resist arrest. He wanted to send a message to the rest of the neighborhood. If we let him off, we can forget about getting the people up there to work with us anytime in the near future."

"And *that*," Russ emphasized, "is exactly why Hamilton should probably start looking for a defense lawyer. The line officers will be pissed off for a while, but the alternative is pissing off the entire black community. We've sided with hothead cops in I don't know how many police shootings, not to mention all the other use-of-force cases. But usually the victim was resisting arrest, or at least a wing nut. Tompkins seems pretty clean."

"If Tompkins wasn't doing anything wrong, how did a cop wind up shooting her in the head?" I asked.

"We're still trying to figure out what happened," Russ explained. "Hamilton's union rep has him clammed up for now, and obviously the woman's not around to tell us anything."

In other words, he had none of the details that might help him decide what was the right, not just the expedient, thing to do.

"Well, I'm about to join the two of you in the hot seat because a bunch of kids can't find anything better to do than run around making trouble." Jessica's change of subject was so abrupt, I wondered whether the thought of a single mother blown away, leaving a one-year-old and three-year-old orphaned, was too much even for her.

"The protest cases again?" I asked.

For Russ's benefit, Jessica repeated what she had told me at the Justice Center about the property damage on Northwest 23rd. "I thought it was bad enough when a few of them looked like they might be felonies. But now it turns out that these losers did more than break a few windows. There were at least two random assaults: bad ones, too. A bystander took some home movies with his camcorder. Hopefully we'll actually find the fuckers, but the media will have a heyday."

"It's always a bigger story when there's video," Russ added.

"Tell me about it. I'm getting calls from the press already, comparing it to the wilding in Central Park. Give me a break. The bureau's telling me they're still getting reports of other incidents up there, which are most likely connected, even though we'll never be able to prove it. It's a total nightmare. Duncan wants me to make sure we put a case together, and I can't get the bureau to decide who's going to do the work."

"What's the problem?" I asked.

"Typical bureaucratic bullshit. It's not a major crime so they won't do anything other than put the pictures out for the public. And the pictures aren't worth a shit, so I know exactly what that'll get us—a ton of calls saying maybe it's this guy, maybe it's not. I'll be back to square one, begging the bureau to do the follow-up."

"What time did all this go down last night?"

"It peaked around nine. Why?"

I thought about the information we had so far on the Crenshaw case. Kids in the parking lot. "Nice car, Snoop." Then I thought about my drive to Percy Crenshaw's condominium earlier that morning, past the Zupan's market on Northwest 23rd. It was only a short jump up the hill to the condos perched above.

I also thought about the time Mike would have on his hands, since he couldn't work on the *Oregonian* search warrant.

"You know Mike Calabrese?" I asked.

"Sure," Jessica said. "Major Crimes Team."

"Want him to help?"

It was a win-win situation for both of us. Or so it seemed.

5

The controversy preceding the search of Percy's office turned out to be the most notable legal aspect of the search. David Bever could have saved us all a lot of time if he'd realized that Percy Crenshaw apparently didn't believe in keeping a record— of anything.

He recorded car mileage only by the distances traveled, no times or locations. He jotted down first names with no other indications of identity or importance. We took copies of the cell phone records and business expense reports we found in his files, hoping they might pan out down the road. But I believe the technical term for the rest of what we found is a whole mess of gobbledy gunk—a seemingly random collection of miscellaneous words, numbers, dates, and codes, the meaning of which most likely left this world with Percy.

Chuck excused himself to make a call while I thanked the young reporter who helped us with the search. When Chuck found me waiting outside the building, he asked me if I had time to make another stop.

I checked my watch, tempted by the idea of a break. Standing in Percy's office just hours after his murder had gotten to me. "Sure, why not? It's my birthday, right?"

"It's nothing fun, I'm afraid. I finally got through to Matt and told him we need to talk. He's at home. Alison's there too. I was thinking you could—"

"Keep her occupied with girl talk while you check out the alibi? Chuck, it's not like we're best friends."

"No, but Matt and I are pretty damn close. He's probably got some idea of what's coming, but it's going to be a hard enough conversation without worrying if Alison's listening in."

He was right. Under the circumstances, the miserable task of sitting awkwardly with Alison fell squarely within both my girlfriend and MCU duties.

Ten minutes later, we pulled into the driveway of their split-level ranch in the Burlingame neighborhood. Chuck smiled sadly at the sight of their mailbox, proudly (and clumsily) announcing the York / Madison-York household.

"Did I ever tell you about the battle over that hyphen?"

"I know Matt mocks her for it." Everyone who knew them knew that. Matt regularly teased his wife, calling her Madison-York for not-so-short.

"Alison wanted Matt to hyphenate too. She was really pushing for it. And, man, guys in the bureau just don't do that. Matt Madison-York? No way." He laughed to himself, no doubt recalling the good-natured shit Matt's friends had given him. "I figured she'd eventually drop it, but to this day they both love to make a point of it." He tapped the box as we passed.

Matt must have heard the county Crown Vic. He met us at the door. I expected him to look a lot worse. When I walked in on Roger with his six-foot-tall plaything, I had driven directly to my parents' house and cried for four hours straight. My face resembled a puff pastry for two days.

Matt seemed resolute by comparison. Aside from telltale shadows beneath his usually bright eyes, his appearance was normal—same neat blond hair, smooth-shaven face, and friendly smile.

"Hey, man," Chuck said, clasping Matt's upper arm. "Thanks for doing this."

"I know the drill," Matt said, opening the door farther to let us in.

Matt took our coats, then told me Alison was out back, gesturing to the rear of the house. "I'm sure she'd appreciate some company."

I found Alison sitting on the porch in a rattan rocker just beyond the sliding glass doors of their kitchen. Her light-brown shoulder-length hair was pulled into a ponytail at the nape of her neck. She had the same clean-cut generic good looks as her husband.

"Aren't you cold out here?" I asked, opening the slider a crack. A green awning covered their back porch, deflecting the rain that Alison appeared to be watching.

"No, this thing's pretty cozy," she said, holding up a U of O stadium blanket from her lap. "Matt told me you guys were coming by. Bureau's got to make sure the jealous husband didn't do it, right?"

Alison had always struck me as more sweet than interesting, but this conversation was even more uncomfortable than anticipated. I doubted that anyone could pull off making light of this situation. Alison surely couldn't.

"Good thing I was at that baby shower, huh?" she added.

"Let's just go ahead and say it," I said. "This is really . . . awkward, to say the least. We obviously feel bad for everyone involved." I didn't mention Percy by name.

She rocked some more, watching the rain again. "I might not seem too sympathetic right now, Sam, but I hope you can leave us out of this," she finally said.

"I assume you understand why the police have to talk to both of you. No one's trying to judge you or punish you."

"No, not that. I mean, after this. I was with my girlfriends. Matt was on duty, and he's going over every last detail with Chuck right now, I'm sure. I hope that can be the end of the story."

She was envisioning an eventual trial against whoever did kill—what was the word for Percy in her life, her lover? Special friend? She was picturing a defense attorney dragging the two of them to the stand, detailing her trips to Vista Heights, using them to create reasonable doubt.

She had reason to worry. I placed my hand lightly on her shoulder. I didn't know Alison well, and I'm the last person to defend what she'd done. But I knew what a criminal trial might put them through, and I knew the Yorks well enough to see that neither of them deserved it.

She covered my hand with hers, as if to say she understood there was only so much I could do. A few silent minutes later, Chuck slid the door open. "Hey, Alison."

She gave him a token wave over her shoulder, clearly not expecting him to reciprocate.

"You about ready?" he asked me. "We're done in here."

"Yeah. I've got to get back," I said to Alison.

She nodded and released her hand from mine, still rocking. I gave her a final squeeze on her shoulder and followed Chuck to the car.

He paused longer than necessary at the stop sign on their

corner, then sighed loudly, physically shaking out his arms, as if that would purge the tension of the York household from his body.

"You OK?"

"I think so. Fuck, that was worse than I expected."

"His alibi's good, though, right?" I was thinking again about trying to protect them at trial.

"Yeah, no problem. He worked swing shift with overtime until two in the morning. I printed out a list of all his calls, and we walked through them one by one. Thanks to the protesters, he was busy."

"And how's he doing?"

That single question launched a response that continued during the entire drive downtown. Despite his rare display of verboseness, my boyfriend never did find the right combination of words to describe either his friend's anguish or his own feelings of disloyalty as he ran through the details of Matt's call-outs, each question a reminder that his wife had been sleeping with another man. Chuck didn't know whether to feel bad for Matt or knock some sense into him for staying with Alison. As he pulled to the curb in front of the courthouse, the best he could manage in conclusion was, "It's just really sad."

By seven o'clock, I was already tired. Apparently you don't need to be legally married to become a boring old married person.

At my father's insistence, we were celebrating my birthday at his house. "No reservations required. No smoking," he had said. At my insistence, only my four favorite people were invited: Dad, Grace, Chuck, and Vinnie. OK, so maybe Vinnie's not a person, but he makes for way better company than most of those who technically qualify.

Dad met Chuck and me at the door in a blue sweater and

chinos. I kissed him on the cheek. "You wore that sweater for me, didn't you?"

"Oh, this old thing?" he said jokingly. I was forever telling my father how handsome he looked in blue. It brought out the color in his kind eyes and contrasted nicely with his silver hair. With his handsome looks and good health, he could probably find himself a girlfriend if he wanted one. But, almost three years after we had lost my mom to cancer, he still wasn't ready, and that was just fine by me.

By the time he and Chuck finished their backslap-not-a-hug thing, Vinnie had finally caught up with us, hoisting his squatty legs and fat little torso over the final porch step. He doesn't like to be carried.

As usual, Dad had fired up mass quantities of hot beef on the Weber. In honor of the special occasion, he had even prepared all the necessary fixin's: garlic bread, mac and Velveeta, and baked potatoes with every imaginable fat form crammed inside. Not a real vegetable in sight.

"Looks yum, Dad, but is there anything for Grace to eat?"

"If she won't eat steak, she can drink her dinner." Dad pointed to the multiple bottles of wine he'd purchased for the evening. "I doubt she'll mind."

Dad had known Grace since we were nine years old and was convinced she was an anorexic lush. The sickening truth was that thin, fit Grace ate as much as she wanted. And she wasn't a lush. She just drank. A lot. Boatloads, really. But a lush can't suck down four martinis and still cut a perfect broom-straight bob.

To my disgust, though, skinny beautiful Grace had just begun a weeklong "purification regime" requiring a mix of all-fruit, all-veggie, and seemingly impossible soy protein days. I didn't care to know all the details, but I was pretty sure that a beef-slab-and-chocolate-cake night was not in the plan.

Chuck was crouched next to the dog bed in the corner of the dining room, coaxing Vinnie to accept a Milk Bone. After years of indifference, Chuck the new roommate was now faced with the difficult task of winning the affections of my little man. In the last week, Vinnie had peed in Chuck's gym bag, pooped in his slippers, and gnawed on every article of clothing that Chuck had left within reach. As far as I could tell, the only training accomplished was strictly canine-to-human. No more dirty man-clothes on my bedroom floor. Good dog.

I wished I knew how to tell a dog to cut a guy some slack, though. Vinnie was usually remarkably in tune with human emotions, but Chuck was doing a good job hiding how upset he was about Matt York's situation. I stared at Vinnie, willing him to take the damn treat.

Chuck finally gave up when Grace walked in. In fact, her barely recognizable appearance stopped us all dead in our tracks. Her natural spiral curls had been straightened to blades, a line of heavy bangs edged her eyebrows, and her ever-changing hair color had morphed to flaming cranberry. Think Vidal Sassoon meets Jolly Rancher.

"You've finally done it," Chuck declared. "You've sucked down enough of those Cosmopolitan martinis to marinate your roots."

Grace looked at him the way you'd look at a child who was intentionally testing your patience—which pretty much describes Chuck. In the time I had learned to let Chuck make me happy instead of nuts, Grace had come to appreciate Chuck, but only for his role in my life.

"As a gift to Sam, I'll refrain from commenting on the smashing ensemble you've selected for this special evening," she said. Chuck was decked out in a black Motorhead T-shirt and faded jeans, complete with a tear beneath the right rear pocket.

"Actually, I kind of like the short part over your forehead like that," Chuck offered. "You look younger somehow. You can't see the wrinkles anymore."

I looked at Chuck and shook my head. Grace just stared at him. "Well, I like it," she announced, flipping a few locks from her shoulder. "Sam's birthday had me feeling old by osmosis. I wanted a bold change."

Mission accomplished, I thought. But like a good best friend, I'd wait until we were alone to break the news: She had officially crossed the fine line that separates fashionably individualistic from drag-queen territory.

And, like a good best friend, Grace broke from her purification regime and defiled herself with macaroni and chocolate cake. She, Chuck, Dad, and I spent the evening around the table, swapping stories, playing pinochle, and, most of all, laughing. Grace even convinced me to join her for a commemorative belting-out of Gloria Gaynor's "I Will Survive," empty cabernet bottles substituting for the hairbrushes we'd once used as microphones.

The revelry was almost enough to make me forget not just the morose silence of the Yorks' house but even the scene in Percy Crenshaw's office earlier that afternoon. Half a year in MCU had hardened me to the horrible acts we humans can commit against each other. Stabbings, shootings, even sex offenses are everyday work now. But death still gets me. The permanence of it. The total, complete finality. And, in the case of a murder, the utter senselessness.

On my first murder call-out, I had felt the magnitude of the loss the minute I saw the woman's body, discarded so hastily at the edge of a construction site. But, as time in the MCU ring has passed, it now takes more blows for me to feel the impact. Today, that moment had come while Chuck and I were standing in Percy's space—the room where he'd researched, created, and written.

The notes we had gone there to scour had been a bust, but we had seen so much more than we intended. The photograph of him with his mother at college graduation, framed and presented so proudly on his desktop. The screen-saver image of two kids in Little League gear—nephews, according to one of the reporters. A Father's Day card drawn for him by one of the fatherless kids at the Boys and Girls Club. Surveying those and the other mementos Percy kept—as we *all* keep near us as tiny glimpses into the lives we are living—was apparently what I needed to regain the passion and compassion I'd felt so instinctively on that first call-out.

And I wanted to find it. To feel it. I have colleagues who have learned to suppress that response forever, and they're grateful for the ability. But that's not who I want to be. Not yet, at least. So after work, and before my birthday party, I had hidden from Chuck in our shower and let myself cry for Percy.

And when I was through, I carefully tucked those feelings back inside, close enough to the surface to help me be there for Percy but deep enough so I could enjoy the people I loved on my birthday. If the time ever came when I could no longer strike that balance, I might have to talk to Grace about my backup plan of shampooing clients at Lockworks. For now, I was managing.

By eleven o'clock, the wine was gone, the dishes were washed, and even Gloria Gaynor was tired. Grace was hugging my father goodbye and Chuck was trying desperately to cajole a sneering Vinnie out of his dog bed, when Chuck's cell phone interrupted.

"Lucky save," I called out behind him, as he left the room to answer. I scooped up my now-compliant Frenchie and placed him in a laundry basket with the gifts I had been given—in spite of my explicit instructions.

Chuck's call was a short one, but I could tell from the look he gave me when he returned to the dining room that something was up. We said a quick final goodbye to Dad; then Chuck broke the news to me on the porch.

The night was still young. We were going to East Precinct.

Before its designation as an interstate freeway, the stretch of I-84 running east from the bridges of downtown Portland to the gorges of the Columbia was labeled Highway 30. Despite the renumbering, the federalization, and the widening and ramping of a freeway through the middle of the city's east-side neighborhoods, longtime locals still call the road the Banfield.

For our drive to East Precinct, Chuck eschewed the Ban-field—as he usually does in favor of a straight shot down Division Street. He has never explained his aversion to the interstate, but I suspect it has something to do with Governor Charles Landon Forbes's opposition to the project's proposal more than twenty years ago. Chuck and his former-governor father aren't what you'd call close these days, but some of a son's earliest impressions are as much a part of him as his blood type and eye color.

From the passenger seat, I observed a blunt reminder that the city's economic rise—and resulting gentrification—had not yet made its way eastward. We passed miles of blocks that had little to do with the Portland I knew and loved but which were mentioned all too frequently in the crime reports that filled my working days. With only a few exceptions, the streets here were suffused with used car lots, biker bars, strip clubs, head shops, discount appliance stores, so-called "lingerie modeling establishments," and motor lodges that advertised the avail-ability of cable. The apartment complexes and small houses that plugged the gaps had been populated for generations by welfare families—primarily white—who produced daughters who bore children to predatory men twice their age who despite so many promises never came around again.

"I feel like shit showing up here from a party," Chuck said, as he parked his '67 Jag in the precinct lot on East 106th. "I didn't think Mike would be working this late."

When I had told Chuck I'd offered Mike as a resource on Jessica Walters's vandalism investigation, he had immediately wanted to serve at his side. I'd guilt-tripped him into staying put. Given what seemed like a tenuous connection between our murder and Jessica's smash-and-grabs, I had feared bureau retribution for using MCT overtime to chase down vandalism leads. And yet here we were.

Fortunately, Chuck's not much of a drinker, so he was good to go on the investigation. I'd had a couple, but the DA's office left it to the attorney's discretion to decide whether we were OK to work after hours. I know, it's frightening.

Mike had called Chuck to notify him that he had arrested Todd Corbett, white male, nineteen years of age. Officially, Corbett had been brought in based on probable cause for the smashing of the front window at Noah's Bagels on Northwest 23rd and Hoyt. The probable cause came from six different citizens who called the bureau's help line after the local ten o'clock news led with a bystander's home video footage of a previously unidentified male running from Noah's, his baseball bat held high.

But the real reason Corbett found himself in the box with an MCT detective, instead of holding the ticket that was standard for most property crimes, was because Mike couldn't help but be curious about a pissed-off kid with a chip on his shoulder, a bat, and a vicious swing, just minutes away from the spot where Percy Crenshaw's head had been smashed in.

■　　■　　■

After showing our respective badges to the woman staffing the reception counter, we were buzzed through the front entrance, then worked our way down a series of hallways to the darkened observation area beside the interrogation room where Calabrese was questioning Corbett.

Through the one-way glass, I got my first glimpse of Todd Corbett. If he was in fact Crenshaw's murderer, the most remarkable aspect of his appearance was how unremarkable it was. Aside from the cuffs that secured his hands behind his back, Corbett looked like any nineteen-year-old kid you might find ringing up cigarettes at a quickie mart. Even seated behind the laminate table, I could tell he was tall and lanky. His brown hair was probably meant to be shorter, but was overdue for a trim, hanging across his eyebrows. His thin upper lip was lined with a layer of facial fuzz, his chin sporting a matching tuft. He wore a small gold hoop through his left earlobe, a Trailblazers wind jacket, oversized blue jeans, and high-tops. A baseball cap—likely backwards when worn—rested on the tabletop, a sign that he had either offered or been forced to show some respect for Calabrese.

"Why's Mike in there alone?" I asked Chuck. It was standard MCT practice to have another detective present during an interrogation, at least outside the room. Always better to have an additional witness.

"Because I was at your dad's house watching you and Grace act like twelve-year-olds," he whispered hurriedly, his attention devoted to the dynamic on the other side of the glass.

"Shouldn't he have found someone else?"

"He was showing mug shots to some witnesses in Northwest when the public information office called him with the info on Corbett. A couple of East Precinct guys helped with the pickup, but I assume they're back out on patrol."

"Why does he still have cuffs on?"

"I'm sure Mike's got a reason. Can't hurt to scare the kid a little, right?"

"Are you going in?" I asked.

He shook his head and hit the button that turned on the sound, so we could hear what was being said on the other side of the glass. "I will if he needs me. He knew we were on our way."

Mike leaned the entirety of his impressive weight toward Corbett's face, supporting himself with both hands against the table. "Here's the problem, Todd. You say you were at home watching TV but you don't know what you were watching, there was no one home with you to help you out on that, and meanwhile I got a videotape that shows you, a baseball bat, and a whole lot of broken glass—"

"And I told you that was bullshit," Corbett said, his narrow chest thrust forward.

Mike leaned in farther still. "Don't interrupt. We still got the best part. See, if you watched as much TV as you claim, Todd, you'd know about Channel Twelve. They aired the home video tonight, including a nice big still of your pretty face—a face that'll be nothing but problems for you inside, by the way. I got seven citizens who tell me it's you."

Corbett sat on that for half a minute, biting his lower lip nervously. "Yeah, well, maybe I got some people out there who don't like me or something."

"Well, I ain't got a grudge against you, and I saw the pictures too. Even I can tell it's you."

Another pause and some more lip gnawing from Corbett. "So maybe I got a long-lost twin out there. I'll talk to my mom about it." He forced a laugh, but his bluster had died down considerably.

Mike stood, gave Corbett some space, then sat in the chair across from him. "Look, you and I are getting off on the wrong foot here. Let me be truthful. I been around long enough to have some perspective. I know damn well there's worse crimes out there. Way worse. You know what I'm saying?"

Mike kept his eyes on Corbett, his new good-cop persona waiting for a response. Corbett shrugged his shoulders and muttered, "I guess."

"And I already checked your records. You're not a bad guy. Maybe a couple juvie pops for drinking, but no real priors. The truth is, Todd, I can see how it probably happened. You're with some buddies downtown. People start getting rowdy. The police show up with gas and everyone starts freaking, am I right?" Corbett said nothing, but his expression showed he was thinking. Mike scooted his chair back from the table and crossed one ankle over the other knee, getting cozy with his new pal. "Actually, when I was your age—a little younger, maybe—me and my crew did something similar back in the Bronx. We got busted spray-painting a dick and some titties on the Kip's Big Boy—you know those big statues of that goofy kid in overalls?"

Corbett let out an uncomfortable chuckle. I couldn't help but wonder whether there even was a Big Boy in the Bronx. I was certain, though, that Calabrese had never been busted for defiling him.

"Anyway, couldn't have been the crime of the century 'cause here I am." Mike paused wistfully, then looked his target directly in the eye. "What I'm trying to say is, I can understand how you might have done something last night that was out of character. What I can't understand, and what's pissing me off, is you sitting here lying to my face about it."

I had noticed that Mike wasn't mentioning the Crenshaw murder. He was probably trying to assure Corbett that we hadn't made the connection yet between Crenshaw's Hillside death and the relatively benign chaos on the streets below. If Mike could lock Corbett in as armed, out of control, and just blocks from Percy's house, he'd have more leverage as the questioning continued.

Corbett was still thinking. Chuck and I exchanged glances. We both recognized the signs: One more go from Calabrese should do it.

Mike saw this too and went for the close. "I'm more likely to cut you loose tonight with a citation if you just come clean with me. Otherwise, I can book you as a custody until a judge arraigns you tomorrow on felony criminal mischief."

To some, that part of Mike's act might sound like a threat to punish a suspect with arrest for refusing to confess. Courts, however, view this common police tactic as a lawful *offer of lenience*—a ticket instead of an arrest—in exchange for cooperation. Mike was being aggressive, but so far so good on the books.

His generous "offer" was enough to get Corbett talking. "So you're saying you'll let me out of here tonight with a ticket if I tell you what happened."

"I see what you're saying. You want to lock me in on that. You're smart. You're thinking," Mike said, tapping his finger against his temple. "Yeah, sure, you've got my word."

I looked at Chuck, worried, but he lifted his chin toward the window to tell me to keep watching. He trusted Mike to know the rules.

"I promise," Mike said, holding up one hand, "if you come clean with me, I'll write you a cite for the crim mischief. I won't book you on that charge."

"For real?"

"That's my absolute word."

I looked away for a moment, coming close to feeling a little sorry for Corbett. He had no clue as to what was about to happen. Then I remembered where my sympathies lay just a few hours earlier in Percy's office, and I steeled myself. Mike's job was to get the evidence, and my only job was to make sure he didn't violate the law getting it. If the law let us sucker Corbett, and Corbett was willing to be suckered, so be it. Corbett's defense attorney could feel sorry for him later.

Then, as I sensed he would, Corbett laid out for Mike the events that led to the rampage down 23rd. Not coincidentally, his version was much like the one Mike had set up for him in advance. Minding his own business. Clashes between cops and protesters. Caught up in the crowd. Not something he'd usually do. Yada yada yada.

He did add one fact—the influence of methamphetamines. The drug of choice for poor white trash like Corbett, crystal meth guarantees at least six hours—if not days—of complete euphoric mind melt. Users lose all control over their judgment, emotions, messianic power complexes, and voracious sexual appetites. Last month, I convicted a defendant who had axed his best friend to death after a meth binge for reasons he would never understand. Once Corbett threw a little meth into the picture, the progression from rowdiness to broken windows to random assaults—and possibly to Percy's murder—seemed almost predictable.

Now that Corbett had admitted the vandalism, Mike just needed him to explain the rest in his own words. "Here's the problem, Todd. Where'd the bat come from?"

A glimmer of worry crossed Corbett's face but quickly disappeared. "That wasn't mine. My friend had it in his car."

"I figured as much," Mike said. He removed a still photograph from a file folder on the table and laid it in front of Corbett. "That's the picture they showed on Channel Twelve tonight. That right there is obviously you"—he pointed at Corbett's face—"but right here on the side is another guy's jean jacket. And on the video, it looks like he's running next to you. Problem is, we can't see his face. If you're going to tell me it's not your bat, you need to tell me whose it is. Otherwise, you take all the blame and you're still a liar."

"You never said anything about giving anyone else up."

"That was before you told me the bat was someone else's. And what did I say about coming clean?"

Corbett paused again, perhaps simply to comfort himself that he had at least hesitated before naming names. "It was Trevor's."

"Last name?"

"Hanks. Trevor Hanks. He lives near me, over on a hundred-fourth and Knight."

Mike scratched the name down in his notebook, then stood again. "Anyone else?"

Corbett shook his head. "Nope. Just me and Trevor. There were plenty of other people acting crazy up there, but I don't know who they were."

"You're not holding back on me, are you?"

"No, man." Mike believed him. "I told you. We were totally fucked up. I don't even remember half of what happened, but I know who I was with."

Chuck called Ray Johnson to pass on the new name. He had already put together a throw-down including Corbett's DMV photo. The plan was to show it to the superintendent who'd seen the men in the parking lot before the murder. They'd create another array now for Hanks, pasting his photograph next to those of five similar-looking men.

"Has Johnson found the super yet?" I asked.

"No luck," Chuck said, flipping his phone shut. "He's not

home. Ray tried his pager number, but nothing yet. Reminds me why I left apartment life behind. Can never find a super when you need one." He glanced at me out of the corner of his eye and smiled.

"Yeah, I thought that's all it was," I said, smiling back.

Back inside the box, Todd Corbett had the erroneous impression he was going home. "So, are we done here?" he asked Mike, reaching for his ball cap.

"Actually, Todd, we're in a bit of a jam." After all Mike's talk about honesty, he sounded genuinely disappointed in Corbett. "Here's the problem. I've got a dead body on Hillside, bashed in with a baseball bat, only a few blocks from where you just told me you were going to town with—guess what? A baseball bat. I really can't ignore that, you know what I'm saying?"

Corbett looked like a train had just come barreling out at him from the inside of a sink drain. Mike's intentionally schizophrenic questioning was probably unsettling enough, but Corbett had undoubtedly confessed to the property crimes only because he was convinced that the police hadn't connected those to Percy's murder. His body slumped in the chair as he realized his mistake.

"You hearing me, Todd? You see my predicament?"

"What about that crap you said about the ticket and your word and all?"

"But that's not what I'm not talking about. We're done with that subject, and I'm still giving you a cite. No booking. But you see the spot I'm in on this killing, don't you?"

"I don't know nothing about that. You never said nothing about a murder."

"Sure, but you also said you didn't know anything about all

the broken windows on Twenty-third. And you're probably going to tell me you don't know anything about these poor people who got walloped at random walking down the street that night, even though I got pictures of that too."

"I told you what you wanted to know about the shit on Twenty-third. But I'm telling you, I didn't kill nobody."

"You're going to have to come up with something better than that, Todd. I mean, what else are people gonna think other than that you and"—he looked at his notebook—"this Hanks guy went a little bit further with the bat a few blocks over. Same time, same neighborhood, same weapon. You said yourself you were so tweaked out you can't even remember what happened. How can you be sure you didn't do it, Todd?"

They went back and forth like that as the minutes, and then the hour, passed. Mike resorted to all the standard interrogation techniques. He covered the tabletop with pictures of Percy, alive and dead. He continually mentioned the witnesses at the apartment, implying that they'd seen more than they had. He suggested that Corbett could reduce his liability if Percy had provoked him in some way, or if Hanks had been the instigator, or if the meth made him do it.

I was growing tired. More important, I was becoming convinced that Mike was wasting his time; Corbett wasn't going to budge. Even Mike looked like he needed a break, which surely meant Corbett needed one too.

But then the dynamic of the conversation shifted.

"So do I need a lawyer or something?" Corbett asked.

Mike slid a piece of paper on the table in front of him toward our viewing window with his fingertips. He was making sure Chuck and I knew that Corbett had already signed a waiver of his Miranda rights. Believe it or not, once that's done, only a crystal-clear request for counsel suffices to invoke a defendant's rights. Corbett's weak-willed question would be seen as an "ambiguous" reference to counsel that Mike was free to ignore, no different legally from a statement about a baseball game.

"That's entirely up to you. You know your rights. But I can tell you one thing, though: a lawyer? He's gonna tell you to clam up and go to trial. And that decision right there would leave you facing capital murder charges. You know what that means, right?"

Corbett shrugged his shoulders.

"That means the State goes for the death penalty, Todd. And once that lawyer of yours tucks you away in a cell tonight to wait for a trial—months down the road—you know what I'm gonna do? I'm gonna go to Trevor's house and have a talk with him, just like this one. And he might not call that lawyer, you see? He might decide to say you were the one who did the whole thing. After all, you're the one with the bat in the pictures, right? Then it's you looking at the needle, and him looking at a plea bargain."

"I don't like where this is going," I said to Chuck.

"He's got the waiver, Sam. And I didn't hear the kid say he wanted a lawyer."

"He can still claim his statements are involuntary. A waiver isn't consent to coercion." And Oregon judges were especially uncomfortable when the threat of lethal injection was thrown around the interrogation room.

"Mike knows what he's doing," Chuck said, "and we need that confession."

I knew Matt was on his mind. Despite his alibi, the cop husband of the victim's girlfriend would be a natural target for the defense at trial—unless, of course, the defendant confessed now. Jurors convict defendants who confess. And defendants don't go to trial when they know a jury will convict.

I looked at him uncertainly. "It's fine," he assured me.

Todd Corbett didn't think so. "They're gonna kill me? You

got to be kidding me. I've told you everything I know. And I'm getting tired, man, and I gotta use the can. I want my ticket, and then I want to go home."

"I'll take you to the men's room, Todd, that's not a problem. I'll walk you down there myself just as soon as you explain to me which of you used the bat. It's only the one with the bat who faces the needle."

"OK, this is getting ridiculous," I said. Chuck tried to reach for my hand as it reached toward the glass, but he was too late. The rap of my knuckles two times against the window made Corbett hop in his seat, but Calabrese only blinked.

"Oh, boy, Todd, now you've really got a problem. You know what that means?" Without warning, Mike hit the switch that illuminated the observation area where Chuck and I stood. Just as quickly, he hit it again. In what had appeared to be the interrogation room's mirror, Corbett would have seen a half-second flash of two strangers watching him through a clear pane of glass. "That knock means the lady in there just ID'd you to my partner. You better get up. It's time to take you downtown."

I started to open the door to interrupt, but this time Chuck was faster. "Think, Sam. If you walk in that room right now, you give Corbett the upper hand. What's done is done. Let's just see what happens."

I pursed my lips and stared into his eyes and at his set jaw. He was right. I was over a barrel. The damage was already done. If I interrupted now to rein Mike in, Corbett would almost certainly invoke his rights, terminating any chance we had of getting an admission. "Fine, but Mike better be wrapping up."

"I'm sure he knows that too."

Corbett's right foot tapped a staccato rhythm against the

linoleum floor, his eyes squeezed shut tightly as his torso rocked front to back in time with his nervous beat. Mike looked at his watch. "I got to get going soon, Todd, so you need to decide what we're doing here."

"Did that lady in there see Trevor too?"

"Just his picture, but my partner knocked twice. That means she ID'd both of you. He's probably being picked up right now as we speak."

Still handcuffed, Corbett was tapping his fingers now against the back edge of the chair, no doubt looking for the out that every defendant thinks he'll find. The story the police will believe. The one that will end his trouble and take him home. The out is something that every defendant thinks he can conjure, but which every cop knows does not exist. It's the belief in the out that convinces suspects to waive their rights and talk to police, locking themselves into an untenable defense from which they cannot escape at trial.

Corbett had lasted longer than most before committing to his out. But what Corbett had displayed in tenacity, he lacked in creativity. He chose the out that Mike had been suggesting all along.

"All right, man, I think we did it," he said, squeezing his eyes shut again, struggling for the right words to convey the truth he was about to admit. "It was the meth. I felt—I don't know, invincible."

"You *think* you did it?"

"Fuck, what do you want from me? Fine, we did it."

"Why?"

"I told you, we were fucked up."

"And the car?"

"Yeah, we were just after the car. It got out of hand."

"When you hit him with the bat," Mike added.

Todd Corbett hesitated, coming to terms with what he was saying. "No. Trevor's the one who hauled off on him with the bat. Check his jacket." He paused again, assuring himself once more before he sank his friend for good. "He called me this morning. There was blood on his jean jacket. Check for yourself."

6

Heidi Hatmaker worked until seven o'clock on Monday night. Nothing new in that.

What made this evening different was that for once she was actually excited to be there. Thrilled, in fact, to hunker down in her tiny cubicle in the news pool offices. To an outside observer, the transformation would go unnoticed. Same room, same chair, same petite frame locked in its studying pose: right leg tucked beneath her, thumbnail between chewing teeth, sandy-blond bangs concealing the direction of her gaze.

But Heidi felt a surge of excitement. She used her forearms to block the source of that excitement from the view of passersby moving frantically, as usual, behind, in front, and beside her in the newsroom. She really needn't have bothered; no one ever paid attention to what she was doing anyway.

It was better, though, she reasoned, to avoid any possible notice of the plan she'd come up with this morning—a plan she thought Percy Crenshaw would approve of. This could be her chance to change the persona she'd been stuck with since she moved to Portland.

As unglamorous as the Portland *Oregonian* might seem, most of the reporters who worked there had paid their dues. They'd slaved for years at community newspapers or as freelance writers. They'd gone into debt, hocked heirlooms, and slept on the same futon for a decade straight.

And they resented the Yale graduate who pulled up in her parents' BMW for an assignment handed to her by their new editor-in-chief. About six months into the job, her father had interfered, and she'd suddenly been offered a regular position on the crime beat. Knowing where the assignment came from, Heidi turned it down and forced her father to promise that his college buddy would never again disrupt her natural career path at the paper.

Since then, she had regularly sat through semiannual job reviews that all delivered the same verdict: She was one of the smartest, most thorough, hardest-working staff members they had. But she had neither spark nor flair. She didn't have the spark that convinced the nonreporters of the world to share secrets she could turn into news. And she didn't have the flair that enabled reporters to take information that was readily available to other news outlets and humanize it in a way that made it Pulitzer Prize–worthy.

Percy Crenshaw had had both. In the months and months she had been relegated to fact-checking and line editing, she had watched him carefully. Once, he'd pulled her aside and told her he had noticed she was hungry. She tried to brush it off with humor, responding, "Thanks, but actually I just had an apple." But because he had the spark, Percy got her talking—and kept her talking—about what it was like to be the only staff member who knew the editor's college friends called him Thor, let alone why. It didn't take him long to realize that she was sick of hearing how dependable and detail-oriented she was, while no one ever let her do anything that came close to reporting the news.

To her surprise, Percy had been kind—almost paternal—but in a manner she had never experienced. He had told her she needed to adopt a new persona, to think of it as acting. He had even teased her about her name, something she usually minded. "You need to act like a Wolf Blitzer or a Hannah Storm, not a Heidi Hatmaker. Heidi Hatmaker's a girl who skips down cobblestone streets and gives presents to children. You need to be ruthless. You need to push those children out of the way to get to your story."

In other words, she needed to *act* like an ambitious reporter even if she still felt like a spoiled-rotten college kid who drove her mother's old car and needed a haircut she refused to let her parents pay for. For the past four months, she'd been trying. But no one seemed to notice.

Then today, after she'd been standing guard outside Percy's office for more than two hours, her editor Tom Runyon finally delivered the instructions he'd received from the newspaper's lawyer. It was yet another task that required a detail-oriented, smart, thorough, hardworking kid to see through—no drive, instinct, or charisma required. The police were going to search Percy's office, and her job was to screen every single file and scrap of paper. She was to make certain nothing revealed a confidential source.

She knew immediately that the stint would be easy. Percy had said it was a mistake—at least for him—to put too much on paper before he knew for sure what his take was. He preferred to store the facts in his head and let them stew until he envisioned his final spin. He only jotted down minutiae that might elude his steel-trap memory. The big-picture stuff stayed upstairs.

In retrospect, Percy Crenshaw had been the yang to her yin. This strong magnetic African-American man had possessed every raw talent that she coveted, while lacking at least some of the learned skills she had mastered. She knew the police wouldn't find much in Percy's office.

But she knew where the minutiae were. She had watched him. She had read every article he had ever written. When the female District Attorney and the good-looking cop were done in Crenshaw's office, she left it just as she'd found it. But first—before she locked the door behind her and returned the key to Lon Hubbard—she and Percy's pocket-sized notebooks made a pit stop at the photocopier.

Now she had pages filled with an intense, nearly illegible scrawl. Heidi might be young, but she knew her strengths and weaknesses. She was patient, and she was smart. She might not have spark or flair, but she had photocopies of Percy Crenshaw's light-blue notebooks. If anyone could reconstruct the reporter's knowledge that Percy had taken with him in death, it would be Heidi. That's cool, Percy would have said.

Back in her studio apartment, Heidi sat Indian-style on the bed, the television turned down low, documents spread around her on the quilt, a larger circle on the floor beneath her.

She had reread several of Percy's older, more notable investigative articles. Now she was searching for any entries in the photocopied notebooks that might line up with the ultimate published work. Scooping carryout chow mein into her mouth as she read, she felt herself recognizing the rhythm of Percy's style.

Heidi was a student of work habits. From what she'd seen, writers were typically funnelers, jotting down their biggest themes and concepts first, filling in the skeleton outline with increasingly specific details down the road. Percy Crenshaw's approach was comparatively spigot-like; first he amassed pages and pages of minutiae; then he decided on the theme that would tie it all together. Percy's earliest notes stuck to basics: numbers, dates, and other specifics he might otherwise forget.

Right now, she was looking at a perfect example of the Crenshaw method. His big magazine article for the *L.A. Times*—the one that got him the movie deal—involved a murdered judge who was blackmailed over an affair she had with an elected official. The earliest notes Heidi had been able to identify on the story didn't include the judge's name or any mention of corruption, murder, or blackmail. Instead, Percy had scrawled *VMI-Van* above a list of dates. Because the published article was long on details about the affair, Heidi eventually realized the note reflected the dates of the couple's liaisons at the Village Motor Inn in Vancouver, Washington. Only later did he begin to fill out the story.

Trying to work Percy's system to her advantage, Heidi had begun compiling a list of cryptic entries from his recent notes. Every time she saw a date, number, or initials, she added them to her list. The problem was, the list was getting longer and longer, and she was no closer to any big ideas.

Most intriguing—and confusing—was Percy's seeming fascination with a set of numbers he had been tracking. Initially, he recorded them in a list-type format. In the first such entry she had found, he had written:

$$\text{NEP } 80 \leq (50 \text{ B}) \ 25 \text{ A} \ (10 \text{ B})$$

The next few entries were similarly headed by the caption NEP but contained different numbers next to the letters s, A, and B. Then the entries became more complicated, throwing in additional numbers marked by the letters L and w.

Heidi had no idea what any of it meant, but she knew Percy had been interested in it. More recently, he had come up with charts, two for each month, from January to August. For each month, Percy had written NEP on top of one chart, and EP on top of the other. On the horizontal axis of the charts were columns titled B, L, W, A, and TOTAL. On the vertical axis, he kept track of rows marked s and A. The numbers on the charts differed, but the labels were always the same.

Heidi stared at the first charts, for the month of January:

NEP

	B	L	W	A	Total
S	120	75	27	8	230
A	34	30	10	3	77

EP

	B	L	W	A	Total
S	32	101	50	27	210
A	12	33	19	10	74

There was definitely a pattern. In the numbers rows, s's always outnumbered A's. In the columns, the TOTALS were always the sum of the figures under B, L, W, and A, indicating that those letters marked a breakdown of the larger whole of whatever Percy was tracking. And the NEP charts always had more B's and fewer L's, W's, and A's than the EP charts.

Now, if only she knew what the letters stood for.

Heidi stretched her cramped legs and looked at the hopeless piles of articles and notes around her. Percy may have taken his current big ideas with him, but Heidi kept telling herself that she had the important details right here somewhere. She could come up with the rest, including the significance of all these numbers and letters.

She needed to remain methodical. She wasn't in a race. She was the only one with Percy's notes. First she needed some sleep. On the television, she was surprised to see Conan wrapping up, a definite sign that she needed to turn in.

7

When Mike finally emerged from the interrogation room with Corbett's signed confession, he raised the palm of his hand for a high-five from his partner. I could have kicked Chuck in the shin for obliging him.

"What the hell was that stunt you pulled in there with the lights?" I demanded, interrupting the celebration.

"What is she talking about?" Calabrese said to Chuck. Then he laughed and held up the confession. "This here's what we call a good thing, Sam. I got you your slam dunk and your co-defendant. That's what I'm saying."

"There's nothing cute about this, Mike. You had to have known that I knocked on the window for a reason." I could tell he was thinking about denying it, which pissed me off even more. "You were teetering dangerously close to the line even then. You pretty much told the guy he'd die if he didn't confess."

"Everything I did in there was about getting you the confession. How many times have I had a case rejected by your office, or dealt down to nothing, because a DA's afraid to try a close case? So, yeah, maybe I walked the line in there, but I didn't cross it."

"You're wrong, Mike, you may very well have crossed it. The defense is going to jump all over that stunt you pulled. But you know what? In court, I'll stick up for you. I'll try to get the confession in. But I don't appreciate what you did. You not only ignored my warning to back off, you used me as a prop to go further."

I had seen Mike get pissy at times when he didn't agree with a call, but I had apparently never seen him angry. Or mean. "Gee, what a surprise: A DA sits on the sideline watching the action, then wants to second-guess every move. Maybe you should sit down with your boy Frist and see if you can prosecute *me* for something." When I didn't respond, he pushed his stack of papers to his partner and stormed away.

"What the hell?" I said to Chuck, once Mike was gone.

"Leave it alone for now," he warned.

"Your partner's totally out of control. Why didn't you say something?"

"Do you realize he's about to ask me the same exact thing about you in a couple of minutes?"

"Maybe, but I'm right, and he's wrong."

"And that's also exactly what he'll say. Look, Sam," he said, touching my shoulder gently with his free hand, "I know you don't want to hear this, but you don't understand the position you just put him in. He's still pumped from getting Corbett to flip. You have no idea what that's like. And to walk out of the box and be told you fucked up—well, now's not a good time. Give him some space."

By two in the morning, we had everything we needed to enter the piece-o'-crap house that Trevor Hanks shared with his father on East 123rd. Officers Craig Todd and Jeff Walls from East Precinct had been perched outside for nearly two hours, watching. According to them, two male heads—one young, one old—were last seen through a gap in the stained sheets that served as living room curtains, watching Howard Stern. The glow of the television faded around one o'clock. Since then, the torn screen doors had remained undisturbed. By all appearances, father and son were quietly tucked away within their home's peeling exterior.

Based on Corbett's statements, we obtained a telephonic arrest warrant for Trevor Hanks. We also secured a no-knock search warrant for the house, authorizing police to force their way in without first announcing their presence. We'd be looking for the bat and any other evidence related to the murder, including the jean jacket and other clothing Hanks was wearing Sunday night.

So far, all I knew about Trevor Hanks had come from his pal Corbett and from reading his PPDS record. That said, I suspected that at some point Corbett's mother, if he had one, must have said to her son, "That Trevor Hanks is a bad influence." While Corbett's only previous run-in with the law was for underage drinking, Trevor had quite the sheet for a twenty-two-year-old.

Although juvie convictions don't show up in the computer, I noted stops for theft, assault, marijuana possession, and—bingo!—unauthorized use of a motor vehicle. Since becoming a grown-up, Hanks had convictions for burglary, forgery, assault, and menacing. Thanks to pleas in exchange for county jail time, Hanks had so far avoided any visits to state prison.

What makes a kid go bad so early? Maybe in Hanks's case there was something in the genes. Daddy Hanks, legally known as—I kid you not—Henry Hanks, had his fair share of troubles too: possession of stolen property, menacing, disorderly conduct, bad checks, and a couple of domestic violence pops—dropped, of course, when the victims refused to testify. Needless to say, we don't have a three-strikes-and-you're-out law in Oregon, and for that the Hanks men should be grateful.

Calabrese had taken Corbett to MCDC—his citation for vandalism in hand—on charges of aggravated murder. Given the tension between us, I was relieved to see him go. The patrol officers outside Hanks's house were ready to help Chuck make the arrest. For good measure, Johnson had paged Walker for the action, and the two partners were on their way there to meet Chuck.

As Chuck was strapping a bulletproof vest over his civilian clothing, he asked if I was coming with him.

"May as well."

"OK, but you're wearing this." Chuck grabbed another vest from a locker.

I hopped into the passenger seat of a white Crown Vic from the precinct detectives' fleet. Rifling through the glove box, I unearthed an old box of Junior Mints from a pile of abandoned notepads, drivers' manuals, receipts, and fast-food coupons. At a different place and time, I might have been grossed out, but given my current hunger pangs, I was willing to compromise culinary standards.

We beat Johnson and Walker to the meeting spot, a corner parking lot behind a car repair shop two doors down from the Hankses'. Waiting in the dark, the stillness was a momentary relief from the manic chaos of the last few hours.

Chuck looked at me and smiled. "Excited?"

"Of course not," I said, popping another crusty mint morsel into my mouth. "I just want Hanks picked up so we can get the hell out of here."

"You're so full of shit," he said jokingly. "Admit it, babe. You came along for the fun of it." He started to sing the theme song from the watch-real-cops-chase-after-real-scumbags show: "Bad boys, bad boys, whatcha gonna do?"

"Sing all you want, reggae boy. You won't be teasing me when you need my legal know-how." He eyed me cynically, then burst out laughing when he realized I had been serious.

So maybe my tag-along wasn't motivated entirely by lawyerly concerns. The truth was, I liked the idea of some real live, not-so-real-life, television prosecutor action. On the rare occasion when I've watched one of those shows, the DA always winds up toe-to-toe with the suspect, telling him he's a "skell" who will "fry" for his crimes. And, of course, if the tough talker's a woman, she's always got cute clothes, a perfect body, and good hair.

My daily reality's a lot less glamorous. I occasionally drop in on crime scenes, but I've never gotten in a suspect's face. Hell, I never even speak to them directly. Even in the third person, I refer to them—boringly and respectfully—by their names or by the generic term *defendant*. And forget the model good looks; I run a minimum of twenty-five miles a week to remain only mildly dissatisfied with my body, and, for me, dressing up means wearing pantyhose and brushing my hair.

Tonight, things could be different. In my ponytail, sweatshirt, and jeans, I might not look the part, but I was ready for action. I was in the front seat of a police car. I was pumped full of aged sugar and chocolate. I even had a vest.

"OK, maybe it sounded just a little bit fun. But can you blame me? Don't I deserve a thrill on my birthday?"

"I'd try to sneak something in before the boys get here, but it's not technically your birthday anymore," he said.

"Not to mention that right now I'm technically way more in the mood for these Junior Mints than for what you've got in mind."

"Ouch."

A second Crown Vic pulled up next to Chuck, and Jack Walker rolled down the passenger window. "All set?" he asked.

"Ready. Got the warrants by phone. No-knock's OK."

"Approach on foot?" he asked.

"Sure," Chuck agreed. "Looks like they're sleeping, but why take a chance?"

I opened my door with the rest of them and felt Chuck grab my left forearm. "No way, Kincaid. You stay here, and I'll tell you when it's clear."

There was neither time for nor any point in arguing, so I slumped back in the seat.

"See this red button here?" Chuck pointed to a button on the computerized terminal that was mounted to the dash. "If anything goes wrong, you push that button and you drive away, OK?" He began walking with the other detectives.

"Wait," I said. "What is it?"

"It's for an officer down."

They never said anything about that on *Cops*.

I looked at my watch again, but it was only a minute later than the last time I checked. *Was this thing working? Where were they?*

As I watched Chuck, Jack, and Ray move to the house twenty minutes ago, there were a tense few seconds when I was grateful for the safety of the locked car. But then, down the street, I saw lights come on inside the Hanks house. No gunfire or other scary sounds. Everything had seemed hunky-dory. I expected Chuck to wave me in or call my cell, then I'd run right over.

Now I wasn't so sure. I looked at my phone, wondering whether to call someone and, if so, whom. I stared at the door, wondering whether I should get out of the car and what I'd do if

I did. I found myself picturing the no-knock entry, wondering whether Chuck had been the one in front, the one to kick the door. And, most of all, I stared at the red button and thought about what I'd be losing if I needed to press it.

I would never say this aloud to anyone—much too sickening—but I still felt overwhelmingly lucky to have this second chance with Chuck. It wasn't just the physical. Don't get me wrong; he turned more heads in a bar than I did. But what I had really found in Chuck was a match. There was nothing he simply tolerated or even just accepted; he actually embraced and genuinely liked everything about me. Sure, my ex-husband Roger had enjoyed dissecting the *New York Times* op-ed page with me. And no doubt the world was replete with men who wouldn't mind a girlfriend who dug football, beer, and the joy of the perfect draw on a golf drive.

But Chuck got all of me. And in him, all the various me's I carry around in my conflicted self had found a partner. In a single Sunday morning, he could scream at the TV during Meet the Talking Heads, bend me over the sink for an X-rated interruption of my morning primp, then laugh when I surprised him with a wet willy while we cooked pancakes in the kitchen. And like me, he'd enjoy every part of it equally, never missing a beat in the unpredictably syncopated rhythm that accompanied our personalities.

And now he was inside the house of a kid who was willing to crush a man's skull with a bat for a car. I was on the verge of calling Calabrese for advice when I saw Chuck emerge from the house, towing a handcuffed Trevor Hanks at his side. Chuck yanked the back door open and guided Trevor in.

"Who the fuck's that?" Hanks asked. Maybe it was the relief of seeing Chuck still alive. Or maybe it was the pressure of worrying that he wasn't. Or maybe it was just the dismissive expression on Hanks's hardened face when he looked at me. Whatever the cause, I snapped into serious skell-confronting mode.

"Who am I? I, Mr. Hanks, am the prosecutor who's going to make sure you just lived your last day of freedom."

He aimed for my face, but the glob of goo that Trevor Hanks spat in my direction was caught in the fencing that separated us. "Fuck you, bitch. No way you're pinning that coon's death on me."

Chuck hopped in the car, strapped on his seatbelt, and hit the gas. Just as quickly, he slammed on the brakes, jerking the unbelted Trevor Hanks forward. Hanks's face thudded against the gate in front of him, still wet from his own saliva. "Act up again, Hanks, and we're making a pit stop under the Burnside Bridge. You got me? Now, just as a reminder, you have the right to shut the fuck up."

Chuck scribbled something on his notepad and passed it to me.

He lawyered up inside the house when we pulled his jacket from the washer. Oh, shit. This never happened to the tough-talking good-hair girls on television.

We finally got home just short of four o'clock in the morning.

Vinnie, whom we had dropped off at the house before our venture east, was unabashedly pissed. And pissing. And gnawing. The vicious pillaging of a 1984 Van Halen T-shirt was, to Chuck, the equivalent of a declaration of war. Acting as this household's Secretary of State, I tried to negotiate a diplomatic solution by pulling Vinnie into the bed to sleep with us.

With the lights out, Vinnie snoring, and my birthday over, I snuggled into the crook of Chuck's arm and held him. Then I pecked a sleepy kiss on his chest and tightened my squeeze.

That kind of sweetness wasn't lost on a guy who knew me as well as Chuck. "Hey, you. What's up?"

I was too exhausted to choose my words. How could I tell him that—as much as I admired him for being a cop, and as much as I had almost refused to date him, precisely because he *was* a cop—I had never truly understood all that his job entailed? Did it make any sense at all that it took an empty police car, twenty minutes, and a little red button for me to understand the instinctual terror that he had to overcome on a daily basis? And if it did, could he possibly understand that for a second—just a second during those twenty minutes—I had selfishly regretted letting him move in with me?

"Just sleepy," I muttered, pulling him even tighter.

Tuesday morning, my alarm blared at 6:30 A.M. as commanded. Chuck might be able to take a few hours of comp time, but my office still expected me in by eight. Maybe the DAs needed to look into unionizing, I thought, smacking the I'm-up-now-so-stop-playing-loud-music button on my clock-radio.

Despite my late night, I was still the first deputy to make it into MCU. They'd arrive soon enough, I thought. Russ Frist would undoubtedly stop by to pepper me for an update on the Crenshaw case. I swear, with his fretting over whatever I was doing, I didn't know when the guy had time to do his own work.

A voice mail from Jessica Walters was waiting for me. "Hey, girl. I saw your defendants on the news this morning. Your instincts paid off, with the added bonus of solving my little PR problem. Good job."

I called her back and gave her the details from the night before, including my confrontation with Calabrese.

"Oh, I see. When you offered to lend me an MCT guy for

my vandalism case, you were farming out the team's biggest hothead?"

"I didn't know that at the time, but, yeah, pretty much. Now we just need to figure out how to merge our cases. My inclination is to get the murder indictment, then use the crime spree on Twenty-third to connect the defendants to the murder. Unless your victims are going to freak, I'd rather not water down the indictment with a bunch of criminal mischief and assault charges."

"Sounds like a plan. I'll explain it to them."

"Thanks." I still needed to talk to Percy's parents in Los Angeles and establish a long-distance rapport with them. "So the television stations have the story already?"

"I saw it this morning," she said. "Nothing detailed. Just that they were suspects in the Twenty-third Avenue mess and in the Crenshaw case."

That's all the radio news had too. The bureau's press release on the arrest must have been bare bones, the best kind as far as I was concerned.

Ten seconds after I hung up, Raymond Johnson's head popped around my door. I wondered if the timing was fortuitous or if he'd arrived earlier and overheard my Calabrese-bashing to Jessica.

"What's your pretty face doing in here?" I asked cheerfully. Was I usually that cheerful, I wondered, or was I trying to be nice in the event he heard me bad-mouthing his colleague? No, I was always that cheerful. Definitely.

And Johnson's face was awfully pretty. At least, it was usually. But this morning, he looked exhausted.

"I was dropping off some evidence across the street, so I figured I'd stop in."

"Are you up early or late?" I asked.

"Way, way too late. Jack and I pulled the all-nighter, since we're the leads. Not that it feels like it, of course. Damn Calabrese, stumbling on the bad guys like that. He did one hell of a job on Corbett, though. Full signed confession."

It was a normal enough comment, but it made me wonder again if he'd heard me on the phone or perhaps spoken to Calabrese.

"He was something, all right," I said. "Anything I need to know about?"

"We finished the searches. Walker oversaw the work at Corbett's house, and I stayed at Hanks's. We took the clothes from the washing machine, still wet. No visible blood, but the lab's working on it."

"Did you find the bat?" According to Corbett, Hanks had thrown the bat into the back of the car he was driving Sunday night.

"Nope." Ray was obviously disappointed. "But the car Corbett described matches a Jeep Liberty that was parked in the driveway, registered to Hanks's dad. Henry Hanks. Can you believe that shit?"

"No kidding. You mean he lives in a house like that and drives a Jeep?"

"A new one too. The lease company already called. Henry's three months behind on the payments, and they're ready to repo it. Anyway, Hanks must have gotten rid of the bat before we showed. We got the Jeep at the lab, though. Maybe they'll find something."

"Very good. So do you finally get to go home now?"

"Ah, if only I could. I just got one last thing to do. Peter Anderson finally paged me back. The condo super? I guess he was out all night with his buddies. Anyway, he says he's in a good enough condition to talk now, so I'm headed up there. You can indict the case either way, though, right?"

"All set," I said, pointing to the charging instrument I was writing on my computer screen. Just as Mike had said, DAs love cases with confessions.

"All right. Catch you later."

"Catch some *sleep!*" I hollered down the hall as he left. I noticed other office lights on, but still no Russ.

Just as I was printing out the charging instruments for Hanks and Corbett, Alice Gerstein walked in. Alice, senior MCU paralegal extraordinaire, has many talents: typing, filing, mailing, printing, researching; the list goes on. But Alice's most important skill—the reason why she is the only indispensable member of the unit—is her ability to force this motley crew of misbehaving children with law degrees to follow the rules. And one of the rules was that I—still, after six months, the newest member of the unit—was supposed to pull screening duty first thing in the morning. Before I touched a single file, I was supposed to review the police reports that had been put aside as potentially major enough for our Major Crimes Unit to handle.

I recognized the familiar Redweld file in her hand. It appeared unusually fat for a Tuesday. "Ahem. Why are these reports still on my desk, Ms. Kincaid?"

"MCT made two arrests last night in the Crenshaw case. The documents are printing as we speak. I was going to grab the screening pile on my way back from the printer."

She eyed me skeptically.

"I swear."

"Well, then, I guess I saved you a trip," she said, handing the file to me. "I'll put a file together for Crenshaw and bring your documents in for you to sign."

"You won't let me leave this office, will you?" I asked.

"Of course I will," she said, "just as soon as you've read every last one of those reports."

How does she do it? I wondered, opening the file. I bet Mike Calabrese would have listened to Alice Gerstein if they had been her knuckles against the glass last night.

At least I'd managed to achieve efficiency in my screening duties. I learned months ago that others in the office used the MCU screening pile to cover their asses. The reports dropped there rarely detailed anything other than minor offenses. But any incident that might arguably fall within the technical definition of a major crime has to be reviewed by an MCU deputy, just to make sure that MCU takes the heat if a big case slips through the cracks. Lucky *moi*.

Some of this morning's gems didn't even pass the straight-face test. Did I really need to see the report about Peter Medina, who ingested enough Ecstasy to seek sexual gratification from a tree in front of an assisted living complex? OK, for pure entertainment value—yes, I did need to see that one. By the time the police arrived, the parking lot was lined with onlookers and their walkers, and the naked and oblivious Medina had found true love, refusing to go to the hospital without his beloved sycamore.

But what about Patricia Roberts? She had just returned from a toy-shopping lunch break when she learned that one of her fellow cubicle-inhabiting Dilberts, Jason Himes, had boosted credit from the boss for one too many of Patricia's ideas. Out came the Nerf missile launcher that Patricia had purchased for her eleven-year-old son. Apparently Himes thought beaning someone in the head with a sponge ball warranted a police response. Perhaps, but it certainly did not constitute assault with a dangerous weapon.

I entered a log note rejecting felony charges against Roberts. And I did it in all caps with lots of underlining. How's that for adamant? I sent the file back to intake to decide whether to proceed on any misdemeanor counts. If it was up to me, I'd give her an oatmeal cookie and a pat on the back for a well-fired f-you. Maybe I'd stop by Toys R Us on the way home for a new office supply.

I delivered the completed screens back to Alice Gerstein. "Still no Mr. Frist?" I asked.

She turned and looked at his darkened office down the hall. "Not yet."

"In light of all the enforcing this morning with my screening duties, you might want to check on him, don't you think?"

"You know, I might just have to track that boy down," Alice said, reaching for her Rolodex.

A few minutes later, my phone rang.

"Kincaid."

"You're sounding awfully perky this morning."

The voice was familiar and yet unfamiliar. "And you sound awfully friendly for someone whose voice I don't recognize."

"It's Russ."

The trademark Frist boom was seriously off. "Wouldn't have known that, but—speak of the devil—Alice and I were just talking about you."

"You sicced that scary woman on me, didn't you?"

"I simply inquired as to your whereabouts. And where exactly are your current abouts?"

"In my bed. I'm sicker than Gary Busey on a bender. It's like what I had yesterday, times a thousand."

"You exert yourself at Gold's again?"

"No way this is from lifting, but talking about it's making it even worse. I saw your arrests on TV this morning. How's it look?"

"Good, I think."

"That's not a voice of confidence," he said.

"Well, one defendant, Todd Corbett, confessed, so that's good. And he lied every step of the way. First he didn't know anything about anything. Then he took some meth and broke some windows but didn't know anything about Percy. Then he tried to steal the car, but Hanks was the one who got violent. Then he finally admitted taking his turn at the vic too, so they're both looking at Agg Murder charges. But Calabrese pushed pretty hard to get every bit of it." I gave him a quick summary of the interrogation.

"Even so," he said, "you put that confession in front of ten judges, and eight of them would let it in."

"Sure, but two wouldn't. Without the confession, we won't have much."

"What did the other defendant say?" he asked.

"Trevor Hanks. He's the tougher of the two. Been through the system a lot. He invoked immediately, but when he came out to the car, he wound up saying we'd 'never pin that coon's death' on him. If I can get that in—arguably to show motive—it also just makes the guy look like a shit."

"So first you say Hanks *wound up* saying something after he invoked. Then you say *if you can get it in*. What aren't you telling me? Did your boyfriend screw something up?"

"You mean Detective Forbes? No, he didn't mess anything up."

"But?"

"Well, I happened to be in the car when Forbes brought Hanks out. Hanks asked who I was, I told him, and then he blurted out his nice little statement."

"You just *happened* to be in the car. I assume you're giving me the edited version."

"I might have left out a few cuss words and some spit—his,

not mine. Anyway, Hanks is the one who initiated the conversation, so I'm pretty sure we can get the statement in. But even so, I'm toast if Corbett's confession gets kicked. Plus, I know his attorney will make a fuss about Percy sleeping with a cop's wife. I even thought about leaving that part out of the discovery—"

"You know you can't do that."

"All I said was that I *thought* about it. Don't worry, I'll do the right thing." The irony wasn't lost on me. Only attorneys would see anything *right* about injecting an innocent couple working to save their marriage into the trial process. "It still comes down to Corbett's confession. I've got to get it in."

"Even if you do, it's only admissible against Corbett."

I didn't need Russ's reminder. One of the few bones thrown to criminal defendants by the current Supreme Court has to do with a defendant's right to confront witnesses. It's hard to confront a codefendant who invokes his right not to testify at trial, so when I tried Hanks I wouldn't be allowed to introduce Corbett's statement at East Precinct. I'd have to convince Corbett to testify in court against Hanks instead.

I explained my strategy to Frist. "If a court upholds Corbett's confession, I sort of assumed he would be willing to testify against Hanks to avoid the death penalty."

"Then make the deal now," he said.

For a second, I thought I'd misheard him. It was not like Russell Frist to start talking about deals before the defendant had even been arraigned.

"I think you better call the doctor, Russ. Whatever you've got really is making you weak."

"I'm serious, Sam. You're in trouble. Call the lab and press them for some kind of estimate on whether they're going to get you any physical evidence. Unless they can tie at least one of the defendants to Percy, I think you should talk to Corbett's attorney sooner rather than later. I doubt we'll pursue this as a death case anyway, so if he's willing to cooperate in exchange for taking the risk off the table, you should do it. No-brainer."

He was right. Duncan would make the official call later, but I doubted he'd go for the death penalty against two kids with no serious priors in a carjacking gone bad. "Still, plead it out already? What if the super at the vic's building can give us an ID?"

"It's still not enough to get you beyond a reasonable doubt," Russ said. "He didn't see them with Percy."

"I don't know—"

"Look, we almost always wind up offering a life sentence for Agg Murder in exchange for a plea. So it's better just to wrap it up now with Corbett, flip him against Hanks, and avoid any possibility of the confession getting suppressed. You may even need to sweeten the pot beyond that, but we can talk about that later."

"All right. I'll go over to the arraignment and talk to Corbett's attorney as soon as he gets one."

"Good. Let me know what happens. In the meantime, I'm going to my doctor. And since you were the one who dimed me up to Alice, you can be the one to cover me."

"For what?"

"A community action meeting about Delores Tompkins. It's at the Kennedy School at eleven. And don't say you're busy. I already asked Alice to check the docket."

"I don't know, Russ, that sounds pretty important. Are you sure you trust me to go?" I asked sarcastically.

"You'll be fine. Just tell them how bad off I am and that the grand jury's scheduled for Friday. Don't make them any promises.

We'll be presenting the evidence and letting the grand jury make the call."

"I think I can handle that."

"Believe it or not, Kincaid, you've actually got pretty good people skills—until someone pisses you off."

8

I called Raymond Johnson midmorning for an update.

"Good timing," he said, when he recognized my voice. "I'm just leaving Vista Heights. I am pleased to report that the seriously hung-over Peter Anderson has just identified Todd Corbett and Trevor Hanks. Picked them both out of the throw-downs. I also showed him a picture of the dad's Jeep, just in case, but no luck there."

Russ's words still rang in my ear. "But Anderson didn't see them near Percy, right?"

"You never cease to amaze me, girl. I rope you a cow and you're, like, *I want the whole damn herd*."

"Sorry," I said. "I just want to make sure I know where things stand."

"No, he didn't actually see them do the deed, but you already knew that. He says he saw a couple kids in the parking lot. His best estimate when I first talked to him was a little after ten o'clock at night. The ME puts time of death between nine and midnight, so we're looking pretty good."

"Did Anderson see a bat?"

"No. But if they brought the dad's car up here, like we think, they probably had the bat in the back while they were scoping out the possibilities."

"And then they saw Percy come in with his shiny car, and they followed him," I said, completing the logical sequence.

"Right."

"So will this Peter Anderson guy make a good witness?"

"I think so. He seems pretty straightforward."

"Did you run him yet? Any priors?"

"He's got some issues."

"So you're telling me he's got priors?"

"No convictions, but let's just say you wouldn't want to marry the guy. There's a pattern of domestic calls culminating in an arrest two months ago. The wife didn't pursue the case. She moved out. She got a restraining order two weeks ago, claiming he was harassing her on the phone. No problems since."

"All right. No impeachables?" You know you've become a trial attorney when you don't think twice about a star witness who beats his wife. According to the rules of evidence, a witness's prior convictions were admissible to impeach his credibility only if they were felonies or involved crimes of dishonesty. Anything else, I didn't need to care about.

"Nope. We've got a law-abiding citizen who picked the defendants from a throw-down. It's about as good as it gets."

"But it only puts them in the parking lot. The defense will say they went up there as part of their other mischief and had nothing to do with the murder."

"That's where the confession comes in." Right, I thought, *if* it comes in. "You need anything else? I need to catch some serious z's."

"You have a number for the victim's parents?"

"Yeah, hold on a second." I cringed at the thought of him half asleep, on the phone, looking through his notebook while he maneuvered the turns down the hill from Vista Heights. He rattled off the number. "Larry and Patricia Crenshaw. You might have missed them, though. I think they were planning on coming up here today."

"OK, thanks." I wished him sweet dreams, hung up, and dialed the bureau's crime lab. I learned that John Fredericks was handling the Crenshaw evidence and asked to be transferred to his line.

"Hey, John, it's Samantha Kincaid. How's the game going?"

"Wet."

Fredericks was a transplant from the Las Vegas Police Department and a rabid golf addict, despite the rain. We were on the same team for last year's Guns, Gavels, and Gurneys tournament, the annual golf gala for cops, prosecutors, and medical examiners. I chalked up the win to John's long drives and my wicked short game, but the sore losers accused us of cheating. Our unfair advantage? We played sober.

"I'm working on the Percy Crenshaw case. What are the chances you're going to find me some blood evidence?"

He exhaled loudly, then clicked his tongue a few times before he spoke. Not a good sign. "I'm not real hopeful right now. The car's definitely clean. Well, not exactly clean, but nothing that helps the good guys. The back was full of old boxes and papers, so a bat dropped in there wouldn't have touched the carpet fibers. I didn't find blood when I ran the black light through."

"They were probably smart enough to dump whatever was next to the bat when they got rid of it," I suggested.

"Right. And so far there's nothing on the clothes, either."

"Not even the jean jacket from Hanks?"

"Nope. Denim's always tricky because of the density, and Hanks probably scrubbed it down before he washed it. I've got one more test to run, but usually that's only good for isolating something testable when I've already got a potential sample. I don't even have a sample yet. Like I said, I'm not hopeful."

"How is that possible? They beat a man to death. I would've thought they'd be covered in blood."

"You should talk to the ME. It depends on how the fight unrolled; I've seen cases without a single drop of blood. You've got a confession, though, right?"

Once again, it all came back to that.

The Kennedy School is just one of the fifty-two links in a micro-brew chain owned by the McMenamin brothers. They started years before the microbrew craze with hippie hangouts cater-ing to Deadheads craving Hammerhead ales, Terminator stouts, and gutbuster sandwiches like the Stormin' Norman. But a few years ago, they started using the beer money to create a local entertainment empire of pubs, theaters, restaurants, hotels—even a winery and a golf course. It was a brilliant move.

Of all of the McMenamins' clever ventures, the most impres-sive might just be the Kennedy School. Until the two beer-brewing brothers stepped in, the former elementary school was shut down and boarded up. Where the children of North Port-land had once studied their three R's, hookers turned tricks and addicts shot up until police chased them out, reboarded the place, and resumed the cycle again the next day. But then the city struck a deal to transfer the building to the brothers for one dollar. In exchange, the neighborhood got a hotel and an enter-tainment complex that not only attracted a new demographic to North Portland but also contained open meeting rooms available to the community.

By the time I walked into the meeting about the Delores Tompkins "incident," as the bureau referred to it, others were taking their seats around a conference table. The meeting wasn't what I had pictured. Other than me, there were only three other women and a man in the room, and they all seemed to know each other. I was the only non-African-American.

I soon learned that an action meeting was more like the planting of a grassroots effort: Only community activists who were most directly involved had been invited. As the participants explained it, they were brainstorming ways to keep pressure on the public, the police, and my office to remember Delores Tompkins, to learn from her death, and to make sure that nothing like it happened again. And they didn't call it an *incident,* they called it Delores's *murder.*

We started with introductions. The man was the Reverend Byron Thomas, pastor of First United Baptist, one of the larger churches on the north side. He looked to be in his mid-forties, wore horn-rimmed glasses, and probably made church a lot more fun than I remembered it. Janelle Rogers was the president of the Buckeye Neighborhood Association. She was about the pastor's age and made a point of telling me that she was a regular participant in the bureau's community policing efforts. Sitting next to Janelle was Selma Gooding, an elderly woman who must have been something of an institution in this neighborhood. For her introduction, she simply said, "And I'm Selma Gooding. I . . . well, I guess you'd say I'm Selma." I smiled, but the rest of the group giggled knowingly.

Rounding out the group was a woman who looked to be Selma Gooding's biological age, but she seemed much older in spirit. I soon learned why when Selma introduced her. "This fine woman beside me is Marla Mavens, my dear friend since we were in middle school at Harriet Tubman. Marla is Delores's mother," she said, looking directly at me.

111

I muttered something about how sorry I was for her loss, realizing how hollow it sounded. I had to give Russ some credit. He must have been doing a good job with the bedside manner to have been included as part of this small group.

I'm not much better with people names than case names, so I came up with a quick mnemonic. The minister was easy; the priest at my church growing up was Father Thomas. Janelle Rogers was the youngest of the other women; JR for junior. Delores's mother, Marla Mavens; M is for mom. And Selma Gooding. S is for senior citizen, and she seemed like a genuinely good person. Silly tricks, but they'd help my short-term problem.

Once introductions were over, Janelle Rogers thanked me for coming. "In light of what happened at the protest on Sunday, we were hoping as a group to have a more open channel of communication with the authorities. An officer from the community policing department was supposed to join us today, but I got a very late phone call saying he couldn't be here. I'm disappointed, to say the least."

I started to offer up a list of possible excuses for this anonymous officer, but thought better of it. "I know Russell Frist was very sorry he couldn't make it. I spoke to him myself this morning, and he sounded terrible. Sicker than Gary Busey on a bender, is how he described it."

That got a good solid chuckle from Dr. Thomas and Mrs. Gooding, who spoke up next. "We had invited Mr. Frist, hoping he could give us some indication of what we could expect in the days to come. We'd like to know whether or not your office intends to bring charges up against Officer Hamilton."

I told them about the upcoming grand jury date and gave them an overview of the process. Seven adults gathered in a small meeting room would hear the evidence presented by Russell Frist regarding the shooting without the formalities of a trial. No defense attorney, no judge. Grand jurors could question witnesses. They also had the power to subpoena additional witnesses and evidence. Once the grand jurors believed they'd gathered sufficient information, they would decide whether or not to indict Officer Hamilton and, if so, for which charges.

That should just about do it, right? After all, the statement was exactly to Russ's specifications. Lesson number one: When someone suckers you into doing something simple, you can be sure it will be anything but.

"I very much appreciate the legal background," Dr. Thompson said with his lilting voice, "but we'd like to know what your office plans to say to those grand jurors before they make the decision. We've known enough boys to go through the system to recognize the realities, you understand?"

I made another attempt to stick with Russ's message. "Like I said, Russ Frist will be the one in the hearing. But I'm confident he'll make sure that the grand jurors understand the required elements for any potential charges. He'll certainly go over the statutes that define a police officer's right to use force, including the requirement that the force has to be reasonable."

As I found myself rambling about the definition of reasonableness, I surveyed the response in the room. I do the same during closing arguments, gauging my audience's reaction as I'm speaking, taking note of who I've got in my corner and who's still on the fence. In trial, I don't sit down until I'm sure I've persuaded them all.

Good thing I was already sitting, because this crowd was not convinced. Byron Thomas shook his head in disappointment. Janelle Rogers rolled her eyes. I heard a serious *tsk* escape Selma Gooding's lips. And Marla Mavens's glance fell to the table, her lips pursed as if she should have known not to get her hopes up.

A hostile audience makes me nervous. Worse, it makes me stray from my prepared points. Once that happens, I never know what will pop out. In one of my first trials in the office, I was taken by surprise when the jury appeared doubtful about my drug case. Before I knew it, I was comparing the defendant's unlikely explanation for carrying drugs to a new paisley-print skirt I had just purchased—it looked good by itself but it didn't match anything else in the closet. Needless to say, the analogy between clothing and evidence didn't go over very well, and the jury handed me my ass with its verdict sheet: *Not guilty. And we didn't care for that prosecutor.*

So far, this gang of four didn't seem to like me any better. My natural unpopularity detector kicked in, and, sure enough, extemporaneous thoughts began tumbling out. Before I knew it, I was babbling; about what, I can't even remember. At one point I decided to be as straight with them as I knew how. And I do know how to be straight. I remember telling them they needed to understand that most people start out with a presumption in favor of police. I know I said something about people viewing a shooting differently when it's committed by an on-duty cop and not a regular citizen.

And I said we'd probably never see eye to eye about many of the confrontations that police have with members of their community. I told them that when a person runs from a police officer or resists an arrest, I tend to support the use of some force. I even think I said something about not paying police officers to lose fights. Janelle Rogers looked alarmed about that.

But I also said that, despite our differences, and even though I wouldn't be handling the grand jury myself, I was pretty sure that the grand jury would notice that, in this particular case, the decedent was an unarmed woman whose only known offense was an attempt to drive away from a traffic stop. It would be up to the grand jurors to decide whether Hamilton should be treated like a criminal, but, if nothing else, they'd know that Delores did not deserve to die.

I don't know which part of the babbling worked. Maybe none of it. Perhaps they just wanted me to shut up. Whatever it was, the eye-rolling, *tsk*ing, lip-pursing, and head-shaking stopped. Instead, I saw pleasant smiles, nods, even an *amen* from Mrs. Gooding. Finally, it seemed safe to stop talking.

When the meeting was over, Janelle invited everyone to stay for some cookies and fruit salad. I said I needed to get back to the courthouse and was on my way out when I made the mistake of looking at the cookies. Home baked. Lots of chocolate. No icky nuts to get in the way of the good stuff.

I could stay a little while, I figured, just to help the office's image.

Before the arraignment on the Crenshaw case, I gave John Fredericks one last try at the crime lab.

"John, it's Samantha Kincaid at the DA's office."

"This is really weird," John said. "I could've sworn that the best darn female golfer at the DA's office called here a few hours ago."

It wasn't saying much. Two years ago at a statewide golf tournament for prosecutors, I had won trophies for both the highest and lowest ladies' scores.

"Sorry, but I'm sort of in a rush."

"We just got the case yesterday."

"I'm trying to decide whether to make a cooperation agreement with one of the defendants. It's a little complicated."

"Well, if you were thinking about doing it before, you're really going to be thinking about it now. I finished that last test

I was telling you about, and it's just like I thought. Not a drop. I got bupkes."

I guess that meant I needed to find Todd Corbett's lawyer as soon as possible. Files in hand, I made the quick damp trek from the courthouse to the Justice Center. Hanks and Corbett were scheduled to be arraigned on the two o'clock docket. From the looks of things, it was safe to say they were indigent and would qualify for court-appointed counsel. Once the lawyers were assigned, I'd pounce on Corbett's.

The arraignment deputy, Ben Bodie, was already at the prosecution's table. Poor Ben. Rumor had it, he was smart as a whip and fearless in trial. He worked hard, but did so modestly and quietly. Not the way to get ahead in this office. So, instead of being fast-tracked into a felony trial unit, here he stood in the JC2 court. A talking monkey could handle JC2. Call the case, hand the clerk the charging instruments, read another lawyer's log notes about the bail recommendation, and you're done. OK, so maybe the arraignment monkey would need to read, too.

"Hey, Ben. I just wanted to let you know that I'll handle the Hanks and Corbett matters."

"Oh, good. Maybe you can talk to that woman in the back row over there. She was asking about Hanks. I told her I didn't know anything."

I turned and saw a young woman with long curly hair sitting in the back of the courtroom. She had a pierced nose and wore a heavy wool sweater, undoubtedly knitted by native peoples somewhere or another.

I introduced myself to her.

"Hey," she said casually. "I'm Annie."

No last name. Interesting. "I was told you were inquiring about Trevor Hanks?"

"Um, yeah. I was wondering if there was any possibility he'd get out?"

"It's up to the judge. But, since it's a murder case, it's unlikely. Extremely unlikely."

"Oh, OK."

"May I ask what your interest is? Do you know him?" She looked like she'd hang with a different kind of crowd, but you never could tell.

"I can't really say."

This was getting suspicious. I told her as much, and she immediately turned on me. "Man, you people always think you know so much. No wonder people don't trust the sytem."

"Annie, you're losing me. What else am I supposed to think when you show up at a court appearance, give me nothing but your first name, and start asking questions about a murder suspect?"

"OK, here's what I can tell you. I'm a volunteer counselor with the Portland Rape Crisis Center, and as a result of my work there I wanted to know if there was any chance he could get out before trial."

Reading between the lines, it was pretty clear I had yet another reason to dislike Trevor Hanks. "I know how serious the center is about confidentiality, but do you think the person who's worried about Hanks would come in and talk to me?"

She shook her head, and I could see from her expression that she had tried. This was frustrating, to say the least. "Look, here's my card. Call me if anything changes."

She fiddled with the card between her fingers. "Is there any way you'd be willing to call me if he does go free? You know, as a sort of heads-up?"

I tried to put myself in the shoes of whoever this woman was that Annie was counseling. Hanks's arrest had probably brought some small hope that there was justice in this world. Karma. If the certainty of his incarceration made her recovery easier, I was all for it. I wrote Annie's name and mobile number in my file with a reminder in bold letters.

Then I waited. Twenty minutes later, sheriff's deputies brought Hanks and Corbett out, and I took the seat next to Ben Bodie and called the two cases together. I handed the clerk a document charging the defendants jointly with aggravated murder for intentionally causing the death of Percy Crenshaw during the course of an armed robbery. The defendants documented their poverty, and the court found that they qualified for counsel.

Since codefendants have inherent conflict of interests, the judge would appoint two separate lawyers. And since those lawyers would owe a duty of loyalty only to their own client, they couldn't both work for the same office, even if that office was the Public Defender. That meant that the judge would need to resort to a contract attorney, a private lawyer who handled indigent defense cases on a contractual basis.

Judge David Lesh perused his list of attorneys, checking to see who was in the room. "All right, let's see here. Mr. Hanks, you'll be represented by Lucas Braun." When a thin lawyer with bad feathered hair rose from the front row, I recognized him as a late-twenty-something eager-beaver solo practitioner. The courts must have only recently approved him for capital cases. "And Mr. Corbett, you'll be represented by Lisa Lopez."

Now Lisa, I knew. She was a hardheaded brat of a public defender and the closest thing I have to a courthouse nemesis. On the rare occasion when I've been able to finagle a compromise from her, it's been like pulling a mouthful of walrus teeth. I could've sworn that Lesh looked at me with a gleam in his eye as he filled out the forms. If only he knew how much easier my job would have been if he switched the appointments around.

Compared to Lisa Lopez, dealing with Braun would have been more like plucking out a few wiggly little baby teeth.

The court appearance itself was quick. I watched Corbett and Hanks out of the corner of my eye as their lawyers tried to make them sound good. Hanks stared straight ahead at nothing in particular, his jaw set firmly. Corbett's gaze, on the other hand, continually darted between me and Hanks. I suspected that I looked familiar to him from the other side of the interrogation room's mirror. He was putting two and two together, and he was trying to make eye contact with the friend he'd dimed up.

Lesh ordered both defendants to be held without bail, the usual in an Agg Murder case. I entered log notes in the files, then made a point of catching up to Lisa quickly, before the deputies had a chance to cart Hanks and Corbett away. "Hey, Lisa. Can we talk about your guy for a sec?"

My comment didn't go unnoticed by the defendants. Corbett's expression was a mix of hopefulness and fear, like a puppy being picked up at the pound. Hanks just looked pissed. Given the unsuccessful spit wad involved in our first encounter, he probably realized I was playing favorites.

And Lisa—well, Lisa looked annoyed and confrontational. In other words, she looked like Lisa. "Yeah, sure. Just a minute," she said, holding up her index finger before turning back to some notes she was scribbling on a legal pad.

While she finished up her thought, I dashed off a note of my own and handed it to one of the sheriff's deputies who'd be walking the boys back to their holding cells on the seventh floor. His name was Jake Meltzer; he used to be assigned to courthouse security and, based on his chronic flirtation with me when I'd walk through the staff entrance, I was pretty sure he thought I was a cutie.

Jake. Keep an eye (and ear) on these guys for me? Sam. I drew a big ear next to two stick figures in jail stripes and finished off with my phone number.

With all notes completed, Lisa and I walked to the hallway outside the courtroom for our little chat.

"What's up?" she asked with a sigh, as if this were the twelfth time she'd been interrupted within the hour. By me.

I felt myself straighten to my full five-eight. Maybe it was a blatant example of discriminatory heightism, but I took tall comfort towering over Lisa's fireplug frame.

"Did you get a chance to read the affidavit?" I asked. I had filed a "just the facts" affidavit to justify the charges against the defendants until a grand jury issued an indictment.

"Just a quick skim," she admitted.

"So you know Corbett confessed. I'm willing to take the death penalty off the table if he'll testify against Hanks." That would leave the maximum sentence as a true life sentence, without parole.

"Are you telling me Griffith has already signed off on this as a death case?"

"Not yet, but obviously it's something we're looking at."

"Then we'll talk about it down the road."

"No. I'm offering it to him now."

"You're kidding, right?" she asked. I said nothing. "Is that all you're taking off the table?"

"It might not mean a lot to you, but I suspect your client will see a big difference between living and dying."

"You want me to plead my guy to true life before we've even talked to a judge about how your cops must have gotten this bullshit confession?" Oh, boy. She hadn't even seen the full reports yet, and I had already triggered the Lisa Lopez Laments button. She was like one of those automated yapping toys. But instead of singing "I love you, you love me" when you touched her belly, she prattled on about the oppression of her clients and the nastiness of the police when you even hinted that she might be representing someone guilty.

On and on she went. If you believed Lisa, she was not only going to get Corbett's confession suppressed but also Peter Anderson's ID, the videotape of her client with a bat, and any mention of the crimes he committed on 23rd Avenue the night of the murder. I let her have a full minute before I interrupted. "I gave you an offer, Lisa. Are you taking it to Corbett or not?"

"You know I'll take it to him. I'm required to. But I'll tell him to walk away from it."

So much for my plan to wrap this case up early.

Even laid up, Russ Frist had a sixth sense. My phone was ringing when I got back from the Justice Center. Sure enough, it was my stay-at-home boss.

"Russ, you need to learn how to take a sick day," I said. "Get yourself a gallon of juice, a box of strudel, a pillow, and your remote control, and stop calling me."

"It could have been worse," he said. "I wanted to call you to find out how things went at the Kennedy School, but I held off until your arraignment on Crenshaw. Any news?"

"Judge Lesh appointed Lisa Lopez to represent Corbett."

"He's the one you wanted to flip?"

"Yep," I confirmed.

"You're screwed."

"Yep," I confirmed again. "She pretty much told me to pound sand."

"So think about sweetening the offer."

There's only three possible sentences once a defendant's convicted of aggravated murder: death, true life—which I'd already offered—and a life sentence with the possibility of parole after thirty years.

"The way I've always seen it, you've got to be willing to take a chance at trial on a close case."

"No way, Sam. No way do you play a gamble like that. This is not a drug case. We don't let people walk away from murders in my unit. You need a conviction, and to get a conviction, you need to convince one of those fuckers to take the stand."

"Fine," I conceded. "If Corbett will agree to thirty years, he can have a deal."

"You're on crack, Kincaid. Chances are, that's the most you'll get even if you go to trial and win. You've got two kids on meth and a robbery gone bad. Flip Corbett, then maybe—*maybe*—you can get Hanks for true life. But if they decide to roll the dice together, which they will if you can't use Corbett's confession, you've got a major problem."

"Well, I can't go back to Lisa yet. If she gets the impression I'm bidding against myself, she'll dig in until I'm offering up probation. I'll wait and see if she comes back with a counteroffer."

"Who's handling the other guy?"

"Lucas Braun."

"That guy? He's a total idiot."

"I had a case against him back in DVD. He seemed OK. Ambitious."

"Exactly," Russ said. "He managed to get himself on the list for agg murder cases when he's still cutting his teeth."

"I was wondering when that happened."

"I'm sure he barely has the minimum requirements. He's got a couple years of felony trials and second-chaired a couple murder cases. Now he thinks he's Gerry Spence, Junior."

"Is he?"

"Only in the strange-coiffure department. You can't even have a serious discussion with the guy about trial issues, because he literally won't understand what the issues are."

"Come on, he can't be that bad." Russ was one of the few people who could outcriticize me.

"Trust me, he's so bad you'll wind up wishing you had another Lisa Lopez to deal with."

"Never. Never, I say."

"We'll see. What is with you two anyway?" It wasn't a big secret around the courthouse that Lisa Lopez drove me nuts. Or that the feeling appeared to be mutual.

"She's evil. Pure, unadulterated evil. And don't you dare make kitty-cat hissing noises." My problem with Lisa had nothing to do with gender; my many run-ins with the other half of the species were a testament to my equal-opportunity bad-mouthing. And, besides, was it my fault that the most irritating lawyer in the defense bar was a woman? I really couldn't help it. Lisa was truly intolerable. She actually flashed a V sign at me once after winning a motion. I asked her what was wrong with her fingers.

"Whatever," Russ said dismissively. "She doesn't seem that bad to me. How was the thing at the Kennedy School?"

"Fine," I said.

"Brevity is never a good sign with you, Kincaid. Were you nice to the other children?"

"Yes, Dad. No sand throwing. No gum in anyone's hair. It really was fine. I sat. I met. I talked. I ate cookies. It was fine."

"Stop saying fine."

"Fine."

I could picture him smiling on the other end of the line. "So, a box of strudel, huh?"

"Works every time," I said. "You want me to call about a delivery?" I realized I didn't know enough about Russ's personal life to know if there was a strudel-delivering type of person in his picture. I guess my ignorance was one of the costs—or benefits—of staying mum at the office about my own off-the-clock time.

"No, thanks," he said. "I'll stop by the store on the way home from the doctor."

"Don't forget the OJ. And don't scrimp. Get the real stuff."

"Got it. Watch the shop for me?"

"No, that's why we've got Alice."

I noticed my message light when I hung up. It was the sheriff's deputy I'd recruited as an eavesdropper. "It's Jake Meltzer from the Sheriff's Office. Hey, I think you missed your calling; I liked your little doodle. Anyway, I got a report for you if you want to page me." I wrote down the numbers he left me.

A few minutes later, Jake answered the page.

"So, are they best buddies again yet?"

"Yeah, right. I thought the mean one was going to jump the dumb one in the transport." I didn't even need to ask: Hanks looks mean; Corbett looks dumb. "I can't remember it all word for word, but the gist of it's that the mean one's pissed as hell. I take it the dumb one confessed?"

"Yeah. Gave up the other one too."

"I figured as much. Anyway, Mean One tells Dumb One something like 'Why didn't you tell them what *really* happened?' and 'Why the f did you open your mouth at all?' Then he said, 'Watch your back, mf,'—but, you know, he actually said the cussing parts. That's about it. I wanted to keep them going to see if they'd say something more, but, like I said, it was getting a little intense."

It was typical. Hanks was pissed, not only that Corbett ratted on him but that he'd undoubtedly managed to understate his own participation along the way. "Did the Dumb One say anything back?"

"Nope. In fact, he kept shushing the other one. He was, like, 'Didn't you hear the lawyers, man? Don't talk to anyone but them, not even each other.'"

I logged an entry into the attorney's notes portion of my file. Maybe the Dumb One wasn't so dumb after all.

9

At five o'clock, Heidi Hatmaker sat in her cubicle, mesmerized by the Portland Police Bureau press release in her hands. These two kids in orange jumpsuits didn't look much older—or meaner, really—than her little brother. The single-page statement offered little: the arrest of two people for a murder. It was no different from the routine press releases that circulated through the office every day.

But this particular piece of news took on a significance that was missing from all the other crime stories the paper covered. This one was personal. It wasn't just a "press release" or "news" now that she knew the person who had been killed. She looked at the faces of Todd Corbett and Trevor Hanks. How could anyone find it in themselves to become so violent— to bludgeon another human being, again and again—just to ride in his car?

She placed the press release beneath a stack of old clippings in her cubicle and turned to Percy's notes. She wished she could work on them full time. Instead, she had spent the entire day on Tom Runyon's latest directive.

Her job had been to hang out at Reed College, a small liberal arts college nestled within an upscale residential area of southeast Portland. For decades, the place had been a bastion of hippie culture, largely isolated from the political changes that had hit the real world since the 1960s. Tom had instructed Heidi to blend in and see whether students really did use marijuana openly on campus, as her editor had heard.

She knew exactly what Tom had in mind. The news departments were under orders from the top to make sure that a "liberal bias" wasn't infecting the paper's coverage. What better way to prove the paper's evenhandedness than to do a cheap exposé targeting pot-smoking by the liberal academic elite?

She wanted to tell Tom Runyon to stuff it. That kids smoking some doob on campus wasn't news. That she was working on something far more important, the re-creation of Percy Crenshaw's pending stories. But, as always, she did as she was told. Fitting in as another student wasn't particularly difficult, given her age and everyday attire. But in her spiral notebook, instead of jotting down notes for a term paper, she documented any activity that could be sexed up into the rich-kids-are-spoiled piece that Tom undoubtedly had in mind: bong hits on the student union porch, kids tripping on acid in the canyon behind Eliot Hall, condoms openly available by the handful in coed dorm bathrooms. Heidi knew it was all stupid non-news but tried to console herself that at least she was being given a chance to write a piece that just might warrant the front page.

When she returned to the office and briefed her editor, Heidi's mood only worsened. "Good job, kid. I'll get Manning on it right away." Dan Manning was the up-and-comer in the newsroom. Heidi was apparently only good for scouting the story, not nailing it down and writing it.

She was finally finished, though. Now she could use her time as she pleased. She grabbed her backpack full of notes and a calculator and walked to the nearest Coffee People.

As Heidi added, divided, and multiplied the various number combinations, she lamented her stunted math skills. When she applied to colleges, it had been a problem. With a 780 verbal and a 500 math on her SATs, her high school academic adviser had warned her that her skills were "skewed." She managed to get into Yale—her status as a legacy undoubtedly helped—but she had avoided even the most basic math classes.

Now it was biting her in the ass. She had taken the figures from Percy's tables for January through August and had calculated grand totals for the eight months. That part was easy; it was simple addition. The numbers in the s rows were always larger than those in the A rows. And the numbers in the B column were larger than the numbers in the L, W, and A columns on the NEP chart. But on the EP chart, the numbers in the L column were largest.

Heidi continued staring at the charts she had made:

NEP

	B	L	W	A	Total
S	1150	751	263	75	2239
A	342	348	98	32	820

EP

	B	L	W	A	Total
S	322	999	489	272	2082
A	121	328	184	98	731

Percy had been keeping track of the total number of s's and A's, and then breaking that down further by whatever the other letters stood for. There must be some sort of interaction between the factors Percy was monitoring, but Heidi was fumbling with the different functions of her calculator to no avail. She took a long sip from the straw of her grande frozen Mocha Mindfreezer and turned back to her notebook, determined to put her finger on a pattern.

If she could change each number in the chart to reflect a percentage of the total, she'd be able to compare the boxes against one another in relative terms. Maybe then she could single out whatever Percy found interesting about these stats.

She probed the limited portion of her memory reserved for algebra. Divide the number in the box by the total, and you get the percentage. She drew new boxes and started punching the keys on her calculator. Filling in each blank square in the new charts with a percentage, she told herself it had better pay off. This was going to exhaust her daily tolerance for math. Maybe even her weekly allotment.

When she was done, she picked up her Mindfreezer again and examined the results of her labor:

NEP

	B	L	W	A
S	51.4	33.5	11.7	3.3
A	41.7	42.4	11.9	4.0

EP

	B	L	W	A
S	15.5	48.0	23.5	13.1
A	16.6	44.5	25.1	13.4

The cold creamy caffeine must have done the trick, because she finally saw what had been bothering her when she was studying the raw numbers. On the EP chart, the percentages beneath each column letter—B, L, W, and A—were pretty much the same in each row. But something weird was going on with the NEP numbers. Whatever B stood for, B's made up more than half of the S's, but only about 40 percent of the A's. The L's, on the other hand, were only about a third of the S's, but were more than 42 percent of the A's.

Great. All this work to know that when NEP was in effect, B's were less likely than L's to be A. That would make a terrific story. She knew she was on to something, though. Percy had gone to the trouble of compiling these numbers for a reason. He had done it carefully and methodically, for eight months, and his notes rarely showed this kind of cautious data gathering. She just needed to figure out what the hell those letters stood for, and she could find the story that Percy had been hunting.

She tossed her empty cup into a nearby trash can, stuffed her notes into her backpack, and returned to the office. Tracking down Percy's last steps was going to require more than just his notes. Fortunately, Heidi had a plan.

10

It was five o'clock and no pending emergencies: my cue to pack up my stuff and head out. I was throwing a couple of files in my briefcase to review at home when Alice walked in.

"Not so fast," she said. "I've got one last thing for you. The public defender's office just faxed this over."

It was a motion to suppress in the case of *State v. Todd Corbett*. Lisa Lopez hadn't wasted any time. I flipped through the pages. Sure enough, it was the same template motion to suppress they filed in every case involving a confession. No facts about this specific defendant, interrogation, or detective. Just a cut-and-paste beneath a new case caption. There was one tricky wrinkle, though: She was asking for a copy of Detective Mike Calabrese's Internal Affairs file, a fishing expedition for anything that might support her claim that Mike had used the psychological equivalent of the rubber hose to get his confession. Cops see a request for their files as the lowest move a defense attorney can make. Given where things stood between Mike and me on this particular subject, I wasn't looking forward to delivering the news.

Lisa had also thrown in a motion to suppress Peter Anderson's identification of the defendants as the men he'd seen in the parking lot before the murder. According to her, the identification process the police had used was so unreliable it violated due process. That was a shock to me, given that the six-photo lineup they'd used was standard procedure.

I had expected Lisa to try to get the confession tossed, but I was suspicious about the timing. I stood at my desk, motion in one hand, open briefcase in the other. I looked out my office door. People were leaving. I could be one of them. Then I looked at my desk and felt the draw of the phone. One quick call to Lisa Lopez, and I'd know why she filed this motion so quickly. I'd still be home early, I told myself, and I wouldn't have to worry all evening about what might be waiting for me in the morning.

I set my briefcase on a chair and dialed Lisa's number.

"This is Lisa Lopez, Esquire."

Even the way the woman answered the telephone made me shudder. "Lisa, it's Samantha Kincaid at the DA's office."

"Did you get my little delivery? I was afraid you might have left with the other government workers."

So much for a stress-free evening. I should have known that a quick call to Lisa was a surefire way to ruin my night. She always managed to be more unpleasant than even I remembered.

I tightened my grip on the handset and imagined smashing it against the desk. I kept my tone even. "Nope. I've still got a couple hours of work to do, but I wanted to make sure I caught you before *you* left. Is there anything I need to know about this motion? Given that it's your standard fill-in-the-caption thing, I really couldn't tell what you had in mind." I couldn't resist the not-so-subtle dig.

"You were the one saying you wanted to move things along. The way I see it, my client's got no incentive to cooperate with you once your only evidence is kicked. So let's get the arguments over the confession and your so-called witness ID out of the way as soon as possible. If I win the motion, the case goes away. If not, then we can talk about what my client wants in exchange for his testimony."

"Lisa, does your guy know the gamble he's taking? Even if you win the motion—which you won't—I still have enough evidence to go forward. And if you lose the motion, what makes you think he can still get a deal?" Telephonic bluster is as vital a skill to litigation as courtroom argument.

"You'll still need Corbett to get to Hanks."

"I won't need him if Hanks takes a deal first," I said. "Maybe I should have talked to Lucas Braun today instead of you."

"Nice try, Sam, but Hanks is way less credible than Corbett, and I think you know who deserves a deal here." I thought again about the visit from the woman who called herself Annie, the Rape Crisis counselor who was asking questions at Hanks's arraignment. "Let's get the motion to suppress out of the way; then we can talk. I plan on calling the presiding judge tomorrow to see when we can get sent out for motions. How much time do you need?"

"I'm ready whenever you are."

I knew better than to trust Lisa, but I also knew that I had little say in the matter. A judge would allow the motion to be scheduled if the defense wanted it done quickly. It would look terrible to suggest that I wasn't ready to defend the admissibility of my own evidence.

"Well, I need to see Calabrese's IA file first." She said it as casually as if she were asking for a copy of the day's paper.

"You know I'm not handing that over to you."

"You always have to make everything difficult, don't you,

Sam? And here I thought I'd been nice by not asking for Matt York's too."

So much for hoping that the defense attorneys might leave Chuck's friend out of the matter. "You think you deserve a gold star for being less of a jerk than you could have been?"

"Fine. We'll meet at the call docket tomorrow for a ruling."

I left a message at IA to send Mike's file over first thing in the morning.

By the time I turned onto my block, I had worked myself into a piss-poor mood. I was still uncomfortable with the way Calabrese had gotten Corbett's confession, and now Lisa Lopez was pushing the issue straight into court. If the confession got suppressed, I was in big trouble. Insufficient evidence against both defendants meant no leverage to flip either one of them. If both planted their feet and insisted on trials, I'd lose and they'd walk.

I had learned that there was only so much I could do as a prosecutor. Even a maximum sentence for the most serious charge does not bring back a murder victim or undo the indescribable damage of a sex offense, and many times I had to settle for far less. Sometimes it was because a jury convicted a defendant on a lesser charge. Other times, it was a result of plea negotiations brought on by doubts about the case. Lord knows I had to hold my nose during some of the deals I had brokered in MCU.

But I hadn't had anyone walk out of the courthouse yet. Not since my time in the drug unit had I heard a judge tell a defendant, "You're free to go." My pride had always made the idea of an acquittal hard to stomach, even back then. But now, with rape cases and murders on the line, I couldn't imagine what it would feel like to watch anyone in my caseload rise from the defense table, shake his lawyer's hand, and simply walk out the door while I sat there wondering what I could have done differently.

I knew it would happen eventually, but it wasn't going to happen with Corbett and Hanks. I had to get that confession in.

When I pulled into my driveway, I saw Chuck on the porch, holding a leash. At the bottom of the porch steps, on the other end of the leash, was a very noncompliant French bulldog named Vinnie.

"What's going on here?" I asked, stepping out of my Jetta.

"We went for a little walk," Chuck explained, "but someone won't come back inside now."

Vinnie was absolutely beside himself to see me. Maybe I should modify that. To describe a dog as beside himself might bring to mind one of those big dumb shaggy animals who jumps, runs, barks, or licks when he's happy. My stout little Vinnie's not one of those. It's more like he waddles a little more briskly. Snorts at a slightly higher pitch. Trust me. He was excited to see me.

He headed straight toward me, and Chuck dropped his end of the leash. *"You don't like your leash, do you, little man?"* I cooed, scratching behind his stiff bat-shaped ears. *"No, you don't. Oh, no, you don't."* Vinnie definitely brings out my sickening side.

"I didn't want to risk him running off," Chuck said. "You'd kick my ass if something happened to him on my watch."

"Yeah, pretty much. Why'd you take him out at all?"

"I was being nice," Chuck protested.

I shook my head and grabbed the straps of my purse and briefcase from the car with my free hand. "You've got to stop trying so hard," I said, heading into the house. "Think of it like being a stepfather."

"And what exactly would I know about being a stepfather?"

"You know, just use some common sense."

"I try to give your fat dog some exercise, and that somehow means I don't have common sense?"

So I could have been more tactful. "I just mean don't try so hard. Give him some time to get used to you being around here. As long as you're not a jerk in the meantime, I think that'll be enough."

"You spoil that thing."

"See? You call him a thing, you call him fat? If you talked about me that way, I'd pee on your stuff too."

"He doesn't know English, Sam. He's a dog. Hell, he's a French dog, for Christ's sake. *I do not parlez ze English. Non. I parlez ze language of ze dog.*" Usually, when Chuck conjures up a voice for Vinnie, he sounds like Buddy Hackett. Now he threw in a touch of Pepe Le Pew. The result was—well, the result was frightening.

As for Vinnie's language abilities, I wasn't so sure. "Keep it up, funny guy," I warned. "I picture puddles of drool forthcoming on your leather jacket. *Isn't that right, little man? You don't let anyone pick on you, do you?*"

"You're encouraging him," Chuck objected.

"Only if he can understand me," I teased, setting Vinnie down next to his self-operated feeder.

He plopped his head over the lip of the bowl and began cherry-picking the moist morsels. Before long, the happy snorts recommenced.

"So how was the rest of your lazy day?"

"Lazy." He wrapped his arms around my waist and kissed my neck. "I was in bed all day, but I could probably make another trip there if you want."

I tried to get into the zone. For a second, I thought I was. It normally doesn't require much effort, especially when Chuck's in full sloppy-kisses-and-roaming-hands mode. But the few minutes of dog talk and foreplay hadn't squelched the bad mood triggered by Lisa Lopez.

Chuck could tell I was distracted. He pulled his head back to look at my face. "What's up?"

"Nothing. I'm fine."

He shook his head. "No, something's wrong," he said, releasing his hold on me.

"Come on, let's go upstairs," I said, pulling him by the arm.

"Oh, man," he said, running his hands through his hair and plopping into one of the dining room chairs. "Listen to us. You want to have sex, and I keep asking you if something's wrong because you seem emotionally distant. Lord," he said, looking up at the ceiling, "I am unworthy of the penis you so kindly granted me."

"I'm sorry," I said. "I thought if we went upstairs, I'd be able to get my mind off things."

"I can't believe I'm saying this, but I don't want you to sleep with me as a distraction. So," he said, placing both hands firmly on the table in front of him, "I am officially holding out on you until you tell me what's wrong."

"You're amazing," I said, kissing the top of his head before taking a seat at the table across from him. It didn't take long to fill him in on the last-minute motion from Lisa and the subsequent phone call.

"You should have waited until tomorrow to call her," he said. "We'd be having sex right now."

That got a chuckle out of me, but I was still feeling stressed.

"I don't think you've got anything to worry about," he said, standing up to squeeze my chronically sore deltoids. Chuck's back rubs are the best. "You're just tired. What did you get, three hours of sleep last night?"

"Not even. And I probably won't sleep tonight either. I'm worried about this motion."

"What's the problem? You put Mike on the stand and ask him, 'What happened?' He tells the judge, and every once in a while you say, 'And then what? And then what?' Defense attorney asks bullshit questions; you get everyone back on track; judge lets the confession in. End of story."

"I don't think this one's going to be that easy, Chuck. I mean, you were there. You saw what happened."

The massaging stopped. I wriggled my shoulders to ask for more. Nothing.

"Yeah, I did see what happened. And if you need someone to back Mike up, call me to the stand. We'll get the confession in."

I turned in my chair to look at him. "Are you suggesting that you and Mike are going to say something other than what we all know actually occurred in the interrogation room?"

He shook his head. "Jesus, Sam. You make it sound like Mike hit the guy across the head with a phone book or something. And, no, I don't *testi-lie,* as your attorney buds call it."

"So what were you talking about when you said I should call you to the stand?"

"Just how things always work. You put two cops up there. We tell it like it is: why each step was called for, cut and dry. It looks a lot better if Mike's not on his own, is all. Just to be safe, since you're having doubts."

"I'm having doubts, Chuck, because I think your partner screwed up. That crap with the lights? I can't withhold that from the defense. Not that I could, in any event, since I'm pretty sure Corbett recognized me today at arraignment. Lisa's going to have a heyday with that in court."

"Oh, so what? So she'll whine a little bit, and maybe the judge will say something to you off the record about reining Mike in. But you'll get to keep the confession. What elected judge wants to be on the front page for suppressing a confession in the Percy Crenshaw case?"

He did have a point. I had noticed that the rules of constitutional criminal procedure seemed to have changed since my promotion from the drug unit into MCU. Judges who routinely suppressed confessions and overruled searches without batting an eye were suddenly siding with the government when a murder trial was at stake.

Still, the possibility that I might squeak past Lisa's motion by drawing a judge who cared more about his low-paying local judicial position than the Constitution he'd been sworn to uphold didn't feel like cause for celebration.

"You really don't have a problem with what Mike did in there with Corbett?"

He paused before answering. "No, Sam. I don't. Look, you'll get used to it. You're still at the point where you feel sorry for these guys. It's because you're looking at him like some kid who—what did you say about him?—he looked like he'd work at the Quickie Mart. Fuck, the guy *killed* someone. He took a bat to Percy Crenshaw so he and his loser friend could joyride in a Benz for a couple of hours. Mike's the good guy here."

"He won't be looking good by the time Lisa gets done with him. We have to fight tomorrow over Mike's IA file. Is she going to find anything in there if she gets it?"

"What's that supposed to mean?"

"Mike's not exactly a light touch. Is there ammunition for the defense in his file? You should know."

"No, Sam. *You* should know that all cops have files that someone like Lisa Lopez can turn into ammunition. Big surprise—bad guys make up shit about the police. That's why the bureau requires your office to contest any request to see IA jackets."

"But sometimes judges order us to produce them. And this is

an aggravated murder trial where Mike's conduct is critical. He confronted Corbett with evidence we didn't have. He pulled out the threat of the death penalty."

"So what should he have done instead? You said yourself, without the confession, they both walk."

"When the calls started coming in to the news, and he knew who Corbett was, he could have held up on the arrest until we got an ID from the victim's super. Then he would have had something legitimate to confront Corbett with in the box."

"What's the difference?" Chuck asked. "We got the ID in the morning. Corbett's still guilty."

"It matters, Chuck, because it makes the interrogation look really bad."

"You've got to get over this, Sam. I've been trying to stay out of it, but both of you keep putting me in the middle. Mike's my partner. He needs to trust me, and you treating him like the bad guy is making it hard between us."

"I know he's your partner. Why do you think I didn't stop him in there? I knew he was going too far, and I knew I should have cut it off, but I didn't. I let you talk me out of it."

Chuck exhaled loudly. "That's what this is about, isn't it? You've got regrets about how you played things last night, and you blame me for it."

"I don't blame you, Chuck."

"Yes, you do."

"No, I don't."

"Yes, you do."

"No, I don't."

Oh, boy. These straight-from-the-playground verbal exchanges had been one of the many reasons I'd kept my Chuck contacts strictly platonic for so long. He has a way of making me absolutely crazy. And not always in a good way.

"You wanted to cut Mike off earlier, and I convinced you not to. You just said so."

"I stated the facts. That doesn't mean I blame you."

"Fine, don't call it blame then, but I know you."

"We both wanted the confession, Chuck. We wanted to avoid a trial where Matt York is defense exhibit A."

"Yeah, but you're thinking to yourself that you wouldn't be in this jam with Lisa and her stupid motion if you weren't involved with me. And I'm thinking I wouldn't be avoiding eye contact with my own partner all day if I weren't involved with you."

"I didn't mean to make this about us. I'm just worried about the case."

I started walking upstairs. He, of course, did the entirely wrong thing and followed me. When I hit the bedroom, I was struck for the first time by the mess of unpacked boxes of summer clothes, sporting gear, and who knew what else. My usually tidy sleigh bed was completely disheveled, the top sheet and comforter entangled with each other in a knot at the foot of the mattress. My reading chair by the window was draped not only with my moss-colored chenille throw, but a couple days' worth of Chuck clothes. And I nearly tripped over two thirty-pound barbells that had been plopped onto the middle of my cute little raglan floor rug.

"Are you ever going to find a place to keep all this stuff?" I asked, rolling the weights near a stack of unopened boxes in the corner.

"So that's what we're talking about now? Whether I've unpacked fast enough?"

"No, I guess it's not." I opened the second drawer of my dresser, grabbed a sports bra and a pair of running shorts, and started to change.

Chuck sat on the bed. "I take it that you're not getting undressed for any fun stuff."

"I just want to go for a quick run. Clear my head. Maybe if I'm not here, you can get some of this stuff put away."

"So we're back to that subject."

"Chuck, look at this room. And it's not just this room; it's the whole house. Do you know how much crap I got rid of to clear out half the closet space and half the drawers in this place? And you don't use any of it. All of your stuff is still hanging out wherever you happened to use it last."

"Whoa," he said. "I had no idea any of this was bothering you."

Neither did I. Until now. "Leave your stuff wherever you want it," I said, stepping into my running shorts. "I just need to get out for a while."

"You mean you need to get away from me."

I pulled my sports bra over my head. "Look, just let me run a few miles and think about some things. You probably think I'm being a big bitch right now anyway."

"Well, you are, Sam."

I stared at him and shook my head.

"What?" he asked.

"I cannot believe you just said that. You called me the b-word."

"You're the one who said it. I was just agreeing with you."

Crazy. He makes me crazy. And, of course, he followed me down the stairs and continued to argue with me as I put my shoes on.

"Don't you see what you're doing?" he asked. "You always do this. Whenever there's the slightest conflict, you pull away from me. I thought that was over."

"I'm just going for a run, Chuck. You're being ridiculous."

"You know I'm right. Jesus, Sam, you shouldn't have said you were ready to live together if your instinct is still always to leave."

"You know what? Maybe you *are* right." As I walked out the door, I let it slam behind me.

I've never known what exactly it is about running that cures my blues—the outside air, the elevated pulse, the rhythm of my stride, the feel of my feet hitting the pavement. Whatever it is, it works. By the end of a third mile, I can send any problem that was eating at me back into the bigger picture. I can visualize solutions. I can realize that even the worst-case scenario isn't so bad. Sometimes, when the endorphins are pumping extra well, I can even find an upside.

But my magical therapy wasn't working for me today. I was twenty-five minutes in, with probably three miles logged, and I still felt like shit. I was worried about the case and even more worried about the exchange between Chuck and me.

I was so inside my own thoughts that I didn't realize I had strayed from the well-worn route I use for my short runs. I was in front of the house I had grown up in. The house where my father now lived alone.

My subconscious must have been telling me something. I climbed the stairs and tried the door, but it was locked. Good, I thought, my father's finally listening to me. I had left the house without my keys, so I knocked.

"Hey! Sammy!" Despite at least weekly visits, my dad always seems excited to see me. "Where's the rest of the family?" He peeked behind me, obviously expecting a boyfriend and dog in tow.

"Just me, Dad." I stepped inside and found Al Fontana, Dad's ninety-year-old neighbor, at the dining room table. He was concentrating hard on the checkerboard in front of him.

"Hi, Mr. Fontana. Sorry to interrupt."

He swatted at an imaginary fly between us. "Aayh, you're not interrupting nothing. I was getting ready to hand your father here his backside again. Wasn't I, Martin?"

"The man cheats," Dad said, pointing an accusing finger in Al's direction. "I walk into the kitchen for some more pretzels. I come back—he's got a handful of my checkers and I owe him a crown."

"Aayh." Again with the hand wave. "So what brings my favorite girl from the block here? Did you finally find me a nice girlfriend?"

Lucky for me, I've known Al Fontana since I was three. As a result, I was one of the few women over the age of twenty who wasn't a target of his affections. Yep, Dad's checker partner is an unabashedly dirty old man.

"Not yet, Mr. Fontana. I'll work on it, though."

"Aayh." This time there was only a small wave. "You work on yourself first. When's that detective going to make an honest woman of you? I knew he was trouble when he was lurking around the first time."

I assumed he meant my high school years, when Chuck was a pretty regular fixture. Apparently, when you're ninety years old, a fifteen-year gap is like a momentary time-out.

"Oh, I don't know about that," I said, realizing my voice sounded off. "We're still happy where things are for now." I heard a distinct crack. I hoped they'd chalk it up to cooling down from the run.

No such luck. "You OK, kid?" Dad asked.

"Yeah, I'm fine."

Dad raised his brows at Al.

Al's response? "Hmph."

Great. How did I find all these men who could read me like a roadside billboard? Al used his cane to prop himself up. I had learned long ago not to offer a helping hand. He had swatted it away, then popped off the bronze hand piece on his cane to reveal a flask of whiskey. "That's the only reason I lug this thing around," he had explained.

"Martin, I suggest we call it a night and agree that another win on my part was imminent."

"Agreed."

I tried to convince them to continue playing, but my protests went ignored. We said our goodbyes to Al at the door, and then Dad told me to come clean.

"As much as I'd like you to, you never drop by here when you're out running. I don't think you'd stop for George Clooney while you're running."

"Are you kidding? I'd throw myself in front of a bus to make *him* stop." I went into the kitchen and poured myself a glass of water from a filtered pitcher in the refrigerator. I took the seat Al had vacated and started completing the moves that would have won him the game.

"All right, smarty," he said, picking up the game's storage box from the nearby buffet. I grinned at Dad over the lip of the glass. "Are you going to tell me what's wrong?" he asked.

After some initial hemming and hawing, I eventually broke down. Dad was patient and let me ramble until I had it all out of my system. It wasn't lost on either of us that my blatherings zigged and zagged interchangeably between the fight with Chuck and my concerns about Corbett's confession.

"You might need to accept that there are going to be things that you and Chuck don't see eye to eye on."

"Maybe it's stupid, but I feel almost like Chuck's ganging up on me with his friends. Why doesn't he see my side on this?"

"He's probably trying, Sammy, but cops are their own kind of animal. You said yourself he was already worried about his friend with the marriage problem. Now you're talking about his partner." My dad spoke from experience. Before he became a ranger for the U.S. Forest Service, he had been a trooper with the Oregon State Police. "And I don't think you're mad at Chuck because he doesn't agree with you. I think you're mad at yourself because you let it affect you."

"It affects me because when I go home and tell the person I live with that I'm worried about work, I want him to have some empathy. I don't want an argument."

"Maybe," Dad said, "but maybe this isn't about what happened when you got home today. It sounds to me like you're upset because you think you might be in a different position on your case if you had followed your own instincts last night instead of Chuck's."

He was right. By the time he said it, I was ready to accept the very notion that had set off the mess at home—Chuck's accusation that part of me blamed him. That was what it boiled down to. Yes, I was worried about losing the motion. And I wondered whether I had done the right thing at the precinct last night. But at the core of my reaction—picking at Chuck's housekeeping skills, walking out on him, stopping here at Dad's—lay that same old concern. Could I really share my life with Chuck and still be good at my job? Could I be with him and still be *me*?

I thanked my father for the visit and began a slow jog back to the house, ready to lick my wounds and come clean with my roommate. I found the door unlocked and a note on the table next to my key chain, a plastic parrot that flashed a purple light when you pinched its beak. It had seemed funny when Grace bought it for me at a cheesy gift shop in Maui.

Sorry about the door, but you left without your pinching parrot. I'm staying at Mike's tonight to give you some space. I'll be home tomorrow night. Chuck.

11

It was nearly 7 P.M., and even the hardest working members of the administrative staff were leaving. If Heidi was going to make her request tonight, she needed to do it soon.

She rode the elevator to the fourth floor, silently rehearsing her speech for Lon Hubbard. She found him at his desk, busy as always. As far as Heidi could tell, Lon was the single most valuable employee at the paper. His title was something like Facilities Manager, but he essentially ran the nuts and bolts of the operation. He figured out how to house all the bodies required to keep the paper afloat in this tiny building. He made sure your phone extension followed you when you transferred departments. He could get you one of those cool keyboard pads that were supposed to prevent carpel tunnel syndrome. And he was the one who had opened Percy's office for Heidi when she'd met with the District Attorney and the detective.

"Hey there, Lon. You working late?"

"Yeah, looks like it," he said, shaking his head. "I keep saying I'm going to start leaving here right at five o'clock, six at the latest. But it seems like there's always something."

"Like I say, 'All roads lead to Lon.'"

He smiled. Heidi had come up with that her third week at the paper. Every time she had one of those new-employee questions—where do I find pencils; can I get a key to the back entrance, how do I change my e-mail password?—she'd start somewhere sensible on the long list of phone extensions. Eventually, and inevitably, someone would tell her, "Oh, that's Lon Hubbard." Ever since, she'd been telling Lon that all roads led to him, and he absolutely loved hearing it.

"What are you working on tonight?" he asked.

"Same old boring stuff. Tom's got me fact-checking a background piece Dan Manning wrote about one of the lawyers reportedly on the President's short list for a vacant judicial spot. Given what Dan turned up, I think Tom wants to make sure we don't get sued. Dan gets the byline; I get to spend the night poring over old law-review articles."

"Makes my life sound fun."

"Exactly. Anyway, I was taking a break from it, and I realized that Percy's family would probably like to have his personal belongings from his office. Since they live in California, I thought I'd offer to pack them up if it hasn't been done yet."

Heidi had expected Lon to allow her to be helpful, but she did not expect his elated response. "You, my dear, are a gift from the heavens. A friend of Percy's called earlier asking about that. I guess the parents are up here for the week. Anyway, she thought it would be a little too much for them to pack up the stuff themselves, so I told her I'd do it and call her when it was ready. But if you're willing to take care of it, that's one less thing on my list."

Lon handed Heidi a scrap of paper with the name *Selma Gooding* and a phone number written on it. "No problem," Heidi chirped. "Just give me a key to his office, and I'll bring it right back up with the boxes when I'm done."

As she turned the key in the lock, she felt a little guilty. Inside Percy's office, with the door closed, she picked up the photograph with his mother that Percy kept on his desk. Looking at his broad smile, she wondered whether he had any way of knowing now what she was doing. Probably not, she thought, but in her shoes, he would have done the same exact thing, she was sure of it.

Heidi went directly to the file drawer of Percy's desk and retrieved the cell phone records and business expense reports that the police had photocopied and she had refiled. After checking the hallway to make sure it was clear, she made copies for herself.

Then she spent the next two hours gingerly organizing and wrapping Percy's belongings, filling each cardboard box with the respectful care of a mortician preparing a coffin for burial.

Back at her apartment, Heidi eyed the business expense reports first. Percy had attended a conference of black journalists in Atlanta four months earlier. He also kept track of his mileage for monthly reimbursement requests, but the paper still used the honor system for these and did not require reporters to itemize each trip and the locations visited.

The cell phone records were slightly more promising. The vast majority of his calls were incoming. Heidi thought about the pattern and decided it made sense. She had seen Percy in his office, dialing potential sources doggedly. He'd use his desk phone to make the calls but invariably give his cell phone number in the messages he left. Unfortunately, the bills did not reflect originating telephone numbers for incoming calls.

They did, however, contain a list of all of the telephone numbers Percy had dialed in the last several months of his life. Two of them she recognized right off the bat: the paper's voice-mail system and a pizza place on Northwest 23rd that she herself called at least weekly. The rest would take some work.

She connected to the Internet on her I-Mac and searched for a reverse phone directory. For the first seven numbers she entered, she got only one hit, and that was for the deli next door to the newspaper. Just as she feared, these directories were no better than they were four years ago when an ex-boyfriend from college had begun crank-calling her obsessively. Unavailable new and unlisted numbers, cell phones, and direct business extensions made for unproductive amateur sleuthing.

There was another way to do this, of course. Heidi grabbed her phone book, confirmed that *67 would block anyone she called from identifying her number, and started dialing.

On the first call, she got a machine. *Hello. You have reached the home of Larry and Patricia Crenshaw. We're not home right now, but—* Percy's parents had been the last number dialed on his phone. She hoped he got through.

She tried another number and got another recording, the service desk of a Mercedes dealership. Percy and his car.

She dialed again. *Berlucci's. Pickup or delivery?*

"Sorry, wrong number."

Heidi reconsidered her plan. Paging through the last three months of Percy's bills, she compiled a list of all of the numbers dialed, keeping tally marks next to those that were repeats.

She picked up the phone again and entered the number he called most often. *Tex-Mex Express. Pickup or delivery?*

This time, she just hung up. *Did Percy ever eat at home?*

She tried the next most frequent number and heard a familiar *Doo-doo-doo. The number you are trying to reach has been disconnected.* Dammit!

She moved down the list to the next one.

"Northeast Precinct. Is this an emergency?"

"Um, no. No emergency. I think I dialed wrong."

She hung up quickly. Northeast Precinct. Or, as Percy had abbreviated it, NEP.

12

I woke up Wednesday morning unrested, unfulfilled, and with a crick in my neck. Great. After a marriage where sleep had been a strictly no-touching activity, I'd finally gotten used to having another human being in my bed—one who liked to spoon me like a Jell-O mold. One night without Chuck's intrusive cuddling, and I was falling apart.

On the way to work, I nearly nodded off on the number 9. I took some occasional ribbing for riding the bus, but as long as I used public transportation more often than not, I felt I was doing my fair share for oil conservation. Unfortunately, for every person like me there's an asshole in a Humvee.

Three people were standing outside the locked entrance to the District Attorney's Office. That's usually my cue to head for the other—unmarked—staff door. As far as I'm concerned, helping out confused people who mistake me for the receptionist is not in my job description.

Before I could turn in the other direction, though, one of the group homed in on me.

"Well, hello there. Samantha, isn't it?"

I recognized the woman's round caramel-colored face from the meeting at the Kennedy School. I reached for my mnemonic to recall her name but couldn't remember it.

"Samantha Kincaid," I said. "We met yesterday. And your name also begins with an S—" I left out the fact that *S* stands for senior citizen.

"That's right," she said warmly. "Selma Gooding. You have a good memory."

Yeah, right. She was accompanied by a man and another woman, both of whom looked to be in their late sixties. The man was tall, with graying hair and a matching mustache. He wore a light gray three-piece suit and held a dress hat in his hands. I suspected the clothes were left over from days long ago, before retirement. The woman next to him had dark skin, piercing eyes, and glossy mahogany lipstick. Her hair was worn in a short natural Afro. She was petite but stood straight as a rail, with the kind of poise young girls practice with books on their heads. The effect was almost regal.

I managed an "I'm sorry" in their direction as I tried to clear my full hands for a well-mannered shake. Tucking my half-eaten croissant away proved to be an impossible task as I struggled with my briefcase, gym bag, and coffee cup.

"Let me help you," the man offered, taking the Marsee's bakery bag and holding it open for me. I dropped the pastry inside and wiped my right hand on my raincoat before offering it to him.

"Samantha Kincaid. I'm one of the attorneys here."

"I'm Larry Crenshaw. This is my wife, Patricia."

Percy's parents. I felt even worse about my disheveled appearance.

"Oh, I had no idea you were coming in. I left a message yesterday at your home. I'm handling the case involving your son." *Why did that sound so bad? Did the case really "involve" their dead son?* "I want to say how sorry I am for your loss. Please let me know if there's anything I can do while you're here in town—"

With the grace I would have expected from her physical appearance, Patricia Crenshaw saved me from my awkward babbling. "How about just a few chairs for now? I'm afraid we're not at the best age for all this standing."

I tapped the security code into the keypad on the door and escorted them to a conference room adjoining the lobby.

"You said you left us a message?" Larry Crenshaw asked, once they were seated.

"I did, at your home in California yesterday."

"We must have left by then," Patricia said.

An awkward silence followed. "I was calling to tell you that the police arrested two suspects in the case."

"Yes, we found out when we arrived last night," Patricia said. She anticipated the apology I was about to offer before I could get to it. "But that's all right. We certainly appreciate that you tried to tell us yourself."

"I'm glad you came in." I gave them a brief summary of the charging process and my typical explanation that you could never tell how long the case might take to get to trial, but that I would consult with them along the way on important developments. I held off mentioning the motion that Lisa Lopez had already filed. I'd call them later if a judge scheduled it for a quick hearing.

"One thing we need to talk about is the potential sentence," I said. "Oregon does have the death penalty, but jurors tend to apply it cautiously. I'll meet with some other attorneys before we make a final decision, but it would certainly help to know what your thoughts are on the subject. Obviously, I can give you some time to think it over together."

"Oh, no, ma'am. We don't need any time on that." Larry took his wife's hand in his on the conference table. "We don't believe in vengeance. Lord knows it will take some time, but, the way Patricia and I see it, we should try someday to find forgiveness for these men."

"You sound fairly certain about that."

"We are," he said gently, his wife nodding beside him.

"Then I will let the District Attorney know." The family's opinion would seal the deal; we would not pursue the death penalty.

"And the two men who have been arrested," Larry said. "You're *sure* these are the men who did it?"

"Yes, we are. The superintendent at Percy's complex identified them as the men he saw in the parking lot at ten o'clock at night, which falls within the medical examiner's estimate of when the confrontation occurred." I paused, wondering whether the word *confrontation* was appropriate, but continued. "We have multiple witnesses who place them in the area adjacent to the complex earlier that night, armed with a baseball bat and using it. We even have videotape of one of them— Todd Corbett—running in the street with the bat. And when Corbett was arrested, he confessed to killing your son and also implicated the other man, Trevor Hanks."

The expression on her face suggested that Patricia was processing the information, but I could tell from the strength of the grip of her husband's hand that she was having a hard time. I kept my eye contact with Larry.

"And this was all about that silly car of his?" he asked.

I nodded. "According to Corbett's admission, yes. Also, a neighbor of your son heard a man's voice mention the car shortly after ten P.M., so it's all consistent. The defendants had taken methamphetamine earlier in the night, and that most likely played a role as well."

The three of them exchanged glances that appeared to hold a secret meaning. Perhaps there was no way for them to hear about two white men killing a black man without wondering if there was more to the story. They would eventually find out at trial about Hanks's comment when he was arrested. It was better for me to break the news now than to have them be surprised later.

"There is an indication that at least one of the two defendants—Trevor Hanks—holds some racial prejudices." I told them about the epithet that Hanks used when he claimed we couldn't prove he killed Percy. The Crenshaws tightened their hand clasp, and Selma simply shook her head. "I'm sorry. I know that's very hard to hear."

Mr. Crenshaw cleared his throat. "Is there any possibility that the story about taking Percy's car could be a cover, perhaps?"

"A cover for what?"

After another pause, Mrs. Crenshaw spoke up. "The last couple of times we spoke to Percy, he seemed a little nervous about something he was working on. He cut Larry off on the phone one night, saying he thought someone was following him in his car."

"When was this?"

"Only a couple of weeks ago. When he called back, he pretended like it was just his crazy imagination, but we could tell there was something wrong."

"Did he ever mention it again?"

"No, but we talked to him a few times after that. He just didn't sound right to us."

It sounded like typical parental worrying to me.

"At this point, there's no evidence that this was connected to your son's work or that the defendants even knew what your son did for a living."

When I stopped talking, more silence followed.

"Do you have any questions for me?" I asked.

No response, but they also didn't appear to be getting ready to leave. I sensed that they needed to think of something other than the aftermath of their son's death. I searched for a change in subject.

"The folks at the paper told me you were from California. Do you mind if I ask how you know Mrs. Gooding?"

Selma Gooding jumped at the opportunity to cut the tension. "I just met the Crenshaws this morning. And please, honey, call me Selma. You see, I had the pleasure of knowing Percy. And when I heard what happened, I called up the paper and made sure to tell them to pass my number to his parents. I knew they didn't have any people up here and figured they could use some."

The Crenshaws smiled appreciatively.

"How did you know Percy?" I asked.

She paused before responding. "I see you don't know me well enough yet to realize what a funny question that is. I just have a way of knowing everyone who comes around my way. Like yesterday. You come up to the school, and now I know you too, don't I? See how easy that is?"

I was smiling now too.

"Anyway, Larry and Patricia called me up last night, and the three of us climbed into a taxi this morning to come down here and find out where things stood. Little did I know I could have just called you."

"Well, I'm sorry you had to come downtown. I can ask one of our investigators to drive you home when you're ready."

Selma looked at her new friends across the table expectantly. The two of them said nothing.

"Fine," Selma announced. "I'll bring it up. What these two aren't saying is that they're not from here, so they can't exactly go home from here, now can they? They tell me the police still have Percy's apartment closed up, so they stayed at a hotel last night. I've offered to let them stay with me, but they won't hear anything of it. I told them to ask about getting some help, but apparently they don't want to."

Selma Gooding deserved her name, indeed.

I hopped on the phone and called the various victims' advocates in the offices until I found one who was in, Jill Holland. Jill met us in the conference room and explained the help that was available from the state's victims' compensation fund, both while they were in town and afterward. I usually don't stick around for these conversations, but I made an exception in this case, happy to feel I was part of something that made a difference, however small.

Back in my office, I couldn't shake off the anxiety of my mucked-up personal life. Another reason not to have a personal life. Every few minutes, I checked my pager and cell, but there were no calls. I stared at my office phone, resisting the urge to pick it up.

I'll be home tomorrow night, his note had read. After twenty minutes of dissecting that one sentence in a phone call to poor, patient Grace, I had concluded that he didn't want to talk to me until we were both home. Part of me wanted to call him anyway, to hear his voice, to know that everything was OK. Why wait until tonight if we could smooth it all over right now? But part of me recognized the possibility that the story begun with my phone call might not have a happy ending.

He might tell me he didn't want to talk about things until later, and I'd be left wondering for the rest of the day what the "things" were that he didn't want to say. Or we might fight again, reigniting the emotions that had flared last night. Or worst of all, maybe he wouldn't answer his cell, and I'd be forced to picture him staring down at my name displayed across the digital readout, ignoring the beckoning chirp. No, thank you. Better to play it cool and hope for the best when we got home. In the meantime, the waiting was hell.

I did have to call Mike Calabrese, though. When he picked up, it was apparent that Chuck had already delivered the news about Lisa's motion.

"You're fighting her on it, aren't you?" Mike demanded. "I mean, even the part about my jacket?"

"Of course I am. You know we've got an agreement with the bureau on that."

"Is that the only reason you're doing it? Because a judge will know if your heart's not in it."

So now Mike was giving me lessons in litigation. "Mike, I'll go to bat for you, but you've got to face facts here. The confession's the heart of our case against Corbett, and you're the one who elicited it. Given what's at stake, a judge might want to see the file. Is there anything I need to worry about?"

"Yeah. I don't want my jacket turned over to some scumbag public defender."

"I get the point. But, if worse comes to worst, how bad is it? The argument's in ninety minutes, and IA still hasn't sent the file over."

Mike gave me the same vague response I'd gotten from Chuck the night before: All cops have complaints against them, and they're all bullshit.

"How many do you think?" When he said he didn't know, I pressed him. "Five? Twenty? A hundred?"

"Yeah, right, a hundred. I've been at PPB for seven years. My guess is maybe fifteen complaints, max, made it to IAD. Mostly from patrol days."

A couple a year seemed a little high but nothing too unusual. "Have any of them been sustained?"

"Not a one," he said proudly.

Of course, if Lisa got the file, she'd flip the numbers around to argue that despite double digits of complaints, the bureau had done nothing to rein Mike in. As long as there are complaints, there is no way to win. That's why we never turn over the files voluntarily.

"I'll call you when I have a ruling."

I had just enough time to get through the MCU screening pile before I had to meet Lisa. Today's lucky sicko to be plucked from the pile was Edward Beattie, a twenty-eight-year-old registered sex offender on parole for a Rape II against a thirteen-year-old girl. He also had four priors for public indecency, all involving victims younger than twelve.

Beattie had been apprehended in a citizen's arrest. A seventeen-year-old boy chased him down the street for peering through the bedroom window of his nine-year-old little sister. I noticed the boxes checked on the police report, indicating that Beattie complained to the responding officer about injuries to his face. That's what I call a good big brother.

The officer had been smart, asking the little girl to describe exactly what she had seen inside her room. She said the magic words: Beattie had slid her unlocked window open, cupped his hands over the ledge, and reached his head through to look down into her bed. That slight entry past the threshold of the house was enough to arrest for criminal trespass.

When the officer searched Beattie, he found condoms in his front coat pocket. On a hunch, I pulled up Beattie's prior rape case on the computer. Sure enough, he had been convicted based on DNA evidence. This time, he was better prepared. Criminal trespass plus the intent to commit a crime inside equals burglary. I also noticed that the address Beattie gave was different from the address filed for his sex offender registration. I added a charge for failing to update his registration.

Surprising a guy like Beattie with two felony charges for poking his head inside a window was my idea of good old-fashioned fun. I handed the file to Alice and headed down to the presiding judge's courtroom.

Thirty short minutes later, I chose to climb the five flights of stairs back to my office—anything to delay having to call Mike Calabrese. The presiding judge, Seymour Gables, had told me in the bluntest terms what he thought of my office's decision to oppose the defense's request for Mike's file.

"It's inexcusable and unethical. You have charged a man with aggravated murder, based almost entirely upon the defendant's own statements, given to a single detective. Ms. Lopez would be committing malpractice if she didn't have some curiosity about the detective himself. The least you can do is get out of the way and let her do her job." Worse, Gables was sending us out for a hearing on Lisa's motion to suppress as soon as he could find an available judge.

More bad news awaited me at MCU. "The boss called," Alice informed me. "He wants to see you."

"Russ is back?"

"No, the Big Boss. Duncan."

Duncan's not exactly the kind of boss who calls just to say hello. I decided to take my lumps from Mike first.

I held the phone three inches from my ear while he vented.

Surely I had not argued stridently enough. Surely Lisa Lopez should be disbarred. Surely Judge Gables had his liberal head stuck up his wrinkled eighty-year-old ass.

I made the mistake of trying to calm him. "It just means Lisa gets to see the file, Mike. It's still up in the air whether she gets to use any of it at trial."

"Don't act like I'm the one who's not getting it. I don't care whether it comes into trial or not. I've got no interest in becoming the defense bar's whipping boy." My other line was ringing, but I wasn't about to interrupt as Mike's pace and volume continued to pick up. "Once word gets out that this bitch has my file, every other defense lawyer in every other case will be questioning me about it. The first time it works, word will hit the street. Every dirtbag I come in contact with will run to IA."

Then he found his own way of ending the call. "Jesus Christ. No wonder Chuck walked out on you." I heard a final clatter in my ear as he slammed his phone down.

"Sam," I heard, as I sat staring at my handset. I turned to find Alice Gerstein in my open door. "That was Duncan's secretary. He's expecting you—now."

Duncan's office is two stories down from mine, just past the main entrance on the sixth floor. His secretary, Donna, stands guard outside like a watchdog, but she waved me in. The one upside to being summoned by Duncan is his office. In contrast to my metal desk and corkboard hutch, Duncan's fancy furniture is dark cherry and forest-green leather. No aged whiskey on the desktop, but it would fit right in.

As did Duncan. I knew for a fact he was close to sixty, but he looked as age-ambiguous as always with his full head of white hair, unnaturally even teeth, and ever reliable perma-tan. He glanced up from a letter he was reading and immediately brought out his politician's smile.

"There she is," he said, although no one else was in the room to hear the third person reference. "Have a seat. Can I get anything for you? Donna, did you offer Samantha some coffee?"

"I'm fine, thank you." I gave a little wave to Donna at her desk outside his office, then settled at the edge of Duncan's leather sofa.

"How's everything been up at MCU lately?"

"Just great," I said. "Well, ever since that little episode where I almost kicked the bucket, it's been great."

He laughed a little too hard. In an office that worked strictly through the chain of command, I hadn't spoken directly to Duncan since he called me six months ago to apologize for not treating the situation more seriously when I initially informed him that one of his buds had tried to kill me—literally. Now he was all hugs and kisses, and I was seriously wondering what the hell was up.

"I hear you're doing a bang-up job. Russ always has good things to say about you, and the judges can't speak highly enough about your trial skills."

"Well, that's nice to hear," I said, not knowing how else to respond. Unsolicited positive reinforcement could only mean one thing: Duncan was about to screw me over.

He must have known I was suspicious, because he tried to lighten the mood. "You must be happy up there, because I can't remember the last time I had someone in here complaining about you."

He was alluding to the isolated run-ins I have had with the occasional defense attorney. And supervisor. And judge. And maybe a police officer or two. I had managed to avoid triggering any tantrums up the ladder for the last few months. "That's me," I said, smiling uncomfortably. "Little Miss Congeniality."

He laughed again. "How's the Crenshaw case going? Have you set a meeting with the death penalty committee?"

Duncan usually calls a gathering of the most senior deputies before making a final decision in capital cases. "Not yet, but I spoke with Percy's parents this morning. They're against it. Religious reasons, I think."

"All right. Honestly, I don't see the need for a meeting on this one. We'll go for the life sentence, unless there's some background I don't know about."

I told him about the visit from Annie, the rape crisis counselor. "Obviously the victim knows who he is, so I suspect she's an ex-girlfriend, or perhaps just a date."

"No conviction?" he asked.

"No. I don't even know who the victim is, but the counselor said she didn't want to prosecute."

"Then we can't use it. Plus there's some drugs involved, right?" I reminded him that the defendants said they were both under the influence of methamphetamine. "That stuff's worse than crack. Yeah, no death penalty on this one."

"I'll tell the parents."

"Very good. Now, the reason I asked you down here: I got a call today from Russ," he said, "and it's going to require some reshuffling of responsibilities in MCU."

Here it comes, I thought. Someone's pulling rank, and I'm getting the boot back to DVD. Or maybe this was about the rumor that the supervisor at intake was retiring. Dear God, no, anything but misdemeanor intake.

"I need you to take over the Delores Tompkins shooting. Russ can't do it."

He paused to read my reaction, but I didn't have one. Not yet. First, I had to process the fact that I wasn't being transferred. When I got to the part about inheriting Russ's big case, I was initially excited. Big cases are challenging. Big cases are fun. Big cases meant I was finally getting some recognition around here.

But then I immediately pictured the backlash from the guys in MCT, one of whom lived with me. What had my father said? Sometimes cops are their own kind of animal. And, like it or not, I was in love with one of those animals, and we were having a hard enough time bridging the gap without me going after one of his own.

I knew better than to ask directly why Russ couldn't keep the case. That kind of talk was seen as work avoidance around here. "Duncan, I'm honored you'd pick me for that case, I really am. But I've also got the Percy Crenshaw case, and Russ thought it was better to have separate lawyers on the two."

"Separating the cases was my call," he said, "but that was before we had an arrest on Crenshaw and before we decided to go ahead with the indictment against Hamilton."

He could tell from the blank expression on my face that I hadn't gotten any better at foreseeing the political issues the way he could. "We're giving the black community what they want on Hamilton, and we arrested two white guys on Crenshaw. We don't need to worry about crossing swords anymore. In fact," he added with a smile, "as hard as this may be to believe, it seems you've actually got some fans out there."

"Am I missing something?" I asked.

"Selma Gooding. She called Donna a couple of hours ago, singing your praises. Apparently you helped her out this morning, but she also went on and on about how wonderful you were when you covered Frist's meeting yesterday on Hamilton. According to her, all those people who've been a pain in Russ's ass for the last two weeks think you're the best thing since sliced bread. Is that about right, Donna?" he hollered toward the doorway.

"More like walking on water, but, yeah, you got it," Donna yelled back.

"Anyway, Donna passed her words on to me, and, given that you were Russ's choice too, it seemed like synchronicity."

I was flattered to know that Selma and her friends approved of me, but I still wasn't sure I wanted the case. "You don't have any concerns about me working on an officer shooting? You know, given my—personal situation?" I knew full well that Duncan had no doubts about the nature of my relationship with Detective Chuck Forbes.

"Have you and your friend had Hamilton over for any barbecues I need to know about?"

"No, sir. They don't actually know each other."

"Then I don't see the problem," he said with confidence. "You assured me long ago that you didn't let your personal life get in the way of work. Are you telling me you can't stand up to your boyfriend?" He smiled broadly. Apparently, *he* was the one he now found amusing.

"Just making sure it was OK by you," I said, realizing there was no acceptable way to turn the case down.

"Well, then," he concluded, "you have inherited the first officer shooting indictment this county has seen since I became DA. Don't mess it up."

He still wore the smile, but I couldn't tell if he was kidding. "I'll do my best, sir—not to mess up, I mean."

"I know what you meant, Kincaid. Relax. Now Russ tells me he could be out for six weeks, but give him a call at home for a briefing."

I finally connected the reassignment to Russ's sick day. "Six weeks? I talked to him yesterday, and it sounded like it was probably just the flu."

"I don't know," Duncan said, shaking his head. "I've learned the hard way: If one of my people utters the phrase *disability leave*, I question no further. Something about Lyme disease. He'll probably tell you more than you want to know when you call him."

Alice Gerstein handed me an oversized envelope when I got back to MCU. "This just came for you. Something from Internal Affairs? Also, Detective Walker called. He wants you to call him ASAP on the Crenshaw case. He sounded very excited."

I cheated and called the MCT line instead of Jack's cell. Maybe Chuck would pick up, and I'd have an excuse to gauge his mood.

"Walker."

"Hey, Jack. It's Samantha."

"Good timing. I just got a call from the crime lab, and things are looking even better than I thought. Back up to the beginning, though: I got a call this morning from the evidence room at East Precinct. Seems some bar owner out in Lents found us a baseball bat in his Dumpster this morning."

"You're kidding. Where in Lents?"

"Hold your horses, I'm getting there. So the bar owner finds a bat in the Dumpster in the alley behind his bar. Apparently, the freaking guy dives it periodically for some recycling thing he does—"

"I thought you were getting there."

"Hey, I spent fifteen minutes listening to this guy preach about recycling. I even looked at his mounted and framed copy of an article the paper ran about him a few weeks ago. I'm surprised you don't appreciate it more, being a bus-riding tree hugger yourself."

"Getting there?"

"Yeah. So anyway he finds the bat and fishes it out to give to Goodwill. Then he sees there's blood on it." I held my breath, waiting for the rest. "So he stashes it in a plastic bag and takes it in to East Precinct, thinking the police might be interested. The cop tossing it into the property room does some thinking of his own and calls Johnson about it. Why? Because the bar's on One-hundred-second and Foster."

"Isn't that—"

"Yep," he said, anticipating my question. "Six short blocks from Trevor Hanks's house."

"The Red Rabbit, or something like that?"

"The Red Raccoon. You got some hangouts I don't know about, Kincaid?"

"No. I just remember driving past it when we were transporting Hanks. I noticed the name."

"Well, that's the place."

"And you said the crime lab just called?"

"Right-ee-o. The blood on the bat's definitely Percy's."

"Anything from the defendants?"

"Nope, only one blood type. And no fingerprints except the bar owner's. But he did find some trace evidence in the blood: two hairs that could be Percy's, four fibers that look like the carpet in his condo, presumably from Percy, and—here's the best part—three fibers that match the carpet in the Jeep."

"Hanks's father's Jeep?"

"Yeah. I believe Fredericks said it was like a two-hundred-yard drive straight down the fairway."

"Except for him that's more like a good five-iron shot, but I get the drift."

Even if nothing else panned out, I was ecstatic. We had a murder weapon. We had the vic's blood. We had fibers from the suspect's car in the blood. And we had a bar owner who digs through garbage just blocks away from one of the defendants.

We had, in short, corroboration for Todd Corbett's confession, if I could just get the confession in.

On that note, I opened the envelope freshly delivered from Internal Affairs and flipped through Mike Calabrese's file. Mike's estimate on the number of complaints had been close: twelve since he arrived from NYPD seven years ago. None of them had gone beyond the initial phase of the investigation. From a cursory review of the complaints and the police reports documenting the incidents, IA had been convinced the allegations lacked merit. I thought of the many complaints filed against me by disgruntled defendants. The bar had dismissed every one, without even requiring me to respond. Lisa's request for the file had been a tempest in a teapot.

As I walked the file to a photocopier, I noticed a single sheet of paper documenting Mike's transfer to PPB from New York. The page was much less complicated than the civil service personnel documents I'd seen for officers who started their careers with the bureau. It was entitled LATERAL TRANSFER and was signed by Terry Schrader, the former commander of Northeast Precinct. As far as I could tell, the form permitted precinct commanders to make lateral hires based solely on a review of the candidate's personnel file and a recommendation from a supervising officer in the transferring jurisdiction.

Schrader had checked boxes to confirm his review of Mike's NYPD file and his personal determination that Mike was suitable for service at PPB. When asked to name the officer recommending Mike for transfer, Schrader had crossed out the words *supervising officer* and replaced them with *officer with knowledge*. With that handwritten change, he had scribbled in the name *Patrick Gallagher*.

Lisa would no doubt have a field day with even this small bit of information. I pictured her with Mike on the stand, probing him for information about Patrick Gallagher and the circumstances that had brought Mike to Portland. Terry Schrader had passed away two years ago, so she'd be free to insinuate any sinister scenario she could conjure.

I started to place the page flat on the photocopier, then looked again at Lisa's motion. She had requested only copies of the complaints filed against Mike with IAD and the bureau's resolution of the complaints, not the entire IAD file.

I skipped the page documenting Mike's transfer and copied the remaining pages. Mike didn't deserve it after the way he spoke to me on the phone, but I'd still do what I could to protect him as my witness.

13

I asked Alice for Frist's home number, then did some quick surfing online before I dialed.

"Hello?" The big booming voice was definitely still out of commission.

"Frist, you sound like shit."

"This must be the lovely and ever-pleasant Miss Kincaid."

"What the heck's wrong with you? Duncan says you're out for six weeks."

"I've got Lyme disease, Kincaid. You wouldn't believe how bad this stuff is."

"How did you go and get Lyme disease? Isn't that when you have sex with a monkey?"

"I see my illness brings out the best in you. As it happens, I developed my little complication helping my stupid uncle on his ranch in upstate New York. If I'd known my vacation was going to kill me, I would have stayed home."

"Relax, Russ. I just read up on Lyme disease on the Internet. You're not going to die."

"Too bad for you, huh?"

"OK, now you're just being a martyr. I won't rat you out to Duncan, but the net says antibiotics wipe that stuff right out."

"That's for people who are smart enough to see a doctor right away. According to mine, I waited too long. She says I'm lucky not to have meningitis."

"You've got a woman doctor?" Every time I thought I had Russ figured, he surprised me again.

"Yeah, she's great. So, has Duncan talked to you yet about Hamilton?"

"Just now. I was sort of hoping you'd be all better when I called so I could dodge the hot potato. And for your own well-being, of course," I added.

"Of course. Trust me, I'd be back if I could, but you'll be fine. A manslaughter indictment will be easy, and I suspect Hamilton's attorney will be willing to work out a plea so long as the penalty's not too stiff."

"There won't be riots in the street if we plead it out?"

"No way. Duncan just wants to get the guy off the force. I've spent enough time talking to the crowd of complainers. They know not to expect much more than that."

"They seemed pretty reasonable when I met with them at the Kennedy School," I said.

"Everyone's reasonable when they get what they want. They're so used to hearing that the cops do no wrong, just having us on their side for once is enough. The end result's less important."

"I saw Selma Gooding again this morning. She was helping Percy Crenshaw's parents find their way around."

"Sounds like Selma. I've only met her a few times, but I got the scoop from Peterson at the last supervisors' meeting." Ken

Peterson was the head of the office's Community Prosecution Unit, our office's contact point with neighborhood activist types. "According to him, Selma's been a ten for us on the community policing stuff up there. He told me, 'Be good to her, and it comes back to you in spades.'"

"Yeah, well, I was good to her, and what I got in return was a case against a cop."

"Tell me if I'm prying, but does this have something to do with Forbes?"

I paused. Despite my feelings about the dividing line between work and home, for reasons I didn't always understand, I occasionally let Frist cross over. "Maybe. I don't know yet."

"He's got to understand it's your job, right? Is he actually pressuring you not to indict Hamilton? That would be seriously inappropriate—"

"No. It's nothing like that." I paused again, feeling the all-important line dissolving further. "In fact, he doesn't know I have the case yet. I haven't told him. Let's just say that, based on the conversations we've had lately, I suspect the reassignment won't go over very well with him. Or his partner, who's under fire in Crenshaw."

"Well, maybe Calabrese doth protest too much. If you ask me, Forbes should be happy for you. You haven't exactly been Duncan's favorite deputy at times, so this is a real sign of faith. Not that you asked me, of course." I was relieved when he promptly changed the subject. "Hey, one more thing about Selma: Peterson tells me she chases the working girls off her corner every night with a broom."

I laughed out loud at the image of round, gentle Selma swinging away at the neighborhood ho cakes.

"We should probably go over the grand jury before Friday," he said.

"Isn't that what we're doing?"

Russ sighed dramatically. "And here I was, convinced you'd called about my serious condition."

"Nope."

"Fine. But I'm no good without a file. Do you mind bringing it out here so we can go over it together?"

"At your house?"

"Get your mind out of the gutter, Kincaid. I'd come to you if I could, but—"

"Yeah, all right. Where am I going?"

I scrawled his address down on a Post-it. "Around six?" he asked.

I thought about Chuck waiting for me after work. "I've got something I have to do tonight, but things are pretty slow around here. I'll try to be there by four. You're not contagious, are you?"

"No, and you're not nearly as funny as you think," he said, laughing. "And bring me some of that strudel you mentioned yesterday."

Alice pulled Frist's Hamilton file for me.

The police reports varied from the standardized incident forms I was used to. Most of the documents were typed memoranda to the Chief of Police from detectives in the bureau's Internal Affairs Department.

From them, I learned that at 3:25 A.M. three Sundays earlier, Officer Geoff Hamilton had indicated with the computer terminal in his patrol car that he was stopping Delores Tompkins's 1999 Oldsmobile Alero at the intersection of Northeast Mallory and Killingsworth. At 3:28 A.M., Hamilton used his radio to call for an emergency response to an officer-involved shooting.

That radio call triggered the complicated procedures required by the Bureau's General Order governing officer-involved shootings. In addition to the swarm of EMTs and police who would respond to any shooting incident, a detective from Internal Affairs, a representative of the police union, and Hamilton's shift sergeant were also dispatched. Hamilton's sergeant promptly seized Hamilton's Glock as evidence and drove him to the precinct to remove him from the immediate scene.

Hamilton was permitted to confer privately with his union delegate before his sergeant and IA Detective Alan Carson saw him. According to the GO, the union rep was supposed to explain the procedures required over the next few days. Hamilton would be placed automatically on paid leave pending completion of both criminal and administrative investigations. There would be media scrutiny and psychological counseling. He would probably never approach the job the same way again.

The EMTs who responded to the scene pronounced Tompkins DOA. According to Detective Carson, Hamilton was noticeably upset, even breaking down and crying when his sergeant confirmed that Tompkins was dead.

Hamilton was advised that he had the right to remain silent and that anything he said could be used against him. His delegate notified Carson that Hamilton was willing to give a brief statement about the shooting but would not answer any follow-up questions until he had a chance to recover. I had never been involved in an officer-involved shooting before, but that part surprised me. When your everyday suspect invokes, police and prosecutors alike assume he must be guilty. If Hamilton had nothing to hide, why wouldn't he open himself up to questioning?

The little that he did say to Carson had been tape-recorded and since transcribed for the file. Hamilton's statement invoked the same skilled formalism that officers tend to use in their reports and on the stand, but without the usual detail:

Earlier tonight, I initiated a stop of a black female now known to me as Delores Tompkins. After I approached her vehicle, she disobeyed orders to turn off her engine and to step away from the vehicle. She then surprised me by attempting to drive away from the scene. Because my person was positioned directly in front of her moving vehicle, I discharged my weapon in an attempt to defend myself.

He provided no explanation for the stop, no explanation for how he came to be standing in front of her car, and—most importantly—no explanation for failing to move out of the way instead of firing his gun three times into the windshield. Before Internal Affairs got a chance to question him again, the media glommed onto the story and Hamilton rightly sensed there could be trouble. Through his union delegate, he declined to speak further about the shooting until the criminal investigation was completed.

The file also contained Hamilton's personnel record. He was three years on the force, currently assigned to night shift. In his short career, he'd made thirty-seven collars for resisting arrest, twenty-one of which involved the additional accusation of assaulting a police officer. He'd already had twelve allegations against him for unlawful use of force, ten resolved by IA in his favor, but two left with no formal determination and small settlements paid out to the complainants to avoid threatened lawsuits.

I was feeling better about inheriting this case. Where there was this much smoke, there was fire. Now that I knew more about the facts, I was sure Russ was right. If Chuck took a little heat around the boys for my role in this, he'd understand. And if Mike put himself in the same camp as Hamilton, that was his problem.

■　■　■

I had one sentencing hearing I had to cover before I could head to Russ's. Eddie Carpenter was a pedophile in denial. His so-called girlfriend ran an in-home day-care chock-full of children he had fondled and photographed. She had walked in on Eddie when he was supposed to be changing a diaper. Suddenly, all those frustrated nights in bed made more sense. Once she came clean with the police, Eddie confessed to other crimes as well and eventually pled guilty to four counts of Sex Abuse I in exchange for a sentencing recommendation of eight years.

Like I said, though, Eddie was in denial. He had been held in custody pending sentencing, and this afternoon's hearing was our fourth attempt to finalize the judgment. Before each of the three prior hearings, he had informed the jail nurses of various ailments that prevented his transport to the courthouse.

But at three o'clock on Wednesday, Judge John DeWitt Gregory's clerk called me to confirm that Eddie had, in fact, entered the building. I took the stairs to Gregory's third-floor courtroom.

Once a conviction is obtained—either by verdict or plea—sentencing should be easy. Defense counsel says his thing; I say mine; judge does what he wants. In this case, where there was a joint recommendation from the parties, the entire hearing should have been a no-brainer.

That's not how things went. I explained the plea agreement to the judge. Eddie's attorney asked the judge to follow it. Then, as the judge started to pronounce the sentence, Eddie Carpenter threw himself to the courtroom floor, spasming like a human cramp. His eyes rolled upward, and choking sounds emerged from his throat, and in case we missed the point, his arms twitched at his side.

Judge Gregory and I stared in disbelief, but Eddie's attorneys, a husband-and-wife team named Jim and Kara Newby, tried to save the day. I'd heard they were dedicated, but still. Kara tried to loosen Eddie's tie, while Jim inserted his fingers in Eddie's throat to clear his air passages. One of the many other defendants awaiting sentencing had his own suggestion: "Get your fingers out of there, man. That's nasty." The concerned litigant jumped the bench in front of him and tried to help by replacing Jim's hand with the eraser tip of his pencil.

All hell broke loose until suddenly Eddie emerged upright, pleading theatrically for water. With a sly grin and a glance in my direction, Judge Gregory appeared to share my suspicions but was understandably reluctant to sentence a defendant who claimed to be suffering from a seizure. The court announced it was calling for medical attention and setting over sentencing, and I left the courtroom, wondering if the remainder of Judge Gregory's docket would be delayed by copycat epileptic episodes.

On my way to the elevator, I heard a woman's voice call out behind me.

"Samantha, wait, you can save me a phone call." I stopped my quick courtroom-walking clip and turned to see Lisa Lopez rushing toward me. "I got a call from Judge Gables. He sent us out to Judge Lesh's courtroom on Thursday for Corbett's motion."

"Thursday? As in tomorrow? You didn't think to get my input on that?"

"We both told him we were ready to go, and the first open court date was tomorrow."

"When exactly were you planning on letting me know?"

"Cut me some slack. I've been in trial all day. We're only taking a break so I can pee."

"What time?" The Crenshaws had been kind enough to invite me to Percy's funeral in the morning, and I wasn't about to miss it because of one of Lisa's stunts.

"Two o'clock. OK?"

"Yeah, sure." The way she'd gone about it pissed me off, but it wasn't worth fighting over.

"You calling anyone other than Calabrese?"

I thought about Chuck's point from our fight the night before: Two cops were always better than one. "Yeah, his partner, Charles Forbes. He's in the reports."

Thanks to Eddie Carpenter's performance, I was running late for my meeting with Frist. On autopilot, I headed to the garage where I usually parked the Jetta. As I was roaming the floors, trying to remember where I had left the car, I realized today had been a bus day. Eventually, before I retired, I'd develop a system for keeping track of these things.

After twenty minutes and a schlep to the county lot, I was finally on the road in a borrowed fleet car. I used my cell to call Mike Calabrese about the hearing. Neither of us acknowledged the nasty way he ended our last conversation. True to form, he was still pissed about Lisa putting him through the wringer, but he didn't sound the least bit worried about losing the confession. "I didn't do anything wrong. She just wants to break my balls."

Five minutes later, I broke down and called Chuck. He also needed to know about the hearing, and I probably needed to tell him I'd be home late.

By the fourth ring, I regretted it. Mike had answered his own phone immediately and hadn't mentioned anything urgent. So why couldn't his partner pick up?

At the tone, I wished I had prepared an appropriate message. "Hey," I said. "It's me. I'm really sorry about this, but Russ Frist is out sick for a few weeks and I have to go to his house to meet with him about something. So I'll be home a little late. I know it's bad timing. I'll be back as soon as I can: seven probably, maybe seven-thirty. Oh, and in case Mike forgets to tell you, the motion to suppress the Corbett confession is scheduled for tomorrow at two before Lesh. I'd like to have you there. OK, I guess that's all. I'll see you tonight. I lo—"

The system cut me off before I could finish telling him I loved him. I thought about calling back, but one rambling message seemed like enough humiliation for the moment.

I followed the Mapquest directions I had printed, making a quick pit stop at Zupan's market. My endpoint was in front of a series of new row houses in John's Landing, just a few miles south of downtown. I found a spot on the street and browsed the house numbers, looking for the right address.

Most of the owners had found a way to personalize their individual residences with flower baskets, season-appropriate nylon flags, cutesy mailboxes, and the like. When my eyes reached 242, I found an unadorned door above a plain brown welcome mat. When I reached the mat, I saw a small sticker on the nearest window: WARNING, THIS HOME PROTECTED BY SMITH AND WESSON. A MESSAGE FROM THE NRA.

I knocked and heard Russ moan, "Come on in."

I cracked the door open a few inches. "You're not going to shoot me, are you?"

"I should be asking *you* that." He was referring to an unfortunate incident at my house a year earlier, after which the entire city knew I kept a handgun in my bedroom. "I saw the sticker at a gun show we were investigating. Seemed like a good deterrent."

I heard a television power off. Russ was comfortably splayed across an overstuffed denim sofa in a gray Marine Corps sweatshirt and navy gym shorts, a carton of OJ open on the coffee table. I placed the Zupan's bag on the glass top of a wrought-iron coffee table. "Fresh cherry strudel, as promised. Where's your kitchen?"

I took the two turns as instructed and retrieved a couple of plates and forks. "Nice place," I said when I returned. "Comfortable."

"You seem surprised. What'd you think? I'd have a futon, a TV, and a weight bench?"

I shrugged my shoulders. "I hadn't thought about it, I guess. It's just that everything seems so . . . together." The furniture was well coordinated and all relatively new. My house, in contrast, was an eclectic mix of hand-me-downs, law school leftovers, and the occasional recent indulgence, selected to fit with the rest of it.

"Yeah, well, let's just say I walked away from most of my belongings a few years ago. You circle a bunch of stuff in the Pottery Barn catalog, and furnishing a place isn't that hard."

I wondered about the comment, imagining that my exhusband's house must be similarly well appointed.

"How's the Crenshaw case?" he asked, as I settled into a chair sized for two across from him. I told him about Lisa's rocket-docket motion to suppress.

"Are you putting your boyfriend on the stand too or just his partner?"

"I am calling both of the detectives who were present for the confession."

"And what's your plan?"

"To win the motion then win the case."

He caught the tone in my voice, the one that only another prosecutor would recognize. It reflected a stubborn willingness to fight the good fight, even if that involved risking a trial and losing, rather than swallow down an unjust plea agreement.

"Shit. I knew I couldn't leave the office. You do know you still need to make a deal, don't you?"

I told him about the carpet fibers on the bat. "Even if I can't use Corbett's confession, I've got a pretty decent case."

"And how do you figure that?" he asked skeptically.

"I've got video proving that an hour before the murder they were out of control, armed with a bat, just blocks away from Percy's house. Despite Lisa's lame motion to kick the ID, I've got a witness who puts them in Percy's parking lot around the time of the murder. And I've got the murder weapon, found just blocks from the homes of the defendants, containing the victim's blood and hair, fibers from the carpet in his apartment, and fibers from Hanks's Jeep."

"You haven't tried enough murders to know how tough jurors can be. Shit, they'll look over at the defendants and see two little boys whose entire lives rest on their verdict. You've only got one witness; it was late at night, and he didn't see the actual crime. And that trace evidence you're so excited about? Fiber comparisons aren't anything like DNA. By the time a defense expert gets done with it, that fiber from the Jeep could be from any manufactured fabric in town."

My case didn't sound so great from that perspective. "One step at a time, OK? We argue the motion tomorrow in front of Lesh." I made a point of letting him see me check my watch. "Let's go over Tompkins so I can skedaddle."

I had already gathered most of the facts from my review of the file, but Russ filled out the dynamic of the investigation after Hamilton had been taken to Northeast Precinct.

"You've got to understand the General Order," he explained. "The bureau writes the procedures on the assumption that the officer is essentially a victim of the person who was shot. Sure, the rules simultaneously facilitate the investigation by securing the crime scene and spelling out the procedures for interrogation and so on, but a primary focus is on the mental health and well-being of the involved officer."

"So that explains why the officer is taken back to the precinct," I said.

"Right. It's all about giving him a psychological break. You get him away from the body; you shield him from the investigation and the media attention."

"Is that why IA waited until Monday morning to question him?"

"That's a little more complicated," he said. "You've basically got two investigations going on after an officer-involved shooting: a criminal investigation into whether charges should be brought and an administrative investigation into whether disciplinary or other actions are warranted. The officer's got his Fifth Amendment rights in the criminal investigation but not in the administrative one."

"Right, but if you force a statement out of him during the administrative process, you can't use it in a criminal trial."

"Plus, you can't use any evidence that the statement leads you to," he added. "And you know how hard it is to prove that evidence isn't tainted by an immunized statement. So we tell the bureau not to compel any statements until the criminal investigation is officially completed. Instead, the officer is notified that he has a right to remain silent. Almost as a matter of course, the union reps advise the officers to give only the briefest of statements—claiming self-defense or whatever—until it's clear what's going on in the criminal process. Here, Hamilton asked for a twenty-four-hour break late Saturday night. By the time IA got to him on Monday morning, it was obvious that he might have some problems in the grand jury, so he clammed up. If he winds up clearing the criminal charges, he'll have to give his side to the bureau if he wants to avoid employment sanctions."

"What do you mean if he clears the charges? I thought you told me to think *plea negotiations*." I had a criminally negligent homicide charge in mind, less serious than the manslaughter charge I'd request from the grand jury.

"Yeah, well, that was before I checked my voice mails this afternoon. I got one from Jerome Black." Black was a former deputy in our office turned high-priced defense lawyer. "He's representing Hamilton, and Hamilton wants to testify before the grand jury."

I processed the information and decided that the news called for a bigger slab of strudel. "He's got to feel pretty confident," I said, shoveling a big cherry-dripping bite of pastry into my mouth.

"He probably figures he'd wind up testifying at trial anyway. May as well do his best to win the grand jury over and nip the whole thing in the bud. Are you going to let him try?"

Because suspects don't have a right to testify before their grand juries in Oregon, I was the one who got to make the call. "Sure."

I sounded confident, but I fed myself an even bulkier chunk of strudel, hoping to find calm in the right combination of fat, sugar, and carbs.

"It's a no-brainer." I used my fingers to tick off the advantages to letting Hamilton testify. "I get to lock in—on the record—his account of the facts before trial. I get a free chance to cross-examine him without his attorney being present. I get the transcript of his testimony if he tries to change his story down the road—"

"And the downside?" Russ interrupted.

I shrugged my shoulders. "So the grand jury gets to hear his side. So what? If I can't get an indictment out of the grand jury, there's no way we'd ever win at trial. May as well get the loss out of the way without the pain of a full trial."

Russ nodded, pleased. "Very good, young padawan."

"You fancy yourself the Yoda of prosecution now? Very modest of you." He had been testing my judgment, apparently.

"*You* got a *Star Wars* reference? Now I really am impressed."

Blame Chuck again. A few more months with him and my IQ points would drop into the double digits.

"Good, because I've got to get out of here," I said, looking at my watch again. "I'll call Black tomorrow to tell him Hamilton can talk to the grand jurors. Anything else?"

"Stop eating my strudel. You're worse than Walters."

It was just past seven by the time I got home. To my surprise, Chuck met me at the door, leather bomber jacket in hand.

"You feel like going out?" he asked. "A burger would hit the spot."

I walked past him, set my briefcase in the hall, and shrugged out of my raincoat. "Are we going to talk about last night?"

"Do we need to?"

"Chuck, you left the house, slept somewhere else, and wouldn't talk to me all day."

"No, you left the house because you wanted time to think. I felt like I was smothering you, so I crashed with Mike to give you some room."

"Did he tell you the nasty thing he said to me today?"

"He mentioned you'd be pissed but didn't give me the specifics."

"He basically used the fact that you 'walked out on me,' in his words, as evidence that I'm a complete bitch."

"If you want me to say something to him, I will, not that things have been particularly great for me at work lately. I hope you realize Mike's got nothing to do with us."

"So why didn't you call me all day?"

"You think I didn't want to? It was killing me. I literally had to put my cell in my desk drawer."

"Is that why you didn't answer when I called?"

"Yeah. By the time I got the message, I figured you were with Russ already. When you pulled up, I thought it would be good for us to get out of the house and eat something."

"So we're OK? You're not moving out?"

"Of course not, babe. You thought that?"

I nodded and felt my eyes start to water.

"Come here, you nut." He held me tightly, cupping one hand behind my head. "We both got a little out of control last night, that's all. We're good, OK?"

When he finally felt me loosen my grip, he looked into my eyes and pushed a loose strand of hair behind my right ear. "Hamburgers now? Please?"

I started to raise all the subjects that had divided us lately, but realized it was not the right time to talk about Matt York, Mike Calabrese, or the jobs that too often defined us. I didn't want to fight anymore. I just wanted to feel like we were OK.

"Promise not to go away again?" I asked.

"Never."

"Then a burger sounds good."

Telling him about my assignment on the Geoff Hamilton case would have to wait.

14

Heidi sat at her desk, reviewing once again the percentages she had compiled from Percy's tables:

NEP

	B	L	W	A
S	51.4	33.5	11.7	3.3
A	41.7	42.4	11.9	4.0

EP

	B	L	W	A
S	15.5	48.0	23.5	13.1
A	16.6	44.5	25.1	13.4

If she was right, NEP referred to Northeast Precinct, and EP referred to East Precinct. For East Precinct, the numbers for the B, L, W, and A columns were roughly the same in both rows. Northeast Precinct's numbers varied more when it came to B's and L's. Percy was keeping track of these numbers to show a screwy pattern in Northeast Precinct that didn't exist in East.

Heidi stared at the notes for a full twenty minutes, jotting down and then scratching out possible explanations for Percy's other abbreviations. Maybe Percy had been keeping track of different kinds of crimes: Burglaries, Loitering, Assaults? But then what did the W stand for?

Heidi had even perused a law enforcement dictionary for that one. As far as she could tell, there were no crimes beginning with the letter W.

So maybe the W stood for something else, Heidi thought. A proper name, perhaps. A cop's name. She wondered how she could get her hands on a complete list of officers, then scratched that possibility from her notepad too. What were the odds that Percy was keeping track of officers with names beginning with the same letters in two separate precincts?

Frustrated, she turned her attention to the mail in her in-box. She threw out three invitations for preapproved credit cards. *No, thank you,* she thought. One more of those, and she'd have to cave in and ask her parents for money. She recycled catalogs from J. Crew and Land's End. *Again, no thank you.* Those were the very things that had led to the maxed-out cards.

She set aside a birth announcement from one of her high school girlfriends back east as a reminder to send a gift. Shopping for baby toys was always fun. The final piece of mail was from her alma mater, gloating about the entering freshman class and, of course, closing with a request for money. Apparently this group of wonder kids included a former National Spelling Bee champion, a silver-medal-winning Olympic gymnast, a fourteen-year-old brainiac, and the lead singer of a pop group with a major recording contract. Fifty-two percent of the entering class was female, and 30 percent identified themselves as part of a racial minority group. To prove their diversity-embracing goodness, the school had gone so far as to list the specific numbers of African-Americans, Latino-Americans, Asian-Americans, and other minorities in the class.

Heidi started to toss the letter but thought again about the racial breakdown. African, Latino, and Asian-Americans. Non-whites. *Why hadn't she seen it before?* When it came to his own racial identity, Percy shunned the language of the academic elite. But in his b, l, w, and a columns, he had been tracking the same statistics.

Now all she had to do was figure out the rows.

The next morning, Thursday, the *Oregonian* temporarily closed its offices at ten o'clock so employees could say goodbye one last time to Percy Crenshaw. Heidi accepted an invitation from Dan Manning to ride up to First Baptist with him. She almost declined but then reminded herself that it wasn't Dan's fault that their editor treated him as up-and-coming crime reporter extraordinaire, and her as a cite-checking peon.

When they walked into the church, she was struck by the enormity of the crowd. As far as she could tell, fewer than half of the attendees were from the paper.

"I wonder who all these people are," she whispered to Dan. Other than her coworkers, Heidi recognized only one person, the woman Deputy District Attorney who had come to search Percy's office.

"Are you kidding? I thought there'd be people lined up around the block. Percy was the man. From every walk of life, he could win you over. How do you think he got so much information out of people?" Dan caught the eye of a tall bulky man entering the church in front of them. The two men exchanged friendly handshakes. "Thanks for coming, man."

"No problem." The stranger offered his hand to Heidi. "Jack Streeter."

"Heidi Hatmaker," she said, trying not to stare. Jack Streeter had dark brown hair, piercing blue eyes, and a jawline straight from superhero central casting. "I work at the paper with Dan."

"Hatmaker?" he asked.

She nodded. "Let the jokes begin."

"No, it's a cute name. Really cute."

Heidi returned his smile shyly, realizing she had reached a new low: flirting at a funeral. "Your name sounds familiar, actually." And cool. Really cool.

"Probably from my job. I'm the PIO for Portland Police."

"Aah. I probably should have known that, being a reporter and all." The Public Information Officer's name and phone number were printed at the bottom of all bureau press releases.

"Well, now you know. You've even got my number, so to speak."

Dan Manning cleared his throat. "We should probably get seated."

"Of course," Jack said. "See you soon, man. And you too, Heidi. Call me if you need anything."

Once Jack was out of earshot, Dan teased Heidi about the encounter. "If I'm not mistaken, my biggest news source was hitting on you."

"He was just being nice."

"Not like I've ever seen him. Count yourself lucky, Hatmaker—you've got at least one advantage over me."

"I'm tempted to be insulted by that."

"I'm kidding. Seriously, though, if you're interested in reporting on crime stuff, you should get to know him. Officially, he's the PIO, but let's just say he forges mutually advantageous relationships with the press. If he wants something out there, he'll give it to the person who'll spin it his way. He's been a great source for me, and I know he did the same for Percy."

"Let's just find seats for now," Heidi said, filing away her colleague's suggestion.

Even after the funeral, Heidi could not stop thinking about Percy's project. Given the neighborhood demographics, it made sense that the numbers under the label B—for black—were higher for Northeast Precinct than they were for East Precinct, while the numbers for L—Latinos—were higher out East than up North. But if she understood Percy's notes, there were some serious anomalies in Northeast Precinct.

In East Precinct, the racial makeup of s's and A's were roughly consistent. But in Northeast Precinct, Blacks made up more than half of the s's but only 40 percent of the A's. And Latinos were only about a third of the s's but more than their share of A's.

Whatever those letters stood for, Percy had been able to compile these statistics on a monthly basis. Heidi couldn't imagine Percy counting thousands of individual occurrences himself each month. He must have been tracking numbers already available through the police department.

The computer in the corner of the research dungeon was free. She logged on to the Internet and pulled up the Portland Police Web site. Before long, she was scrolling through monthly arrest statistics, by offense, for each precinct, through August. The postings must run a couple of months behind. She compared the total number of A's tracked in Percy's charts with the arrest statistics on the Web site. One crime lined up with Percy's numbers to the digit: drug offenses.

The charts were beginning to make sense. There were always more s's than A's. In order to make a drug arrest, the police usually had to search the person first. s's and A's: searches and arrests. Percy was keeping track of the number of drug searches and arrests in each precinct, broken down by the race of the suspect.

Heidi could not find the number of drug searches on the bureau's Web site, let alone by race, but she did have a vague recollection that police officers were required to keep track of that information. She pulled up the *Oregonian*'s Web page and searched for articles on racial profiling. Two years ago, a liberal lawmaker had tried to restrict the ability of police officers to search for drugs, arguing that police were targeting minorities disproportionately. Instead of changing the rules, the legislature voted to study the problem further. As part of the study, police departments were required to keep records of all searches, including the race of the person searched. With a simple request, Percy could have gotten his hands on those numbers.

If Heidi was right, the police in Northeast Precinct were searching black suspects for drugs, but then arresting them at a lower rate than other suspects, particularly Latinos. Heidi thought through the implications. Maybe police were simply less accurate when they decided to search black suspects, finding drugs less frequently than with other racial groups. But why would that occur only in Northeast Precinct and not East Precinct?

Another possibility was that the officers in Northeast Precinct were not arresting black defendants even when they found drugs on them. Now *that* was interesting.

First, though, Heidi needed to make sure she was on the right track. She needed to get the bureau's search statistics and make sure they matched Percy's numbers. She walked back to her cubicle, picked up the phone, and dialed the number at the bottom of a bureau press release, the number for Public Information Officer Jack Streeter.

"Um, I'm not sure if you remember, but we met this morning at First Baptist."

"Of course I remember you. Cute name. Cute reporter, if you don't mind me saying."

"Well, honestly, I'm a reporter in name only. Dan and Percy do most of the crime stuff here at the paper—well, *did*, I guess—"

"I know what you mean."

"So anyway, you know, I try every once in a while to get my own stories. Otherwise, it's just neighborhood garden parties and stuff."

"Reminds me of patrol days. I was always keeping my eye out for something other than car alarms and bar fights."

"Exactly. Anyway, I've been thinking of doing a follow-up story on that law a couple of years ago that requires the police to keep track of all their stops and searches by race. At the time, when racial profiling was such a hot topic, it seemed like someone was going to keep track of all that information and go back to the legislature with proposed legal changes. But then nothing happened. I thought it might be interesting to look at the numbers. I suspect there's nothing there, and maybe that's interesting in its own right. You know, sort of a 'Why'd the state make police do this just to prove there aren't any problems' kind of story."

"So is that why you were calling me? You need something for the story?"

"Um, yeah, if that's OK."

"I was sort of hoping you were calling me for dinner."

Heidi laughed nervously. "Um, I don't really call people for dinner. But I do accept invitations from nice public information officers who help me with stories."

"Is that right?"

"For the most part."

"How about a monthly breakdown of our stop-and-search numbers by precinct? And dinner tonight at Papa Haydn?"

"Perfect."

"The reports will be ready for you in an hour at the reception desk at Central Precinct. And I'll be ready for you at the restaurant at seven."

15

Percy Crenshaw's funeral was, to my mind, all you could want if you had to have your own. Flowers, ceremony, and framed portraits—these were easy enough to procure with the right price and planning. But the morning had been at once commemorative, respectful, solemn, and celebratory. It was an intensely personal ending to Percy's life and the beginning of a community's remembrance of it.

Sitting in my Jetta afterward, I actually had to dig a dusty pack of Kleenex from the bottom of the glove box. It's not often that I well up. I had called Percy's parents at their hotel the night before to make sure they knew that Todd Corbett's motion was being heard. I could not bear the thought of having to report, just hours after the burial of their son, that a jury would not hear the confession of Percy's killer. It was not an option. Once I was done sniffling, I returned to my office more resolved than ever to make sure I didn't blow the case.

Upon my arrival, I learned that Russ Frist had been right. Lisa Lopez was irritating, but Lucas Braun won the award for worst attorney in the courthouse. The previous afternoon, while I was at Russ's, Braun had served me with a copy of two motions. One was a motion to suppress the racial epithet and the spit that Hanks had hurled upon his arrest. Even with the spelling errors, bad prose, and chronic comma overuse, the motion was a reasonable one; Hanks might have behaved himself if I hadn't spoken to him after he invoked his right to counsel. It was the other filing that had me doubting Braun's competence to handle a capital murder trial.

Braun had filed a Notice of Defense, advising the state that Hanks would be asserting a claim of self-defense. According to Braun, Hanks was entitled to use reasonable force if "the victim used excessive unlawful force against the defendants while protecting his property, to wit: one Mercedes-Benz." I was tempted to draft a response entitled Three Reasons Why the Defendant's Lawyer—to wit: one Lucas Braun—Is an Idiot. First, defendants claiming self-defense in Oregon don't need to file notice. Second, beating a man with a baseball bat in order to steal his Benz did not constitute self-defense under any definition of the term. And, third, a claim of self-defense only flies if the defendant concedes that he was the killer. Right now, my biggest problem was proving that Hanks and Corbett were, in fact, the killers.

Braun's mistakes were only going to wind up helping me. Fifteen minutes after I was done reading Braun's motions, Lisa Lopez called.

"Did you get Braun's motions?" she asked.

"I've got them right here."

"You must be licking your chops over that Notice of Defense."

"Believe it or not, Lisa, I don't take pleasure winning an unfair fight."

"Whatever. Lucas Braun's an idiot." For once, Lisa and I agreed. "He just called. He wants to piggyback his motion to suppress onto our hearing today. You OK with that?"

"I'll need to make sure he doesn't plan on making me testify." I was the one who had spoken to Hanks after he invoked his right to counsel.

"I already asked him. He's willing to stipulate to the facts as written in the police report. The judge is OK with it too."

I told her I'd go along with it. Better to get both motions over with at once.

"You really said what's in the report? 'I'm the prosecutor who's going to make sure you just lived your last day of freedom'?"

I had insisted that Chuck include my faux pax in the police reports to avoid the embarrassment of having to disclose it myself.

"That's what we're stipulating to."

"You really need to get over yourself."

Even though I had prepared and re-prepared for the pretrial motions, I reviewed my notes one last time before the hearing. I felt confident that Lucas Braun's motion would go nowhere. Hanks may have invoked his right to counsel, but I had spoken to him only after *he* asked who I was. According to case law, a defendant who initiates the conversation is shit out of luck.

The problem, though, was that my case against Hanks was still weak. Hanks could be a spitter and a racist without being a murderer, and I couldn't use Corbett's confession against him.

On the other hand, I assumed that if Corbett lost his motion to suppress his own confession, Lisa would come to her senses. Corbett would agree to testify against Hanks in exchange for leniency. All would be well in the world.

The entire case turned on whether the court thought Corbett's confession was voluntary. With that comforting thought, I headed to Judge David Lesh's courtroom.

Mike and Chuck were waiting outside in the hall. "Is Peter Anderson here yet?" I asked.

"In the courtroom," Mike told me.

My eyewitness had worn a suit and tie for the occasion, placing him already in the upper quarter of civilian witnesses, at least for common sense. He had a dark mustache and was losing his hair at the temples, and I knew from his PPDS that he was thirty-nine years old. As I approached to introduce myself, I was overpowered by a strong whiff of eau de ashtray.

I explained the hearing. Lisa was trying to prevent him from testifying at trial and to exclude all evidence of his identification of the defendants. She was going to argue that the procedure we had used to get the out-of-court IDs was unreliable and that his memory was now tainted from having seen the defendants' photographs in the throw-downs.

"I don't get it."

At least he was honest. "What exactly don't you get?"

"Well, how am I unreliable?"

"It's not that *you're* unreliable. She's saying that the police used bad procedures. Like, let's say Detective Johnson had shown you six photographs in the throw-downs, but that the defendants had been the only men, or the only white men. That would be an unreliable procedure, since it would basically tell you who the police wanted you to pick, right?"

"Yeah. OK, I get it."

"Honestly, I'm not worried about this. The attorney's much more focused on attacking some other evidence that's at issue."

"OK. So what do I need to do?"

"I'll call you to the stand and you'll be sworn in. We'll talk about what you saw in the parking lot. Was there light, by the way?"

"Yeah, somewhat. You know, it was dark outside, but we've got light poles all around."

"And where were the defendants with respect to the lights?"

"Not right under them, but walking through the lot no area is pitch black or anything."

"And how good of a look at them did you get?"

"Just a couple seconds at first. You know, they caught my eye while I was taking out my garbage. Then I did sort of a double-take because I didn't recognize them. I watched them, wondering if I should ask who they were or something. But, you know, I try not to pry too much with the residents, and they looked decent enough, so I let it be."

"How long do you think you saw them in total?"

"Maybe ten or fifteen seconds after they first caught my eye."

"What angle did you see them from, head on? From the side?"

"Well, they were walking up the hill, which was pretty much right at me."

"Do you remember what they were wearing?"

"Like I told the detective that first morning, I thought it was just jeans and rain jackets."

Close enough. Trevor's jacket had been denim, but eyewitnesses were rarely perfect. "You'll be fine."

"Am I going to have to talk about the light in Percy's carport? Because I feel . . . well, I don't think I can find the right words for it—"

"You can't look at it that way. You could imagine changing a thousand different things about that day and never know if the ending would differ. And, no—the defense will probably ask generally about the lighting where you saw the defendants, but not about the carport."

He seemed relieved, but I did have some bad news for him.

"There *is* one thing we should probably talk about." I pulled a copy of Anderson's PPDS record from the file. "This particular attorney is very aggressive, and she's likely to ask about the occasions when police were called to your home, particularly the arrest two months ago."

His agitation was apparent. "That was all a bunch of stuff with my liar of a wife. What in Pete's sake does that have to do with—"

"It doesn't," I explained calmly, "but this isn't a trial. There's no jury here. The judge is likely to let her ask the questions so he can decide for himself whether any of it's relevant, which, I agree, it's not. I just wanted you to be aware that she'll probably ask. It's best if you simply answer the questions, making clear that you were never prosecuted and have no convictions. OK?"

"It's still a bunch of crap."

"I understand. The system's not always fair to witnesses."

He nodded, realizing he'd be put through the wringer merely because he happened to be taking his trash out shortly before Hanks and Corbett decided to kill someone. I was in no position to know the truth about what happened between Anderson and his wife, but I'd had my job long enough to carry suspicions. Even so, I wasn't about to defend a system that let a lawyer like Lisa Lopez scrutinize every aspect of this man's life, searching for a diversion from her client's guilt.

"You'll be fine," I told him. "And, really, thank you for doing this."

David Lesh runs a tighter ship than most judges. He emerged from chambers just five minutes past the promised hour, then apologized for running late. As usual, his blond hair could have used a cut, and his bemused expression suggested an unspoken joke lingering beneath the surface. Having heard colorful stories of Lesh's happy-hour days as a prosecutor and city attorney, it was probably for the best that he rarely shared his sense of humor in court.

Once Lesh took the bench, I suggested dealing with the eyewitness testimony first. The least I could do was get Anderson out of here.

Once the bailiff swore Anderson in, I walked him through the testimony as I'd prepped him: the garbage, the parking lot, the defendants, Detective Johnson, and the throw-downs. Anderson was a good witness: articulate, straightforward, and responsive.

Then it was Lisa's turn to cross-examine. "You supposedly saw the men you described in the parking lot on Sunday night, the night of Percy Crenshaw's murder. Is that correct?"

"Yes."

"And Detective Johnson came to you on Tuesday morning with the photographic lineups, correct?"

"Yes."

"Isn't it true that on Monday you spent the day with the police looking through books of mug shots?"

"That's right."

"Did the police have those narrowed down in any way for you, by hair color, perhaps, or even by height or age?"

"I'm not sure. I don't think so. There were a lot of pictures."

"Let me put this another way. When you talked to police on Monday, did you tell them the ages or the heights or the hair colors of the men you saw?"

"Well, I said they were young. White. Average build, which they are, at least to me."

"What about hair color?"

"I wasn't sure."

"But nevertheless you picked these men from the photo arrays that the prosecutor has submitted as evidence."

"Yes. Right away. Once I saw their pictures, I recognized them."

"Two days after you'd seen them for a few seconds in a dark parking lot?"

"Objection, your honor," I said, rising slightly.

Judge Lesh sustained the objection. "I recall the witness's testimony. Don't worry."

"I'll rephrase," Lisa offered. "You say you recognized the defendants when Detective Johnson showed you the photos on Tuesday?"

"Yes."

"Do you remember what time it was on Tuesday when Detective Johnson showed you the lineups?"

"Midmorning, I think."

Lisa glanced at the supplemental report Johnson had written about the ID. "Eleven fifteen A.M. Does that sound about right?"

"Yeah. I mean yes."

Lisa carried a videotape to the clerk and had it marked as an exhibit, then inserted it into a TV/VCR near the stand. I recognized the local news anchor. According to the network marker in the lower corner of the screen, it was broadcast at 9:32 A.M., the Tuesday after Percy's murder. The anchor reported that two men had been arrested in the case. Their booking photos from the night before appeared on the screen, part of the press release issued by the bureau. Both looked pretty nasty. Not surprising, I thought. Corbett had started out as a normal-looking kid. But even a normal guy looks like shit after such an abnormal night.

Lisa stopped the tape when the anchor moved on to the next story. "Now, according to that tape, the local news was publicizing the defendants' arrests by nine-thirty on Tuesday morning, nearly two hours before you were interviewed again by Detective Johnson. Is that correct?"

"Yes, but—"

"Thank you. You've answered the question posed. Now, Detective Johnson's not the first police officer you've encountered at your home, is he?"

"No," Anderson replied, looking to me for help.

"In fact, you've had some problems with law enforcement recently, haven't you?"

"I wouldn't call them problems, no."

"No? You were arrested just two months ago, weren't you, Mr. Anderson? Isn't that a problem?"

Anderson shook his head, frustrated. "Given the things my wife was saying at the time, it was probably good for me to be gone for the night. No charges were filed, and she moved out a couple of weeks later."

"Just to be clear, you were arrested for assaulting your wife, correct?"

"That was the accusation, but, no, I did not assault her."

"And the police had been to your home several times prior to that over the course of the last year to investigate other domestic disturbances, correct?"

"Objection, your honor," I said. "Ms. Lopez has already moved beyond any possible definition of relevance by inquiring about an arrest. This is simply harassment."

"Goes to bias, your honor."

"I'm wary, Ms. Lopez, but there's no jury here. Mr. Anderson, I'd appreciate it if you'd continue to answer the questions, even though I may very well decide they're irrelevant."

Anderson nodded, and Lisa restated her question.

"One of the neighbors called the police a few times about arguments my wife and me were having. Let's just say they were loud, and we're better off separated. My wife made clear that everything was fine, and the police left. I guess the last time she really wanted me out. She told them I'd hit her, and, like I said, I got arrested."

It was plausible. Oregon has a mandatory arrest law for domestic violence. Even if it's a shaky case, the police are required to remove the aggressor from the home if there's probable cause for a domestic assault.

Lisa marked a document as evidence, handing me a copy in the process. The caption read MARCY WELLINGTON V. PETER ANDERSON, FAMILY ABUSE ORDER OF PROTECTION.

"Could you please identify this document for the court, Mr. Anderson?"

"Why don't you tell me what you want to call it?" So Anderson had a temper after all.

"This is a restraining order that your wife obtained against you after she moved out. Is that correct?"

"Yep."

"You objected to it?"

"Of course I did. She made up a bunch of lies in the application. Made me sound like a wife beater or something."

"And, despite your objections, the order was issued?"

"Her word against mine. I told the judge I didn't care whether I saw her or not, I just wanted to clear my name. The judge said, 'If you don't care, then you won't mind me issuing the order.' And that was that."

Again, it was plausible. No family court judge wants to be the one who denies a restraining order, then reads about a homicide two weeks later.

"So you're aware that if you contact your wife in violation of that order, you would be arrested?"

"That's the law as it was explained to me, yes."

"No further questions, your honor."

I saw where Lisa was going. She'd argue that Anderson saw the defendants on the news and fabricated the identifications to get in good with the bureau, just in case he was arrested down the road. It was farfetched even for Lisa.

I went straight to what mattered on rebuttal. "I noticed that Ms. Lopez cut you off earlier. You were trying to say something about the fact that the news report she showed you aired before Detective Johnson interviewed you. What were you trying to say?"

"That I never saw it. I was sleeping until right before the detective came up. Honestly?" Anderson looked at Judge Lesh. "I was hung over. Things haven't been going so well with me lately, in case you haven't figured that out already."

Once Lisa and I had finished submitting our evidence, Judge Lesh announced he was ready to rule.

"I am denying the defense's motion to suppress the witness Peter Anderson's identification of the defendants. The procedures used by the police were standard and permissible. At its heart, the defense's argument is that the witness's memory was tainted by media coverage of the defendants' arrest. Although the publication of the defendants' photographs may raise colorable arguments about the source of the witness's recollection, those will be for the jury to consider. Mr. Anderson, you're excused."

Ironically, my best hope of bolstering Anderson's ID at trial would be to remind the jury that he was hung over and pathetic. Before he left, I thanked him again for coming in and assured him that I'd do my best to keep Lisa from questioning him about his wife again at trial.

"Now," Lesh said, once Anderson was gone, "should we get down to what we really came for?"

Three hours later, the evidence was in. No real surprises, since I had insisted that Mike and Chuck disclose the entire truth about the night Corbett and Hanks were arrested. If we were going to win, I wanted it to be because we were right, not because the judge had a mistaken impression of the facts.

The tension between Mike and me was palpable. I tried to hide my discomfort with his tactics, knowing it would be the death knell of the confession if Lesh sensed it. Mike tried to conceal his disgust with my detailed questions, pretending he was at ease divulging every aspect of the investigation.

So out came the entire story. The lengthy interrogation, with Corbett held incommunicado, in cuffs, through its entirety. Lying to him in every possible way: about the nature of the investigation, the strength of the evidence, even the identity of the very prosecutor in the courtroom. The threat of the death penalty hung over his head. Corbett's ambiguous reference to an attorney, ignored. His own apparent uncertainty about the events of that night, thanks to good old reliable crystal meth.

When Chuck got to the part about my comment to Hanks, I watched Lesh carefully. To the casual eye, he kept right on with his notes. To an eye paranoid about its holder's professional reputation, however, he paused, just momentarily. Uh-oh.

When the lawyers were done, Lesh announced that he needed some time in chambers. Thirty minutes later, he emerged, legal pad still in hand.

"I'm ready to rule. First, let me address Mr. Braun's motion to suppress both the statement and the—well, let's call it what it was—the spitting, by defendant Hanks upon his arrest. By that time, Hanks was clearly in police custody. He had been Mirandized and had unambiguously asserted his right to counsel. As a result, the state was prohibited from deliberately eliciting any further information from him. However, I find that the state did in fact respect the defendant's rights. Although the defendant's remark to DDA Kincaid was in response to a statement by her, it was actually the defendant who initiated the entire exchange. It was the defendant who first broke the silence by inquiring as to Ms. Kincaid's identity, in his own colorful words. Although Ms. Kincaid's response was undoubtedly provocative, it was in fact responsive to the defendant's question. Accordingly, I find that the defendant's statement, including the conduct that accompanied it, to be lawfully obtained and admissible evidence.

"Now, with that said, let me turn to the signed confession and the oral statements of defendant Corbett, which Ms. Lopez has moved to suppress. Here, in combination with the conduct of the detectives, I view Ms. Kincaid's comments in a subtly different light, and I'll explain what I mean momentarily."

I was already on the edge of my seat, but now my heart was racing.

"Let me be very clear here: I see this as an extremely close case. The law in this area is difficult to apply, but the critical question is whether this confession was obtained voluntarily. There is a great deal about this interrogation that troubles me. I myself was a prosecutor and am well aware that police officers have tools they use to loosen up a suspect. Nothing about that is unconstitutional per se. In fact, some would say the Supreme Court encourages a little trickiness. My problem here is that Detective Calabrese appears to have used not just one or some of these tools but every one he could think of. It's as if he had an agenda when he went in that room, regardless of process and regardless of whether the defendant was in fact guilty.

"Let me explain the factors that tip the balance for me.

First, I take judicial notice of the fact that this is a high-profile case. The victim was well known, and the media had already begun to cover the story. I imagine that creates pressure to get a confession. My second observation has to do with Ms. Kincaid's behavior on the night of the arrest. I have had the pleasure of knowing Ms. Kincaid and seeing her work as a prosecutor in this courthouse for some time now. She has always been, and continues to be, a consummate professional.

"So I cannot help but notice that her conduct on the night of the arrest—your conduct, Ms. Kincaid, as it has been described by your own witnesses—was somewhat atypical. I say that not to embarrass you, Ms. Kincaid, or to condemn your supervision of this case. I say it because I have the utmost respect for you, and ordinarily your presence during the interrogation would probably have tipped the balance in favor of ruling for the state. But what I have heard only reinforces my impression that the government was willing to be extremely aggressive to get the evidence it needed in this case. That aggressiveness translated into police conduct that renders defendant Corbett's confession—both the signed statement and his oral statements preceding it—inadmissible."

I heard Mike grumble behind me and turned to find him storming from the courtroom. I could see that Chuck was torn. I looked to the courtroom door, signaling him to go after his partner.

"In light of my rulings, are there other motions I need to entertain?" Judge Lesh asked.

Both defense attorneys rose, but Lisa shot Lucas Braun a look that sat him right back down. "Yes, your honor. The defendants make a joint motion to dismiss count one of their joint indictment, the charge of murder. Without Mr. Corbett's confession, there is insufficient evidence to proceed against either defendant."

It was a standard request once evidence was suppressed, but I nevertheless found my voice shaking as I recited the remaining evidence for the court. As nervous as I had been about Lisa's motion to suppress, I had expected in the end to win it. I thought the court would dress me down, warning me to keep a closer watch on my cops, but I didn't think a judge would actually have the guts to kick a murder confession. And yet here I was, clinging to a single eyewitness and a couple of carpet fibers to avoid an outright dismissal.

When I was done, Lisa and Lucas each argued separately that the case I laid out amounted to coincidence, smoke and mirrors, and, in Lucas's words, "a few circumstantial evidences." Lesh, however, recognized how little it takes to proceed with charges, even as a case is falling apart.

"Based on the evidence proffered by the state, a reasonable jury could find the defendants guilty. Accordingly, I deny the motion to dismiss count one. The defendants are bound over for trial. Anything further?"

"No, your honor," the lawyers said as one.

"Very good. Counsel, please remain during recess." Once the court reporter started packing up her gear, and the sheriffs' deputies had removed Corbett and Hanks from the courtroom, Lesh explained the request. "First, although I ruled for Corbett on the motion to suppress, nothing I heard today changes my very high opinion of Ms. Kincaid. I know the realities of investigative work. Second, although I ruled for the State on the motion to dismiss the charges, that's only because the standard for getting in front of a jury is low. I think the prosecutor knows this isn't a slam dunk. I encourage the three of you to sit down and work something out. Now you guys get out of here and have a good weekend. I need a beer."

■ ■ ■

Lisa Lopez and Lucas Braun packed up their briefcases and walked out of Judge Lesh's courtroom separately. Apparently there was no love lost between them.

I caught up to Lisa in the hall, prepared to suck it up and grovel for a plea. "OK, so you won the motion. My offer still stands."

"You're kidding, right? Your offer, if you can call it that, was made before Duncan took the death penalty off the table. And, more important, that was *before* I won the motion, when you still had a confession. You'll have to do a hell of a lot better than a life sentence."

"Calm down. I meant my offer to give your guy the deal. If Corbett will testify, I'll agree to the possibility of parole after thirty. What more can you ask for? That's the minimum sentence."

"Yeah, the minimum for *aggravated* murder, which you can't prove. You're off your rocker, Kincaid. I'm looking for something more like Man Two with probation."

Lisa was skipping quickly over a few levels of homicide, like Man One and garden-variety unaggravated Murder. "You know that's unreasonable."

"You know what's unreasonable? I've got an innocent client, and you don't seem to care about that for a second."

She was truly unbelievable. "Lisa, you say everyone is innocent. In fact, the last time you said that, your so-called 'innocent' client tried to kill me." Talk about a trump card.

"You know I've admitted I was wrong about that." The aftermath of that case was, in fact, the closest Lisa and I had ever come to getting along. "But I mean it this time. Corbett and Hanks did not kill Percy Crenshaw."

I shook my head. Some defense lawyers could pique my attention by insisting the police got the wrong guy, but Lisa wasn't one of them. "Then why did your guy confess, Lisa? And why are you even talking about pleading someone out if he's innocent?"

"He confessed because your thumper cop didn't give him any choices. And the only reason he's even willing to consider a plea is to avoid the risk—the very real risk—that innocent people can still get convicted."

"This conversation isn't getting us anywhere, Lisa."

"Well, the only thing I'm willing to talk about is Man Two and probation."

"We both know there's always something to talk about." I may have started at a thirty-year sentence for Agg Murder, but negotiations were part of the game.

"You can throw out all the numbers you want. You're wasting your time." She turned and started walking away.

"You don't have a monopoly on the market, Lisa. I can always go to Braun."

"And he'll tell you the same thing," she said, turning to face me. "We met this morning. It's a united front. With no confession and no cooperation from either of us, we're willing to take our chances in court."

When I returned to my office, I found a handwritten note on my chair. *Russ wants you to call him. Sorry.—Alice.*

Poor Alice. Russ had been calling her every couple of hours for updates on the entire unit's work. Not surprisingly, he wanted information on Crenshaw.

"I'm fine here. Get back down on the couch and tend to your bull's-eye rash and flulike symptoms."

"What happened on the motion?"

When I filled him in on Lesh's ruling and my conversation with Lisa afterward, he provided his expert legal analysis. "You are totally fucked."

"I've still got a lot of evidence."

"We've talked about this. It's not enough. You *will* broker a deal, and I don't care which one of those assholes gets it."

Not so long ago, my response to a direct order at work was to think about, and most often threaten, quitting. But at some point during my time in MCU, I had come to see my relationship with the DA's office as a marriage. Or, more aptly put in my case, a marriage where one of the partners wasn't misusing his penis. The point is, I had come to accept that I wasn't leaving, even in rough times.

On the other hand, even the best couples argue. "I can't. She made it clear I'd be bargaining with myself until I got down to Man Two, which I'm not about to offer."

"And I'm not telling you to give her Man Two. I'm telling you to make a deal. Man One with six to ten is fairly standard when you need a guy to flip. Offer it. That united front she built? Your job is to break it. If Lopez is being a stickler, I know you can out-scare a pussy like Braun."

"No way. Hanks is the one who brought the bat." He was also the one with prior convictions, the one who reduced a man like Percy Crenshaw to a racist epithet, the one who'd spit at me when he was arrested, and the one who was most likely a date rapist to boot. I did *not* want to give him a deal.

"Then convince Lopez."

"Trust me. I know her. I just talked to her. It's not going to happen."

"Jesus, Kincaid. You're worse than this rash. Pick one of them. I don't care who it is. Or call them both and tell them your rock bottom offer goes to the first one who takes it. Just get one of them to turn."

Alice Gerstein walked into my office and handed me a note. *An attorney is waiting to see you—Lucas Braun.*

"Russ, I've got to go. I'll call you right back." I could still hear him in the handset when I disconnected.

I didn't even know Lucas Braun, and I could tell he was nervous. It's basic body language. Through the glass window of the room where he waited, I watched him fiddle with the pad on which he'd written his notes, his lips moving subtly as he rehearsed the lines he'd composed for himself. When I walked in, he couldn't even rise to shake my hand without adjusting his out-of-character striped tie and stroking the tips of his shoulder-length hair like a security blanket.

"What can I do for you, Mr. Braun?"

"Well, first let me thank you for taking the time to see me without an appointment. I know how busy the DDAs get in MCU."

Inwardly, I winced at his attempt to impress me with law-enforcement acronyms. "Not a problem. What's up?"

"I couldn't help but notice you speaking with Ms. Lopez after the hearing in Judge Lesh's courtroom."

"Uh-huh."

"I know the two of you handle more cases than I do, so you're probably quite comfortable with each other by now. I just wanted to stop by to talk—you know, to make sure my client wasn't at a disadvantage when it came to communications among the lawyers."

He apparently didn't know the personality dynamics well enough to realize that Lisa and I weren't exactly girlfriends, but he had picked up on the possibility that Lisa was a snake who'd sell out her united front in a heartbeat to benefit her client. So here he was, selling her out first. I knew what he wanted—a deal for his racist, spitting, date-raping, murderer client.

There were plenty of reasons why I'd hate to be a defense attorney, but this struck me as one of them. My ethical obligations aren't particularly complicated: Get bad guys, don't get good ones. But in the shoes of Lopez or Braun, I'm not sure where my loyalties would lie. If both defendants kept quiet, both stood a good shot at an acquittal. But if one stepped to the plate, he could buy his way out of the gamble at the other's expense. Which one should go home feeling guilty? Lucas— ready to take the one and only deal I was willing to put on the table—or Lisa, who had turned it down moments ago?

"If there's something you want to say, Lucas, you should probably get to the point."

"I've spoken to Trevor. He's willing to testify against Corbett. In exchange, you accept a plea to Robbery One with a sentencing recommendation of three years."

"You need to quintuple that number and start talking about a homicide charge."

"My guy says it was Corbett who took all the swings."

"And you know that doesn't matter. Robbery plus dead body equals felony murder."

"Man Two, three years."

"No, Lucas."

"Man One, four years."

"Didn't you hear me before? You're still way off."

"Man One, five years. That's my final offer."

He'd finally stopped bidding against himself. It was time for me to get specific. "Man One, ten years."

"I won't recommend that to him. We've already talked about the options. Any more than seven years, and he wants a trial."

"He'll do the seven? Waive all rights to appeal? Contingent on truthful testimony?"

"Yeah."

I thought about Russ's directive. I had to make a deal, and seven years was in the suggested range. I thought about the possibility of getting something better from Lisa. No, I'd seen how determined she was; given time, she might even be able to pull Braun back into the united front. This was my only choice.

"Have your guy ready to talk to me tomorrow at two. If I don't like what he has to say, no deal."

As soon as I left the conference room, Alice informed me that Russ had called twice since I hung up on him.

"Sam?" he answered.

"Yeah."

"Don't hang up on me when I'm trying to supervise you."

"Sorry about that. Alice—"

"Alice doesn't run the unit. You know, I've put up with a lot of shit from you this year. And I haven't gone running to Duncan with it like Rocco used to."

Russ didn't need to remind me that he was the only supervisor I'd managed to get along with—for the most part. "I know, but—"

"And I know you don't want to cut a deal, but when I'm giving you a direct order—"

"Russ. I hung up because Lucas Braun was here to see me. I did what you told me. Hanks is testifying. Man One, seven years."

"Really?"

"Yes."

"Just like that? You listened to me?"

"Yes."

"OK! Very good. All right, just make sure you tell your cops before they find out somewhere else. Warning: They'll be pissed."

■ ■ ■

As it turned out, they already were, but for an entirely different reason.

When I called MCU to check if the guys were around, I could tell from Mike Calabrese's tone that something was up, but I assumed he was still mad about Lesh's ruling. If I'd known there was more to the story, perhaps I would have been less breezy when I walked into the MCU office.

"Hey, guys," I said casually. "I had a chance to talk to both of the defense attorneys on Crenshaw, and I wanted to tell you in person where things stand."

It was when Mike Calabrese grunted under his breath that I realized he was staring coldly at me, arms crossed in front of his chest. Ray Johnson was still typing at a computer terminal, apparently ignoring my entrance. Jack Walker was fiddling with his pants pockets, avoiding my eyes. And Chuck—well, Chuck did his best to save me from my own mistake.

"Sam, I think there's been some kind of misunderstanding. A court reminder came into the property room today for a grand jury appearance on Geoff Hamilton. It had your name on it, so everyone's sort of wondering—but I know your guys' names wind up on each other's files all the time."

This was bad. Very bad. In a perfect world, I would have mitigated the conflict with MCT by telling them all up front I had inherited the Hamilton situation. As it stood, I hadn't even told Chuck.

"Um, yeah, they do, but actually I *am* covering that hearing. I'm sorry. I should have mentioned it earlier," I said, looking directly at Chuck. "It just happened yesterday. Russ is out sick for a while."

This morning, Chuck had been paged away before I woke, staying just long enough to kiss me goodbye and wish me luck on the Crenshaw motion.

My apology was met with silence from everyone but Chuck. "Well, all the better for Hamilton. Better you than Russ, right?"

This time, I was the one who was silent. And now the guys were staring at Chuck, not just me.

"All I'm saying is that Hamilton stands a better chance with Sam. At least she knows what it's like for a cop out there."

"Is that true, Sam?" Mike asked derisively. "Does Hamilton really stand any better chance with you in the room instead of Russ Frist?"

"Look, I told you guys, I'm sorry I didn't bring up the reassignment. I knew there were strong feelings in this room about the case, and as your friend I should have said something." I pretended not to hear Mike's scoff at my use of the word *friend*. "Beyond that, it would be incredibly inappropriate—and in fact illegal—to comment on the impaneling of a grand jury. I came over here to talk to you about the Crenshaw case, and, if it's OK, that is what I would still like to do."

Chuck closed his eyes and pinched the bridge of his nose.

"As I'm sure the rest of you know by now," I said, looking at Walker and Johnson, "Judge Lesh suppressed Corbett's confession. I managed to avoid a motion to dismiss the case outright." Mike sighed from his seat at the table, and Chuck threw him a correcting glance. "You didn't get to see Lesh's reaction, because you rushed out of the courtroom. He may have denied the motion to dismiss, but he made it clear that without the confession he didn't think much of the State's case. I agree with him. Long story short, Hanks agreed to flip. I had to give him a rock-bottom deal, but this way we're assured convictions for both of them."

"And what's a rock-bottom deal?" Mike demanded.

"Seven years. It's not that unusual when we need the cooperation."

"You mean when you don't want to go to trial."

It was times like these that I wished prosecutors occupied a link somewhere squarely within the chain of command of the police hierarchy. It was never quite clear where we stood with one another when push came to shove. Sure, rookie cops knew not to cross a Russ Frist, but only because they'd eventually feel the heat from someone on high. And baby DAs knew not to rankle a captain, or Duncan would hear about it. But in a straight-up pissing match between Calabrese and me, I didn't know whether to dress him down or not.

"That is totally unfair. If anyone should know I'm willing to go out on a limb, it's you guys. But walking into a trial to crash and burn is not an option. Without that confession, we were screwed."

"We lost that confession because you did all Lopez's work for her. What was up with all those questions? And why didn't you get her off my back about my IA file?"

"I didn't ask you for anything other than the truth, Mike. It's not my fault the facts were what they were. And I told you she had the complaints. If it weren't for me, she would have had the entire file; she would have been all over you about your transfer from NYPD."

"What the fuck does that mean?"

"This is getting out of control," Chuck interjected.

We both ignored him. "It means I left out the part of the file where a precinct commander might have cut a couple of corners to get you into the bureau. I was trying to protect you, and it still wasn't enough."

"Protect me? You don't know shit about why I moved here, and you'd be smart never to mention it again." Mike's voice was louder and shriller than I'd ever heard it. "You cut a deal, and you want to blame it all on me."

"I didn't say anything to blame you, Mike. And, in case you didn't notice, I took a beating in there at least as much as you did over that entire fucked-up interrogation, so don't pretend like I don't have something riding on this too. And, more important than either of our fragile fucking egos is the fact that I'm the one who has to call Percy's parents tonight and explain to them why a redneck piece of shit like Trevor Hanks will be out by his twenty-fifth birthday."

The room was silent. None of them—except Chuck, of course—had seen me truly angry before. I knew from experience what they were seeing: my cheeks reddened, my eyes piercing, my jaw set, and the white cotton of my blouse seriously pitted. I had, in short, lost it in front of them for the first time.

"OK, then," I said. "I've told you what I came to say. I'll let you get back to work."

Chuck actually caught up with me in the Justice Center staircase. Damn heels.

"Talk to me, OK? I think you owe me at least that. Do you know how stupid I felt when they asked me about that grand jury notice?"

"I know. I fucked up, and I'm sorry. But I was so relieved last night when you weren't mad at me, and I just wanted to be with you and get a hamburger, and—" I felt tears starting to form, threatening to violate my hard-held no-crying-in-the-courthouse-halls rule. "Please, Chuck," I said quietly, "just please let me go. I promise we'll talk at home. I've got a ton of work I have to wrap up, and then I really do just want to be at home with you."

"Well, I won't be there." He could tell from my expression that I was confused. "I called Matt to see how he's holding up. We're meeting for a beer a little later."

"Two cops commiserating about their broken relationships?"

"We're not broken, Sam. Talk to me about what's going on with you, please?"

"After you get home. I promise."

He looked at me with that expression I'd seen so many times now—too many times. It was a look of frustration and helplessness, resulting from his mistaken certainty that he could make everything better if I'd just let him.

"If you want to do something for me, talk to Mike. He's prideful, and he's taking it out on me."

"I could say the same thing about you."

"That I'm taking it out on you or on Mike?"

He shook his head. "I'll see you at home."

16

Heidi showed up at Papa Haydn on 23rd Avenue and Irving at seven o'clock, prompt as usual. To her surprise, Jack Streeter was already waiting for her in the cramped alcove. A relationship with the trusted public face of the police bureau already had its advantages. Heidi had spent countless hours over the years waiting for overage, trust-fund hippie kids.

"Hey, there you are," he said, kissing her cheek. "Believe it or not, they've actually got the table ready for us, but I was afraid you wouldn't find me."

They followed their hostess past a crowd of waiting bodies to a table adjacent to the front window.

"I still love this place," Heidi said. Papa Haydn had been an old standby for years, outlasting many trendy hot spots.

"Good. It's important, you know, that the site of our first date still be open years from now." He clinked his water glass against hers and smiled.

Heidi didn't know whether that was the best first-date opening line she'd ever heard or a reason to be wary. She decided to give him the benefit of the doubt but to keep one eye open.

"I never even look at the menu. French onion soup to start, gorganzola pasta for dinner; then I evaluate the good stuff," she said, looking over her shoulder at the long case of pies, cakes, custards, mousses, tortes, and tarts at the front counter.

When the waitress stopped at the table, Jack ordered for both of them, throwing in a bottle of Pinot Gris. Again, Heidi was torn between believing she'd found the man she was going to marry or the cheesiest chick magnet on the planet.

When the wine arrived and two glasses were filled, Jack lifted his for a toast. "To the prettiest crime-beat reporter I've ever met."

"No, to the best," she said, tapping her glass against his. Oh, God, she thought, was that confident and sophisticated or just really embarrassing?

"So how come I've never met you before?" Jack asked, setting down his glass.

"Honestly? Because I've been here for three years and never written a single inch of significant type." Heidi gave him a quick overview of her paper résumé, skipping the part where she could have had a much more powerful position if she'd left it up to her parents.

"Got it. Not too different than life on patrol, where a quiet guy with a master's degree in psychology gets less attention than a muscle head who shakes things up on the corner a little more than he should."

"I take it you're the psych degree?"

He filled her in on his credentials. "I thought I was going to be the male Clarice Starling, chasing down serial killers with my dead-on criminal profiles. Then I realized the FBI's like joining the military; for all I knew, they'd send me off to investigate bank robberies in Alabama. I didn't want to leave the Northwest—the mountains, the ocean, my family. So I joined the Portland Police. They decided they liked the way I talk," he said, moving into a exaggerated announcer voice, "and look," he added, striking an anchorly pose, "and here I am."

"Do you miss the police work? I mean, not to say that what you do isn't police—"

"I know what you mean. Yeah, I miss the adrenaline sometimes. But I think I do a lot of good as it stands. I control the message, and as you know that can mean everything. Not that I'd ever spin *you*, of course," he said, smiling.

"Of course not. But, I guess I've heard it said that cops and reporters can have mutually beneficial relationships."

"Exactly."

Heidi had no idea whether this was intense flirting or grooming for a future story. "Is that what your friendship with Percy was like?"

Jack almost spit out his wine laughing. "I was sort of hoping that you and I would have something a little different than what I had with Percy."

Heidi blushed. "I'm sorry. It's just the most obvious topic, given how we met."

"Right. So years from now, if we're happily paired up, we'll have to come up with another cover story, OK?"

"Agreed."

"Good. But, to answer your question, yeah, I got along real well with Percy. We mostly knew each other through PAL." He caught Heidi's quizzical look. "Police Activities League. We do summer camps and after-school programs for kids. The bureau runs it, but we've got all kinds of volunteers. Percy was an absolute ten for us during the summers. OK, maybe a nine-point-eight. Man couldn't play Ping-Pong for shit."

"Wow. I don't think I ever heard him talk about that stuff."

Jack smiled. "No, I guess he wouldn't. Can't spoil that hard-nosed-reporter image, right?"

"Is that what he was like in your experience? Hard-nosed?"

"Yeah, I guess. But reasonable, for the most part. You knew him, so you know he never pulled his punches. But he always at least heard me out on the bureau's side. And a couple of times, I think he actually toned a story down because of it."

"You know those numbers I asked you for today?"

"Yeah. Did you get them all right?"

"No problem. Thanks. I asked for them because I think Percy was working on something involving them, but he never wrote the story, from what I can tell. I was hoping to put the pieces together, sort of like a posthumous thing for Percy. Did he ever talk to you about it?"

"No, but he could get those numbers without going to me. A public information request, maybe, or any of the sources you know the guy had."

"Right, I'm just making sure. He might not have even put it in terms of these numbers, but did he say anything having to do with the racial makeup of arrests or anything like that? He seemed really interested in it."

Jack shook his head. "Sorry. I can ask around the department—check with some of the guys who knew him—if you want."

"No," she said quickly. "It's probably better if I figure out a little bit more before I start asking questions. I wouldn't even know what to ask at this point," she added, laughing.

"All right. Just let me know if I can help you."

"It would help to know how exactly the information you gave me is compiled. Like, do the officers enter their own numbers, or do they report this stuff from their cars, or—"

"Boy, you don't let up, do you?"

"I'm sorry," Heidi said, meaning it. "It can take me awhile to get my head out of work sometimes."

"I'll tell you what: I'll give you whatever you want to know about stop-and-search cards, if you promise to let me ask you a question next."

"Deal."

"It's really very complicated," he said, pretending to be deadly serious. "The officer makes a stop, maybe conducts a search, then fills out a little card that we keep in the patrol cars, saying what kind of stop it was, whether there was a search, and the race of the person involved. Then, at the end of the shift, they all drop their cards in a box in the report writing room. The shift sergeant reviews them—if he or she so chooses—and then delivers them to the records desk. Someone there enters each card into the computer. I hit PRINT, and you pick up your reports. Voilà! We are a well-oiled machine at PPB."

"But can you pull the information up by individual officers?"

"No, just by precinct. The troops were mad enough about having to do it at all. You can imagine if we kept track of this stuff by individual officer."

"If the cops don't like it, why do they bother filling out the cards?"

"Because their sergeants want to make sure they're doing what they're supposed to. I don't know where you live—yet." He smiled, and she smiled back. "But in our hot spots, our most frequent calls aren't for robbery or rape. They're for stuff like loitering, graffiti, and street-level drug crimes. That's the kind of stuff that makes a neighborhood *feel* unsafe. And, once it feels unsafe, the good guys start hiding inside and the bad guys take over. All the warm, fuzzy talk about community policing aside, our whole philosophy right now is to get our guys out there, talking to these kids on the corners, and stopping and searching them when necessary. The cards were required as part of the racial profiling stuff, but sergeants have been using them as a way to make sure the patrol guys are being proactive instead of sitting around eating doughnuts."

It made sense to Heidi. "What about the cards? What happens to those?"

"Garbage. Or, hopefully, the recycling bin. Once it goes in the computer, we don't need the card."

"What about the officer's police reports? Would those have the stops on them?"

"Nope. We don't write reports for every encounter, just arrests or other incidents that need to be documented. That's why they passed the law about the cards."

"Can the press see those?"

"Usually, unless the case is sealed during the investigation. We keep a press binder in the records departments at the precincts with copies of recent reports. Your buddy Dan Manning trolls those every week. So did Percy, probably closer to every day."

"So I could look through them too."

"Just show your ID at the front desk. Are we done now? Can I ask my question?"

Heidi figured she better stop grilling Jack about record-keeping if she had any hope of a second dinner invitation. "Ask away."

"What was it like growing up with a name like Heidi Hatmaker?"

It was the perfect question. Heidi told him stories about growing up with two sisters and a brother in Woodstock, Vermont, where the closest she ever came to evil were kids on the playground who called her Hearty Fartmaker. When he was still laughing by the time she'd finished the last drop of her

French onion soup, she knew it was the beginning of a really good date.

Heidi was full of energy when she got back to her apartment after dinner. And coffee. And a walk through the Rose Gardens and the sweetest good-night kiss at her car door. There was no way she was going to fall asleep.

She took another look at the search-record printouts Jack had given her, comparing them to the identical numbers that Percy had recorded in his notes. The trend was clear: The cops were searching plenty of African-Americans in Northeast Precinct, then arresting them at lower rates than their Latino, white, and Asian counterparts. But without access to more information, Heidi had no idea who was responsible for the disparity or what it meant.

She thought about driving out to Northeast Precinct to look at the press binder of police reports, but it was a little too late to start a job like that. Then she realized she had been so focused on cracking the numbers Percy had been tracking that she hadn't gone back to his original notes.

She had been able to rule out some of Percy's entries because of their apparent connection to other projects, like the recent team-written article about Nike and Percy's ongoing coverage of a former mayor's newly emerged sex scandal. But there were more than a few odds and ends that could relate to Northeast Precinct.

Meeting dates and time were scribbled in the margins. Names, but apparently only first names: Tom, Peter, Amy. Recently, Percy had added a reference to Powell and Foster streets. Did he meet someone at that intersection? Had something important happened there? Percy had definitely never intended for these notes to be interpreted by anyone other than him. They could relate to anything.

Heidi did understand some of them, though. *Sat. 2:00 Kennedy School.* Given its placement in Percy's book, the note had probably been made in the last month or so. The Kennedy School was the big McMenamin's complex in North Portland. Chances are, he'd met someone at the bar, in which case she'd never know who it was or whether the meeting related to his investigation. On the other hand, the Kennedy School had meeting rooms.

She looked up the telephone number and dialed.

"Hi. I'm wondering if someone there could help me with sort of an odd request. I've got a monthly report due to my boss tomorrow where I'm supposed to summarize all of the meetings and conferences and things I've gone to, and I'm having a hard time reconstructing a few dates from my calendar. Is there someone there who could help me figure out what meeting I might have had there a few Saturdays ago?"

After several minutes of the loud background noise of Thursday night partiers, someone else picked up the phone. "Yeah. You need some help with the events calendar?"

She repeated her cover story.

"What Saturday was it?"

"I'm not even sure. Probably about a month ago. I think I'm getting early Alzheimer's."

"Happens to everyone. OK, let's see here. Actually, we don't have a lot of Saturday events. It probably wasn't a kids' party, right?"

"No." It could have been, of course, but not if it was related to this story.

"Oh, was it the Buckeye Neighborhood Association meeting? Second Saturday of every month, two o'clock. Contact person: Selma Gooding."

"Yeah, that was it." Buckeye was a Northeast hot spot. "I can't believe I forgot about that."

"Well, the next one's day after tomorrow, so don't forget that one either."

"I won't. Thanks."

17

Between losing the motion in Crenshaw, cutting a deal with a loser like Hanks, my blowup at MCT, and the fallout with Chuck at home, I had been grateful when one of the worst days in recent years had finally come to a close. Chuck and I had talked for hours but had gotten nowhere. The discussion had begun reasonably enough, with me explaining that I really had meant to tell him about my inheritance of the Hamilton case. But as we moved from topic to topic—covering the tensions between me and the other detectives, him and Mike, and him and me—it quickly dissolved into a long, frustrating night where we argued more about the things we said during the argument than any of the things that had necessitated the we-need-to-talk talk in the first place.

In the end, he wound up outside, tinkering with his car in the dark and leaving me to watch the *Daily Show* alone. He came to bed eventually, but the night was spent without the usual spooning.

If I had any hopes of things looking up with a new day, they were quickly squashed. When I woke Friday, Chuck had already left. A note on his pillow said he wanted to hit the gym before work.

Then, on the drive to the courthouse, I was pulled over for a rolling stop at the corner of my block. I didn't recognize the young officer, but I made a point of holding out my District Attorney badge while I was pretending to fumble with my driver's license and registration.

As he was writing out a ticket for running the stop sign, I was more explicit. "I don't think we've met before. I'm at the DA's office, in MCU. I live just back there," I said, gesturing to my bungalow at the middle of the block.

"Nice place," he said, smiling and handing me my citation. "I'd cut you some slack, but I wouldn't want you to prosecute me for shirking my duties."

Apparently word of the Hamilton case had gotten out.

Then came the grand jury hearing itself—the one I'd taken so much grief for, the one Russ Frist had told me not to worry about. My first witness was Marla Mavens, Delores Tompkins's mother. She knew nothing about the shooting itself, but I thought the grand jurors needed to hear something about Delores other than the fact that she was shot by a cop. Mrs. Mavens brought a picture of her daughter and her two grand-sons with her.

She told the grand jury that Delores's only flaw in life had been her pattern of picking bad men for herself instead of find-ing her own way. The separate fathers of her two children were both long gone. More recently, she'd been seeing someone who seemed like a good man until Delores figured out that he was deeply involved in drugs, yet another disappointment.

Tragically, Delores finally seemed to be turning things around for herself in the weeks before her death. She had broken up with the louse in question, had gotten a job with benefits at a home improvement store, and had said she was working on something that made her feel special—something Marla had never heard her daughter express before. Marla had pushed to hear more about it, but Delores had wanted to keep it private. Now that she was gone, Marla would never know.

"Do you know why your daughter was in her car at three-thirty in the morning?"

Marla shook her head. "No, I can't figure it. I was keeping the boys for her that night, like I do once a week or so. Or did. I've got them full-time now. But it wasn't like her to be out late like that."

"Can you think of any reason why she would try to drive away from a police officer during a traffic stop?" That was the kind of question I could never ask in court, where the rules of evidence actually applied.

"Delores? Oh, no. I can't even imagine why she'd be pulled over, she was such a careful driver. But she certainly wouldn't cause any trouble."

After Marla left the room, I made a point of showing Delores's PPDS printout to the grand jurors. No arrests, no convictions.

My next witness was Alan Carson, the Internal Affairs detective who responded to the scene of the shooting. With helmet hair and doughy skin, he looked like he'd sell Bibles door-to-door. From his assignment alone, I doubted that many cops outside his unit were friendly with him. But so far he had struck me as reasonable and competent, expertly reconstructing the incident based on the ballistics evidence.

He covered the few facts we knew about that night: Hamilton had discharged his weapon until it was empty, firing a total of seven bullets. Six of them penetrated the windshield of Delores's Alero; three of them struck her—two in the head, one in the neck. No weapon or drugs were found in the car. Based on the car's location when it was stopped and Hamilton's location when he discharged the gun, the car could not have been moving faster than fifteen miles an hour when Hamilton started shooting. I might never be able to explain exactly why Hamilton had panicked that night, but I had enough to show he was at least reckless about the shooting, the standard for the manslaughter charge I was asking for.

When I walked Carson out of the room, I watched him pass the final witness waiting outside, Officer Geoff Hamilton. If looks could kill—well, it's a damn good thing they can't.

Hamilton didn't have the right to an attorney during the hearing, so Jerome Black had to wait in the hall. I watched the grand jurors eye Hamilton while the foreman swore him in. He'd worn his uniform, much to my annoyance. His chubby face, stocky build, and boyish blond hair added to the appearance of earnest innocence.

"Mr. Hamilton," I said, avoiding any mention of his official position, "we've already heard testimony establishing that you discharged your service weapon on the night in question, and that Delores Tompkins died as a consequence."

"Yes, ma'am."

"Shortly after the shooting, you had this to say." I read the grand jury the terse statement Hamilton had given at the precinct. "Now you have asked for an opportunity to provide additional information to the grand jurors that you chose not to share with your own sergeant or with the officers investigating the shooting?"

"That's correct, ma'am, after consulting with counsel."

"Why don't you go ahead and say what you'd like to say, then."

"Well, I'll start from the beginning. I initially noticed a black female now known to me as Delores Tompkins because she was crying in her vehicle, close to hysterical." He had shifted into the formal tone officers tend to use during trial testimony. "Based on my experience, I thought she might have fled a recent domestic encounter, and I wanted to make sure she was not in any danger. I pulled my car to the left of hers at the red light at the intersection of Ainsworth and MLK, then rolled down my passenger's side window and waved at her in an attempt to get her attention. The subject—"

"You mean Delores Tompkins," I interrupted, trying to remind the grand jurors that she was the victim, not the suspect.

"That's correct. Ms. Tompkins looked in my direction but abruptly drove away when the light changed. She then proceeded to turn right, moving westbound on Ainsworth. She then took a quick left on Garfield, then her next right. Based on her demeanor, the neighborhood we were in, and her erratic driving patterns, I suspected that the subject may have been under the influence of drugs and attempting to elude me. I activated my overhead lights, and the subject finally pulled over at Killingsworth and Mallory."

"But we know that she was not in fact under the influence of drugs, isn't that correct?"

"Correct, but I'm trying to explain what I thought at the time, based on my observations. Because she appeared to be attempting to evade me, I was interpreting the emotional demeanor I had witnessed earlier in a different light. Given the high-drug neighborhood, I thought it was at least a possibility that she was under the influence or perhaps looking to score."

I nodded for him to continue, realizing that the training we give cops to withstand cross-examination was backfiring.

"She did finally pull over. When I approached the vehicle, I realized that her engine was still running. I ordered her to turn off the engine and step out of the car, but she attempted to drive away. Apparently, she had stopped too close to a vehicle parked in front of her to pull out. I then saw her reverse lights go on, and I stepped to the left to avoid being hit by the car. Once she backed up—barely missing me—I was situated in front of the subject's vehicle. I unholstered my weapon and again ordered her to stop and to step away from the vehicle."

Hamilton's voice had taken on a new urgency. The grand jurors were listening intently, pens in hand but taking no notes lest they lose a word of the story.

"What happened then?" the foreman asked.

"I don't know how to explain it, but she drove her vehicle directly toward me. It was so quick. I discharged my weapon, and to this day I replay it in my head, wondering if I could have done something different, but I couldn't. She would have run right into me." His voice cracked, and for a moment I thought he might actually cry.

I did my best to cross-examine him, but Black had earned whatever fees Hamilton had paid him. This was a well-prepped witness. He deflected all my questions about why he didn't move out of the way, why he fired seven times, why he aimed at the driver instead of the tires, returning each time to the same theme: All of a sudden, I had a car gunning right at me, and I responded. He swore he didn't even realize he'd fired all his bullets until he was told later.

He was a better witness than I'd expected, which indicated that a trial would be tough if it ever came to that. But despite Hamilton's skills on the stand, I was confident that the hearing was headed toward an indictment.

Then the grand jury foreman asked the question that changed everything.

"Do you regret what happened?"

Hamilton paused for nearly a minute. When he opened his mouth to speak, he broke down. "Oh, God, you have no idea. I wake up every night wishing I'd let her hit me. You know, maybe I would have made it. But even if I didn't, at least I wouldn't be suffering like this. I can't eat. I can't sleep. I won't let myself drink because I'm too afraid of what will happen. I took my weapons to my dad's house, so I'm not near them. Even if I get reinstated, I can't imagine ever being a cop again." At that point, he finally did shed tears. One of the women handed Hamilton a package of tissues from her purse, and I knew I was in trouble.

When Hamilton left the room, I did my best to shift the tide. I reminded the grand jury how low the standard was for an indictment. I emphasized that Hamilton wasn't being accused of intentionally causing Delores's death, only of recklessness. I even pulled out pictures I had from the file of Delores's head injuries.

But, a full hour later—the longest grand jury deliberation I'd ever witnessed—the foreman walked out of the room and handed me a slip of paper. No indictment, by a vote of four to three.

I walked back to MCU in a daze, wondering how I was going to break the news to Marla Mavens that a grand jury had decided her daughter's killing did not even warrant a full trial. And, of course, I'd feel the wrath of Russ Frist. He had called Alice Gerstein four times in the last hour wondering why I was taking so long with a grand jury hearing.

"Oh," Alice added, "that annoying little Lisa Lopez came by twice looking for you. I didn't tell her where you were, but she assured me she'd be back soon."

Of course she would. I thanked Alice for protecting me. Lisa's the type who'd bang down the grand jury's door if she thought her need to see me was urgent.

My plan was to call Russ first. As harsh a critic as he could be, I knew it would be less painful than calling Mrs. Mavens. As it turned out, a ringing phone awaited me.

"Kincaid."

"Dammit, Kincaid, why didn't you call me back? And don't tell me for a second that Alice didn't give you my messages."

"She did, Russ. And, literally, I just walked into my office. I was just about to call you." I really was.

"Yeah, right. You really need to keep me in the loop on things, Sam."

Great. He was mad at me before I even got to the bad stuff. I broke the news anyway. When he was done yelling about brain-dead grand jurors, Russ was surprisingly understanding. "I'll call Duncan."

"No, I'll take my lumps."

"Don't look a gift horse in the mouth, Sam. He'll blow a gasket when he gets the news, no matter who tells him. If you're there, he'll rip into you, and the two of you will butt heads as usual. I can be a buffer and walk him through the stuff he really cares about."

"Like—"

"You know, the fallout. Who's going to be pissed and why."

"Start by explaining it to me."

"It's not that bad. The cops might think we cut Hamilton a break. As far as the community goes, we can lay the blame for the loss on those lame-ass grand jurors. The split vote shows we tried."

"Thanks, Russ." I would make the compassionate call to Mrs. Mavens and leave the political massaging to my boss.

"No problem. Besides, how bad can he be to a guy sitting at home with Lyme disease?"

Alice Gerstein walked in just seconds after my call to Mrs. Mavens, when the lump that had formed in my throat was still threatening to squeeze up and burst into a sob.

"I'm sorry, Samantha, but Lisa Lopez is back. Do you want me to tell her you're in a meeting?"

"No, send her in."

"You sure?" Alice was careful never to pry, but she could clearly tell that I was upset.

"I'm having the worst thirty-six hours of my career. Why stop now?"

She smiled sympathetically and sent in the beast.

Lisa made herself comfortable in one of my guest chairs and pulled a thin file folder from her briefcase.

"Lucas Braun called me yesterday. I can't believe that idiot was going to have Hanks testify."

I couldn't believe that Lucas had told Lisa about our deal before I'd even debriefed his client. "So now you're here shopping a plea for Corbett? Forget it. You're too late, Lisa."

"No, I'm here to get the charges dismissed."

"You really have caught me at the worst possible time for game playing—"

"I have ironclad proof of innocence." She handed me a printed page of paper with a notarized signature at the bottom. "This is an affidavit from a girl named Tamara Lyons. She was with the defendants from a quarter to ten until one in the morning the night Percy Crenshaw was killed."

I gave the document a perfunctory perusal and handed it back to her. "In case you haven't noticed, Lisa, little girlfriends willing to serve as bogus alibis are a dime a dozen around here."

"She's not a little girlfriend. She's Hanks's ex, and she called her best friend a little after one in the morning because she'd just been raped by Hanks and Corbett. She called the crisis center two hours later."

"No way, Lisa. Both defendants have confessed at one point or another to killing Percy. You might have gotten your guy's statement tossed, but that doesn't change the fact that he made it." I was arguing on reflex, but internally I flashed back to the rape crisis counselor, Annie of the pierced nose, asking at the arraignment whether the defendants had any chance of release pending trial.

"My guy confessed because your detective gave him no choice. What was he going to say? Offer up an alibi of 'Sorry, officer, but I think I was busy raping someone?' It lands him with a mandatory minimum sentence of a hundred months, and only makes him look worse. Your detective gave him the out of shifting the blame to Trevor Hanks, and that's what he did."

"But even after he blamed it on Trevor, we still arrested him. Why didn't he say something then?"

"Honestly? He started to think maybe they did do it. He was high out of his mind and couldn't remember everything that happened between Twenty-third Avenue and Tamara. When Hanks called him in the morning, saying he found blood on his jean jacket, Todd assumed it was from Tamara. But when Calabrese confronted him about Percy, he started to wonder."

"And what about Hanks? According to Lucas Braun, I've got the right men."

"That's because Lucas is an unethical idiot who figures seven years for manslaughter is better than eight and a half years for rape, truth be damned."

"Why didn't this girl Tamara Lyons say anything?"

"Because those wackos at the Rape Crisis Center told her no one would believe her. Corbett and Hanks showed up at Fred Meyer right before closing. She works there. Her coworkers will confirm that she said she was leaving with her ex and one of his friends. Hanks had some meth, and she was willing to kiss and make up for the night to get in on the action. When they went out to the river by the airport, things got out of hand. Both of them raped her. When she realized Tuesday morning they'd been arrested for something even worse, she figured it was kismet or something. I talked to her myself last night."

I thought about the methamphetamine-related date rapes I'd seen at MCU, like so many alcohol-induced cases, but rougher and more prolonged. "So how'd you get her to sign the affidavit?"

"It wasn't easy. I assured her that Corbett would plead to Rape One and testify against Hanks so she wouldn't have to go through a trial. I also gave her my opinion that Hanks would probably plead guilty once he realized Corbett was coming clean, and that the likely sentence was the mandatory minimum."

"And you've talked to the people at the Rape Crisis Center?"

She nodded. "This morning. Tamara agreed to it. They confirmed that the call came in Sunday morning around three. Tamara told the counselor she'd left with the perpetrators from work. Fred Meyer confirms she clocked out at ten. That means Corbett and Hanks weren't in the parking lot when the super saw two men there and when the neighbor heard the comment about the car."

I shook my head. "I don't get it, Lisa. How long have you known about this?"

"You know I don't have to tell you that."

"And you know that it affects whether I choose to trust you."

"I've known the whole time." Her voice rose over my protests. "What was I going to do, Sam? Try to help my client by telling you he's a gang rapist when he takes too much meth? Hanks and Corbett couldn't give us a firm enough timeline to provide an alibi. If I'd mentioned it earlier, you would have tacked on a rape charge to the indictment and argued they did everything as one big crime spree. Tamara's affidavit changes that."

I shook my head. "I don't know, Lisa. Maybe the girl's messed up on the timing. Or who knows? Maybe Hanks called her at two in the morning and talked her into cooking this up as a worst-case defense."

"Oh, come on. Do either of these kids strike you as that smart?"

No, they didn't. But there was too much evidence: Peter Anderson's eyewitness testimony, the baseball bat near Hanks's house, the fibers from his Jeep. I wasn't buying it, and I told her so.

"That's what's been bothering me too," she said. "From the first time I sat down with Todd, I was never really worried about the case. I had a get-out-of-jail-free card if the case really fell apart. But then you seemed to keep finding more evidence. I think you've got a serious problem on your hands."

"Like what, Lisa, a secret evidence maker? You know, you're so quick to put the blame on everyone else instead of just coming to terms with the fact that your clients lie to you."

Still, in the back of my head and, more importantly, in my gut, I felt that Tamara Lyons was telling the truth. I remembered Annie's secrecy and obvious discomfort at the arraignment. I thought about the look of shock and fear on Todd Corbett's face when Calabrese had brought up Percy's murder. It was an entirely different look than the nervous, defensive expression he bore when Mike initially accused him of the vandalisms.

"Trust me," she said, without the slightest irony, "I've looked at this from every angle. Don't you think I went back to my client when new evidence kept trickling in? But I talked to Tamara myself. You should too. She's the last one who would lie to help these guys; her hatred for them just oozes from her. So, yeah, I've been scrutinizing the evidence like crazy. Your eyewitness? I'm not saying he's an outright liar. He could have seen the news report while he was shaving or something without even thinking about it. Then, when he saw the throw-downs, two of the guys looked familiar. He assumed it was from the parking lot."

"Even if I were to buy that, Lisa, there's the bat."

"I know," she said, nodding. "And I really have no way of knowing whether it's the same bat they used for the vandalisms. They both say they got so high they must have lost it somewhere in the night. But how hard is it to buy a baseball bat and dump it in an alley near one of the suspects' houses?"

"And put Percy Crenshaw's blood and your client's car fibers on it?"

"That's why I said you might have a problem on your hands. Let me be real clear here: I think I can get a dismissal of the murder charges just on Tamara's testimony. And, like I said, my guy's fully prepared to admit the rape. This next part you can take for what it's worth, because I know how you protect your cops."

"Attacking me's not helping, Lisa."

"All right, fine. If this thing had gone to trial—which it's not—I was going to go after the girlfriend's husband."

"Matt York? He was on duty."

"Right. And I got the call-out records from Central Precinct for that night. He and someone named Ben Hayden both logged in as responding to a call of protesters blocking the entrances at the City Grill at nine-thirty that night. York didn't clear until eleven."

I recalled my conversation with Chuck after our visit to Matt York's house. The discussion itself had been lengthy as Chuck struggled to describe his friend's pain and his own discomfort raising the questions that had to be asked. But as a briefing from a detective to a prosecutor, it had been quick; the alibi checked out. I had a vague memory of the printout Chuck had run of Matt's calls that night. "So? Something like that could easily take a couple hours."

"But Hayden's report shows he cleared from the call before ten, and no one else was sent to that address after he left. So either York stayed alone at the site of a confrontation—which cops are always testifying on the stand that they don't do—or we don't know where York was after Hayden cleared. And the bat? I looked at the autopsy report. The ME never said the weapon was a bat, just a blunt instrument. My expert said it could have been anything, like maybe a police baton. And when word got out that Calabrese had a couple of bat-wielding suspects in custody, how hard would it have been for a cop to wipe some blood on a bat and get a few fibers from the Jeep in the impound lot?"

I wasn't buying it. I'd had dinner with Matt York. The man I lived with loved him like a brother. No way.

Lisa must have sensed my resistance. "The other possibility is that whoever killed Crenshaw was smart enough to dump the bat near Hanks's house after the news was out. Then, afterward, looking for something to shore up the case, one of your MCU detectives let a few fibers touch the bat."

I sighed loudly.

"Come on, Sam. You know that kind of stuff happens. They get convinced they've got the right guy and want to make sure they seal the deal. Can you honestly tell me it's not at least a possibility with a guy like Calabrese?"

I took the affidavit back from her. "Is this all you've got?"

She opened the file in her hand and began handing me more documents. "This is the printout from the call with York and Hayden, showing Hayden cleared more than an hour before York. These are my investigator's notes from a phone interview with Annie Hunter at the Rape Crisis Center. And these are his notes from interviews with two of Tamara's coworkers at Fred Meyer, confirming she said she was leaving with an ex-boyfriend and his friend."

"All right. I'll get back to you."

"He didn't do it, Sam. You need to do the right thing. Despite our history, I'm trusting you on this."

The second Lisa left, I began a furious review of the file, searching for something to contradict her version of the story. Instead, I found what in hindsight appeared to be obvious signs that Corbett's so-called confession was indeed false. I read the statement that he signed. Every fact contained in it—the car, the bat, the carport—had been mentioned directly by Calabrese during the prolonged questioning. Corbett had offered absolutely no independent detail that could be corroborated. We should have insisted that he provide verifiable specifics. But we were stressed, exhausted, and relieved to get the statement. We got sloppy.

Then there were the notes from my conversation with Jake Meltzer, the sheriff's deputy who transported the defendants back to holding after arraignment. The mean one didn't ask the stupid one why he told the police what happened. Rather, he asked him why he *didn't* tell the police what *really* happened. At the time, I thought Hanks was angry that Corbett hadn't taken more of the responsibility in his so-called confession. Now it sounded like he'd been referring to Tamara.

I read everything about Peter Anderson's identification again. His initial description appeared to match the defendants. On the other hand, it was vague enough to describe most young white men. As for the throw-downs, human memories are notoriously malleable. Anderson could very well have caught a glimpse of the defendants' pictures on television during the fog of his hangover, without even realizing the distortion of his own recollections.

I studied Tamara Lyons's affidavit. The defendants showed up at Fred Meyer at a quarter to ten, rowdy and ready to party. She told them to get lost, having tired long ago of Hanks's unreliability. When Hanks threw in the promise of meth, she changed her mind. Two hours later, she was bent over the backseat of Hanks's Jeep, the defendants taking turns on her from behind. An hour after that, she called her girlfriend; then it was on to Annie the counselor. I'd have one of the detectives verify it, but I could tell it would all check out.

I turned to the physical evidence. The discrepancy between the amount of blood in Percy's carport and the absence of blood on the defendants' clothing was newly troubling. Whatever small amount of blood that had been on Hanks's jean jacket was gone, and it could have been Tamara's. No blood in the Jeep. That left just the bat.

I called John Fredericks at the crime lab. "Tell me about carpet fibers."

"They're these fibers, and they come off of carpets."

Sarcasm's the price you pay in my business. "I'm serious. About that bat: I know fiber comparisons aren't as reliable as DNA, but how good are they?"

"When done well, they're good. And we do them well. Between me and you, is it *possible* that the fibers came from somewhere other than the Jeep? Sure, because, like you said, carpet's not unique, like DNA. But I can tell you that whatever carpet the fibers came from, it was the same kind and color as the carpet in the car. Why all the questions?"

"I've got a defense attorney crying bullshit, that's all." There was no need to fill Fredericks in on the details yet. "So if she argues at trial that someone put the fibers on the bat after the fact to frame the defendant, is that even possible?"

"Again? Between the two of us? Yeah, because the blood on the bat was in fact smeared, most likely against the victim's own clothing, which was smooth microfiber and didn't shed any fibers. So the bad guy could take the bat, rub it against the Jeep's carpet, and there you go. The problem with that scenario is there's no blood transfer to the Jeep. Not a problem for us, though, because of all the crap in the truck. The fibers were probably loose, and whatever garbage was beneath the bat got tossed at the same time."

"So could someone have rubbed loose fibers onto the bat?" I asked.

"Maybe, but that raises the even bigger problem your defense lawyer's going to have. How'd the bad guy get into the Jeep? No one was looking at your guy until right before he was arrested. The Jeep's been in the impound lot ever since. So unless she's saying *we* tampered with evidence after we seized the bat—"

He let the idea dangle as inconceivable. I thanked him and hung up, keeping Lisa's suspicions about Matt York and Mike Calabrese to myself. For now.

18

At work on Friday, Heidi hid in the research dungeon reading old newspaper articles online about drug arrests in Portland. Unfortunately, the coverage was sporadic at best. Every few months, a high-profile sweep or a major bust would make the paper. These occasional articles weren't going to give Heidi the kind of expertise she needed. She wanted to know who the officers were who were making the arrests and why arrest patterns were screwy in Northeast Precinct.

Then she found an article written by Percy a year earlier about a federal bust of a major Dominican heroin ring in East Portland. To place the arrests within a bigger picture, Percy had dissected the racial lines that tended to split the city's drug trade. Black dealers controlled the crack and powder cocaine, Latinos dominated heroin, and whites handled the crystal meth and hallucinogens.

Drugs manufactured in the States—like speed, acid, and Ecstasy—could be distributed by diverse, independent, relatively small-time dealers. But according to Percy's story, police suspected that the control of cocaine and heroin was centralized. There might be hundreds of kids on the corners conducting hand-to-hand deals, but the police theorized that all the cocaine and heroin coming into the city was first received, cut, and distributed by two small, separate, competing cabals—one using black dealers for coke, the other using Latinos for heroin.

Heidi thought again about Percy's charts. She assumed he was looking into the possibility that police were discriminating on the basis of race by searching more black suspects than warranted, but there was an alternative explanation. Maybe a few cops had been recruited by whatever group controlled the crack trade in North Portland. These cops might be searching neighborhood dealers as required by the precinct sergeants, and filling out the cards to show they were doing their work. But if they weren't actually arresting the dealers who were carrying crack, that would explain the trend in the numbers.

Gut instinct told her she was on the right track. Now, if only she had the right contacts. She needed to learn more about the drug scene.

It felt awkward to ask anything further of Jack Streeter after a first date. Who else did she know in law enforcement? She recalled the District Attorney who was handling Percy's case. She had seemed pleasant enough in Percy's office, and she had to be relatively nice to take the time to attend the funeral. The worst she could do was blow Heidi off.

Heidi flipped through her Rolodex until she came to the prosecutor's business card, then entered the name in the newspaper's internal database. Soon, she found multiple stories about a shooting at Samantha Kincaid's house earlier in the year. Heidi remembered it but hadn't made the connection. She read with interest that Kincaid had been assigned at the time to the Drug and Vice Division of her office. She had apparently been so tenacious on a case that she was nearly killed. Maybe she'd admire Heidi's quest for Percy's truth.

Heidi picked up the phone, then remembered the rule that her editor in Vermont had always emphasized: Don't start interviewing until you've learned as much as you possibly can on your own. She remembered the press binders of police reports that Jack Streeter had mentioned. The least she could do was get a feel for them—to learn the names of the officers working Northeast Precinct, to see who was making crack arrests and who wasn't—before turning empty-handed to her one potential source.

She found her editor, Tom Runyon, in his office.

"Hey, Tom. I'm feeling major-league crummy. I think I need to go home for the rest of the day."

"Are you really sick? Because I was just about to look for you. They're opening the new wing of the airport. I thought you could interview some travelers, see how they like it."

"Tom, I'm really not up to walking around the airport right now." Tom looked put out. "You know, it's sort of a female thing," she whispered.

The trump card did the trick. Without further questioning, Heidi was out the door and on her way to Northeast Precinct. As she detoured through the residential streets adjacent to MLK Boulevard, she couldn't help but notice the gradual deterioration of the housing. Just north of the trendy restaurants and shops on Broadway, young couples enjoyed their restored bungalows, decorating their porches with hanging flower baskets. Farther north, the grass was longer, the walks unedged, the paint jobs less consistent. Still farther on, cars were abandoned on the streets, fences and stop signs were laced with graffiti, and the occasionally well-kept house carried bars on its first-floor windows.

Even though she was parked in the precinct lot, Heidi

tucked all her CDs beneath the passenger seat before locking up. She approached a middle-aged woman sitting behind a glass window at the reception desk.

"Hi. My name's Heidi Hatmaker. I'm from the *Oregonian*. Jack Streeter told me there were police reports here that the press can look at?"

"Here you go," the receptionist said, reaching beneath the counter and producing a six-inch stack of reports held together on a clipboard containing two huge metal binder rings. "So you're the new Percy Crenshaw?"

"Pardon me?"

"We just got word this morning." She handed Heidi a memorandum. "Someone's certainly fond of you."

The PPB header declared that it was a note to all precinct officers from the Office of Public Information. "As most of you know, good media relationships can be part of good police work. Many of you, like me, trusted, worked with, and genuinely liked our lost friend Percy Crenshaw. For those looking to reach out to the media, Heidi Hatmaker at the *Oregonian* is trustworthy and interested in pursuing any joint efforts you had with Crenshaw." It ended with Heidi's telephone number.

"This went out to every single police officer this morning?" Heidi asked.

"No, but it's posted in the report writing room. Oh, and it's also on the roll-call board so the sergeants read it to everyone when shift starts."

Apparently this was Jack Streeter's version of sending flowers the morning after a good date. She'd call him later to reprimand him for sending word out, despite her objection. And to thank him.

"Well, I definitely can't fill Percy's shoes," Heidi said to the receptionist, "but, yeah, I'm picking up a couple of things he was working on."

She thanked the woman again, took a seat at a round table in the public area of the precinct, and flipped through the pages of the press binder. Reports as recent as last night's were on top. She jumped ahead to the page at the bottom of the stack. Three weeks ago. Not a long-term picture but certainly a lot of incidents.

She gave special attention to drug cases, dwelling on every detail of the first few reports: the events leading the police to stop the person, the justification for conducting the search for drugs, the description of the substance seized, the defendant's statements once he was arrested—it was all fascinating.

Halfway through the binder, she was skimming quickly. Seen one drug case, seen them all. Cop initiates contact, either on the street or in a traffic stop. Cop finds drugs, usually because the person agrees to be searched or while the cop is frisking for weapons. Cop makes an arrest. Arrested person admits he had drugs, sometimes claiming they belonged to a friend.

She did notice the trend Percy had highlighted in his article about last year's Dominican heroin bust. Crack cases tended to involve black suspects; heroin cases involved Latinos. It also became clear that some cops worked harder than others. Most officers' names had appeared only once so far at the bottom of the reports. But a few seemed to be real go-getters, making the traffic stops and pounding the corners. One officer was so active that she began to recognize the block capital-letter print in his reports: Curt Foster.

She found herself making a mental scratch mark for each of Foster's cases. By the eighth scratch, she realized that five had involved heroin, two speed, and one marijuana. No rocks of cocaine in a neighborhood that appeared from other officers' reports to be plagued by crack. She flipped back through Foster's reports. She'd been right. Plus, all the defendants were

Latino and white. No African-Americans. She whizzed through the rest of Foster's reports in the binder. Same pattern.

Just then, a youngish-looking officer with dark brown wavy hair walked out of the card-protected door that separated the secured part of the precinct from the lobby. He seemed to glance at the binder as he passed. It was probably a natural curiosity, but Heidi found herself instinctively huddling over the pages, averting her eyes. After he left the building, she kept her eyes on the glass doors, checking to see if he looked back. He didn't. She was being paranoid.

She flipped the open pages of the binder together, ready to return it to the front window. She wrote *Curt Foster* on a notepad she pulled from her backpack. She'd have to figure out a way to find out more about him.

As she was putting the pad back into her bag, she found herself looking at the officer's last name more carefully. Foster. Where had she heard that recently?

Then she remembered. She turned the pages of Percy's original notes furiously until she found it. *Powell/Foster,* he'd written. She had assumed it was a reference to the intersection of Foster and Powell streets. Now, she wondered.

She began flipping through the bound reports again. A third of the way through, she hit upon what she knew in her gut she would find—the name *Powell,* scrawled at the bottom of a report. This one was for a fight at Jay-J's, an up-and-coming hangout for the too-cool-for-the-west-side types. She searched the bottoms of more pages and found more reports written by Officer Jamie Powell, including drug cases. Powell hadn't been quite as active as Foster. But, like Foster, Powell had also managed to work Northeast Precinct for three weeks without crossing paths with a single rock of cocaine.

When she returned the binder to the receptionist, she engaged her in small talk about her scarf, the pace of her job, and, finally, about the subject that truly interested Heidi. "I got the impression from the reports that most of the drug problem around here is from crack, but I know that's only for the last three weeks."

"Yeah, but the last three weeks are like any other three weeks, you know? My guess is, like, maybe sixty percent crack and cocaine. East Precinct's got more of the meth and heroin."

Heidi nodded, thanked the woman again, and left. As she walked to her BMW, she noticed the cop with the brown wavy hair standing against a squad car in the fleet parking lot, smoking a cigarette. She tried looking away quickly, but not before he removed his cigarette-free hand from his holster and waved.

Before she even realized she was nervous, Heidi had ducked into her car, started the engine, and driven six blocks. Only when she stopped for a light did she register her quickened pulse, her rushed and shallow breathing.

Forget nervous. She was actually scared. The officer was probably being friendly, but she couldn't ignore the possibility that he wasn't. Her imagination soared wildly as she navigated her way downtown. That Percy was killed while tracking this story was not helping matters. In the battle between her intellect and anxiety, Heidi reminded herself that the police had already solved Percy's murder. Rubbing cops and drug dealers the wrong way was certainly not the safest activity, but so far there was no reason to believe she'd meet the same fate as Percy.

So why was she afraid to turn around, return to the precinct, and ask for the name of the officer with the brown wavy hair? Because of her damn imagination, that's why.

She was convinced she was on to something, but she had no next step to confirming her suspicions about Powell and Foster.

She needed help from someone inside the system, who could access more than just a few weeks of police reports, who might even know something about the officers' reputations and who else might be involved. And she needed someone she could trust.

She couldn't go back to work. Tom thought she was out with a deadly case of cramps. Feeling emboldened by her research at the precinct, she decided it was time to talk to Samantha Kincaid, the woman prosecutor who used to be in the Drug and Vice Division.

She started to dial information, then flipped her cell shut, remembering another rule of reporting: People are more likely to talk to the press when surprised in person. She hopped onto the Morrison Bridge, just a few blocks from the county courthouse.

19

Within thirty minutes of Lisa Lopez's departure from my office, Lucas Braun called.

"Lopez tells me the two of you are talking," he said. I was surprised Lisa had bothered to give him a heads-up.

"Yes, Lucas, we certainly are. Pretty fascinating stuff, as I'm sure you can imagine." He deserved to be disbarred. The least I could do was let him know I was annoyed.

"Do we still have our deal?"

"You're kidding me, right?"

"Corbett's got his story, but Hanks has his, and he's still willing to testify. We had an agreement, regardless of Corbett's defense strategy."

"*Defense strategy?* That's what you're calling this? According to Lisa, you were in on this little secret. She says you knew damn well this entire time that when Percy was killed, the defendants were committing a different crime on the opposite side of town. Are you telling me Lisa's lying?"

A couple of deputies chatting in the hall peered into my office. I used my toe to kick the door shut.

"What do you want me to say?"

"The truth, Lucas. You can't put Hanks on the stand if you know he's lying."

"How do I *know* anything? I know what my clients tell me, and I know their stories go back and forth."

It was the standard line that all defense lawyers recite when asked how they can justify defending a person they know is guilty. I never bought the rationalization, but it was particularly perverse when Braun was trying to plead his client out for a murder he didn't commit, send another young man to prison for life, and leave whoever actually killed Percy Crenshaw walking the streets.

"So you admit that Hanks initially said he was with Tamara Lyons?" There was a long pause. In person, I could have stared him down, but on the phone he needed some encouragement. "I'm not going forward with any deal until you tell me what's going on."

"Whatever. Yeah, that was the first story he gave. Later, he said he made it up and was willing to give up Corbett on the Crenshaw case."

"And let me take a guess. He changed his story after you told him what the mandatory minimum sentence was for Rape One compared to what you could get him if he cooperated on the murder. I remember exactly what you told me, Lucas: absolutely no more than seven years: eighty-four months. That was the trade, wasn't it? He'd rather accept the sure seven and lie than face a hundred months on the rape."

"Off the record?"

Who the hell was this guy? "We're not in court, Lucas. There is no record."

"I talked to him about the sentences. But that's my job as his lawyer."

I read him the critical sentences from Lyons's affidavit. "Is this girl telling the truth or not?"

"Everyone sees the truth differently."

I had to end this call before my head exploded. "I'm hanging up, Lucas. And once I fix the cluster fuck you and Lisa have created, I'm writing a letter to the bar."

"Do we have a deal or not?"

I resisted the temptation to slam the phone down and instead took a deep breath and began counting to ten, returning the handpiece gently to its cradle.

I was up to twenty-five by the time I regained a cool enough head to deal with the outside world.

My first call was to Annie Hunter, the rape crisis counselor. As offhandedly as a restaurant hostess confirming a reservation, she substantiated Lisa's claims about Tamara Lyons's version of Sunday night's events.

"And you didn't think to tell me when you were in court on Tuesday morning that I was charging two innocent men with aggravated murder?"

"Innocent? Give me a break. Didn't you hear what I just told you?"

"Then the charge should have been rape."

"She was high on meth, she left with them from work voluntarily, one of the guys is her ex-boyfriend, and some of the initial contact was consensual. Are you telling me you would have taken the case? Please, I've been there with enough women while some cop or DA tells them why a jury won't believe them."

As Annie spoke, I quietly typed her full name into a search of victims stored in the DA system. One result: a declined Rape Two, four years ago.

"Cases can be hard to prove, even when we believe the victim's telling the truth," I said. "But making Corbett and Hanks pay for a different crime isn't the answer. If they didn't kill Percy Crenshaw, someone else did. I need the police to be out looking for the killer."

When Annie spoke again, her voice was lower. "I did talk to Tamara about that. At length. Before I went to court and after. But, come on, it was less than two days since she'd been raped by these guys, and she wakes up and finds out one of them has confessed to murder? It would take a saint to rush to their defense."

Regardless of whether I agreed with Tamara Lyons's notion of rough justice, I could understand it. From the looks of things, she was telling the truth now. But, before I concluded that I had charged the wrong men with Percy's murder, I wanted to be sure.

"Do you think she'd be willing to take a polygraph?" Annie started to protest. "It would be very brief," I insisted, "and it would make it much easier for us to convince a court to accept the defendants' pleas on the rape case. It's not exactly an everyday occurrence to dismiss murder charges."

She relented. "Fine. She's actually holding up pretty well. I'll explain it to her."

"Thanks. Tell her to expect to hear from a detective to set it up."

My next call was to Chuck. He sounded relieved when he realized I was calling him about the case instead of capital-U Us—until I filled him in on the details.

"Hold up. You don't really think they're innocent, do you?"

I remembered Annie's outrage about the use of that word to

describe the men who assailed Tamara Lyons's body and trust. "Chuck, I don't think they killed Percy. They couldn't have, not if Tamara's telling the truth. And she gave prompt reports to her best friend and to the Rape Crisis Center. That's more than what we've got in most of the rape cases we prosecute. But we need a statement. The counselor's talking to her now about doing a poly. Can you follow up on it? Hopefully today, if possible."

"Yeah, OK, I'll do it, but have you really thought this through? The timing of it all seems fishy, and we've got a solid case against them on the murder."

"No, we really don't." I began to run through the evidence, explaining how no single piece was incontrovertible.

"What about the fibers on the bat?" he challenged.

Lisa's words still nagged at me like a bumblebee in summer: *I think you've got a serious problem on your hands.* "Maybe it's just a coincidence," I offered tentatively. "Fibers aren't DNA or fingerprints."

"A *coincidence*? You sound like a defense attorney. What are the odds that the so-called *real killer* just happened to place the weapon on a carpet whose fibers are microscopically indistinguishable from the carpet in Hanks's Jeep? What did the lab say?"

"That it was a pretty good match."

"OK, then. How does Lisa Lopez explain that?"

"What if someone else killed Crenshaw, read about the defendants' arrest, and *then* dumped a bat in their neighborhood to help the case along? Is it possible that fibers from the Jeep could have gotten mixed up with the bat during the processing of the evidence?"

"Sam, we know how to preserve evidence. So unless you're saying that one of us did something intentionally—"

"No, I'm just telling you what *Lisa* said."

"Then tell me what the alternative is. I know you. You wouldn't have me setting up a poly for this girl if you didn't have a theory about those fibers."

"I'm setting up the polygraph, Chuck, precisely because I don't want to believe any of Lisa's explanations about the fibers, all right? Please, let's get the poly done first, then figure out the rest of it."

"What other explanations did she have?"

"I told you. She thinks someone tampered with the evidence after the bat and the Jeep were seized."

"That's one explanation. What else is there?"

When it came to hammering out the inconsistencies in a statement, no one—lawyers, detectives, angry pit bulls—was more persistent than my boyfriend. I chose my next words carefully, trying to get the job done without starting another fight.

"Apparently Lisa found a problem with Matt's alibi."

"I checked it myself, Sam."

"I know. But apparently the officer who was covering that call with Matt was clear half an hour later. Matt—at least according to the reports—was checked out to the call for an additional hour by himself."

"So what? Cops forget to enter their status in their terminals all the time. She's going to jump from that to Matt killing Crenshaw in a jealous rage, sneaking into the impound lot, and framing her client? That's classic."

"I didn't say I believed her."

"You're kidding me, right? That's the most you can say? Did you tell her you *didn't* believe her?"

"Stop yelling at me. Do you know how stressful this is, how hard it is for me?"

"For *you*? Does everything always have to be about you? Matt's our friend. He's one of my best friends. This isn't just some defense maneuver in one of your cases, this is personal. He's having a hard enough time with his marriage right now. He doesn't need some attorney making him out to be a murderer. You should have kicked that crazy bitch out of your office. Instead, you're telling me that you're keeping an open mind?"

"I don't believe it, Chuck, OK? But we need to find out what the hell's going on. If Tamara Lyons passes that polygraph, we've got the wrong guys for the Crenshaw case and we have to look at everything again. I don't like what that means for Matt either, but we'll deal with it. Chances are, he'll explain the discrepancy about the call."

"Chances are?"

"You know, it's like there's nothing I can say right now that would be good enough for you."

"You can promise me you're on Matt's side on this. If this girl passes the poly, you and I both know there will be pressure to look at him. When that happens, are you willing to tell Griffith and Frist to go to hell?"

I thought about it. "Yes, if Matt can explain where he was during that call, I will go back to my days of being the boat rocker around here."

"What if he can't, Sam? Do you know how chaotic patrol must have been Sunday night?"

"Chuck, I can't see into the future. Can you please just call Tamara Lyons, and we'll take things from there? I called you because I trust your judgment. I need you to tell me whether this girl's telling the truth."

"Fine, we'll do it your way. What else is new, right?"

Chuck usually has a unique ability to return us to a state of relative normalcy in the simplest ways. He was trying to be light, but I sensed the resentment—resentment that only worsened when I updated my request.

"I need you to go without Mike."

A long silent pause followed, about ten beats. Chuck, after all, had been the one who taught me the anger-management technique of counting silently.

"Are you going to explain that?" he asked finally.

"I don't want him on the case anymore. He went ape shit in that interrogation room."

"And what am I supposed to say to Mike?"

"You don't have to say anything. I'm calling your lieutenant. He can't keep working MCT cases until we're sure."

"You're having him pulled? You can't do that, Sam. You'll totally fuck him over."

"His credibility is sunk since Lesh tossed the confession, and if there was evidence contamination you can bet he'll be suspected."

"Suspected by you or by Lisa Lopez?"

"By anyone looking at the case, Chuck."

"Jesus, first Matt, now Mike. Do you trust anyone?"

"I told you I didn't think Matt had anything to do with this, and I'm not saying Mike tampered with evidence. I'm saying it's better to avoid any problems by keeping him away from the investigation until we know what's up. If anyone knows how this works, it's you."

It hadn't been long since the bureau tried to suspend Chuck during an investigation into the viability of one of his own confessions. As a compromise, he worked patrol until he was cleared back into MCT, but he knew the process.

"It's funny. When it happened to me, you thought it was bullshit."

"That was different," I said, knowing in my heart that it wasn't. "I don't have a choice. Please, I called you because I trust you. I need you to interview Tamara."

■ ■ ■

As soon as I hung up, I heard a tap against my closed office door. Terrific. Whoever was waiting for me on the other side had undoubtedly heard at least part of the exchange with Chuck.

"Yeah, come on in."

Alice peered tentatively through the door. "I'm very sorry to disturb you again, but there's a woman named Heidi Hatmaker here to see you. She's from the *Oregonian*."

The name didn't sound familiar. It sounded funny but not familiar. "Did she say what it was about?"

"No. She said she met you when you were at the newspaper recently."

I vaguely recalled a woman at Percy's office when Chuck and I conducted the search. "Can she call me later?"

"I suggested that already, and she insisted on waiting until you were free."

Crap. It had only been an hour since I learned that my case was falling apart. Could the press possibly be on to the story already?

"Go ahead and send her in. And Alice—thanks, you know, for not saying anything."

"About what?" she asked, and winked before she walked away.

I felt a momentary sense of relief once Heidi Hatmaker left my office. She didn't know anything about the case against Corbett and Hanks after all. She had come fishing for background about street-level drug sales in northeast Portland for an article Percy left unfinished.

I felt more than a little guilty about the way the encounter had unfolded. I had been picturing the angle a reporter in her shoes might take: Manipulative detective coerces young men's confessions, crime lab tampers with evidence, love-struck prosecutor looks the other way. When she initially said she hoped to get a minute of my time for a story, I nearly took her head off. In light of her actual objective, I must have come across like the coldest of ice queens.

Still, what was she thinking? That I'd offer up a one-hour private tutorial on the Portland drug market? Percy had been around long enough to have a feel for the streets himself. Maybe he could have pulled off a story about the subtle ways police can manipulate the market by cracking down in one hot spot or on one particular drug, focusing street resources and reverse buys accordingly. But it would take more than an hour to give a novice the kind of background information needed for that story. I told her to call me Monday, or, better yet, to call the bureau's DVD, but I'm sure she realized I was blowing her off.

I didn't have a choice. I had no time to spare. There was only so much I could do on the Crenshaw case while I waited for Chuck to interview Tamara, but I was expecting one of Russ's bi-hourly checkups any minute. I'd be dumping colossally bad news on him for the second time in as many calls, and I wanted to be as prepared as possible.

I called Jeffrey Sandler, the medical examiner who had conducted Percy's autopsy. Just as I'd assumed, multiple blows from a blunt instrument was as specific as he could be about the cause of Percy's injuries. He was prepared to testify that the injuries were consistent with a bat; however, he would have to concede on cross-examination that any number of items could also have been the weapon of choice.

"Based on the injuries I observed, I am fairly confident that the weapon had a rounded rather than a hard, square edge. And from the size of the injuries, I imagine this weapon to be of a substantial width, something more like a baseball bat than, say, a crowbar."

"What about a baton?"

"Like a child's baton? I'd have to see it, but I suspect it would be too narrow to create the victim's injuries."

"No, I meant more like a police baton."

"I see."

"Not specifically," I added quickly. "I'm just trying to get an idea how thin an instrument the defense could hypothesize without contradicting the physical evidence. It was the first thing that came to mind between a bat and a crowbar."

"Yes, of course. Well, I'd have to measure a baton and go back and look at the photographs of the injuries, but, yes, I imagine it's within the realm of what we're talking about. That's nothing to worry about, of course. Physical evidence must always be viewed as part of the larger evidentiary picture. The blood evidence, the fibers, the nonphysical evidence against the defendants."

"Obviously," I said. "I just need to be prepared. It always helps to anticipate the defense."

"They do make the job more interesting, don't they?"

My next call was to Peter Anderson. He sounded groggy when he picked up. I looked at my watch: three o'clock. He was some eyewitness, all right.

"Hi, Peter. It's Samantha Kincaid from the DA's office. I just wanted to touch base with you on the status of the case since the hearing yesterday."

"It went OK, don't you think?"

"You were great. In fact, it looks like one of the defendants is going to be pleading guilty. The other one will either take a deal soon or, if not, we'll have his codefendant's testimony against him."

"So will you still need me to testify?"

"We'll play it by ear, but it's possible we won't need you after all. I did want to go through some of the questions the defense attorney was asking you, though."

"You mean that junk about my ex?"

"No. Like I said, that really isn't a subject that would be admissible in front of a jury."

"That's good, 'cause, man, it is a mess. We got attorneys fighting over the divorce and the money, plus, you know, it just sucks to split up."

"I can imagine. Like I said, we really don't need to go over it." *Take a hint, dude. I do not want to hear anything more about your nasty divorce.* "But I've been thinking about what the defense attorney said—about how the defendants' pictures had been all over the news the morning Detective Johnson talked to you."

"Yeah, she said that. But, man, I was out of it. The last thing I was doing was watching the news. Plus, I'd remember if I heard anything about the case. It's not every day someone gets killed at Vista Heights."

"Oh, I know. I don't think you were actually watching the coverage. But I was thinking about how sometimes if I'm puttering around the house, I'll have the TV on in the background and won't even be watching it. Sometimes I even turn the volume off. Is there a remote chance that you could have caught even a glimpse of the story?"

"I hadn't thought about it, but, yeah, I guess I might have had the television on. I know I wasn't watching it, though."

"But you might have seen something?" I was leading him, but I needed to know if the possibility existed, no matter how unlikely. "If so, it's fine. We've got one of the defendants on board now, so it might be better not to use your testimony if the defense attorney's going to be able to confuse the jury with it."

"Sure, I see what you're saying. Yeah, I guess I'm like you. I keep the TV on almost all the time, especially now that Marcy's gone. Maybe I had it on that morning, I'm really not sure."

That was all I needed to know.

I preempted Russ and dialed his home number. At least this way he'd know I was trying to keep him in the loop—a seriously screwed-up loop, unfortunately, but one in which I was indeed keeping him tightly encircled.

"We've got another problem," I said. I brought him up to speed. Then, just as Chuck and I had, we walked through the evidence I thought we'd had against Corbett and Hanks, trying to determine whether each piece was reconcilable with the new defense story.

"If Anderson's memory was tainted by media coverage, and we buy the notion that the defendants were willing to confess to murder to avoid the rape charge, that really only leaves the bat," I concluded. "Someone put that bat in the Dumpster behind the Red Raccoon, and whoever it was had access to Percy Crenshaw's blood and fibers from his condo and Hanks's Jeep."

"If that's the only thing your case is hanging on, you don't have a case."

"Russ, I know I don't have a case anymore. I'm trying to figure out what happened. If the defendants were assaulting Tamara Lyons when Percy was killed—and it's starting to look like they were—how do we explain the bat? If we can figure that out, maybe we can figure out who actually killed Percy."

"It could be anyone, Sam. By the time that bat was pulled out of the Dumpster, the arrests were all over the news, including their addresses. Bad guy takes the weapon and drops it, sealing up the case. End of story."

"And the fibers?"

"Your vic probably had fibers from his condo somewhere on him, and those transferred onto the bat. The other fibers? You drew a bad break. They happened to look like the Jeep's carpet. Shit happens."

"So you really think they're innocent?"

"I don't think in those terms anymore. What matters is that you no longer have enough evidence to pursue the murder charge. Period." It had been six months, yet I was still surprised to have a supervisor who appeared to exercise fair judgment and sound reason. "It's good to set up the poly first, though. I assume under the circumstances the defendants are willing to sit tight for a few days."

"They're not going anywhere."

"What are you planning to do about Calabrese?"

So I hadn't been alone in my instincts. "If he got a confession from an innocent suspect—and there's even a question about the processing of the trace evidence—I don't think I have a choice."

"No, you don't. We pull him from MCT."

"Just temporarily though, right?"

"Well, at least until this is sorted out."

"What do you mean, 'at least'?"

"I mean, maybe he shouldn't be there at all. Even if you get an explanation for the fiber evidence being hinky, you've got a coerced confession from a kid who didn't do it."

"Kicking him entirely out of the unit seems a little severe."

"Out of the unit? Try out of the bureau. His credibility's shot. First, Lopez gets a look at his IA file, and now this. From here on out, you can bet this case will bite us in the ass every time he gets a statement. Besides, you said it yourself—he was totally out of control in there."

I paused, considering the other side of the picture, the one my father said I might never understand.

"Right, Sam?"

"From our perspective, yes. Not from theirs."

"Well, unless you want your ass on the line, too, ours is the perspective that matters. Are you calling his lieutenant?"

"Are you telling me that he'll definitely be kicked out? Not just from MCT, but from the bureau?"

"What do you want me to say, Sam? No, not *definitely*. You know how hard it can be to fire a cop. If it makes you feel better, when this shakes out, you won't be the one to make the decision. It'll be up to the bureau, and they'll probably talk to Duncan, who will consult with me. Now are you calling the lieutenant or not?"

"Like I said, I don't think I have a choice."

"Good, I thought I was going to have to fight you on that one."

There was a time when I would have met his expectations. And Chuck's.

"So that's all you can do for now," he said. "That, and break the news to Duncan."

"You won't call him for me again?"

"Are you kidding? Word to the wise: The last time I spoke to him, he was pretty damn grumpy."

I called Duncan's keeper, Donna, to check if he was available and headed downstairs to deliver the bad news.

Duncan was affable, at first.

"Thanks for coming by, Sam, but I don't think there's anything we need to cover here. The grand jurors got sucked in by Hamilton, and that's all there is to it. I talked to Selma Gooding.

She says the victim's mom was pretty shaken up but made a point of emphasizing how well you treated her. I've called the press in for a public statement at four. Do you want to stand with me for that?"

"Whatever you prefer."

"I don't think it will be necessary. Very good."

"I'm actually here about something else. The defendants in the Crenshaw case have come forward with an alibi of sorts for the time of the murder."

He was initially as incredulous as I was, until I explained how the defendants themselves had been fuzzy about their own timeline until Tamara cooperated.

"Christ, Kincaid, sometimes I think you let more people out of jail than you put in. Does anything ever go right on your cases?"

"Occasionally, sir, when the police arrest the right people."

"Touché. Well, all I can say is, what a cluster fuck. There's nothing at all in the Corbett kid's confession that can be corroborated? It all came from Calabrese?"

"Right."

"And you were there for the interrogation?"

"Yes, sir." He stared at me blankly. "I know, it was a screwup. I should have made Calabrese go back in and get more detail."

"So why didn't you?"

"What do you want me to say, Duncan? I told you, I know I made a mistake. It was late, we were tired, I chewed out Calabrese for his tactics, and I wasn't focusing on the content of the confession."

"And your boyfriend was there."

"Honestly, Duncan, I don't see how that's relevant." Arguing with Duncan on this point was pure biological reflex.

"You shouldn't think of yourself as one of the gang, Sam. Your job when it comes to the cops is to get in their faces when you need to, tell Calabrese to get the hell back into the box and get a confession that can be verified later if the defendant retracts it. I know you can do that—hell, I can't count the number of lawyers I've talked to who've been on the receiving side of one of your outbursts. But you want these guys to like you for some reason; maybe it's because they're Forbes's buddies. Will you at least think about that? Maybe we need to reconsider your decision to work cases with him."

"Fine," I said, realizing it was time for me to start facing my own concerns on this issue, as much as I hated hearing them voiced by someone else.

Duncan looked at me skeptically.

"I will think about it. I promise." I held up three fingers: scout's honor.

"All right. So when's this poly going to happen?"

"I told MCT to get it as soon as possible, but who knows." The few trained polygraphers in Portland have erratic schedules, and they insist on time to study the case and develop the decoy and material questions.

"Let's do what we can to keep this under wraps right now. Make sure the defense lawyers know we won't be happy if the story gets out before we've nailed it all down."

"What about Percy's family?"

"There's no need to tell them anything as long as we're in a holding pattern. Obviously, you can fill them in before we dismiss the charges, if that in fact occurs. And that won't be an easy conversation. We may have to face the reality that this case could be left unsolved."

"That seems overly pessimistic. The bureau can keep working it."

"Oh, I'm sure they will. But they better find a videotape of the murder if they want a conviction. Anyone we ultimately charge is going to point to the evidence we had against Corbett and Hanks and argue reasonable doubt."

I didn't think I could feel any worse about my failure to prevent this mess when I had the chance, but I was wrong.

By the time I got home, every channel was opening their six o'clock news broadcasts with the Hamilton case. Duncan really was the master of spin, proudly defending the decision to take a difficult case to the grand jury because it was "the right thing to do, even if we couldn't win it." The Chief of Police stood at Duncan's side at the lectern, nodding, then announced that the bureau was terminating Hamilton for cause and was prepared to defend its decision in the courts. Duncan had even brought in Selma Gooding for the press conference, as a friend of Delores Tompkins's family. She thanked the bureau, Duncan, and his "very able assistant, Samantha Kincaid," for trying to do what was right.

Once again, Duncan had not only avoided a potential land mine but had turned it around in his favor. Perhaps that was why, seventeen years into his tenure as District Attorney, no one even bothered running against him anymore.

I clicked off the television when I heard Chuck's key in the lock.

"Hey," I called.

"Hey."

I picked up the *New York Times* crossword from the coffee table and feigned concentration as he walked into the room.

"I heard about the grand jury's decision on Hamilton," he said. "When you didn't mention it, I assumed it had gone all right."

"Nope. I guess I was so preoccupied by Lisa's little bomb-shell that I forgot to tell you."

"How are you holding up?"

I shrugged my shoulders.

"I'm sorry, Sam. For what it's worth, it looked to me like a bad shooting. I should've spoken up for you with the guys."

"Did you get a chance to talk to Tamara Lyons?" We were back to cop and prosecutor talk.

"Yeah, I caught her at home, if you can call it that. She lives in that shitty trailer park on a hundred twenty-second."

East Portland had more than its fair share of shitty trailer parks, but I knew the one he was referring to. "And?"

"And . . . I think she's telling the truth," he said, obviously disappointed, plopping down on the sofa across from me. "When she was describing the rape, it definitely seemed legiti-mate. Plus, I could tell she still had mixed feelings about help-ing them out of their current predicament. Can't say I blame her."

Me neither.

"Then I gave her a ride to work. She didn't tell the Fred Meyer people what happened, so I said I was tracking down the timeline of a couple guys she knew. Anyway, two of her cowork-ers remember her saying she was going out to party with her ex-boyfriend and one of his friends. And I also talked to the girl that Tamara called Sunday night. I couldn't get a poly set until Tuesday, but so far it all adds up."

I nodded. "How's Mike?"

He pursed his lips. "Mad. Very mad. At you, specifically. They didn't just transfer him. They suspended him. And it looks like they're going to try to make it stick."

"I ran it by my office, Chuck. It was going to happen, whether I fought it or not. It's probably just temporary."

"Probably?" he said, clearly taken aback.

I couldn't bring myself to explain it to Chuck. Instead, I just shrugged my shoulders again. "Most likely. I don't know. It remains to be determined. And not by me. That kind of thing's over my head."

"Jesus, Sam. You could have at least called him yourself."

"After the way he's treated me lately? I haven't forgotten that comment he made about you walking out on me."

"He's sorry he said that."

"Well, he hasn't told me he's sorry."

"The two of you," he said, shaking his head. "Let's just say you've both got some seriously whacked tantrum-to-contrition ratios, and I'm stuck in the middle."

I moved to the sofa and stretched myself out next to him, hoping he'd accept the gesture.

"Hard day, huh?" he said.

"Hard week. I hate the way things have been with us."

"Yeah, me too. I should have listened when you said this was hard on you. Is Duncan pissed?"

"We wound up looking OK on Hamilton, so that was OK. But, yeah, he was upset about Crenshaw. He thinks you and I are a little too cozy," I said, wrapping my arms around his neck.

"He does, does he?"

"He says I would have sent Calabrese back in for a better confession if he hadn't been your partner."

"Ah. And what do you think about that theory?"

"I haven't decided."

He pushed a lock of hair that was tickling his face behind my ear. "You're good at what you do, Sam. The guy's lucky to have you in his office."

"I know, but I made a mistake."

"We all did. Christ, it was three in the morning. When was the last time Duncan tried working at that time of the night?"

"You always defend me."

274

"That's because I know you're perfect."

"And I feel the same way about you. And maybe that's why Duncan might have a point."

"So what are we supposed to do? Stop working together?"

"No, I'm just saying it's something we should both think about," I said, kissing his neck and rubbing my foot against his ankle.

"I see. And in this hypothetical world where we didn't work together, would I still get to live here with you? And do this to you?" He slipped his hands under my blouse and ran his fingertips along the small of my back.

"But of course," I said, pressing my body against him.

"Keep doing that, and I'll work property cases the rest of my life if that's what makes you happy."

Still, when neither of us made the next move, it was clear we had taken a step backward.

"I'm sorry I let Lisa get me all worked up with her conspiracy theories."

"No, I'm the one who's sorry." He paused before explaining. "I went back and talked to Matt again about his timeline Sunday night."

"Already?"

"Hey, I messed it up. I should have pulled his partner's call sheet too."

"What did he say?"

"That's what's bothering me. At first, everything seemed fine. Patrol was smoking, and he must have gone to another call from City Grill. Then, when I started pushing him to name the guys he took calls with that night, he freaked out on me, like I was an ass just for posing the questions. I tried explaining that I was trying to jog his memory, and he said something like *You're in IA mode.*"

"*Matt* said that? To *you*?"

"I know. Totally fucked up. When I called him out on it, he starts making weird comments like maybe Alison wasn't the only one with secrets."

"Like maybe *he* was fooling around too, on duty?"

"That's what he was suggesting, but he never even hinted at that when he seemed so upset about her and Percy before. I don't know. I mean, it's not like he killed Percy—"

"No, of course not."

"—but he seemed weird. So: bad news if Russ and Duncan start looking at him."

I was disappointed. "If he does come under the microscope—and hopefully it won't get to that—I assume he'd fess up to whatever he had going on the side."

"Let's just hope it doesn't get to that."

20

At two o'clock on Saturday afternoon, Heidi attended the monthly meeting of the Buckeye Neighborhood Association at the Kennedy School.

Even before the meeting was called to order, the room was filled with noisy talk about the grand jury's decision not to indict Geoff Hamilton. Who were these grand jurors? people wanted to know. How could they just let him go without at least having a trial? Was it true that the man was suing and that the bureau was going to fold, putting him back on the street with a gun and a badge? And why did the District Attorney let the officer testify? None of the men they knew was ever allowed to meet the grand jurors who weighed his fate.

Once the meeting was called to order, the president, a woman named Janelle Rogers, filled everyone in on the previous day's events, separating fact from fiction, reality from rumor. But it wasn't until the group's secretary, Selma Gooding, weighed in that the group seemed convinced. Selma spoke especially highly of the woman prosecutor on the case, Samantha Kincaid, emphasizing how wonderful she had been to Delores's mother. Heidi kept her opinion to herself.

At the end of the meeting, Janelle asked if anyone had any announcements or new business for the group. Heidi rose from the seat she had taken in the back of the room and introduced herself. "I'm a reporter from the *Oregonian*. I'm working on a story about drug enforcement in the Portland neighborhoods. If any of you are willing to stay afterward, I'd love to speak with you about what you've seen in the Buckeye district: drug activity in the streets, your experiences with the police department, that kind of thing."

"What's there to say?" an older man called out. "Everyone in Portland knows Buckeye's the place to go when you're looking for drugs. So we got lots of po-lice up there creating a *presence,* as they say. But when you got all them people driving around with money in their pockets, willing to spend it, and no good jobs, there's going to be other people willing to sell all those drugs no matter what you tell them."

Several in the group expressed their agreement with *Uh-huh, You said it,* and *Go on.*

"If they want to find drugs," one woman offered, "they should go on up to that Jay-J's. My niece tells me there's all kinds of dope going in and out of that joint. The owner Andre knows all about it, but the police don't do nothing because it's all the rage now with the rich white people from the west side."

Heidi wasn't the least bit surprised that the occasional drug deal went down at a club as popular as Jay-J's.

"But in your experience, do the police generally try to do something about drugs in Buckeye? One of the things I've been looking into is the fact that the police seem to do a lot of searches, but that doesn't necessarily translate into arrests."

There were knowing laughs in the room.

Selma Gooding spoke up. "It ain't nothing but a revolving door. We see these people hanging out on the corners—and at places like Jay-J's"—she added for the benefit of the previous speaker. "Sellers looking for buyers, buyers looking for sellers. The police come by and run them off, but they just come right on back. Even when someone gets arrested, you see them back out there—on the same corner—two hours later. Then you've got the police stopping innocent people all the time, searching them for drugs they don't have."

More sounds of agreement.

"But why do you think that happens? Are the police trying and failing, or do you think they intentionally let people go?"

At that point, the room broke out into cacophony. As people spoke and even yelled over one another, Heidi sensed a deep divide in the neighborhood between those who respected the police and wanted more help from them and those who saw the police as nothing more than state-backed gangsters. To Janelle Rogers, for example, the police appeared to be doing every-thing they could do. The problem was judges who cared more about the rights of criminals and overcrowded jails than her community's need to feel safe. As others told it, the police were haphazard in their enforcement, shaking down every young black man on the street, guilt be damned. One man went so far as to suggest that cops were simply stealing drugs and money off suspects for themselves.

Eventually, impatient participants began leaving the room, and Janelle Rogers announced a formal adjournment of the meeting, inviting those who wanted to continue the discussion to stay. Everyone left except Selma Gooding.

"Didn't realize you were opening up such a can of worms, did you?"

"Absolutely not. I'm sorry. I feel like I totally took over your meeting."

"Those kinds of things happen when people are angry and fed up and feel like nothing they ever do is going to change anything."

Heidi followed Selma as she walked to the parking lot. "I didn't mean to stir up a controversy. I wish there was something I could do to help."

"Well, there is," she said, unlocking the door to an older green Chevy Cavalier. "Once you figure out what you want to say, you can write a story about it. Did you know Percy Crenshaw?"

"I did. Not well, but he was very good to me at the paper. In fact, I was the one who packed his office up for his family. I talked to you when the boxes were ready."

Selma's face glowed with the recognition. "Well, bless your heart, darling. Yes, you are indeed the one who called me."

"So you knew Percy well?"

"I don't know what you mean by well, but, yes, I suppose we thought of him as a part of our little family up here. But the reason I asked you about him is that he did people an awful lot of good with the stories he'd write. Now, I know how things worked. He'd tend to come up with a good guy who wasn't so good, and a bad guy who wasn't so bad, and sometimes he'd jazz the whole thing up to get some attention. But the point is, he used his position to open people's eyes to things they were blind to. That's a mighty powerful thing. We're going to miss Percy dearly, and we are really going to miss the help he gave us too."

As Selma launched into specific stories Percy had written about race and class in Portland and about the Buckeye neighborhood in particular, Heidi noticed a police patrol car on Ainsworth slow as it passed the parking lot. Heidi did not want to look away from Selma while she was speaking, but as the car turned onto 33rd Avenue in front of the school, she noticed that the officer had wavy brown hair. Before she could tell if it was the same officer from Northeast Precinct, the car was gone.

"Is everything all right?" Selma asked. Heidi's attention had clearly drifted.

"Fine. Sorry. Actually, the story I was thinking of writing about drug enforcement was something that Percy was working on." Heidi began to describe it in the same vague terms she'd used with the district attorney and the neighborhood association, but then she realized that hadn't gotten her anywhere so far. This woman seemed trustworthy enough, and, besides, it wasn't like she could beat her to the story.

"Percy compiled evidence showing disparities in enforcement between Northeast Precinct and East Precinct." She explained how searches didn't necessarily turn into arrests in Northeast Precinct, particularly for African-American suspects.

"Well, isn't that a new twist?" Selma laughed, slapping the top of her car hood. "We're the ones getting the breaks? Don't hear that too often."

Heidi explained her theory that some police officers might be working with the dealers who controlled the crack trade in the neighborhood, filling out their stop-and-search cards as required but letting the drugs and the dealers stay on the streets.

"*Hhmph, hhmph*—so we get the short end of the stick after all. That would certainly explain why there seems to be more and more of that rock cocaine around here, no matter how much we call the police."

"Well, as you can imagine, I'm eager to put everything together, but it's difficult to prove. Did Percy ever talk to you about it? He had a couple of names written in his notes that seem to be connected. If I could just figure out who his sources were, maybe I could pick up where he left off."

"Oh, I don't know anything about that."

"He never mentioned it at all? I got the impression that he came to a neighborhood association meeting recently, either last month or maybe the month before."

"That's right, he most certainly did. Two months ago, he was here. He was fairly regular about attending, just to see what was going on. And, you know, that was one of the things everyone was talking about the last time he was here. About how you'd call up the police about some drug dealer outside your house. And it's just like people were telling you today: The police come, you see them with the boys spread-eagle on the car, and then, soon enough, you see those same boys out on the same corner just a couple hours later. We didn't know if the police were letting them go, or if the jail was too full, or what was going on. But, yeah, I guess I could see Percy looking into something like that."

"Do you know who he might have spoken to about it? He seemed particularly interested in two officers named Powell and Foster."

"Now I don't know who they are. Janelle, she works with the community policing officers, but I don't think those are their names. And Percy—well, he knew so many people. I can only imagine. I'm sorry I can't be more helpful, but Percy didn't get where he was by telling stories to an old woman like me."

"You don't seem so old to me," Heidi said. Just then, she saw the patrol car turn the corner onto Ainsworth, pausing again near the parking lot.

"Well, aren't you sweet?"

Heidi craned her neck to get a good look at the driver, but she was just too far away. This time, the car turned right on 33rd, heading away from the school.

"Selma, did you notice that officer loop around the school twice, just since we were standing here?"

"Welcome to the neighborhood, child."

Heidi watched Selma climb rigidly into her little car, a trail of exhaust following her down Ainsworth. On the drive back to northwest Portland, Selma's words echoed in Heidi's head. *Once you figure out what you want to say, you can write a story about it.* As Heidi was falling asleep that night, she thought about Selma's reverent tone as she spoke about the way Percy used journalism to help people. With just a few words, Selma had reminded Heidi why she'd chosen this low-paying, uncelebrated career path in the first place.

And, on Sunday morning, Heidi thought about Selma again when she opened the front door of her townhouse and found a story from that morning's *Oregonian* taped to it. According to a short In Crime sidebar, community activists Selma Gooding and Janelle Rogers had been shot in a late-night drive-by.

21

I had big plans for Sunday. After a long run, I'd gorge myself on dim sum at Fong Chong over a leisurely read of the *New York Times,* then top it all off with a large bucket of balls at the Westmoreland driving range. Perfect.

It started well enough. I woke to kisses on my neck from the back half of my bed spoon. Before long, Vinnie had been evicted to the hallway, and Chuck, in his own special way, was loosening up my back for my golf swing.

The start of the optimistic day came to an end, however, when I walked into the house after my run, damp with drizzle and sweat. Chuck was at the dining room table with a Coffee People java, black, and Vinnie unusually content at his feet. Progress.

"Hey, what was the name of that woman you were telling me about?"

"Um, a little more specificity please?" I kicked my shoes off at the door and pulled off my shell, stripping down to my sports bra and tights.

"The one you met at that thing about the Tompkins shooting, who called Duncan saying how great you were?"

"Oh. Selma Gooding. Salt of the earth, that woman."

"Then you need to see this." He pushed the open Metro section of the *Oregonian* across the table toward me and pointed to a short side column. The headline—Drive-by Shooting Targets Activists—leaped out, along with two familiar faces. Late Saturday night, an unidentified gunman had fired multiple bullets through the window of Selma Gooding's house, landing her and her houseguest, Buckeye Neighborhood Association president Janelle Rogers, in critical condition. Although the article was too brief to draw any conclusions, the mention of the women's activism against the neighborhood gangs and street crime suggested the possibility of retribution.

"You haven't heard anything?" I asked Chuck.

"Nothing. Pager's been quiet."

"Can you find out what's up?"

"Yeah, sure, no problem." He made a few phone calls from the kitchen as I eavesdropped, trying to ascertain from his *uh-huh*s and *yeah*s what was going on. A few minutes later, he told me that Selma was in serious but stable condition at Emanuel Legacy Hospital. He interrupted my sigh of relief with a second piece of news: Janelle Rogers was dead. An image of her offering me cookies and fruit salad flashed in my mind like a hologram.

Two detectives from the Gang Team had been assigned to the shooting. I pulled my DA call list from my briefcase and dialed Jessica Walters's home number. "Jessica, it's Sam Kincaid. Sorry to call you, but did the Gang Team happen to call you about a shooting last night? In Buckeye?"

"They paged me last night around one. Might not actually be a gang thing, but we're handling it for now. What's up?"

"I just wanted to make sure someone in our office had it. I've met both the victims, and—well, I guess I was shocked this morning when I read about the shooting."

"The younger one didn't make it, but the old lady's fine." Another shooting wasn't much to Jessica.

"Are you sure?"

"Yeah, the detectives tell me she's totally out of the woods. Don't worry, we've got it under control. You done interrupting my weekend, Kincaid?"

"Yeah. Sorry."

"Not a problem. Go run a marathon now or whatever the hell you do on Sunday." She hung up without saying goodbye.

I showered, dressed, and placed my fat bundle of a *New York Times* into a backpack, but I couldn't quite ready myself for the drive to Chinatown for dumplings. Instead, I called the front desk at Emanuel Legacy. After a few requests, I was connected to the ICU. The doctors had cleared Selma for visitors. The hours were from two to four in the afternoon. My sports watch was approaching one o'clock when I hung up.

"Chuck, do you mind if we skip the dim sum today?"

I found a small crowd of people standing in the hall outside Selma's hospital room. Among them was a familiar face—the young reporter from the *Oregonian,* the one with the nauseatingly sweet name.

"Holly?" I asked.

"Heidi, actually." I peeked over the shoulder of a woman blocking the entrance to Room 328. Selma was sleeping, tubes running from a bandage over her left arm. Importantly, though, I saw a rise and fall in her chest, a slight smile on her restful face.

"You know Selma too?" I asked.

"I think I need to tell you more about that story I was talking about."

An hour and a Jell-O pudding parfait later in the hospital cafeteria, I had heard Heidi Hatmaker's story. Percy's notes. The statistics. Officers Powell and Foster. The theory. Heidi's conversation with Selma in the Kennedy School parking lot just hours before the shooting. And, most importantly, the article taped to Heidi's front door that morning.

"Can you think of anyone—*anyone*—who might have left that article for you, just to make sure you saw it?" I asked. "Someone at the paper who knew you were talking to Selma about the story?"

"No. I didn't even know I would talk to Selma about the story until I went to the meeting yesterday. And as it turns out, she didn't know anything."

"You hadn't met Selma at all before yesterday?"

"Met her? No. I called her once—"

"About the story?"

Heidi shook her head. "After you guys searched Percy's office, Selma contacted the paper trying to get Percy's belongings for the family. I packed them up and then called her."

"And who knew about that?"

"Only the facilities manager. I think this has something to do with my talking to her yesterday about Percy's story. I saw that patrol car swing around twice in—literally—like three minutes. Then, just like that, Selma and Janelle get shot, and someone wants to make sure I know about it."

In a moment of frankness, Percy had told his parents that someone was following him. In hindsight, I should have taken the comment more seriously.

"Did you talk to Janelle about the story too?"

"No, just Selma."

"Let's try to find out what else Selma knows."

■　　■　　■

The patient was awake by the time we walked back to her room. "Well, look at the two of you," Selma said, brightening slightly with the addition of two new people to her get-well entourage. "How did I get so lucky to have all these visitors?"

She was doing her best to appear perky, but her friend's death hung heavily over the room. Heidi and I smiled uncomfortably at the sea of faces staring at us through the doorway, wondering who the hell we were and why we were visiting their beloved survivor.

"We both heard what happened last night and just wanted to wish you well and tell you we're so sorry about Janelle."

"Sweet, sweet Janelle. Only one shot hit me and, wouldn't you know it, my big old thigh came in handy for once. Poor little Janelle wasn't so lucky."

"Yes, well, I'm sorry for your loss. For all of you," I said, nodding to the others in the room. "I know it's not the best time, but when you've got a chance, Selma, I do want to ask you a few questions." She knew I was from the DA's office. I wouldn't have to be any more specific for her to infer my questions were investigative.

Within a few minutes, Selma had emptied out her hospital room, explaining she was tired but just fine. Once we were alone, I told her that someone had left a copy of the newspaper article about the shooting on Heidi's front door.

"Well, what in the world could that be about? Maybe one of your reporter friends making sure you saw the article?" she asked.

Heidi shook her head. "No one at the paper knows I talked to you yesterday."

"After you saw Heidi, did you talk to anyone about what she told you? About the story Percy had been working on?"

Selma didn't hesitate. "I talk to everyone about everything

all the time. Heidi told me Percy was working on something having to do with Buckeye, so I called around when I got home to see if anyone knew those police officers she brought up. What were their names?"

"Jamie Powell and Curt Foster," Heidi reminder her.

"Those are the ones. Funny how I knew those names yesterday right after we talked. Can't remember either one of them today. But I didn't find anything out for you. The downside of our little group is we tend to be pretty law-abiding. We see the community policing officers, and that's about it."

"Who did you talk to about them?" I asked.

"Just the group. You met a couple of them—Janelle, of course, and Reverend Byron. I called a couple more, but then, of course, they may have talked to people beyond that. We're grassroots that way."

I looked at Heidi. What was she thinking, disclosing the specific targets of her story with someone like Selma, plugged into the neighborhood network like an overloaded power strip?

"Why was Janelle over?"

"Oh, she was always just so intrigued by anything having to do with the neighborhood and the police. After I called her, she wanted to know if anyone else had heard anything, what Heidi was working on—just gossip, really."

"And Percy never mentioned anything at all to you about this story?" I asked.

"Like I told Heidi the other day, Percy would talk to us about our problems and show us his stories when they were done, but we never really knew exactly what he was up to until we saw it right there in black-and-white. Why are you asking me all this?"

"Just trying to make sure it doesn't have anything to do with what happened last night," I explained.

"The police sent someone from a special gang team to see me. They thought maybe all my days of chasing people off the stoop might have finally caught up with me. I hope that wasn't it. God help me if I did something to hurt Janelle."

Heidi and I exchanged a look across Selma's bed. No, this definitely had something to do with Percy's story.

I stepped into the lobby and used my cell phone to call Jessica again.

"My God, Kincaid. If you haven't noticed, I'm trying to enjoy my last few weekends of childless freedom here."

"Well, how about I help you out a little? Do you mind if I take the Buckeye shooting from you?"

"Let's see . . . do I mind if you do my work for me? Am I missing something?"

"I don't think it's a gang case." I told her about Heidi's theory of a conspiracy between Northeast Portland drug dealers and officers at the precinct. "Do you know anything about Jamie Powell or Curt Foster? Percy had their names down in his notes."

"Vaguely, but just as the initial responders to some gang cases. From there the detectives take over. You don't know them from DVD?"

"The names sound vaguely familiar, but nothing stands out. Anyway, the reporter talked to Selma about the story, mentioned Powell and Foster, and then Selma made a bunch of phone calls asking around about them, including one to Janelle Rogers. A few hours later, her house gets shot up, and Janelle's dead."

"Oh, come on, you think a cop would shoot some old women for poking around?"

"Maybe, or a freaked-out dealer. Maybe they meant to miss; I don't know."

"Or your Percy Crenshaw story could be totally unrelated. From what my detectives told me, there are some people in the 'hood who wouldn't mind losing the assistance of people like Ms. Gooding."

"I haven't mentioned the best part." I told her about the newspaper article on Heidi's door.

"OK, now that *is* a little weird."

"Uh-huh."

"You really don't mind taking the case?"

"It makes sense that I should." Briefly, I told her about the disintegration of my case against Corbett and Hanks. "MCT's going to have to look at Percy's murder again anyway, and this could be part of the big picture." Lisa Lopez had suggested Matt York as a suspect because he had motive, access to Hanks's Jeep in the impound lot, and the kind of knowledge suggested by an evidence-laden bat planted in a suspect's neighborhood. The same could be said of Powell and Foster.

"Fine with me," Jessica said. "I'm warning you, though. We haven't found a single witness yet. It's starting to look like just another Buckeye misdemeanor."

I had heard the term before around the Gang Unit. When one gangbanger shoots another, the only witnesses tend to be still other gangbangers who have their own ideas about the right way to identify and punish wrongdoers. As a result, deputies in the Gang Unit get used to pleading out their cases, big-time.

"Hopefully, if I follow the trail on Percy's story, we'll find our shooter."

"And maybe Percy's killer. You'll leave a message for the boss?"

"No problem."

I called Duncan's frequently checked voice mail immediately to make sure I didn't forget. Only the unit supervisors are entrusted with Duncan's pager number, and they know better than to use it except for a catastrophic emergency.

My next call was a little tougher. As I dialed the home number for the Yorks, I wondered if there was a tactful way to question a woman whose marriage was falling apart and whose husband had been treated as a possible murder suspect. Just my luck; the betrayed husband answered.

"Matt? It's Samantha Kincaid." I felt like I had to say something before asking for Alison. "I can't imagine what the last week has been like for you. I hope you understand—"

"Jealous husband's always a possibility," he observed bluntly.

"Well, never a real possibility in this case." I was struggling for some other consolation, but Matt apparently didn't want to hear it.

"What's up, Sam?"

"I was actually calling for Alison."

"May I ask what it's about?"

"Something has come up on the case. I wanted to see if she might know anything about it. You know, from talking to Percy." Yikes, this was worse than I imagined.

"I see. Um, I guess it's up to her." He must have hit the mute button. A full minute went by before Alison picked up.

"Hello?"

"Hey. Matt told you why I was calling?"

"Sort of."

"I'm tracking down a story Percy was working on. Did Percy ever say anything to you about suspecting police officers of being involved in drug traffic?"

"No. Doesn't sound familiar."

"He never mentioned it to you?"

"No. It wasn't that kind of a thing. Not a lot of talking, you know?"

"Anything about Officers Jamie Powell or Curt Foster?"

She lowered her voice. "Do you know the position you're putting me in right now? I can't exactly give you the details, but it was only a few times in a few weeks. He never told me anything about his stories. Now, please, just leave us alone."

"I'm sorry, Alison. I—"

"Goodbye, Sam. Tell Chuck I said hello."

I closed my phone, ashamed. Percy didn't get where he was by sharing the facts he dug up with other people, yet I had called Alison anyway. Just because I could.

Selma Gooding and Janelle Rogers had already paid the price for being dragged into this story. I knew I could decipher a few notes in a reporter's book and do it without hurting the innocent people around him even more. I just needed to think.

From memory, I dialed the cell number of my favorite sergeant in the Drug and Vice Division.

"Yo, what's up in the big MCT? Have you forgotten about us little people yet?"

"Tommy, I just saw you two weeks ago in the pit." Thanks to similar eating habits, Tommy Garcia and I run into each other frequently in the food court at the mall next to the courthouse. And every time he hassles me about my promotion into the big leagues.

"Yeah, but you never call me anymore."

"Until just now. How much do you know about what's going on with street-level crack sales up in Northeast Precinct?"

"I know we're not finding as much of it as we want to."

"How so?"

"The whole year, we just haven't been pulling as much crack off the streets as we used to, although North and Northeast Portland are the main districts for crack, at least traditionally."

"Maybe it's just fallen out of favor. More heroin and meth?"

"Yeah, right," he said, laughing. "You and I both know that crack doesn't fall out of favor until you take so much of it off the streets that it's no longer a cheap high. And in those long-ass joint task force meetings with the Feds, they keep telling us that, if anything, the amount of crack coming into the entire Pacific Northwest has been going up."

"So the question is, with all the policing we throw at street-level drug sales, why aren't you finding the rocks?"

"Precisely. It's frustrating as hell. Now that I've enlightened you, are you going to tell me what's up?"

"How much do you care if a few cops get pissed at you?" Tommy was familiar enough with my penchant for understatement to know that *a few* meant *a lot* and *pissed* meant *bloodthirsty*.

"I forgot how much trouble you cause, Kincaid. Let's see, are these angry cops going to be good cops?"

"No."

"Then I don't give a shit."

"Good. Meet me at Northeast Precinct in an hour. And I might have a reporter there."

"You're fucking with me, right?"

"Serious as a heart attack," I said, flipping my phone shut. From what I could tell, Heidi Hatmaker was going to snoop around with or without official cooperation. Given that her last attempt at amateur sleuthing had gotten Selma shot, I'd rather keep an eye on her myself.

I made one last phone call and then found Heidi in the lobby, freeing a Snickers bar from the slot of the vending machine. "Late breakfast," she explained.

A woman after my own heart. "Let's go, little miss Jessica Fletcher."

"Who?" she asked through her first enormous bite of candy bar.

I shook my head. "You don't watch nearly enough television."

"Where are we going?"

"First, we're getting some lunch." I had skipped my Sunday dumplings, and a pudding parfait plus machine-issued hospital food just wasn't going to cut it. "Then you're going to meet some cops."

Heidi and I grabbed sandwiches at the Tin Shed Café; then she followed me to the precinct in a cute little BMW that looked like something Chuck would want to take apart and put back together again.

When we arrived, Alan Carson was waiting for us in the lobby, hair still stiffly in helmet formation. When you only know one Internal Affairs detective, it's not hard to decide whom to call.

"I didn't think you'd get here that quickly."

"I told you, if there's one thing we can do well at IA, it's organize some files," he said, holding up two legal-sized manila folders. "Pulling a couple of them for you was the least I could do after you jumped into Frist's shoes on Hamilton."

"That went real well until it fell apart."

"Hey, you went for it; sometimes that's all we can do." He lowered his voice, even though the lobby was empty at the moment except for us. "Trust me, I know it's not easy being on the other side of a case from a cop."

A few minutes later, Tommy Garcia arrived wearing an Oregon Ducks sweatshirt, jeans, and his always-perfect white smile. "You're off duty?"

"Yeah, finally got rid of Sundays. But for you, anything. If it pans out, I'll get some OT, right?"

Garcia, Carson, and I showed ID to the front receptionist as I asked for an open room. "She's with me," I said, pointing to Heidi. I made a point of saying hello to a couple of familiar faces in the hallways once we were buzzed inside. Good. Let word seep out that the new crime reporter was running around with DVD, IA, and a DDA. The more acronyms, the hotter the action.

I pulled the blinds in the interrogation room, and we got down to business. I introduced Heidi and asked her to explain the theory she had pieced together from Percy's notes. It started with the fact that cops in Northeast Precinct were stopping and searching black suspects, but then arresting them at lower rates than other suspects. Heidi initially thought Percy was looking into racial profiling or another form of discrimination.

"But then," she explained, "I found out that sergeants review the patrol officers' stop-and-search statistics to gauge their work effort. I also learned—as I'm sure you already know—that different racial cliques control different drugs. When I put it all together, I realized cops might be stopping and searching as required but then underarresting when it came to crack cocaine. Maybe their allegiances were somewhere other than the war on drugs. After I had a theory in place, I realized that two names in Percy's notes—Powell and Foster—weren't street names at all, like I had figured, but the names of two officers in Northeast Precinct. So I started looking for more information to nail down the theory."

"Like what?" Tommy asked.

"I came here and read a couple weeks of reports. I went to a Buckeye Neighborhood Association meeting yesterday and then talked to Selma Gooding afterward, in the parking lot."

"Now Selma's in the hospital," I said, "a friend of hers is dead, Heidi's getting creepy stories fastened to her front door, and the four of us are going to figure out what to do about it. And, Heidi, there's one thing I haven't told you yet. You're obviously going to have the lead on this once we put it together, but I swear to God, if you go to print before we're ready, I'll never talk to you again, and I'll make sure no one else does either."

"I can live with that."

Trusting her was the right thing to do. She was scared enough over the shooting, but she needed to know the extent of the danger she was looking at.

"I found out Friday that the defendants charged with killing Percy have an alibi," I told her. "We're still checking it out, but it looks solid. That means we're back to square one."

I saw a swallow in Heidi's throat and a fearful blink of her eyes as she realized the implication of what I was telling her.

"Heidi, you need to watch your back. No more running around the city asking questions and stirring up neighbors. You get the story through us, not on your own."

"Trust me. After what I've seen today, that's just fine."

"OK. Tommy, does this sound like something that fits in with what you've seen on the drug side?"

"There's no doubt we've been stumped by some of the patterns. Still lots of meth, pot, heroin, X, you name it, but crack arrests are down."

"And, before today, any theories?"

He folded his arms in front of him. "Depends on who you ask. Some guys write off the Feds as having their heads squarely up their asses and insist there must be less crack coming into the city, with other drugs filling the void. I for one don't put any stock in that, because the price of a rock's still steady on the street. Cheaper, if anything."

"So no crack shortage," I said.

"No way. Personally, I chalked it up to those stupid stop-and-search cards. The way I saw it, if a guy's afraid of looking like a racist, he might think twice about following his instincts when the target's black. If we have enough guys doing that, given how the market's divided up, down go the crack busts and up go the other busts. Problem with that, though, is exactly what you pointed out." He looked to Heidi.

"The numbers show that cops are doing the stop-and-searches and filling out the cards. But they're not arresting."

"Right. That leaves the theory that the black guys have just gotten better at this. They hide the dope behind a bush while they're dealing, or they use a kid across the street to hold product and shuttle it deal-by-deal on a signal. Even if we bust someone on a hand-to-hand, the product stays protected. You never see that kind of stealth with meth and X because, honestly, white people don't need to worry as much about getting stopped in the first place."

"And what about Heidi's theory?"

Tommy's eyes grew big, and he sighed before speaking. "Well, I hate to think that's what we're looking at. But if Percy Crenshaw's writing down the names of cops in his book before he gets killed, and now two women have been shot. . . ."

"So let's assume Heidi's right. If cops were taking money to look the other way, who'd be paying it? Not the kids on the corners. They don't have the kind of cash it takes to get to an officer, and the pattern's too widespread."

"It's got to be someone big. But part of the reason I can't give you a definitive answer on who the key players are is because the fewer street people we pop, the less chance we've got flipping someone to work our way up the chain. We've got a theory, though—" Tommy cut himself off.

"And?" I prompted.

He looked at Heidi, then at me again. Heidi caught the drift. "I'm not going to write a story exposing law enforcement's plans on an ongoing investigation. That's not how I operate."

Tommy looked at me, and I nodded. He went on. "We've heard a lot about a guy named Andre Brouse. Thirty years old. He was a street kid up here back in the day, but on paper at least he's become mister legitimate businessman. Owns a night-club called Jay-J's."

"I've heard of it," I said. Grace was more connected to the club scene than I. According to her, the downtown crowd headed over to North Portland in the wee hours for Jay-J's thumping blend of hip-hop, rap, and world music. The fact that Jay-J's was willing to pour after the better-known bars stopped serving also helped.

"A lady at the Buckeye meeting said there were rumors about drugs there," Heidi volunteered. "She said the owner knew about it, too."

"And rumors are pretty much all we've got on Brouse other than a bunch of liquor law violations, which we've ignored so far. Let him think he's still off the radar."

"What makes you think he's dealing?" Alan asked.

"Word on the street, to start. He's surrounded by an armed entourage and a ton of cash. And, by all appearances, he had the money before the club, and no one knows where the money came from. Some people say it's from his dad. I guess his daddy was a one-hit wonder—one of those songs where they spelled some stupid word out in letters. Anyway, we don't buy it. His mom moved him up here alone from California as a kid, and they were poor. Plus, rumor is, he'll smack the shit out of any-one who even asks him about that song."

"So the story about the father might be something put out there to make him seem legit?" I asked.

"Exactly, like the old-school gangster's sanitation manage-ment business. He looks like a law-abiding bar owner, but meanwhile he's sitting on top of the city's crack trade. Plus, from what we hear, the network's totally out of control. Too many kids trying to climb too fast. Supposedly there's infighting among the managers who sit just above the corner dealers, all battling for Andre's attention. The problem is, these guys aren't Andre's age, and they're not as smooth. Andre's thirty years old, has never spent a day in prison as an adult, and has never taken a bullet. His people? They're thugs, and the way they get attention is by thugging. The Gang Unit's been hopping with unsolved shootings. We hadn't heard about cops in the picture, but if Brouse is as smart as he seems to be, it's possible."

"Which brings us to Powell and Foster. What do we know about them?" I asked Carson.

"Well, I pulled their rookie file photos," he said, tossing copies of two photographs across the table to Heidi. "Do either of these men look like the officer who watched you read the reports?"

"Yeah, that one," she said, pointing to the darker of the two men.

"Curt Foster."

"He was the one whose reports were most out of whack," Heidi explained. "Lots of arrests but no crack cases."

He opened the two personnel files in front of him. "Now these I can't let you have access to," he said to Heidi.

"City rules," I explained. "Any external releases have to go through the City Attorney."

"You know what? I'm just going to go home." She stood and started pulling on her rain jacket.

"No, it's just the personnel records," I said.

"Seriously, given the state of Percy's notes when I found them, I'm just happy to see the three of you work out the rest of it from here. And in exchange for keeping my mouth shut, I trust you to give me the story when you're done. Besides, I'm scared out of my pants right now. Honestly, I'm tempted to wash my hands of this and become a day-care teacher or something."

"Don't do that," Tommy said. "Little kids are far more dangerous."

Before she left, I walked her to the hallway. "You'll be careful, yes? You've got my cell number?"

"I'm fine. In fact, a guy who's safe and protective has been trying to call me all day. The thought of dinner, movie, and a very large companion sounds pretty good right now."

After she left, Alan, Tommy, and I pored over Foster's and Powell's personnel records. Neither one of them was what you'd call a star. Mediocre scores on the civil service entrance exam. None of the special letters of recognition that come when a supervisor spots the promise of advancement through the ranks. Powell had early run-ins several years ago with suspects, marked by a disproportionate number of resisting-arrest complaints by—and excessive-force complaints against—him. Recently, though, he seemed to have mellowed out, making fewer arrests than the typical patrol officers on his same shifts and beats. Was it the laziness that often sets in with experience or something more nefarious?

"Wait, here's something," Carson announced. "Two years ago, Powell was one of the last remaining moonlighters. Threatened with discipline, settled when he voluntary terminated his non-PPB employment." Unlike a lot of departments, Portland's bureau prohibits officers from accepting independent gigs as private security. Roughhousing on their off-hours creates too many questions about the city's liability. "All it says here is a tavern at 4112 Coving."

Tommy Garcia smiled and smacked the table. "Otherwise known, boys and girls, as Jay-J's."

I grabbed Foster's file from Garcia, paging through it

quickly, hoping to find the club mentioned there as well. Instead, I read with surprise the name of a young officer with whom Curt Foster was partnered five years ago, when the bureau could still afford two-man patrols. It was a piece of evidence I couldn't ignore, as much as I wanted to.

"Alan, I need one more file. I just sent it back to IA on Thursday."

22

That night, hidden away with Vinnie in the small cluttered room I call my home office, I was still studying the three IA files Alan Carson had entrusted to me. I had learned nothing new about Curt Foster or Jamie Powell, but I was, unfortunately, piecing together new information about Chuck's partner.

When Mike Calabrese joined PPB seven years ago, he started out in Northeast Precinct, partnered with Curt Foster. According to Carson, Calabrese was brought in when the bureau, struggling to meet hiring needs, created a laundry list of exceptions to the usual requirements of civil service exams and background checks.

Calabrese was hired under an exception for lateral hires, which explained the personnel forms I had neglected to photocopy for Lopez. In lieu of the usual procedures, the precinct commanders could rely on a review of the candidate's personnel file and a recommendation from a supervising officer in the transferring jurisdiction.

I wasn't surprised when Carson told me that this short-lived experiment was wracked with political, familial, and personal patronage. But Mike's file was more troubling than the hiring of someone's Gomer Pyle nephew. For starters, there was no documentation whatsoever from NYPD. Carson insisted that Mike's file should have contained a complete copy of his former records.

Even more troubling, I had done my own investigation into Patrick Gallagher, the"officer with knowledge" upon whom the precinct commander had relied when he hired Mike. An Internet search of news articles in New York about Patrick Gallagher turned up years of references to a lieutenant consistently assigned to the Internal Affairs Bureau of the NYPD.

I seriously doubted that Mike worked IAB in New York. He wouldn't have had enough years on the job by then, it didn't suit his temperament, and I would have heard about it. But somehow an IAB lieutenant had "knowledge" about Mike and had helped ship him out to Portland.

I dug my old Rolodex from the back of my desk drawer, the one I'd used at the U.S. Attorney's Office in New York. I dialed the number for Ed Devlin, an NYPD sergeant who was my local police contact when I was a federal prosecutor. He had been close to retirement even then, so I was surprised when I heard his familiar voice on the outgoing message.

"Ed, it's Samantha Kincaid from the U.S. Attorney's Office, back in the day. I'm at the DA's Office in Oregon now, and a question has come up about one of our officers who used to be NYPD. I need you to get me the scoop." I left Mike's name, NYPD badge number, and my home phone, hoping he was still working graveyards.

As I tried to make sense of the gaps in Mike's file, I thought about the lessons I learned on the Hamilton case. It's not easy to prosecute cops. It's not even easy to fire them. If Mike had trouble in New York—but not enough trouble to lose the support of his union—was it that farfetched to imagine the city settling the case by finding him a place with another bureau, one desperate for new hires?

I heard a tap on the door and, before it opened, quickly pushed Mike's file beneath a stack of old legal magazines I kept telling myself I'd read someday.

"Good game. You sure you can't take a break?"

"Not quite yet. I'd rather wait just a little longer until my brain dries up completely. Then I can enjoy the rest of the night."

"Okay. I ordered Pizzacata, half gourmet for you." Chuck's a pepperoni guy, I'm goat cheese and artichoke. "Want me to bring it up when it gets here?"

"Hopefully I'll be done by then."

He started to leave, then turned around. "Are those IA files?"

Uh-oh. Chuck knew I was working on something Percy had been researching. I had mentioned Heidi, the Buckeye shooting, and the newspaper article. Beyond that, I hadn't gotten specific.

"Yeah, that story Percy was working on involved two patrol officers at Northeast Precinct."

He reached over my shoulder and separated the files to see the names on the tabs. "Oh, shit. Curt Foster was Mike's partner back on patrol for a while."

I didn't want to lie by feigning surprise, but I didn't want to get into this, either. Instead, I said nothing.

"You should call him. Mike didn't like that guy at all."

"Really?"

"Yeah. I don't know the details, but it came up a few times when he said how glad he was to get out of patrol."

"All right."

"You want his number?"

"I've got it somewhere."

"Babe, you and Mike can't stay angry forever, and it's stupid for you to spend all night on files when Mike can give you the skinny. Let's call him together," he said, picking up the phone on my desk and starting to dial.

I cut the call with the click of a finger on the phone base. "Chuck, wait."

"Sam, c'mon, I'm just trying to help you. Why won't you—?" He replaced the phone in its cradle. "Is that another IA file?" he asked, looking beneath my pile of magazines.

I looked at him, trying to figure out the best way to tell him what I needed to say.

"Whose file is it, Sam?"

I bit my lower lip and reached for his hand. He pulled it away. "Is that what I think it is?"

I unearthed the file and extended it toward him. He looked at it as if it were food I'd stolen for him from a child. "Why do you still have that? You've been up here with that for hours while I'm watching football and calling in a pizza order?"

"Chuck, I'm sorry. His name came up because he was Foster's partner." He also happened to be the detective who extracted Todd Corbett's murder confession—the confession that closed off any suspicions that Percy's killing was related to a story. "I had to at least look at it, and I didn't want to upset you."

"When are you ever going to get it? I only get upset with you when you isolate yourself from me. You never trust me. You never trust anyone. First, it's Matt York. Now it's Mike. You look at these guys—my friends, *our* friends—like they're anyone else in your caseload, like you don't even know them."

"That's not true, Chuck. Do you think I want those names to turn up on our cases? But am I supposed to just ignore the fact that Matt's wife was sleeping with Percy and Matt himself happens to have a bunk alibi? I've been busting my ass all day to prove that Foster and Powell did it instead, and every second, in the back of my mind, part of my motivation has been to clear Matt. Now it turns out that the detective who coerced Corbett's confession in the first place happens to be connected to Foster. And you should see this, Chuck. Mike's hire was very strange. Do you know anything about why he left New York?"

The look on his face cut straight to my heart. "Have you even stopped to think about the position you're putting me in?"

"Of course. Why do you think I put the file where you couldn't see it?"

He shook his head. "That's your version of caring about me? Doing exactly what you want but hiding it? Now that I know, what am I supposed to do?"

"Well, you certainly can't tell Mike about it. It's a pending investigation."

"An investigation by whom, Sam? By you. So you can be the one to call it off."

"OK, I shouldn't have even called it an investigation. I just want to make sure I'm not missing something."

"You're not, Sam. I know Mike. You know Mike. And you should have enough faith in him—and in my judgment about him—to know that you don't need to go down that road."

"All I'm doing is asking some questions."

"You are so naive sometimes. A DA and IA don't just 'ask questions.' Mike's already suspended, and now you've got IA looking at him for corruption? Once your name even comes up with something like that, your reputation? It's over."

"Well, it's pretty much over for Mike anyway, no matter what I do."

"What the hell does that mean?" When I didn't respond immediately, he jumped back in. "I knew it. I knew it on Friday when you said this was 'probably' only temporary, but I gave you the benefit of the doubt. Are you telling me that my partner's out? For good?"

"I don't know that for sure. It depends how this all falls out."

"You mean it depends on whether your boss needs a scapegoat."

"That's not fair, Chuck. He's certainly more responsible for this cluster fuck than either of us."

"No. Todd Corbett and Trevor Hanks are the ones responsible."

"Fine, yes, to some extent, but they didn't kill Percy. I'm trying to find out who did, and I'd appreciate it if you wouldn't criticize me for that."

"I'm criticizing you for running over Mike's career in the process. Give his file back to IA and leave him out of it, before you get him kicked out of the bureau entirely."

"I can't do that."

"Then I can't know about this and keep it from Mike. He's my partner."

"And I'm your girlfriend."

"And I'm your boyfriend, Sam. Jesus, these things go both ways. For once, why can't you be the one to have a little faith in *me* and make an adjustment?"

"I can't believe you're asking me to do that. Are you saying you're going to leave me if I don't ignore my job?"

"You really want me to put it in those terms, don't you? It's always about whether I'll forgive you, whether we're over. Fine, yes, that's what I'm saying. I will see you differently if you won't trust me on this."

"I do trust you. But we have different jobs. I have to—"

"I can't do this anymore. I'm sorry. If I stay here, we're both going to say things we regret."

He headed for the bedroom. "Chuck, please don't leave."

"Why not? You do it all the time." He was throwing things haphazardly into a gym bag. "Maybe I'm the one who gets to have a temper tantrum for once and say we'll work it out tomorrow."

Following him down the stairs, I asked where he was going.

"Mike's." Then, before I could say anything else, he was slamming the front door. As I heard the Jag's engine rev, I knew there was something wrong with me. The words I would have spoken if he had stayed a second longer? *Are you going to tell Mike?*

I made three back-to-back calls to his cell. No answer. I had never seen him this angry before. Then I realized there was something worse than anger. Maybe this time I had actually blown it. Maybe he was finally through putting up with my shit.

A knock at the door stole my attention. I wondered hopefully if perhaps Chuck had come home and forgotten his keys. I looked out the glass pane in the door. The pizza boy. Crap. I let him in, then went hunting for my purse. Where the hell was my purse?

I retraced my steps from the precinct. I must have left it in the car. And, of course I had parked my car in the street so as not to block Chuck in the driveway. If he ever did come back, I'd start blocking him.

I slipped my bare feet into a pair of Chuck's tennies by the door, dashed to the car, and unlocked the passenger-side door. If my purse had been there, it was gone now. I checked the backseat. Not there either. As I was shutting the door, I looked up and saw that my driver's-side window was open. No, it was broken. And my CDs were all gone. And there was glass every-where.

Portland and property crime. This was the fourth time my car had been prowled since I moved back from New York. The pizza boy was eyeing me suspiciously from the door.

I ran inside, retrieved a new book of checks from my office, and finally convinced him with my DA badge and repeated gestures toward my smashed-in car window to accept it.

I did my best in the rain to clean the glass from my car and the street, move the Jetta into the driveway, and catch an old tarp in the door to block the open window. Back inside, I called the bureau's nonemergency number to report the break-in. Then I called Grace, who immediately offered to stay with me. When I hung up, I sat at my dining room table with Vinnie in my lap, waiting, and stared at my large pizza going cold as I picked the artichokes off one by one.

The sound of Grace's TT pulling into the driveway instantly comforted me. I met her at the door.

"How are you holding up?"

"Piss-poorly. I never should have let myself need another person like this. You know, people can say they won't leave, and it doesn't mean shit. He left and now I'm here, a complete and total wreck."

I could tell from the expression on her face that I must have looked absolutely miserable. She hugged me. "You guys will be fine. You need an occasional shit day so you don't stop appreciating all the good ones."

I poured myself a glass of wine and asked her if she wanted to violate her purification by joining me in a soggy cold pizza.

"As appetizing as that sounds, I already ate. Half glass of wine, though. So where are the cops?"

"So that's why you came over," I said, trying to smile. "I called, but it's a low priority."

"Fuck that. You're a DA, and your car gets broken into right in front of your house? They should at least take a report."

True. Just as they had the three other times. I had wondered myself about the timing. Heidi talks to Selma. Selma talks to Janelle. Selma and Janelle get shot. Heidi talks to me. My car gets broken into. On the other hand, I was the one who'd been stupid enough to leave my purse in the front seat, the Portland equivalent of a BREAK ME sign on the car window.

I called the nonemergency number again. "I entered it in the queue, ma'am," the dispatcher explained, "but I can't guarantee when they'll get to it. If the calls are busy tonight—"

"I understand."

When I called an hour later and got the same response, I took matters into my own hands. I left a message for the shift lieutenant at the precinct asking him to at least have a desk officer call me so I could file a report over the phone.

By the time I finally hit the sheets around one, I still hadn't heard a peep. Apparently Friday morning's traffic ticket was just the beginning of the fuck-you I was getting from PPB. Throughout the night, as I woke up to each quiet house shift and tree branch squeak, I questioned the wisdom of conducting my little meeting at Northeast Precinct.

At eight-thirty-five the next morning, Alice Gerstein informed me that two detectives were waiting in my office. "I told them to go to the lobby, but one of them insisted you wouldn't mind."

I found Alan Carson sitting quietly in one guest chair, reading the paper, and Tommy Garcia in the other, helping himself to my Stanford Law School alumni magazine, complete with acknowledgments of recent donations.

"Hundred-dollar donation to the alma mater, huh? You got some money for me too?"

"Last time I checked, Starvin' Marvin, you made more than I did once you figure in OT."

"So did you take care of whatever you needed to do last night?" Carson asked.

Did I? "No, not really. But we need to make a decision anyway, don't we?"

Here was our problem. Usually we're at an advantage when we've got multiple conspiring suspects. Bring them all in. Tell them whoever flips first gets the deal. Wonder Twin Powers, Activate. Form of: a cooperating witness. That wasn't going to work here. Our suspects were cops, and we didn't have enough evidence to hold them in the event they both called our bluff and held strong.

And, as it turned out, time was of the essence. "You saw this, didn't you?" Carson held up the front page of the Metro section.

I hadn't had a chance to bring in the newspapers, let alone read them. Dan Manning broke the story. Trevor Hanks's father, the distinguished Henry Hanks, was bitching up a storm about the continued detention of his son, insisting that the police had verified his "alibi." So much for keeping quiet. Mr. Hanks, of course, didn't bother disclosing details about the so-called alibi, or the fact that it would still land his son in prison for the next eight and a half years.

"I can't get a break. I was going to suggest setting up surveillance on Foster and Powell, but if they know we're taking a new look at Crenshaw—"

"Way too risky," Carson said.

Once again, I wondered if we'd been too bold barging through the precinct yesterday with Heidi. I had wanted to stir things up, but now I'd boxed us in. We had to act soon.

"What about a wiretap at Jay-J's?" Carson suggested.

"Man, if we had probable cause, don't you think we would've done that by now?" Tommy said. "No, we need to figure out which one of these dudes is likely to cooperate and bring him in. I pulled their drug stats from the last year. Foster's by far the worse. Somehow this guy is managing to work the single largest crack market in the state, but keeps stumbling on pot, meth, acid, heroin, powder cocaine, Drano, whatever. He's got some crack cases, but hardly any black kids. He manages to find the only Ecuadorans and Mexicans who've been bold enough to try to crack that market."

"So to speak," I added. "OK, so here's the question: Do we have enough to confront them? And, if so, which one?"

"There's a third way," Carson offered. "We go to Brouse. Give him the deal to hand us the cops."

"This guy's kidding, right?" Tommy scoffed. "Brouse is a gangster. If anyone did a drive-by on Selma, it was one of his people, not a couple patrol officers."

I didn't have the energy for the debate they were having over who was worse: the organized criminals or the cops who turned a blind eye. Garcia finally won when he convinced Carson that, from everything he knew about Andre, he'd never cut a deal.

Then Carson made a suggestion that caught me off guard. "What if we go after Calabrese? He's pretty much toast with the bureau over that Corbett confession, but if he's still hanging on to hopes of staying in MCT, we could use that. He might be able to give us something to flip Foster."

It was just as Chuck had warned. What had started as a temporary break for Mike from MCT had rapidly become part of the bureau's institutional memory. Calabrese's one mistake— the one Chuck and I were also a part of—had rendered him a bad apple, to be thrown out or traded on, however we saw fit. I wanted to defend Mike to Carson, to say there was no way he could possibly be involved in any of this. I heard Chuck's words from last night: *You should have enough faith in him—and in my judgment about him—to know.* So why didn't I know?

Instead, it was Tommy who held Carson back. "That's not something I want any part of. Not until you show me something concrete against him."

"Tommy's right," I said. "We're stretching for evidence as it is, and what we've got points to Powell and Foster."

In the end, we realized it was a draw. Both Powell and Foster had their names in Percy's book. Both had been on duty when he was killed, but without any documented call-outs to provide an airtight alibi. Foster had the arrest pattern that most obviously needed explaining. He had been the one to eyeball Heidi at the precinct. But Powell had a direct connection to Brouse through Jay-J's. The sad truth was, we had little against either one. Just a shared gut instinct.

Finally, it fell to Carson, with his experience convincing bad cops to do the right thing, to make the decision. "We go after Powell. He's married with four kids. Foster's a bachelor."

The implications were immediate. You could threaten either one of them with an IA investigation. But you could threaten Powell with his family. No job means no benefits and no pension. It was cold, no doubt, but was it any worse than the games we play in every case to get cooperation?

"Fine, let's do it. How long do you need?" I asked Carson.

"I need to run it by my lieutenant. We should aim for picking him up by two. His shift starts at four, and we want to catch him at home. It's more unsettling, and if we're lucky the family will be there. He won't want to get too loud."

"I need to run it by Duncan too, but let's assume it's a go."

I checked my voice mail once they left. A bunch of junk that could wait, a message from Lisa Lopez emphasizing that it wasn't her client who'd blabbed, and one from Duncan scolding me for "letting the story get out." Apparently I was supposed to tape the defendants' mouths shut.

I didn't hear the voice I was hoping for. I dialed into the voice mail of my stolen cell phone. Nothing. While I was in the system, I changed my outgoing message: *Hey, it's me. If you get this message, you've dialed a cell that now belongs to whatever desperate lowlife broke into my car last night. I'll try to check messages, but you might want to try my other numbers instead. Have a better day than I'm having. 'Bye.*

When I hung up, I felt myself start to cry. But then I did what I always do when that happens at the office. I pushed the pain down as far as I could, forcing myself to focus on work. Healthy, I know.

Once I gave the requisite mea culpa to the boss about the newspaper article and got his permission to go forward with the plan to confront Jamie Powell, I turned to the rest of my regular duties, starting with screening. When that was done, I handled my grand juries, then a sentencing hearing. I was fine as long as I was running around the courthouse. But back in the office, I couldn't help it. I stared at the silent phone on my desk, wondering when Chuck would call.

I considered calling Alison York to apologize for phoning her at home the day before to ask about Percy. No, better to leave well enough alone. She and Matt were trying to salvage their marriage, and every call from me was just a reminder of what had compromised it in the first place.

That thought brought me squarely back to the problems in my own home life. I called my cell phone one more time, checking for a message I knew was not there.

Desperately seeking a distraction, I turned to the Crenshaw file, reviewing once again his notes on the Northeast Precinct story. Looking at everything we knew now, Heidi's theory added up, but how in the world had Percy pieced it together from just these numbers and a few comments at neighborhood association meetings? He must have had a source who fed him information on the side, someone we hadn't found yet—maybe one of these people whose first names Percy scrawled randomly in his margins. Whoever they were, I hoped they were watching their backs.

Or maybe Percy didn't have a source. Maybe he hadn't yet made sense of these numbers himself. I flipped through the pages, saddened by the thought of Percy being killed for information he didn't even have.

Then I stopped at a name in the margin: a first name, or at least it had seemed, in all-capital print letters. Nothing special, just another small detail in this vast collection of minutiae. But this time, those three letters took on new significance: AMY.

There was nothing wrong with the York marriage after all.

23

I dialed their home number, but there was no answer. I tracked down Matt's cell phone with the bureau and tried it instead. He sounded unnerved when he answered.

"Matt, it's Sam Kincaid. We need to talk."

I heard static in the heavy pause, then Alison's faint voice in the background. "We were actually thinking about calling you. We've been driving around for hours."

"No more thinking," I said. "I've got officers in place ready to pick up Powell and Foster this afternoon. The lies end now." It was tough talk from a friend, but it came with the implicit threat and power of the District Attorney's Office.

"Can you give us any assurances?"

"Matt, you know how this works. I need the cooperation first." My tone softened slightly. "But, as your friend, I promise you: A couple of hours from now, your help won't mean as much."

I heard a muffled exchange between them as I prayed silently that I wouldn't need to have them picked up by force.

"Yeah, OK. But, please, not at the courthouse. Can you meet us somewhere?" He directed me to a hole-in-the-wall diner on the far west end of downtown. "And make sure no one follows you."

Alison and Matt sat side by side in the back booth of Jake's Diner, sharing a chocolate malt like two high school kids in letter jackets.

I dropped Percy's open notebook on the table in front of them. "That's you: Alison Madison-York." I pointed for emphasis at each of the three initials that had tipped me off. "You two apparently spent enough time with Percy for him to pick up on the joke."

Alison turned anxiously to her husband.

"You weren't sleeping with Percy. You were his source. You were at his apartment to give him information."

Matt looked nervously around the diner, calmed not in the least by its limited and geriatric customer base. "Can you please just sit for a second," he said in a hushed tone.

I took a seat across from them in the booth.

"How much do you have without us?" Matt asked.

"Unh-unh. If you want my help, you tell me everything." I glanced at my watch. "And I meant it about being pressed for time. That shooting in Buckeye Saturday night? A coworker of Percy's had contacted those women earlier in the day, trying to track the story."

Alison nudged Matt with her elbow. "I told you it could be related," she said to her husband. "I've been on edge since you called last night. When I saw the story this morning about Percy's case being reopened, I was too scared to stay in the house. We've been driving around for hours."

"You *should* be scared." I immediately regretted the harshness of the words. "We figured it out. Powell and Foster have been going through the motions on searches, then cutting Andre Brouse's people loose if they're carrying. Obviously, someone doesn't want that information out, and they may have killed Percy over it."

Alison looked confused. "Then you know more than we do. I've never even heard of that person."

"Start by telling me what you do know." Mentally, I kicked myself. I had been thinking of Alison solely as Matt's wife and Percy's lover, not as a potentially valuable source in the records department of Northeast Precinct, which processes search-and-seizure cards.

"I swear to you, I didn't know what was going on at first. A few months ago, I noticed they had plenty of searches going into the system, but their arrests were down. I said something to them about slacking off. I was only joking around, but they totally freaked out and told me to stick to data entry and mind my own business. A couple days later, Powell came to me all nice and apologetic, and asked if I'd disregard a few of their searches of black males every once in a while."

They must have realized that if Alison could spot the discrepancy between the numbers of searches shown on their stop-and-search cards and the number of arrests they were making, so could anyone who might actually look.

"And so you did it?"

"No, of course not. I said I didn't want to get involved in anything like that. But Powell said they were just worried after my comment that some left-wing liberal might make them out to be racist cops using searches to harass people in Buckeye. He said they were only doing their job in a neighborhood that happens to be mostly black. My husband's a cop, too, and I didn't see the harm in ignoring a few of the searches when I was doing data entry."

"When was this? When did you start cutting back on their numbers?" I asked.

"Around the end of August." The bureau had only published the statistics through August on its Web site. Apparently the numbers would be less skewed in the months since, thanks to Alison's assistance.

"Is that everything?"

Alison looked at her husband. "No. A couple of weeks later, the sergeants started to get on the officers for letting low-level dealers off with warnings instead of taking them in. Right after that, Powell asked me to destroy actual arrest records for him and Foster—always on drug cases. They'd bring people in and make it look like they were processing them for arrests, paper work and all. But then instead of transporting them to the jail, they'd cut them loose in the neighborhood. They wanted me to make sure the arrest reports didn't get processed." The practice explained the complaints from residents that dealers who were arrested would magically reappear on the same corner within the hour.

"You had to have known something was up, Alison."

"I figured it out eventually."

"And you did this for them out of—what? Friendship? Loyalty?" I asked.

"No. I told them I wouldn't throw out arrest records. But they didn't seem to want to accept that answer and then— well, then they offered to pay me." I started to ask why she needed the money, then remembered a frustrated conversation during the summer about infertility treatment. "We already took a second mortgage on the house for shots that weren't working. We need in vitro."

"Alison," I said, shaking my head sadly at her desperation.

"I know, it was stupid. So incredibly stupid."

"How long have you known?" I asked Matt. He said nothing.

"I told him about a month ago. It's not his fault. He was— well, angry, to say the least."

"Why didn't you come forward?"

This time Matt answered. "I couldn't think of a safe way to get her out of it. Think about it: I didn't know who else was involved or how things would play out with her word against theirs." He paused, struggling for the right words to convey the complexity of their dilemma. "Have you ever heard of *slow cover*?"

My blank expression told him I hadn't.

"Cops who make enemies of other cops don't necessarily get help when they push their panic buttons."

I thought about the red button I had nearly triggered the night Chuck arrested Trevor Hanks, and Chuck's unwillingness to see my side of the police–district attorney divide. If scorned cops will imperil one of their own, could Chuck have worried— consciously or not—about living with a prosecutor who wasn't part of the code?

"How'd you get involved with Percy?"

"Powell and Foster told me that Percy Crenshaw was asking questions. We needed to be even more careful about the records. I had to make sure their numbers looked normal. Instead, I called Percy and started giving him information."

"You never heard either of them mention Andre Brouse?"

She shook her head.

"Can you help her?" Matt asked.

"It's not just her, Matt. You withheld information in a murder investigation."

"I know. I'll handle whatever needs to be done, but I want you to do what you can for Alison."

Alison started to argue, and I immediately understood what they must have been discussing during the daylong car ride.

"Is there something else I need to know, Matt? Chuck says you were more than a little sensitive about your whereabouts on Sunday night."

"I still feel like shit for the way I talked to him. I really did forget to log back in after the call at City Grill. But the more he pushed, the more I started to think he actually suspected me of killing Percy. I lost it."

"I'll let you explain that to him yourself," I said. I didn't mention that Chuck apparently wasn't speaking to me directly anymore.

"If it makes any difference, we really were close to calling Chuck—and you—on our own before."

I nodded, realizing none of us could know what they would have done if I hadn't made the connection first.

"It was because of Chuck's partner, actually," Matt added. "I guess Chuck told him how I acted Friday. Lo and behold, Calabrese was waiting for me later at the precinct. Said he figured I wasn't being straight with my buddy, and I'd only do that to Chuck if I was worried about diming someone else up."

"You think he knew about this?"

"No, not like that. I got the feeling he thought it was minor, like I was off having a drink with another cop or something. But everything he said about it hit me right inside—that one lie would start another, that it was better just to be honest and take the consequences, that I was putting Chuck in a bind. I don't know; it just got to me. Then when we saw the story this morning about the investigation into Percy's murder being reopened, we knew we had to say something."

With that one story from Matt York, I finally had the confidence in my gut that Chuck had implored me to feel earlier. Mike Calabrese might be rough around the edges, but at his core he was one of the good ones. And Chuck had been right. By going to his lieutenant, I had screwed them both over.

■   ■   ■

By the time I met Tommy Garcia and Alan Carson at the Internal Affairs Division offices in Central Precinct as scheduled, I had an arrest warrant in hand for Powell based on information provided by two confidential and reliable informants.

"I know you're capable of great things, Kincaid, but you've got a *what*?" Garcia apparently wasn't certain he'd heard me right.

"An arrest warrant, signed by one Judge David Lesh after reviewing the fastest affidavit I've ever drafted."

"I can't imagine any judge signing off for an arrest on what we've got."

I backed up and told them about the Yorks.

"They could be in deeper than they're admitting," Carson suggested.

I shook my head. "I don't think so. Alison was desperate for money and didn't realize how bad it would get. By the time she was in, they couldn't think of a way out."

"They could have come to us," Carson protested.

"Yeah, well, according to what I heard from Matt today, they didn't think that was realistic. Something about *slow cover*?"

"Urban legend," Carson said.

Tommy scoffed, and I couldn't help but think of my recent ticket and the ignored attempts to report the car prowl at my house.

"Anyway, that's part of what they were afraid of. Then Alison hears Powell and Foster saying that Percy's on to the connection between them and Brouse."

"Wait," Tommy said. "Alison York can give us Brouse? She heard them use his name?"

"No, sorry, that was me filling in the blanks. She heard them say Percy had figured *it* out. She and Matt talked it through and saw Percy as a way of getting the problem to end without her having to come forward."

"The plan didn't exactly work," Garcia said dryly.

"And now they're truly contrite, appealing for lenience from the DA?" Carson asked sarcastically.

"I didn't make any deals other than to say I'd go to bat for them."

"You done good, Sammie," Garcia said. "Let's pick up Jamie Powell."

Powell wasn't exactly calling attention to whatever money he received for his complicity. We arrived in two separate detective vehicles at a modest ranch house in the suburb of Beaverton. The open garage door revealed a Dodge Caravan and a Chevy Malibu.

The idea of a corrupt cop with four kids brings to mind a certain age, but I knew from his file that he was younger than I was. Still, the boyish face that answered the door came as a surprise.

Carson introduced the three of us, including respective titles. Internal Affairs, the Drug Unit, and the DA's Major Crimes Unit. The implication was clear. "Do you want to come with us, or do you want to talk here?"

Powell initially feigned confusion, but his expression quickly changed when a woman inside asked who was at the door. The moment he'd dreaded had finally come. "Can I tell my wife I'm going?"

"I can't leave you by yourself," Carson said. Too many cops end the problem on their own with their service weapon.

"Yeah, all right. Come on in." Alan stepped inside while we waited on the porch. "Hon, this is Alan, my buddy from work.

Something's come up. I got to go in early. . . . No, everything's fine."

Thirty minutes later, the four of us were back at IAD with a union delegate for Powell. Carson was laying out the case against him, along with Powell's options. Even the union rep conceded that Powell had an incentive to cooperate. We were offering an extraordinary deal under the circumstances: full immunity from prosecution. He would leave the force, keep his pension, and stay insured for a year. Not a single day as a former cop behind bars. In exchange, he would corroborate the case against Foster and, most importantly, wear a wire to give us Brouse. The deal was good for half an hour. After that, we were booking him and trying our luck with Foster.

"Give you Andre for what?" he asked.

"Everything." The scope of the drug activity alone could land Brouse in prison for life if we convinced the Feds to remand him. I wanted him in state prison, though. "What do you know about Percy Crenshaw?"

"Andre didn't do that."

"That's not what I asked you. I asked you what you knew about it."

"Andre heard Crenshaw had been asking about him. He obviously wasn't pleased. When I found out he'd been killed, I confronted Andre at Jay-J's. Regardless of what you might think of me, no way was I willing to look the other way on a murder."

Tommy and Alan exchanged skeptical glances.

"He didn't even know about it. Don't get me wrong—he was happy when I told him, like he couldn't believe his own stupid luck—but he was obviously surprised. He didn't do it."

"What about Selma Gooding and Janelle Rogers?"

His body slumped as he exhaled, realizing we had tied in the Buckeye shooting.

"The clock's ticking," Carson prompted.

Powell looked to his delegate, who said nothing. We clearly had the power here. "On that one, I think Andre at least knows who did it. Foster saw that new female reporter talking to Selma on Saturday and told Andre about it. When the call came in about the drive-by, Foster called Andre, pissed off. Andre blamed it on some kid getting crazy, trying to gain favor with him. He said he was *going to take care of it,* in his words. Foster told him not to do anything stupid, but everything was obviously getting out of control."

Just like Foster and Powell had convinced themselves they were just a little bit corrupt, Andre Brouse had probably allowed them to live that illusion, letting them in on the drug operation but leaving them out of the messy details.

"When do you wear the wire?" I asked. He didn't respond to the question. "Do we need to talk to Foster or not?"

Powell had seen perps in a similar position and knew he had no choice. If he didn't take the deal, Foster would. "I'm supposed to meet Brouse at the club at the start of shift. Four o'clock."

Forty-five minutes. "Can we get him wired by then?" I asked Carson.

"We can do it right now."

"Let's do it," Powell said. "Can I call my wife? Get her to take the kids to her mother's?"

Alan nodded. "I'll send an escort with them if you want."

"Brouse doesn't check you?" I asked.

"Not for a couple of years."

Carson assured me that would be the case. "Are you kidding?" he said. "No one's more trustworthy to a guy like Brouse than a guy like Powell. A dirty cop's got more to lose."

■ ■ ■

I checked for messages back at the office while Carson and a technician wired Powell for sound. With Frist out and me away for more than four hours, the unit could be falling apart. And maybe Chuck had called.

Only one new message. "Hi, this is Marcy Wellington. My husband—or I guess soon-to-be ex-husband—is Peter Anderson? A witness for you on the Percy Crenshaw case? Anyway, we've been having some problems, and"—I heard her sniffle into the phone—"anyway, I need to talk to someone. Can you please call me back?"

I'd heard plenty of complaints from DV deputies about these kinds of calls—domestic violence victims turning futilely to prosecutors to understand the confusing combination of fear, anger, betrayal, and sadness that came with being hit by someone you still loved.

I started to save the message for later, then stopped. Janelle Rogers had been killed the day after I blew off a request for help from Heidi Hatmaker. Shit. For all I knew, Anderson could be threatening his wife and claiming he'd get away with it because he knew a DA. I didn't want to read about Marcy Wellington's murder in the paper tomorrow morning, knowing I could've stopped it. I scribbled Marcy's number on a legal pad.

"How are we looking?" I asked Carson.

"Just a minute. He's putting on his uniform."

I called the bureau switchboard and asked to be connected to the Domestic Violence Unit. The unit's assistant told me no one was in; she'd have an officer call me back later. I explained I was out of the office and left my pager number.

"We're about ready," Tommy said.

As we were getting ready to walk out, Powell said, "What about my gun?"

"We can't let you have that," Carson explained. Powell's

union rep protested, but Carson held strong. "As far as we're concerned, he's not even a cop anymore."

Powell spoke up for himself. "I can't go in on duty, in uniform, without my gun. He'll know immediately."

Carson and I exchanged glances. We'd been moving so quickly we hadn't thought all the details through. "Then we take the bullets out," I said.

"No way," the union rep said. "You can't send him into a club full of gangbangers, with them thinking he's armed, when he's not."

"And we can't let him have a loaded gun," Carson said.

The union rep started to ask for time to consult with Powell privately, but Powell waved him off. "That's a deal killer," he said. "My kids are better off with me on trial than me dead."

For a guy who'd blown it all, today Jamie Powell had shown good judgment. When it came to cutting the deal, he needed us more than we needed him. But we needed him enough, and were moving quickly enough, to grant him this one. Carson made the call, and I approved it. We were ready to go.

Tailing Jamie Powell's patrol vehicle to the club in a unmarked van with Tommy Garcia, Alan Carson, and the technician, I still hadn't heard anything from the DV unit. Whether it was the adrenaline from what was about to happen, my anal-retentive desire to square away the loose end of Marcy Wellington's phone call, or simply an excuse, I used Tommy's cell to call Chuck.

"Hey, I can't really talk right now."

"Neither can I."

Tommy Garcia was sitting next to me, and I had approximately three minutes before Powell walked into Jay-J's. I wasn't calling about our relationship.

I walked him through the situation with Marcy Wellington. "I tried calling DV, but they're not getting back to me. Can you call them for me? Just stay on them until they go out there."

"Sure. Are you all right? You sound frantic."

Now wasn't the time. "It's that thing I was working on yesterday. A lot has happened today, though. We should talk."

"Yeah, OK," he said, sounding rushed. "Can I call you later?"

Music to my ears. "Yeah, or just come home."

"I'll call you."

So much for the music. "Um, OK. You'll probably get voice mail, but I've been checking them all day. Someone stole my purse last night, so I don't have my cell—"

"Last night? Someone broke into the house?"

"No, my car. And then no one from fucking Northeast Precinct would come to the house to take a report. They said it was policy, but I got the whole cold-shoulder gist, if that's what they were aiming for."

Chuck was clearly annoyed at the police response—or lack thereof—and, for once, I actually appreciated his protectiveness.

Unfortunately, his irritation wasn't limited to the precinct. "Why didn't you call me? Were you trying to make me feel even worse about leaving?"

"How did I do anything to make you feel bad?" In the driver's seat, Tommy looked out his window when we stopped at a light. "Look, I'm in the middle of a million things right now. Can you please just call DV for me? I don't have anyone else to call." My voice broke slightly as I realized the truth carried in that single sentence.

"Yeah, fine. I'll talk to you later."

He hung up just as Powell's patrol car pulled into the Jay-J's parking lot.

"Here we go," Garcia said, cutting the engine.

24

As planned, we monitored electronically from the parking lot of an Italian restaurant across the street from the club. In the back of the van, Carson and the technician hit a button to feed Powell's audio to our speaker.

"Getting out now," Powell said, just as his car door opened. We were clear.

We watched him enter Jay-J's, and soon the van was filled with the thumping beat of a rap artist who'd survived multiple gunshots to the face. "At four in the afternoon?" I asked.

"Consider that Muzak, Kincaid," Tommy said. "Twelve hours from now, you can't hear yourself think in that place."

The sound of the bass line dulled as we heard a door shut. Powell had walked into the back office. According to Powell, he had demanded this meeting with Brouse last week. With Percy's prying and then his murder, it was all becoming too much for him. Powell's plan, if you believed what he said, was to pull out, to tell Andre he was going to do his job right from now on.

As we listened, what he did instead—and what I suspected he planned to do all along—was demand additional money. He wouldn't get to keep the cash, but we'd get the corroboration we needed to nail Brouse.

"I'm paying y'all enough." It was Andre. "Shit, dealing with the po-po's worse than the mob. That's what it is. You're shaking me down for security money."

"Well, for the kind of security you're getting, it's not enough. We go out of our way to take the calls about your guys on the corners, then they get to walk away."

Andre laughed. "You know what's cracking me up? You really are acting like this is a bunch of mafia shit. Foster, now, he's easy—he could be any one of them, so let's make him Michael Corleone, how about? Now you? You'd have to be Tom Hagen with that light hair of yours. Before Bobby D went bald, obviously. But now here's the funny part: Don't no one in those movies look like me. You know what I'm saying?"

It really was true. All men loved the Godfather.

"Don't give me that movie bullshit, Andre. You're getting a piece of every rock that's sold in this city—"

"Not *every* rock—" Andre interrupted.

"Well, pretty fucking close. And now you've dragged me into something I never signed on for. People are getting hurt—"

"You rather they figured out the shit you've been doing?"

"We never talked about witnesses getting killed."

"Now if that ain't some hypocritical shit, I don't know what the fuck is. If you want to talk about fucked up—"

"Shooting an old lady's fucked up."

"And I told Foster I'd take care of it. You think I want some dumb-ass kid popping ladies from the neighborhood? Talk to your boy—"

"You know you wouldn't have this club and all the other shit you have if we hadn't been watching your back."

"You're less valuable than you think," Andre said.

"Who else is going to do this crap for you?"

They went back and forth like that, arguing about whether Powell had been paid fairly. Tommy even managed to find some humor in the situation. "Sounds like every workplace in America."

What happened next was over so fast, it took the many replays of the audio later to help me understand what we had heard.

"Stop!" It was Powell's voice, and it was panicked. "Don't do it! Don't!"

Two distinct pops followed. Before I could even process what was happening, the other occupants of the van reacted on pure police instinct. Tommy Garcia and Alan Carson jumped from the back doors, drawing their weapons and yelling commands into the radios on their chests. Backup teams in two separate cars on the street poured out as well, descending on Jay-J's. Just a few minutes later, Tommy Garcia radioed the audio technician to give the clear.

In retrospect, we were lucky. Only a few employees were in the bar with Brouse. Two of the men were armed, but the stereo's pounding rhythms had drowned out the sound of Powell's shots. The scene was secured without incident.

That would have been little consolation to Andre Brouse, who was declared DOA. Two bullets—one in the head, one in the chest.

We followed the protocol for an officer-involved shooting. Powell was transported to the precinct with his union rep. He told us that he fired when Andre reached for a gun in his top drawer. He said he intended to keep his end of our deal, but he wouldn't be discussing the incident further until he spoke with an attorney. We found a Glock in the open desk drawer, but we also knew the discovery would never be enough to resolve what happened in that office. Powell had been around Brouse enough to know where he kept his gun.

When the crime scene was secured and the evidence-gathering process under way, I took a breather to call Duncan, who at least appeared to be understanding. "We're just the lawyers," he said. "This was a decision about the implementation of an undercover operation, and the bureau made a reasonable call. We've got enough to show the guy was dirty, right?" I accepted his support with one eye open, realizing that if the debacle came with political damage, he'd sacrifice Carson and Garcia in a heartbeat—then me, if necessary.

He did explain that he was going to send Jessica Walters to handle the shooting, since I was technically a witness. I tried to argue, emphasizing the entanglement of the shooting with the Crenshaw investigation.

"And if Walters comes across anything on Crenshaw, I'm sure she'll fill you in. What I need right now is a deputy who's going to deal with the immediate issue—a cop shot a suspect—and you're not going to be that lawyer. Consider it a lucky break. After the day you've had, I'd think you'd be grateful for the rest."

I should have been, of course, but I wasn't. As much as I usually hate a sports analogy, when Jessica showed up, I felt like a pitcher getting pulled in the middle of an important game. I didn't care if it was a morass of confusion. It was my morass, and I wanted to be in the middle of it.

Jessica finally gave me a choice: I could leave on my own, or she would have me forcibly evicted. I didn't think she'd actually go through with it, but I got the point. "Can I take a copy of the tape with me?" I asked, as a final negotiating point.

"Jesus, Kincaid, why the hell do you want to do that to yourself?"

Because I feel guilty, I thought. *Because I sat in a van and listened while the person who could have answered all my questions was killed, possibly executed. Because if I listen to the tape, I might be able to convince myself there was nothing else I could do.*

"I should add it to my Crenshaw file," I said, "just in case."

"Yeah, whatever. Have the tech dupe it for you, then get the hell out of here."

A patrol officer gave me a ride home as instructed, speaking not a single word once he had my address. As we turned onto my block, I eyed the street eagerly, hoping to spot Chuck's car. My disappointment was complete when the officer pulled into my driveway. Nothing other than my Jetta, the tarp I'd used to cover the window loose now, blowing in the wind.

In one tiny bow to normalcy, Vinnie was eagerly waiting for me when I opened the door. I scooped him up and cuddled him on my way to the kitchen. My message light was blinking.

Well, good evening, Samantha Kincaid. Or I guess it's afternoon out there in Oregon. Ed Devlin here, NYPD. It wasn't easy, but I did finally find a friend of mine who's a friend of Patrick Gallagher. Gallagher was the IA officer who'd vouched for Mike when PPB hired him. *I couldn't get the full story, but apparently a couple of officers thumped up a suspect pretty good. Everyone was supposed to give the same story—you know how it goes—but Calabrese went his own way. He told it like it was and—well, it didn't go over so good. The bureau transferred him around a couple times, but a story like that follows a guy. He wanted out, and I guess Gallagher helped him. Give me a call if you need more. Hell, you're a beautiful young lady. Give an old guy a break and call me anyway.*

As the machine moved on to the next message, I smiled, thinking back to the many times Ed had encouraged me to dump my then-husband and run away with him instead.

Hey, it's me. I noticed the absence of Chuck's usual *hey, babe* at the start of the message. *I can't get anyone in DV either, so I finally called this Marcy Wellington chick myself. She was freaking out, so I'll head over myself to take a report. I'll call you when I'm done. You owe me one.*

I tried to keep occupied with TV, but my mind kept returning to the scene in the van. Tommy Garcia, making a joke about the banter between Andre and Powell. Then panic in Powell's voice. Two shots. The van doors spilling open. It was so damn fast.

I retrieved my Walkman from my gym bag and inserted the tape of the shooting. I hit STOP and REWIND over and over again, trying to calculate the time that passed between the argument about money and the end of Andre Brouse's life. Somewhere between two or three seconds, by my watch. Not enough to stop Powell. Not even enough for Andre Brouse to speak.

The tape did at least corroborate the evidence we'd gotten from Powell and the Yorks. Jay-J's would most likely be seized by the state in a drug forfeiture action. Hopefully, Jessica would find evidence identifying Brouse's source and key distributors.

Still, I kept fiddling with the buttons of the tape player, searching for some clue about the murders of Percy Crenshaw and Janelle Rogers.

"We never talked about witnesses getting killed," Powell had said. *Now if that ain't some hypocritical shit, I don't know what the fuck is. If you want to talk about fucked up—* "Shooting an old lady's fucked up," Powell interrupted. *And I told Foster I'd take care of it. You think I want some dumb-ass kid popping ladies from the neighborhood? Talk to your boy—*

I listened to Brouse's words again and again, knowing I was missing something. Snippets of the tape started to come together. *Now if that ain't some hypocritical shit . . . talk about fucked up . . . talk to your boy—*

I had figured out what was bothering me. Brouse had something on Powell, or at least on someone close to him. Powell was supposed to cajole Brouse into talking about Percy and the drive-by at Selma's, but Brouse kept turning the tables on him. And each time, Powell had interrupted. There was only one explanation: Brouse was mad at Powell's *boy* for something serious, and Powell didn't want us to know about it.

I plucked off my headphones. *Talk to your boy. Talk to your boy.* Why did that seem so familiar? I was close to making sense of Brouse's words. Something about the sentence echoing in my head would pull the pieces together.

Then it came to me: Mike's hostile reaction when we had first talked about the Hamilton shooting. *Your buddy Frist's looking to shine by going after our boy Hamilton.* Geoff Hamilton worked out of Northeast Precinct with Powell and Foster.

I logged on to the District Attorney data system from my computer, pulled up the Hamilton case, and dialed the phone number for Marla Mavens, Delores Tompkins's mother. She assumed I was calling to see how she was faring in the aftermath of the grand jury's decision, but I got straight to the point.

"You mentioned during the grand jury that Delores had been dating a man who was involved with drugs."

"Well, she didn't know that at first. And, like I said, she was trying to get a fresh start."

"I remember. She had the new home improvement job and something she was working on that made her feel special." Marla clearly found comfort in the fact that her daughter seemed finally to find the right track before her death.

"That's right," she said proudly.

"Do you remember the name of the boyfriend?"

"Oh, shoot. I should, but—"

"Was it Andre Brouse?" I prompted.

"Yes, that was it. She called him Dre sometimes for short."

"Did she know a man named Percy Crenshaw?"

"The reporter?"

"That's the one. Did your daughter know him? The special thing she was doing—could she have been helping Percy with a story?"

"Oh, I don't know about that. I didn't keep track of all her friends, but she never mentioned him. Does this have anything to do with the grand jury?"

I knew in my gut that I was right about this. I just needed to prove the connection. "No, I'm sorry," I said, not wanting to get her hopes up about reopening the case. "I'm just tying up some loose ends before I can put the file away."

"I guess you could say I've been doing the same thing," she said.

"Would you mind if I asked what phone numbers someone might have used if they were talking to your daughter?"

"Not at all. I still remember them. Probably always will, I suspect." She rattled off the digits for Delores's home and cell phones, and I jotted them down on a legal pad from my briefcase.

My next call was to Heidi Hatmaker.

"How have you been holding up?" I asked when she answered her cell. We hadn't spoken since she left the precinct the day before.

"Honestly? I lasted about five minutes in my apartment by myself before I packed a bag. I went on a date, haven't been home since, and couldn't feel any safer." I heard a man say something in the background, and Heidi shushed him. "What have I missed?"

Where could I even begin? I told her briefly that we'd flipped Powell and about the shooting at Jay-J's. "And you didn't call me?" she protested. "You swore you weren't going to leave me out of the story."

"And I didn't. Only the sanitized version gets released today: An officer returned fire when a suspect reached for a weapon. We're still putting the rest of it together. On that note, do you happen to have Percy's cell phone records?" The ones we seized were in the police evidence room.

"Are you kidding? After this weekend, I wasn't about to leave anything having to do with Percy in my unoccupied apartment."

I thought about asking her to check for Delores's numbers, but I wasn't ready to give Heidi all of the pieces to the puzzle yet. Not before I'd put them together. "Do you mind if I come by and get them?"

"I guess not. From what I could tell, it was just a bunch of carryout places."

I had a feeling there was more to it if you knew what to look for.

I pulled into the driveway of the address she'd given me, a well-kept home in the Hawthorne district. Fortunately, given my high-class cellophaned car window, it was only a five-minute drive from my place.

A vaguely familiar face greeted me at the door. "You must be Samantha Kincaid."

"Wait a second," I said, pointing at him. "I know this one. The bureau's PIO?"

"You've got it. Jack Streeter." We shook hands and exchanged the requisite good-to-meet-yous as he welcomed me in. Heidi looked comfy on a sofa in the front room, legs crossed beneath her, documents spread out on the coffee table.

"Are those the phone records?" I asked.

She nodded. "I was just putting them in order." She piled a stack together. "Most recent are on top."

"Great. Thanks."

"What are you looking for?" she asked inquisitively.

I shrugged my shoulders. "With Andre Brouse dead, we're pretty much back to square one." I felt bad leaving her in the dark, but I held strong. She'd get it all before the rest of the media, and that's what really counted.

In my car, I double-checked the Saran Wrap on my window. Then I scanned the list of calls in Percy's records, comparing them against the numbers I'd gotten from Marla Mavens. It didn't take long to find what I was looking for. In the two weeks before Delores Tompkins's death, her cell phone number was one of the most frequently dialed by Percy Crenshaw. I saw that Heidi had written *disc'd* on the bill, most likely after she'd tried the disconnected number.

I was just about to return the papers to my bag when I noticed something else—another match between Percy's cell phone records and my legal pad. I checked the records and found the number listed three additional times within the same month.

I knocked on Jack Streeter's door again. "Sorry. Do you mind if I use your phone real quick? Someone stole my mobile."

"Wish that would happen to me," he joked, pointing me to a phone in his kitchen.

I tried Chuck's cell, but there was no answer. I hit REDIAL, but still nothing. Either he had Motorhead blasting as he drove or he was still taking the report from Marcy Wellington.

Back in my car, I flipped through the Crenshaw file until I found what I was looking for: the restraining order against Peter Anderson, with Marcy Wellington's current residential address. I'd ask her myself what she and Percy Crenshaw had been discussing so frequently.

■　　■　　■

The route took me east on Hawthorne, past the earthy coffee shops and breakfast bistros in Streeter's neighborhood to the used car lots, gun shops, and cement strip malls on 82nd Avenue. A couple of quick turns and I was on Marcy Wellington's street.

Chuck's familiar car was in the driveway. Good, I hadn't missed him. I parked the Jetta on the street and started to get out. Then I took another look at the house. A Toyota Celica was pulled to the front of the double driveway, on the side closest to the house. Chuck was parked on the opposite side. A third car, a Geo Prizm, blocked the Celica from behind.

I looked through the Crenshaw file again and found Peter Anderson's PPDS printout. Sure enough, he was the registered owner of a 1996 Geo Prizm.

I automatically reached to the floor of my passenger compartment for my purse. Shit. I'd need to find a pay phone. I reinserted my key in the ignition but couldn't bring myself to drive away. Who knew how long the three of them had been in there? I had called Chuck's cell nearly fifteen minutes ago, and he hadn't answered. At the very least, Anderson was violating the restraining order against him, and I refused to consider the other possibilities in any detail. I knew how many police officers were killed each year at the scene of domestic assaults.

I stepped from the car and shut the door lightly behind me. I scurried next to the Prizm, ducking low for cover as I worked my way to Chuck's Jag. I checked the dash. No flashing light. Good, he hadn't bothered arming his alarm. I fumbled with the bulky ring in my hand until I found my copy of the key. I slid into the car and used the next key to open Chuck's glove box, flashing back to the day two weeks ago at Home Depot when Chuck had insisted that we copy our car keys for each other.

"We live together now," he'd said, as if that was an obvious explanation. I had dangled my overstuffed purple parrot key chain and asked why in the world I needed to make room for a key that started a car he wouldn't let me drive, let alone the glove box. "Think of it as a symbolic gesture, a token of our commitment to one another," he responded with self-mocking flourish.

Right now, the keys beat a wedding ring, hands down. I opened the glove box and removed the case I knew I would find there, the one that cradled Chuck's off-duty weapon. He had insisted on keeping his Colt .45 after the bureau replaced its service weapons with Glocks. I checked it. Full magazine, empty chamber. I secured the gun snugly in the back of my waistband and worked my way to the front porch.

I pretended to knock on the door as I peered cautiously through its glass panes. I could see a front hallway and the door of what was probably a coat closet. I tried to get a peripheral view, but could only make out some beige carpet and the arm of a blue sofa.

Walking to the side of the house, I found a window where the vinyl blinds hadn't dropped completely. Through the three-inch gap, I saw Peter Anderson standing behind a woman I assumed was Marcy Wellington. His left arm was wrapped around her waist, almost intimately. His right clenched the handle of a knife, pressing its six-inch stainless steel blade against his wife's throat. From her disheveled appearance and flushed face, I suspected that she had been slapped recently, or worse. Her eyes were wide with fear, and her entire body seemed tucked against her husband's, as if trying to shrink from the cool metal of the blade.

Chuck stood fifteen feet away, his arms held palms out in front of him. I could tell that he and Anderson were both talking, at and over each other. It was obviously intense, but I couldn't make out the words. I thought through what must have occurred to bring the four of us here.

It would have all started with the article that morning starring Henry Hanks and his claim that the police had cleared his son and Corbett in the Percy Crenshaw case. The article mentioned that the building superintendent had identified the defendants. With Hanks and Corbett cleared, the article must have raised new questions for Marcy Wellington about her violent husband and his reaction to the kindness shown to her by a neighbor, a former PI who knew about things like restraining orders. She called me to make sure I knew that Anderson had a beef with Percy. For Peter Anderson, the article had created an incentive to confirm his wife wasn't a problem. He came here to make sure she knew he could still get to her.

And Chuck had walked into the middle of it. I knew Chuck still had his Glock in his holster. He would never give up his weapon. He knew better. But I'd heard enough about murder-suicides in the DV unit to know he and Marcy were in trouble. Chuck was good, but Peter Anderson was not going to drop that knife voluntarily.

I removed the .45 from my waistband and cocked the hammer, sliding an active round into the chamber. I had no idea what to do next. I could shoot through the glass, but the thought of randomly ricocheted bullets seemed unwise. I couldn't pull this off alone.

I held the gun in my right hand and fished my keys from my pocket with my left. Carefully, at the bottom of the window, I flashed the souvenir Grace had bought me in Hawaii, my little parrot with its pulsing purple beak. *Please let this work.* Chuck had made fun of my parrot enough times to recognize the light, if he would just notice it in the window.

After about a minute, his eyes darted briefly to his periphery. Then I caught it. A blink. Just a flicker of recognition, a hint of relief. He knew I was out here.

Chuck's voice became louder, even more urgent. *Yes!* I could make out the words. "Think about it, Peter. You don't want to do this. Not to Marcy. Percy was an act of rage; the law calls it heat of passion. But this is premeditated. And it's *Marcy*. You still love her, don't you?"

Peter was speaking more heatedly now, and Marcy was sobbing hysterically. With emotions escalating in both the victim and perpetrator, there was no status quo to preserve. This needed to end soon.

"Then let's all three of us walk through that *front door. Right now,* Peter. Just put the knife down, and we walk right out the *front door.*"

Chuck was telling me what to do. He was telling me Anderson had left the front door unlocked. I moved to the porch and reached for the knob. I turned it as slowly as I could until I felt the latch give way. I pressed gently, opening the door just a crack. Chuck's voice continued to boom, loud enough to cover any squeaking. Quickly, I pushed the door ajar and stepped inside the hallway, flattening my back against the closet door.

I envisioned the layout of the living room. Once I went in, Anderson would be standing twenty-five feet away, facing me at a 45-degree angle. His head would be higher than Marcy's, but it was a risky shot, and Chuck would probably be in the way of a clear hit.

"Where the fuck are you going? Stop moving, stop moving." It was Peter Anderson. He was freaking out, and apparently Chuck had read my mind.

"Don't panic," Chuck reassured him. "I just want to get a better look at Marcy. You're scaring her, Peter. You OK there?" he asked in a gentle voice.

I heard a frightened whimper.

"I'm OK too," Chuck said. "We're all OK."

He was telling me it was clear. I had to go now. I remembered what it felt like to fire the .45 at the range. I had been good with it, better than Chuck.

I took a deep breath and rotated my body around the corner, pulling my arms in front of me as I turned. I kept a firm grip on the gun, preparing for the strength of the recoil.

The scene lasted no longer than the shooting at Jay-J's, but it felt like an eternity. Marcy saw me first and panicked. She pulled the weight of her small frame down and away from her husband. Anderson's body convulsed with hers as he struggled to maintain his firm embrace of her waist. A perplexed look of recognition, surprise, and fear registered in his eyes as the bullet I had aimed at his head sailed over them, penetrating a china cabinet against the back wall.

A confusing succession of sounds filled my head: the blast of the gun; shattering glass and china; the terrified scream of Marcy Wellington, piercing at first, then muffled by her husband's body against her mouth as he turned her to face him as they fell forward. I followed the arc of their movement with the .45, impotently searching for a shot that would not catch Marcy. Peter pulled his right elbow beside him, and I foresaw the momentum of the knife thrust planned for his wife's abdomen.

The sounds of the room seemed impossibly loud as I struggled to ignore a popping noise I couldn't make sense of—a ricochet from the cabinet, perhaps, or an imagined echo of my first shot. I felt my finger stiffen against the trigger, willing to take the risk of another.

Then Marcy screamed again as her husband collapsed in a heap on top of her, slowly releasing the knife. Blood and brain matter burst from an exit wound in the left side of his skull. To my right, Chuck stood staring at the scene, his Glock trembling in front of him.

I quickly surveyed the three people in the room, weighing who needed me first. I ran straight to Chuck.

25

Two Sundays later, a little bit of luck and a tremendous amount of follow-up work had helped fill the gaps in what we knew. Selma Gooding had confirmed that Percy Crenshaw knew Delores Tompkins. "Of course he did," she had told Raymond Johnson and me from her hospital bed, as if we should have made the connection long ago. "I introduced them—why, not quite two months ago. Delores came to me one day and said she wanted to talk to a reporter. Her mother had bragged about Delores turning over a new leaf, so I figured she had a new career in mind. It wasn't for me to tell her she needed to go to college first, but I figured Percy would set her straight."

It had never dawned on Selma that Delores had gone to Percy about her ex-boyfriend, Andre Brouse. When Alison Madison-York came forward as well, Percy would have had the second source he needed. But before he even started putting pen to paper—or fingers to keyboard—Delores Tompkins was killed. According to the Yorks, even Percy had been nervous.

■ ■ ■

IA reopened the case against Geoff Hamilton. An assistant to Andre Brouse was willing to testify that Hamilton was in on the Northeast Precinct scam, and other witnesses placed him as a frequent visitor to Jay-J's. According to the assistant, Hamilton told Brouse that he pulled Delores over, intending to scare her into silence. Instead, she had punched the engine, and the rest had happened pretty much as he'd claimed at grand jury, but without all the remorse. If the story was true, he was guilty of felony murder. I didn't know yet whether I'd be able to prove my case, but I knew one thing: He wasn't getting a deal.

Peter Anderson, needless to say, did not recover from his injuries. My father chuckled at that one.

"Stop laughing," I protested. "I told you I wanted to read this to you." We sat at my dining room table with Helen Bernhard sticky buns and the morning's paper, featuring a front-page story by Heidi Hatmaker about Delores Tompkins, Percy Crenshaw, and the two back-to-back officer-involved shootings nearly two weeks earlier, one at Jay-J's and one at a home in southeast Portland.

"Did you really say that to her?" my father asked. *"He didn't recover from his injuries?* You mean the hole Chuck shot through his head?"

My father's law-enforcement days were long behind him, but he still had the sick sense of humor that comes with the job. All that mattered to him was that Peter Anderson was a murderer. He had admitted it to Marcy and Chuck before the shooting. Jack Walker even found Anderson's name on a list of customers who recently test-drove a Jeep Liberty from a dealer out in Beaverton. The way we figured, Anderson had helped himself to a few carpet fibers before dumping the baseball bat at the Red Raccoon. The bar owner is now rethinking his decision to publicize his Dumpster diving habits.

The last time I saw Chuck, he was dealing with the aftermath of Anderson's shooting with humor as well. I used the same kinds of reassuring words that had comforted me when I was once in his position—he could never have convinced Anderson to drop the knife; there were no nondeadly options; Anderson gave him no choice. Chuck's response? "When you sit down for that interview, just don't tell her I'm a punk-ass bitch who had to be rescued by his woman."

"What does the story say about the women from the neighborhood association?" Dad asked.

"Just that the investigation remains open." Jessica Walters had tried to console me by explaining that sometimes years pass before a suspect in custody offers to clear up an old gang shooting in exchange for leniency. Maybe, but, absent such fortuity, the murder of Janelle Rogers and the attempted murder of Selma Gooding were starting to look like yet another unsolved Buckeye drive-by.

"Good," I said, reading further, "she didn't name Matt and Alison. I was worried about that." It took a fight to persuade Duncan not to pursue charges against either of them—him for obstruction of justice, her for far worse. In exchange, Alison gladly resigned her position at the bureau, and Matt accepted a six-month suspension without pay. Russ Frist, who was over the worst of his Lyme disease, frowned upon the deal, but I did it anyway. So far, I still had my job.

"It looks like she talked to Tommy Garcia too:

A sergeant in the bureau's Drug and Vice Division believes that the business records from Jay-J's will lead to some of the largest drug busts in his unit's history."

Perhaps, but he was going to have to do the work with the acting senior deputy in the Gang Unit. Jessica Walters's water had broken yesterday. Last night, I'd received an e-mail from her partner about a baby girl named Bridget.

When I got to the part about seizing Jay-J's as a state forfeiture asset, Dad interrupted my enthusiastic monologue. "Put the paper down, Sammie."

"But I'm reading—"

"No, you're avoiding conversation. It's an easily identifiable Kincaid trait."

I lowered the paper slightly and eyed him warily over its pages.

"Are you getting through this OK?" he asked quietly.

"Yeah, Dad, I'm fine." I took another bite from my sticky bun.

"Fine, huh?"

No one ever believes me when I use that word, but I suppose my father had particularly good reasons for scrutinizing it now. Some of the events of the past week didn't make their way into the article. The wall that traditionally divides prosecutors from cops had formally been erected between me and MCT. Walker and Johnson were polite, but they spoke to me only on an as-needed basis.

For Mike Calabrese, speaking to me on an as-needed basis meant not speaking to me at all, other than a terse e-mail conceding he'd been wrong about Geoff Hamilton. He was still suspended, and the bureau was trying to demote him to patrol because of the faulty confession from Corbett. The union was backing Mike up, but, from what I heard, Mike was talking to a department near Bend about a transfer. Even if he could force his way back into MCT, he wasn't interested in a career—and the resulting cross-examinations—defined by his prior suspension, union grievance, and Todd Corbett. He wasn't taking my calls, and two e-mail messages had so far gone unacknowledged: one, a thank-you for talking to Matt York about coming forward; the other, a clumsy and apparently insufficient apology.

"Obviously things aren't perfect," I said finally, softening to my father's concerned face, my voice cracking.

"He's going to come back, Sam. You guys will be fine."

I hadn't given Dad the play-by-play of Chuck's departure, but I remembered every minute of it. His self-deprecating request that I not dime him up to Heidi as a wussy boy had been the one last joke. Then his tone changed.

"Well, I think I've got everything."

He held the final box, packed from our bedroom. A mini U-Haul was waiting out front, full of the belongings he had moved in only a month earlier. They were presumably going into the apartment he had rented in his old neighborhood, along with the furniture we had placed in storage just before Halloween.

"You don't have to do this, Chuck."

"I know, but I need to."

When I replayed the scene each night in bed alone, I could still feel the shortness of breath and the pain in my stomach. I had fought my hardest, but in the end I broke down. It was heartbreak, and it was happening. I really was losing him.

"No, you don't need to," I had argued. Begged, really. "You need to be here with me. In our house."

"Not ours, Sam. Yours. It was always yours. We finally tried it, and now we know—it's not enough. We just didn't work." He kissed me on the head one last time. Then, just like that, he left.

I swallowed now against the lump forming in my throat. "No, Dad. He's not coming back." I blotted my eyes with the end of my shirt sleeve, absorbing the dampness before tears could form. I had cried every day for a week. I needed to make it through one dry day.

"Maybe—"

I shook my head adamantly. Privately, though, I was also keeping a small window of hope open for the maybes. Maybe if I stopped trying to fit in at MCU at the expense of my own instincts about the officers in MCT. Maybe if I earned Mike's forgiveness, even if I couldn't repair the harm I'd done to his reputation—and feelings. Maybe if I promised to sign the piece of paper with the rings and the death-do-you-part stuff. Maybe if I swore to quit MCU, if that's what it took.

A lot of maybes. I had no idea where to start, but I knew I'd give it a shot. I had to.

Acknowledgments

To my delight, I have been fortunate enough now to have written three novels about Samantha Kincaid, the police officers she works with, and the cases she prosecutes in my favorite city, Portland, Oregon. I could fill another book trying to express my gratitude to those to whom it is owed, but I'll use this one small publishable page instead.

Thank you to the many wonderful, diverse, hospitable bookstore folks who have hosted me for readings and helped personally move the books from boxes to shelves to curious fingers that turn pages. Thank you to those who have welcomed me as a friend along the way, even if our meetings were through your web browser. Most important, thank you—whoever *you* are—for reading this. I am forever grateful for the opportunity I have been given to write fiction, and I know it comes directly from readers.

As always, I thank my tireless agent, Philip Spitzer, and the incredible team at Henry Holt: John Sterling, Jennifer Barth, Maggie Richards, Annsley Rosner, Sam Douglas, Donna Holstein, and Richard Rhorer. Thank you, Jane Wood, Gaby Young, and company at Orion Books, and Matthew Shear, Marc Resnick, and Jennifer Enderlin at St. Martin's Press for taking Samantha overseas and to paperback. I am also thankful to my students and colleagues at Hofstra Law School.

Thank you, Danielle Holley and Maggie Griffin. Any remaining typos are entirely your fault.

Finally, thank you, Sean Simpson. You're the best.

About the Author

A former deputy district attorney in Portland, Oregon, ALAFAIR BURKE now teaches criminal law at Hofstra Law School. The daughter of acclaimed crime writer James Lee Burke, she is a graduate of Stanford Law School and currently lives in New York City. *Close Case* is the third in the Samantha Kincaid series.